Ashes of Vengeance

Yoeland stood at the window watching the dawn.

Ashes of Vengeance

A Romance of Old France. By
H. B. Somerville.

ILLUSTRATED

ROBERT M. McBRIDE & COMPANY
NEW YORK : : : : 1923

TO
MRS. H. N. FALKNER
MRS. ARCHD. AND MURIEL McCOMAS
AS "A SMALL TOKEN OF ESTEEM"

The publishers wish to acknowledge their indebtedness to the courtesy of The Norma Talmadge Film Company and First National Pictures, Inc., for permission to use scenes from the motion picture of this story as illustrations in this book.

ASHES OF VENGEANCE

CHAPTER I

MADEMOISELLE DE VAINÇEOIRE looked discontentedly about her at the crowd of gayly chatting people in the King's antechamber.

"No, Monsieur," she said, looking up at Rupert de Vrieac, her betrothed, who stood beside her, "I hate Paris and I do not thank you for bringing me here. For it was you who first proposed that I should come, who persuaded my father to consent. I would now that I had remained at Vainçeoire."

Rupert flushed at the reproach in her voice, as he protested:

"But, Margot, you who begged to come. I wished to please you. I told you——"

"You told me that Paris was gay, Rupert, and that I should see here many gallant gentlemen and beautiful ladies. You told me that I should find laughter and friendship and admiration. Oh, it was a pretty enough picture that you painted for me. But observe the reality, Monsieur. My aunt finds the Court wicked, forsooth, so she will not enter it. Monsieur, my betrothed, is of the Admiral's party, whereas it is the friends of the duc de Guise who are in favor. So here we sit by ourselves while painted insolents and laughing fools make merry about us."

It was not without reason that Mademoiselle was discontented. She had been led to expect many things of Paris. In her home, in that grim castle at the foot of the Pyrenees, where the Vidame de Vainçeoire rested after many battles, lavishing all his love upon her, his only daughter, where Rupert de Vrieac, seeing in her nothing but perfection, had

1

told her in a thousand ways how great her beauty was and how she had only to be seen to become the admired of all men, she had dreamed endless dreams of the day when she might go to Court to score an easy triumph over other less fortunate women. So, in this August of 1572, when the Court celebrated the marriage of Marguerite de Valois to Henri, King of Navarre, she had persuaded her father to let her go to Paris to visit her aunt that she might witness the festivities; and with Rupert, who had seconded her pleadings, she had ridden north, her head filled with dreams of the conquests she would make.

But in Paris disappointment awaited her. Her beauty, which shone so brightly at home, found many rivals here; her loveliest gowns seemed drab beside the splendor of many of the women of the Court; and Mademoiselle, who had dreamed of triumph, found herself almost unnoticed, her only cavalier Rupert, of whose devotion she was already too well assured. In a word, Mademoiselle was bored. Paris was dull; and, however innocent, Rupert must pay for it.

Her eyes roamed away again restlessly at the throng about her. Suddenly she started slightly, and a flush of pleased surprise colored her cheeks. Two eyes had caught her own; eyes that smiled at her across the room, and which, she felt, had been waiting many minutes to catch her glance. For a moment she gazed at the stranger, welcoming his admiration. Then she turned away her head.

"Rupert," she said in a low voice, "who is the tall, fair man in the violet doublet, standing beside M. Teligny? No, more to the left. There, just—"

She paused, startled, for Rupert's face had flushed with sudden rage and a gleam of hatred shone in the stranger's eyes as he looked at her betrothed. For a moment the two men glared at one another across the room. Then, with an ironic bow, the stranger turned away and was lost in the crowd. Rupert watched him depart in silence, then he looked down into Marguerite's face with a grim smile.

"That, Margot," he said slowly, "is the Comte de la Roche."

The Comte de la Roche! She understood, then, the hatred that flamed in the eyes of the two men as they gazed at each other. It was no personal enmity that animated them, but a feud that had existed for generations, ever since that far-off day when Raoul de Vrieac had made a willing captive of the lovely Yvonne de Marbleu, carrying her off on the eve of her wedding to the then Comte de la Roche, whose suit Yvonne's father had favored over that of his penniless rival. They were proud, the men of La Roche, and had not forgiven the insult to their pride. Raoul de Vrieac had lived in happiness with his stolen bride, but many a man of his blood had fallen at the hands of them of La Roche, and on many a descendant of La Roche had a Vrieac taken vengeance. So hatred grew between them, becoming ever more powerful with the years, until, indeed, it became a point of honor with the men of either house that never should any quarrel find them ranged except on opposite sides.

Between Rupert and the tall stranger who had gazed so boldly at Marguerite there was a new cause for enmity. For now, in France, religious warfare threatened. Huguenot and Catholic had passed from silent antagonism into open hatred. The Duc de Guise, whose power had grown until it seemed greater than that of the King himself, had formed, in the Catholic League, an organization whose existence was a threat to all of the Huguenot faith. There was terror and distrust and hatred in every heart during that August of 1572; and behind the festive mask lurked a shadowy horror, as yet imperceptible but growing ever larger—the shadow of St. Bartholomew.

And Marguerite, who watched the tall figure of the Comte de la Roche disappear in the throng, knew that she should feel for him a twofold hatred. For not only was he the enemy of her lover's house, he was a Catholic, a friend of Guise, and thus an enemy of her own faith, as well.

Enemy or no, this Charles de Breux, Comte de la Roche, had singled her out for his admiration when others had ignored her, and Marguerite was not the woman to think ill of him for that reason. Nor did she regard him the less highly for his gallant air or the brilliance of his doublet, so different from Rupert's Huguenot sobriety. There was little thought of the obligations of loyalty when, somewhat later that day, during a brief absence of Rupert, the Comte suddenly appeared before her, and begged the lady in whose charge she had been left to present him to Mademoiselle.

"And does Mademoiselle enjoy her first visit to Paris?" asked the Comte, as they sat together in the embrasure of a window.

"What," she countered, "am I then so much the country lass that the fact is apparent to a stranger's eyes?"

"Pardon, Mademoiselle," he answered. "You wrong my eyes to call them strange, when they have been bent upon you all the day. For the rest, it is a simple matter. Even so poor a courtier as I knows by sight the half-dozen women at Court whom one may call beautiful. How then, when a lovelier lady than they appears, can one fail to know that it is her neglect of Paris which makes her face so strange, or the privilege of admiring her so belated."

Thus the Comte, who found it not at all an unpleasant amusement to talk nonsense to the betrothed of his enemy; and if there was little of sincerity in his flattering words, Marguerite was in no mood to detect it. There was a heightened color in her cheeks as she listened, and a light in her eyes which not even Rupert's adoration had created; nor did she give a thought to de Vrieac or wonder how he might regard her too ready acceptance of his enemy's attentions.

So they laughed and talked through many moments, until La Roche wearying for a time of his conquest, pleaded business elsewhere and withdrew.

"For a little time, Mademoiselle," he whispered, as he made his adieux. "We shall meet again? You have made Paris gay for me this afternoon. May I not dream of to-morrow, then?"

He bowed himself away, while Marguerite watched him, her eyes shining with gratification.

But they did not meet on the morrow. Rupert arrived early, with an anxious look in his eyes and ill news upon his lips. Coligny, the beloved Admiral, had been treacherously attacked that morning, as he returned from the Louvre. A shot from an arquebus had wounded him, and, although he had suffered little ill from the attack, the assassin had been permitted to escape. Men saw in the affair the hand of Guise, arch-enemy of all Huguenots, and wondered what greater danger, what new outrage threatened. And the shadow, the shadow of a horror to come, grew larger as the day passed.

Yet the next day dawned calmly enough. There had been street riots, it was true. Bands of Huguenots had paraded before the Hotel de Guise muttering threats against the Duc. Yet the King had given new promises of safety to his Huguenot subjects; he had visited Coligny and had taken measures to have the assassin apprehended. The streets grew quiet once more. And only Guise, plotting in his chamber, only the Queen-Mother, Catherine de Medici, pacing her apartments in the Louvre, cursing Maurevert's poor aim and the skill of Ambroise Paré the surgeon, vowing greater vengeance against the heretics, knew what this quiet portended.

So for a time the terror passed, and Marguerite, who had kept within all the day, breathed freely once more, and prepared for the evening's festivities. Toward dusk, Rupert came with reassuring tidings. There had been a stormy interview between the King and de Guise, and the latter, with his brother, the Duc d'Aumale, had prepared to leave Paris, followed by a number of their adherents. Finally, they had turned back at the Porte St. Antoine,

and had barricaded themselves in their hotel, outside which
armed Huguenots still marched, threatening vengeance.
The Admiral was greatly improved, and had received many
messages from His Majesty, whose graciousness toward
his Huguenot subjects increased hourly with his resentment
against the Guises. The Queen-Mother and M. d'Anjou
were together at the Louvre and would see no one. But
all danger had passed and there were to be great festivities
at the palace that night, to which Marguerite might safely
go.

"And here," he said, offering her a bouquet of red Pro-
vence roses, "are fitting companions for your beauty. Will
you wear them, sweet, to-night?"

But it was not these or the knowledge of Rupert's love
which made her eyes shine happily as they entered the
great ballroom that evening.

Never had there been such gayety as on that evening of
the 23rd of August. There was relief in the heart of every
one, and a fevered desire to forget the turmoil of the past
two days and to ignore whatever might be forthcoming.
So they danced and made merry, while the Queen-Mother
watched their revels with an evil smile.

None among the merrymakers was more gay than Marguerite, her discontent of the days past forgotten in the triumph
of the present. For, to-night her beauty brought her many
admiring glances and not a few cavaliers would have been
glad to exchange places with Rupert who stood proudly
at her side. Then came a summons for M. de Vrieac to
attend the King of Navarre; and Marguerite, for a moment left alone in the care of the Duchesse d'Aumarde,
looked up to find the Comte de la Roche bowing before
her.

"Mademoiselle is kind," he was saying, "or is it a more
than gracious fortune I must thank for this sight of her?
I had feared I should not see you again."

"I stayed within yesterday," she said, "for M. de Vrieac

considered it safer. Indeed I came near to leaving Paris. I may do so at any day now."

As she spoke she watched him intently, curious to learn how great his interest in her might be. She was not disappointed, for a look of what might well have been genuine disappointment passed over the face of the Comte.

"Leave Paris, Mademoiselle?" he exclaimed. "In heaven's name, why?"

"M. de Vrieac fears that the air of Paris may not be healthy for us Huguenots," she replied. "As for me, I find your city dull, Monsieur."

For a second the Count regarded her gravely, dismay in his eyes. Then a smile broke over his face.

"You are mocking me, Mademoiselle. Paris dull! Would you make it desolate also? Surely you will not go away just at this moment when I—when all Paris has discovered you."

And then, perhaps because her blonde loveliness was a potent intoxicant on this fever-ridden night, perhaps because the game of making love to the betrothed of his enemy proved enjoyable beyond discretion, La Roche grew bolder. Now his words were no longer the polite currency of the courtier. It was of love he whispered to her, of a love that was greater than prudence, greater than honor. Marguerite listened, a sense of triumph in her, as she watched his impassioned eyes. She could not discern the contempt that lay behind his passion, or the mockery his words concealed.

Yet she was too wise to forget caution or to promise too ready a victory to so new a suitor. There was dignity in her manner as she rose to her feet.

"You go fast, Monsieur le Comte. Almost, I think, you forget that I am betrothed to M. de Vrieac——"

Now there was hatred unconcealed in the Comte's eyes.

"I had not forgotten," he said. "But you, Mademoiselle? Is it so high a destiny, to be Madame de Vrieac, that you must always remember? Could so fair a lady go without regret to so ill a mating?" He smiled oddly as he stood before her. "You do not answer," he said, "and I will not press you. I ask for no words to-day; only a token, a rose, that I may wear it proudly and, perhaps, dream mad dreams upon it. Will you give me this, Mademoiselle?"

He stood above her, one hand upon her own, the other outstretched for the flower he had begged. For a moment Marguerite hesitated. She had forgotten Rupert, forgotten loyalty, a new ambition in her thoughts as she listened to the Comte's words. But this was imprudent—mad. Then, on impulse, she broke a bud from its stem and offered it to the man before her.

"Take it, then," she said, laughing. "Who knows——"

She broke off, terror in her eyes, her hand still clutching the rosebud. A shadow had fallen upon the two, as they stood in the recess of the ballroom; and Rupert, his face white with fury, stood watching them.

For a moment no word was spoken. Then Rupert, his eyes still upon the Comte's face, his hand upon his sword, stepped forward.

It was the woman who spoke first.

"Rupert," she cried, and there was a sick fear in her voice. "Oh, not here, not here. Take me home." She clung to him, sobbing, crying out that she had meant no harm, begging him to take her home, in her heart fear and a sense of pride struggling together.

"I will take you home, Mademoiselle," said Rupert's voice at last. "And you, Monsieur, will you await me at the inn of La Touchette in the Rue des Toules. I shall be there in half an hour. I and my second."

With a bow, he led Marguerite away, silent but with murder in his eyes. The Comte smiled. Half an hour, then. One must hurry. Oh, decidedly one must not be late for such a pleasure as that of killing M. de Vrieac.

CHAPTER II

THE inn, La Touchette, in the Rue des Toules, was a long, rambling building, part house, part stables, where several of the less wealthy young Huguenots had their lodging, and where Rupert de Vrieac was himself staying.

Here appeared, exactly half an hour after they had left the Louvre, the Comte, accompanied by his friend, Paul de Voes, asking for M. de Vrieac. The two were at once shown to a room on the second floor, where Rupert and a young Huguenot, Geoffrey Lefevre, were waiting.

It was a long, low room, brilliantly lighted by many candles. The furniture had been pushed aside, leaving the center of the room clear. A screen had been placed before the fire, that its flickering light might not baulk the swordsmen; the rugs had been rolled back. Glancing quickly round, the Comte noticed that the windows were heavily curtained, shutting out any observing eyes. Rupert had already taken off his shoes and stood ready in shirt and hose, a pleasant anticipation shining in his eyes.

The Comte, noting the look, smiled to himself, and made his preparations quickly, whilst the seconds measured their principals' weapons and drew lots for their positions. At a nod from Rupert, Lefevre crossed to the door and, locking it, laid the key on the table.

"Now, Monsieur," said Rupert gravely, "we are secure from interruption, so if you are ready, let us begin."

"Certainly," replied the Comte, taking his place with a gay bow. "I ask nothing better than to have the killing of you as soon as possible, M. de Vrieac."

Both stood ready, waiting in their places. At the word from de Voes, they set to.

Under the keen, silent observation of their seconds they fought, each watching the other with alert eyes, their stockinged feet moving noiselessly on the polished floor, only their breathing and the sharp clink of steel on steel breaking the silence.

They were well matched, each active and highly-trained. The Comte had a slight advantage in reach which was balanced by the dexterity of Rupert's wristplay. Supple and strong, he met every lunge with a repulse of iron, getting in a counterthrust with great swiftness. At first each fought with caution, feeling the strength of his opponent. Then the Comte, tiring of this, attacked suddenly with great fierceness. So quick was his swordplay that it might have confused a less skillful fencer; but Rupert met each trick firmly, his defense never failing for a second, the quick brain and iron wrist foreseeing and defeating every stroke of his adversary.

After a few minutes the Comte cooled off, trying to get by caution what his swift assault had failed to win. Then Rupert began to attack, pressing him hard. It seemed as if the fight would have to be settled by the combatants' endurance, their skill was so equal. Once the Comte, stepping back to avoid a lunge of Rupert's, slipped a little; but Rupert, unwilling to avail himself of his opponent's mischance, stood off quickly until he had regained his balance, the Comte acknowledging his courtesy gravely.

Both men were beginning to feel the strain of the contest. Their breath was coming in short gasps, perspiration trickled down their faces, whilst the hatred in their eyes had given place to a dogged determination in each, not to be conquered by the other.

Then, very slowly, after much maneuvering, the Comte began to drive his enemy slowly backwards towards the table, where his movements would necessarily be hampered. Fiercely Rupert tried to fight his way to the left, contesting each inch hardly before he gave way. Twice he almost touched his opponent, missing his stroke by a hair-breadth.

And then, baulked by the knowledge that the table was just behind him, that any moment he might feel it, he took his eyes for a second from his opponent's, and in that second the Comte got beyond his guard, touching him on the left forearm.

The wound was only slight, but the Comte's smile and his triumphant "My point! First blood!" roused Rupert's flagging energies, stirring his hatred into a blazing flame. With a sudden, fierce rally he drove back the Comte's attack, compelling him to withdraw a little. With set face and eyes blazing with the lust to kill, Rupert fought desperately, pressing the Comte hard and making him keep strictly on the defensive. Backwards and forwards they moved, the seconds watching their fierce struggle intently. Slowly a little stream of red grew on the left arm of Rupert's shirt, but he was barely aware of his wound, every feeling was taken up by his determination to conquer. Twice he almost drove the Comte back against the table. Then, quite suddenly, by a beautiful bit of swordplay quicker than the eye could follow, Rupert gained his point— the Comte's sword flew from his hand, shot across the room like a flash of light and fell with a clatter on the floor, leaving its master with only a poniard, and practically in Rupert's power.

In the instant's pause which followed, Rupert flung his own sword away and sprang forward. The Comte, dazed by the jar and suddenness of his misfortune, made a quick rally, but it was too late. Rupert was within his guard, his left hand seized the Comte's wrist, thrusting it back, whilst with his right he struck his adversary on the forehead with the pummel of his dagger, sending him staggering against the table behind him. By a quick wrench of his wrist, Rupert compelled the Comte to drop his weapon and then, like a flash, his hand gripped the Comte's throat, forcing him down on the table, the dagger in his right hand ready to strike.

A great silence held the room. The two seconds waited

motionless, watching in fascinated silence, and Rupert, leaning over his prisoner, holding him fiercely down, noted with satisfaction his strained muscles, and laughed triumphantly. At last the victory was his, and the Comte utterly in his power. By the rules of dueling then held, Rupert had the right to do as he would with him. And as the Comte, looking into his enemy's eyes, read Death there, his lips twisted into a whimsical smile. Rupert's hand pressed a little harder on his throat, the hatred in his eyes deepened; for a minute longer they gazed at each other in silence.

Then, with an oath, Rupert relaxed his grip and stood up, driving his poniard back into its sheath with a snap. The Comte, raising his head, looked at him with surprise. What was coming now, he wondered? Lefevre had picked up their swords and laid them together on a chair. Putting his own back in its place, Rupert took up the Comte's and stood for a moment holding it in his hand, watching his enemy with brooding eyes; the Comte, his head raised from the table across which he was practically lying, and believing every moment to be his last, still smiled with courageous indifference.

"You may rise, Monsieur," said Rupert suddenly, in a harsh voice, and when the Comte had done so, handed him back his sword. "Your poniard is on that chair, take it too," he continued, his tones trembling with passion. "A moment since I meant to kill you, as it was my right to do. Now I give you your life. You were not afraid to die. I could see that. You will suffer more by living, with the knowledge that your life is my gift, that it was my pleasure to spare you. You may go." And he made a gesture towards the door.

The Comte, who had taken the sword and listened to Rupert in surprised silence, gave a sudden cry as he realized his enemy's meaning, and Rupert smiled grimly at the sound, for he knew his guess had been right, that he had chosen the bitterest revenge. With a violent movement the Comte flung down his weapon.

"No!" he cried. "Ten thousand times, no! I will not take my life from you."

Leaning forward, with a quick movement he struck Rupert on the cheek.

An evil light blazed into Rupert's eyes, and his hand fell on his sword-hilt. Then as the Comte stood waiting with quiet expectation for the thrust, he drew his hand back and laughed softly.

"So!" he said. "I was right. You do suffer, Monsieur. Then most certainly I will not kill you." Striding to the door he flung it open. "You may go, unless you wish to stay and thank me for my mercy."

At this de Voes, who had picked up the Comte's sword, caught his principal by the arm before he could reply.

"Come away," he whispered, pushing him gently towards the door, "and do not say another word. You are only pleasing him by protesting." And the Comte, seeing the truth of this, allowed himself to be led forward.

Rupert bowed them through the door with mocking courtesy, and the Comte, stumbling down the stairs, his eyes full of bitter shame, flushed hotly as the Huguenot's taunting laugh followed him.

He and de Voes passed into the street and walked along in silence. The Comte strode along, trembling with rage, his eyes like smoldering fires. Never had he hated Rupert de Vrieac so bitterly. The feud which had existed between them before had been a heritage; there had been no actual cause for quarrel between the men. But now this was changed. If Rupert had given hours of thought to the subject he could not have devised any plan which would have hurt his enemy's pride more keenly, or have roused a more deadly hatred within him. That he, Charles de Breux, should be compelled to take his life as a gift from the hands of Rupert de Vrieac! The thought almost choked

him and he walked on with clenched hands and a passion
for revenge in his heart. Once or twice he muttered fiercely
to himself, but it was not until they had almost reached the
Louvre that he stopped, and laying his hand on his companion's arm, spoke to him.

"De Voes," he said, and there was a mingling of shame
and passion in his voice, "I ask as the greatest favor to
myself, that you should not mention to-night what—what
has just happened to any one. I only ask for twelve hours.
Give me till then to get my revenge on Rupert de Vrieac,
and after that you can say what you will."

De Voes nodded assent gravely.

"Most certainly, La Roche," he replied. "As far as I am
concerned the whole affair is forgotten. Your luck was
against you to-night, though to-morrow it may be de Vrieac's
turn. In the meantime, however, he will talk."

The Comte laughed bitterly.

"He will and he may," he replied. "But to-morrow
something may happen at which he will neither talk—
nor laugh. It will be my turn then. And so I ask that
when you tell the story of to-night you should also be able
to tell that of my revenge. Good-night, Paul. I am going
to de Guise."

So they parted. The Comte, entering the palace, went
to the King's antechamber. Here he found a group of the
King's gentlemen with one or two ladies of the Court. The
evening had turned cold and a wood fire burned brightly on
the great hearth. Round it the talk flowed gayly, but under
all there ran a strong current of excitement, of expectation,
of speculation.

Henri de Guise had, with M. d'Anjou and the Marshal
de Tavannes, been in conference with the Queen-Mother
for several hours, and they were now all with His Majesty
in his bedchamber, La Roche was told. The door was
locked, and no one, be the matter never so urgent, was
to disturb them, by Catherine's special orders. That famous conference at which had been arranged one of the

darkest deeds in history, and whose members were even then trying to persuade their poor, mad King, distraught by fear, horror and the clamor of warring interests around him, to break his most solemn promise and condemn thousands of his unsuspecting subjects to torture and death; that with the semblance of his power, the reality of which they had long since taken from him, Catherine de Medici and her fellow-plotters might be free to wreak vengeance on their enemies, to glut their lust for cruelty and murder to the utmost, under a cloak of serving God's pleasure and the King's good.

Those who live during great events are seldom able to realize how wide-spreading may be the consequences, or how, under their very eyes, momentous history is shaping itself. So the Comte, although as one of Henri de Guise's most intimate friends he was fully aware of what was brewing, gave little thought to the general result of the plot. With the exception of Rupert de Vrieac, he bore no malice against the Huguenots, merely feeling contemptuous amusement for their sober manners and religious observances. As far as he was concerned they might live and thrive in peace, all, that is, save one. And here his interest in the plot began, for he saw how it might be made to serve his own ends, saw in it a wonderful chance to wreak vengeance upon his enemy, vengeance such as is given into the hands of few.

Impatiently he awaited the close of that gathering in the King's bedchamber. He realized that sooner or later, Charles, sick in body and soul and ready to turn wherever he might have peace, would yield to the Queen-Mother's desire and sanction the massacre, but for his plan the sooner was very much the better.

Shortly before midnight the Provost of Paris, who had been hastily summoned by Catherine, left the King's room, bearing with him an order signed by Charles, and was shortly followed by de Guise and the Marshal.

As the Duke walked quickly through the antechamber,

the Comte called to him to join a game. But de Guise, whose eyes were blazing with excitement, shook his head.

"Not to-night," he cried; adding in a low tone as La Roche moved closer: "We have another game to play. Charles has signed the order."

"Signed! For when?"

"It will be to-night, as soon as may be. We must strike at once. He must have no time to cancel it."

"To-night!" whispered the Comte. "St. Denis be praised!"

De Guise looked at him in sudden surprise.

"Why that thanksgiving? You did not seem so anxious over the affair before, Charles—otherwise, I thought."

Slipping his hand through de Guise's arm, the Comte drew him into an embrasure of one of the windows, away from the rest of the room.

"Is it a general order? They are all to go?" he asked softly.

De Guise's eyes glowed.

"All," he replied, "all, except Paré and His Majesty's old nurse and one or two more who are of no value. The rest——" and he drew his hand across his throat with an expressive gesture. "Coligny first, then Navarre, and the others to follow. The King was for saving Rochefoucauld and Navarre, but they are down on the list now."

The Comte was breathing heavily, as though under some great excitement, and he paid no attention to the latter part of de Guise's speech.

"Henri," he said, choosing his words very carefully, "I do not ask it as anything but the greatest favor, but there is one thing I want, and you can give me. When 'the others' are being dealt with there is a house which will not have a cross on it, that the rabble must not touch."

Henri de Guise, who was in high good humor at the success of his plans, nevertheless drew his brows together in sudden annoyance. He wished the affair to be carried through thoroughly, and he knew how many of his enemies this one house might hold.

"It is in the Rue de Valois, next to the butcher's, on the right hand side," the Comte continued quietly. "There are only two women in it and a few servants, no one of importance; but I want your word that they will be unmolested, that some soldiers in your livery—nothing else will keep back the rabble, once they have tasted blood—will guard it till I come, for I shall have to make another call first and I do not want the place sacked before I get there. I saved your life from that mad fool, de Vert's, dagger last year," he added. "I did that as your friend and you owe me no debt, but I ask this as a favor in return."

De Guise's face cleared and he laid his hand on his companion's shoulder.

"You shall have it," he said. "There are a few houses to be kept for my own use too, and yours shall go on the list. Perhaps I will call in and see how the ladies like you. Here's luck to your visit. I shall have many to pay to-night myself. I tell you there will be some scores settled before to-morrow dawns. Paris will be rid of a lot of rats by to-morrow."

And he walked away with a grim laugh of satisfaction.

The Comte stood for a few moments wrapt in thought, then he turned and quickly left the room also. On the stairs he met Paul de Voes and caught him by the arm.

"I was going to fetch you, Paul," he said. "So that you may tell the story better I want you to come with me and see how I revenge myself on Rupert de Vrieac."

CHAPTER III

RUPERT, having watched the Comte and his second descend the stairs, closed the door and drawing a chair to the fire, sank into it moodily. All his triumphant satisfaction had passed away. It was true that he had conquered and humbled his enemy.

Had she chosen to cast a passing favor on any other man, he would, though displeased and jealous, have comprehended the innocence of her intentions and forgiven. But that Marguerite, perfectly aware who he was and how he and her betrothed regarded each other, should have encouraged the Comte's attentions, filled him with bitter anger. No child, however innocent, would have done such a thing; she must have had some deliberate reason.

Thus Rupert, moodily staring into the fire, was filled with no pleasant expectations of his interview with Marguerite on the morrow. The more he thought over the affair the more indignant he became. The picture of the Comte wearing one of Marguerite's red roses, and smiling unrebuked into her eyes, kept recurring to his mind, and it was only partly consoling to remember another picture of the same man, ashamed and conquered, as he had left Rupert's room a little later.

Geoffrey Lefevre, finding his presence unnoticed and unwanted by his friend, had long ago slipped out of the room; and Rupert, suddenly becoming aware of this and the flight of time, decided to go to bed. His thoughts seemed to be racing round in a circle, with an enormous and unanswerable "Why?" as their center. Perhaps the morning would bring clearness and a solution.

So carrying his light, he mounted to his room, and having

Rupert bowed La Roche down the stairs with mocking courtesy.

undressed and laid his sword near at hand, got into bed.
And in the street below, a ·man who had been lounging
against the opposite wall for nearly an hour, noted the fact
that M. de Vrieac had gone to his bed, and that as his candle
had been put out, he would probably shortly go to sleep in
the darkness, and be so found should any one require him
suddenly during the next few hours.

Rupert had not meant to sleep. In the dark silence
he had hoped to see things more clearly, to be able to
judge of their true proportions, but being a healthy man
who took plenty of exercise and lived a busy life, drowsi-
ness overtook him, his eyes closed gradually and very soon
he slept.

And in his sleep strange dreams came to him. He
seemed, far off, to hear a great tumult, hoarse cries, the
tolling of bells, and in the streets a sound of men running
to and fro. Then, above the clamor some one was calling
his name urgently, and he awoke with a start to find his
servant, Martin, white-faced and only partly dressed, shaking him roughly by the shoulder.

"Wake up, Monsieur, for the love of God, wake up!"
he cried. "The Catholics are out and murdering our
people everywhere. They say it is an order from the
King and that we are all to die. Here is your sword, dress
quickly, they may be on us any second. My God! what are
we to do?"

Startled into instant wakefulness, Rupert sprang up.

All Huguenots to die! But it was impossible, there was
the King's promise! And yet into his mind flashed in-
cidents hardly noticed at the time—meaning glances; groups
whose whispers had hushed when he, a Huguenot, approached, and he knew that the horror was true—the King's
word stood for nothing. And Marguerite! Good God,
what might not be happening to her! The Rue de Valois,
where her aunt lived, was nearly a quarter of a mile away,
and who knew what carnage lay between them. But at all
costs he must get to her.

Hurriedly he flung on some clothes, Martin, though shivering with fear, remembering to fetch his steel corselet, whilst from the street below and even from the very house they were in, came hoarse cries and sounds of carnage.

"We must get to Mlle. de Vainçeoire, Martin, whatever happens. Have your sword ready and follow me close."

And catching up his own, Rupert sprang to the door.

But before he could reach it, there was a sound of men on the stairs, the door was flung open and the Comte de La Roche, followed by Paul de Voes and a dozen soldiers, burst into the room.

The Comte paused when he saw Rupert standing sword in hand, then he bowed. He and his companions all wore white bands on their left arms, and La Roche's eyes burned with excitement.

"So you are up, de Vrieac! All the better, it will save time. Now oblige me by putting down your sword and tying this white band round your left arm. Be quick, there's no time to lose."

Though knowing that he was hopelessly outnumbered, Rupert did not speak or lower his guard, and it was then that Martin, believing that the Comte was about to kill his master, flung down his sword, and stepping quickly forward, knelt before La Roche with outstretched, pleading hands.

"Monseigneur," he cried, "let me die for him. Why should you kill so good a gentleman? Take my life instead and spare——"

And then Rupert's hand shot out, and seizing him by the collar, dragged him roughly back.

"You insolent dog!" whispered his master furiously. "Be silent. Who gave you leave to speak?"

But the Comte nodded gravely to Martin.

"I was not thinking of killing M. de Vrieac, my man, but you were a good fellow to offer. I wonder how many of my knaves would have done the same for me. And as loyalty is uncommon now-a-days, you can come with us.

I had not included you in the scheme, but it seems a pity
that the rabble should have the killing of you.

"Now, Monsieur," he continued, turning angrily to Rupert, "will you tie on that bandage or shall three of my
men do it for you? God's death! Are you going to stand
there scowling at me all night when they are killing your
friends down by the hundred. I tell you there is no time to
be lost. Mlle. de Vainçeoire is safe—so far; for how long
she will remain safe is another matter. Death is having a
grand carnival to-night, and the rabble are devils loose from
hell. It will take a good few pikes to keep them back from a
house with no cross upon it, and I do not know how many
men de Guise sent. So hurry. Put down your sword, you'll
not need it, and tie on that bandage, for without one no
man goes safe in the streets of Paris to-night. Hurry!
We must go to Mlle. de Vainçeoire as soon as may be."

Lowering his sword, Rupert took a step forward.

"To Mlle. de Vainçeoire?" he faltered.

"Yes, yes, to Mlle. de Vainçeoire," cried the Comte impatiently. "I am going to take you to her. Do as I tell
you quickly and that lean-faced fellow of yours too. In
God's name, must I tell you again to hurry?"

Like a man in a dream, Rupert laid down his sword and
tied the white bandage on his left arm, signing to Martin
to do the same. The Comte watched them in silence.

"Now follow me," he said, "and whatever happens or
you may see, pass on and be silent. Remember that unless
you obey my orders implicitly I will not take you to Mlle.
de Vainçeoire."

Then he and de Voes left the room, and as Rupert and
Martin moved forward the soldiers closed round, keeping
them in the middle, whilst one, picking up the two swords,
brought them with him. They passed down to the second
landing. Here the marks of the carnage were very plain.
Doors stood open, showing the rooms beyond in wild dis-
order. Every cupboard and crevice which could conceal a
Huguenot had been ruthlessly searched, no barrier had been

strong enough to keep out their pursuers. In one doorway, round which a fierce fight had evidently been waged, lay the body of a man, the eyes staring fixed and vacant in the stillness of death, and at sight of it Rupert paused with a sharp cry. His murderers had found Geoffrey Lefevre asleep, but springing up, he had seized his sword and fought fiercely, until he was finally borne down by numbers. Rupert gazed at his friend's body in horror, until a soldier behind pushed him gently forward.

"There is no time to stop, Monsieur," he said, and Rupert moved on.

Lefevre was dead, nothing could help him now, but Marguerite was safe—"so far," and at all costs Rupert must get to her.

Further down the passage lay a woman, young and pretty, several of whose fingers had been cut off that the rabble might more quickly get her rings, dead across the body of the husband to whom she had only been married one short month.

Without hesitation the Comte stepped quickly over the bodies, the others following, and Rupert with a shudder did the same. They passed out at the back of the inn to a small courtyard. Here were several troopers holding some horses. The Comte and his company mounted, a spare horse having been kept for Rupert, and Martin was put up behind one of the soldiers. Then they trotted quickly down the street, the Comte and de Voes leading, with Rupert and Martin placed in the middle of the troop.

On all sides dreadful sounds and more dreadful sights met them. A systematic house-to-house search for the heretics was being organized, and the unfortunates when discovered were hunted down without mercy—men, women and children, old and young. Twice they encountered bands of soldiers with an attendant rabble, their faces distorted with the lust to kill, holding flaming torches in hands which, like their weapons, were red with blood.

But the Comte, leading his men forward at a sharp trot, did not hesitate, and the rabble had to give way, trampling back on each other in their hurry to get out of his path.

They turned at last into a quiet side street and moved forward more swiftly. Then suddenly the far end of it was blocked by a shouting, running crowd before which fled a girl, a child of eight or nine, with fair streaming hair and a face blanched with terror. The Comte checked his horse and flung up his hand. Instantly the troop behind him halted and stood waiting. The child ran on, blind with fear, unmindful of the horsemen until she was up to them. Then the Comte bent over and, catching her in his arms, swung her up before him with a low laugh. Feeling his hands on her, the child gave a shriek of terror and began to struggle. But the Comte, holding her firmly, smiled.

"Do not be afraid, little lady," he said, "those devils shall not touch you now. You are quite safe up here, so keep still."

Then as the child gazed wonderingly at him in silence, he moved his horse forward and the rest followed.

The crowd, seeing it was to be baulked of its prey, drew across the road with threatening shouts, but the Comte only quickened his horse's pace and came on with the evident determination of riding some of the men down if they did not clear a road. Not till the horses were almost on them did they give way, moving reluctantly aside, and the Comte led his men steadily through a muttering, scowling sea of furies. Only one man, however, madder than the rest, moved to stop them. With a long knife clutched fiercely, he sprang forward, and, seizing the Comte's saddle, reached up to stab at the child.

"You cannot save the brat," he yelled with an oath. "It is the King's order. All are to die."

"Very well," replied the Comte, slipping out his poniard, "then you shall be her proxy," and plunged the dagger through the man's throat.

With a choking cry the man relaxed his grip and fell back on the road, whilst the Comte, one arm round the sobbing child, sheathed his weapon and rode on.

They reached the Rue de Valois at last, and here, as everywhere, the signs of Death's carnival were plain to be seen. The house of Madame de Saxe had, however, escaped so far, for before it stood a body of pike-men in the livery of de Guise.

The corporal in charge saluted the Comte respectfully.

"Our orders were to guard the house until you came, Monsieur, and then take your instructions," he said.

The Comte nodded.

"Go on guarding it," he said. "Have you had any trouble?"

"Yes, Monsieur, we've had several callers. The scum saw the house had no cross but we soon showed them that what their betters kept was not for them."

And he nodded to three corpses which lay in a heap in the gutter.

The Comte turned in his saddle.

"You will come into the house with me, M. de Vrieac, and you, Carlote," to the leader of his troop. "The rest of you wait out here." Then catching Martin's pleading gaze, "Yes, you may go with your master. Now, de Voes, will you come?"

And dismounting, he crossed to the door of Madame de Saxe's house, carrying the Huguenot child in his arms. The handle yielded to his touch, and, followed by de Voes, Rupert de Vrieac and Martin, Carlote, with the two extra swords, bringing up the rear, he entered the house.

The dimly lighted hall was empty, but from under a door on their left came a streak of light. Going to this, the Comte knocked sharply and then opened it.

Beyond was a long, high room, lit by many candles, and at the far end, in a high-backed chair, sat Madame de Saxe, very straight and calm, dressed in priceless lace and black velvet, her white hair elaborately coiffed, as though she

were about to attend some great Court function. Kneeling at her side, her face buried in the elder woman's lap,
crouched Marguerite de Vainçeoire. Behind them, a little
to one side, stood six servants in a frightened, huddled
group.

At the sound of their entrance, Marguerite raised her
head with a sharp scream of terror, then the Comte felt himself pushed roughly to one side, and Rupert sprang forward towards her.

"Margot!" he cried, and caught her in his arms, while
she clung to him convulsively, her head against his shoulder.

"Rupert! Rupert!" she moaned, "something dreadful
has happened. They are killing people—all the Huguenots! Aunt says they may come in at any moment and
kill us too. And when you did not come I thought that—
that—— The soldiers outside told us to keep all the windows shuttered or the mob would try to break in. They
said that M. de La Roche had sent them to guard the
house till he came. But now that you and he are both here
we shall be quite safe. Nothing dreadful can happen to us
now, can it?" And she lifted her face, smiling into his
eyes.

Rupert did not reply. He kissed the upturned face
gently, whilst his clasp tightened round her. The Comte
was his bitter enemy, and he had too much common sense
to deceive himself or draw any comforting hope from his
presence. When his bedroom door had been flung open
and Charles de La Roche with his men burst in, Rupert
had expected to be killed instantly. Great had been his
surprise then, when not only had precautions been taken to
guard his life, but he had been brought safely to the very
house where he wished to be, and which he would most
certainly not otherwise have reached. And this house had
been carefully guarded from all danger by the Comte's
orders. Why? The arrangements showed premeditation.
The Comte had obviously some definite, organized plan.
What could it be?

A ghastly suspicion flashed through his brain, only to be immediately dismissed as groundless. Charles de La Roche did not love Marguerite, of that Rupert was certain. An expert love-maker, he had only been trifling with her for his own amusement and to annoy his enemy. Then what could be his reason for saving them in defiance of the King's order, "Spare none!"? It was obvious that he could only wait and see.

Meanwhile the Comte, apparently unconscious of Rupert's action, advanced down the room and bowed gravely to Madame de Saxe. He had put the child out of his arms and led her forward by the hand.

"I trust that you will forgive our intrusion, Madame," he said, "and that you have not been greatly disturbed by the—er—events of to-night. There is no cause for alarm, the soldiers will prevent any one from entering." Then he looked down at the child holding tightly to his hand. "This," he continued, "is one of your religion. There are those who like their pleasures to be without risk to themselves and some butchers were hunting her, but we cheated them of their game then, did we not, little one? The saints alone know where her mother is. Perhaps you——" and he looked questioningly at Madame de Saxe.

Without a word she put out her arms and the proud old face softened as she lifted the child on to her knees. And over the head lying trustingly against her breast, her eyes met those of Charles de La Roche. The Comte was a Catholic and the bitterest enemy of her niece's betrothed, why then had he saved them? Like Rupert, she drew neither hope nor comfort from his action.

"Why have you done all this, Monsieur?" she asked quietly.

And as quietly he answered her: "Because of Rupert de Vrieac."

Then he turned to the others.

"Mademoiselle," he said, bowing to Marguerite, "may

I beg of you to be seated? There is something important which I have to say and which may take a little time."

Then when she had taken a chair, with Rupert standing very close beside her, and holding her hands protectingly, the Comte continued:

"You know that to-day His Majesty signed an edict condemning all Huguenots to death. To-night thousands of your religion have been killed, and there will be more to follow. The King's edict said 'Spare none; all are to die,' and yet in spite of that, I sent soldiers to guard this house. I had men posted outside your inn, de Vrieac, to see that no one harmed you before I came, and then I brought you here in safety. Why? Madame de Saxe asked me that question just now, and I said that you, Rupert de Vrieac, were the answer. This evening you humiliated me, and before witnesses. You taunted me and tried to make my life unbearable. You know that I could never forget that or cease to wish for revenge. And to-night, I shall have it—before witnesses also. M. Lefevre is, I regret, dead, but M. de Voes is here, and others. His Majesty's edict was, I believe, a great surprise; it came in the nature of a shock—to your leaders, but some acted very promptly and so saved their lives. De Biron and others held the Arsenal, and there they have strongly entrenched themselves. The place is practically impregnable, and should the King's advisers refuse to grant his terms of surrender, de Biron has it in his power to blow most of Paris to pieces, therefore the Huguenots at the Arsenal are safe. Now I am prepared to convey Madame de Saxe, her servants and Mlle. de Vainçeoire under a strong and sufficient escort, safely to the Arsenal, and to risk His Majesty's consequent displeasure —on one condition."

"And that condition?" Rupert asked quietly.

"That you become my servant, the slave of my word and wish, for five years, and that during that time you will not attempt to injure me, or permit any one to do so for you. Of course, I could take you by force and compel you to obey me, but I do not like unwilling servants; besides, you would be always trying to murder me. And I think it will hurt your pride more to take my orders pleasantly, for I will not tolerate any glum or scowling looks from you, remember. That is my condition. Now what is your answer?"

For a moment Rupert did not reply.

"And if I do not agree to that condition?" he asked at last.

The Comte shrugged his shoulders.

"In that case Carlote will give you and your servant back your swords and M. de Voes and I will leave the house, the soldiers with us. The guard once removed, it will not take the rabble long to discover that this covert has not been drawn, or to force an entrance. Once inside, you have seen enough to-night to know what they will do then, and your two swords will not count for much. That is what will happen if you do not agree to my condition, M. de Vrieac."

Rupert took a step towards him with blazing eyes.

"You devil!" he said hoarsely; and the Comte laughed.

"Is that your answer?" he asked.

Rupert hesitated. Had only his own life been concerned, his choice would have been simple. There are things more bitter and hard to bear than death. But there were the others—Marguerite, Madame de Saxe; and as he remembered some of the horrors he had seen that night he shuddered. Better anything should happen to him than that such a fate should come to them. But to serve Charles de La Roche, to voluntarily put himself into his enemy's power for five years! Was there no loophole, no third way of escape, from such a choice?

"And if—if I consent, how am I to know that the others will reach the Arsenal, or be safe there?" he said slowly.

"I will provide for that," the Comte replied with a grave nod. "Once at the Arsenal they will most assuredly be safe, but so that you may be certain they have arrived there,

I am prepared to do my share of the bargain first. You are intimate with de Biron, I believe, and know his handwriting? Very well. Madame, Mademoiselle, and the servants shall go to the Arsenal under a strong escort, and I will not claim the fulfillment of your promise until you have received word, in de Biron's own writing, that they are safely under his care. Does that content you?"

Desperately Rupert looked around him. There was no escape. Marguerite, only half understanding the Comte's demand and what fate held in the balance for her, watched him very trustfully. Madame de Saxe was bending over the child on her lap and would not meet his glance. Martin, his eyes on the floor, stood very still beside him. With a sudden impulse of emotion Rupert laid his hand affectionately on the servant's shoulder.

"You will save Martin, and the child, too?" he asked.

Again the Comte nodded.

"You bargain like a Jew," he said, "but they shall be included. All the Huguenots in this room shall be safely taken to the Arsenal, I promise you—on that one condition."

"Then I agree," Rupert replied in a low voice.

CHAPTER IV

A GLEAM of triumph shone in the eyes of La Roche. "I thought you would accept," he said. "Now I carry out my part of the bargain. It would be better if the ladies did not start until daylight. The streets will be quieter then, and they will not be so likely to see things which might shock them; besides, there are no doubt preparations which they will wish to make and they would feel the better for a few hours' rest. So I propose that they and the others shall leave for the Arsenal at seven o'clock. It will be perfectly safe to remain here till then. The soldiers outside will keep off the rabble. Now with your permission, ladies," and he bowed to Madame and Marguerite, "M. de Voes and I will retire. I shall return at seven o'clock to see that all preparations for your departure are correct; until then I beg to take my leave. You, de Vrieac, I should advise to stay here, although as your promise does not become binding until de Biron acknowledges the ladies' safe arrival, you are free to go out if you wish, providing that you are here when the letter arrives. As the streets are somewhat unsafe for one of your religion to-night, perhaps it would be better for you to keep within." Then struck by a sudden thought. "Carlote," he called, "bring me M. de Vrieac's sword," and taking it from him handed it to Rupert. "In case you should go out and until de Biron's letter comes, you had better have this. Adieu, ladies, until seven o'clock. Are you ready, de Voes? Come, Carlote." And he left the room.

They heard the three men cross the hall, the outer door closed, the Comte's voice spoke to the soldiers and was followed by the sound of horses trotting away up the street.

There was silence in the room for a long minute. Madame de Saxe watched Rupert, a kind smile on the lips which were usually so grave and proud, and from him her glance traveled to Marguerite, who, with bent head, was looking at a ring upon her finger. Shrugging her shoulders impatiently Madame rose.

She dismissed her servants with a few short instructions and putting the child into Martin's arms, bade him carry her upstairs; then with another glance at the lovers, turned to follow. But in the doorway she paused, looking back. Neither had moved nor seemed conscious of her movements. Then very swiftly Madame went to Marguerite and there was an angry sparkle in her eyes.

"Marguerite," she whispered, laying her hand on the girl's shoulder, "M. de Vrieac has given more than his life to save us and have you no comfort to give him? Cease thinking of yourself, child, and go to him." Then she left the room, closing the door firmly behind her.

Marguerite stared after her. Given more than his life! What could her aunt mean? Surely one could not pay a bigger price than death? To her that was the greatest fear, the supreme horror. But that escaped, what could there be so very dreadful to endure, with life and senses, the sunshine and a thousand things to please and love, remaining? She was utterly incapable of understanding that the suffering endured by a proud man's soul could be ten thousand times more acute than any agony which could be inflicted upon his body. She could not see anything very dreadful in the bargain which Rupert had made. The arrangement was not going to last forever, only a few years. She could not see why he should have hesitated to consent, or why Madame de Saxe should have thought the price so terrible for him to pay. It was almost as bad for herself. Of course she would wait for him, spend the best years of her life lonely and faithful, till he could be free to claim her. And now she thought it over, it was almost worse for her. Five years in a man's life were not long, but in a

woman's they passed with leaden feet. She would be quite
old, almost gray-haired, by the time her constancy could gain
its reward. And she saw herself a heroine, sitting in the
tower at Vainçeoire, waiting with patient, tired eyes for
Rupert's coming. The picture soothed her wounded con-
ceit and, her temper cooler, she looked round at Rupert.
Poor boy! How very unhappy he seemed, standing there,
staring at nothing. But of course he was unhappy, no doubt
he believed that he would have to part with her forever,
that she would not be brave enough to wait for him all that
long time. Well, she would show him what a strong,
splendid love hers was. And rising, she went softly to him.

"Rupert," she whispered, laying her hand caressingly
on his shoulder, "you must not be so unhappy. I will
wait for you, dear. Even if you do not come for years
and years it will make no difference, I shall go on loving
you just the same, always."

Lifting his white, tortured face from the shelter of his
arms, Rupert turned and caught her to him with a passionate cry.

"Margot! Margot! My brave little sweetheart!"

And then, because she found that picture of herself in
the tower at Vainçeoire very alluring, they sat down close
together and Marguerite told him just how those five years
of waiting would be spent. They were to be a continuous
vigil, with little time for food and less for sleep; her eyes
turned ever on the road along which he must come, her
hands busy with some delicate piece of embroidery, she
would sit at her open window, the sun shining upon her by
day, a burning candle at her side by night. And Rupert,
trying to keep from his mind the thought of how he would
spend those years, listened enraptured and felt his love for
her growing into adoration.

"I will give you a token," she said, "and you must
always wear it on your heart, and then if you should ever
cease to love me I shall know, for it will fly back to me."

"God's pity!" he cried, "how could I ever cease to love you, my brave Margot?"

She laughed happily as she unfastened a knot of blue ribbons from her dress, and having lifted it lightly to her lips, gave it to him, watching him contentedly as he kissed it and bestowed it safely in his doublet. Then he knelt before her, and slipping the signet-ring from his little finger, placed it on one of hers, lifting the ring and finger reverently to his lips. And as his kisses fell passionately the clock of St. Marc le Vau near by struck the hour loudly. One—two—three—four—five—six.

Marguerite started and withdrew her hand.

"I must go," she said quickly, "we leave at seven and I must make some preparations. Aunt has been upstairs these last three hours. Oh, my dear, I must! Let us say our 'Good-by' now, before any one comes."

She would not let him go further than the hall, but as he stood watching her mount the stairs she turned and descended a few steps. He sprang up to meet her, and with her head against his shoulder, his arms round her, she whispered:

"It is not really 'Good-by,' only 'Au revoir.' We shall meet again and the time will go quite quickly, for you. I shall be always waiting. So you must not be unhappy any more. It is not as if M. de La Roche were going to put you in a dungeon. No doubt he will let you ride and hunt and you will go about quite freely. It will be almost like being at Vrieac. Au revoir."

Then she sprang from his arms and ran up the stairs, turning at the top to wave, whilst he smiled at her bravely. But when she had gone the smile faded and a very bitter look crossed his face.

" 'Almost like being at Vrieac,' " he muttered, returning to his old position before the dead fire. "Ah! Margot, Margot! Thank God you can never know what it cost me to accept La Roche's condition."

As he stood there a thought, vague at first, then growing more definite, crept into his brain. He had not yet given his promise to the Comte, the start was not to be made for another hour; he had his sword and was free to go out if he chose. Once in the street with no bandage on his left arm it would not be long before he met a band of the murderers. A short, sharp fight, a few good thrusts with his sword, perhaps one or two of the scum sent after their victims, then they would bear him down by force of numbers and he would be beyond the fulfilling of La Roche's condition. And the Comte could not, would not carry out his threat in case of unfulfillment. The rescue of the Huguenot child had shown Rupert new possibilities in his character. If he were dead and so beyond the reach of the Comte's revenge, Rupert believed that the others would still be conveyed to safety. It was obvious that the Comte's quarrel was not with them, that he was practically indifferent where they went. It was only in the power which they gave to hurt Rupert through them that they were of value. Then Rupert set his shoulders and put the thought very firmly from him. Honor can forge a stronger chain than was ever wrought from steel or silver. "What Vrieac owes, Vrieac pays." It was the motto of his house. His promise had not been given in actual words, but the chain of honor held him firmly nevertheless. He must remain and pay the price.

Some twenty minutes later, the Comte, accompanied by Paul de Voes, entered the room. A quick satisfaction shone in his eyes when he saw the man standing motionless, with bowed head, before the fire. The same thoughts which had been in Rupert's mind had occurred to him, and it relieved him to see that the honor upon which he relied had stood the test. The more honorable de Vrieac was, the more likely those five years were to smart, and the less need there would be for the Comte to keep a watch on him.

A coach was in readiness outside, and as the little baggage which the ladies wished to take with them was being carried to it, Rupert drew Martin aside.

"I want you to attach yourself to Mlle. de Vainçeoire, Martin. Look after her and guard her with your life. You have been a good servant to me, be as faithful to her. I dare not give you my sword, they might notice and take it from you, but here is my poniard. Hide it in your sleeve, and, if need be, use it in Mademoiselle's service. Good-by, my friend. I have not been a perfect master, but I hope you will forgive any harshness or injustice I have shown you."

And he held out his hand frankly.

"Monsieur! Monsieur!" murmured Martin, with tears in his eyes, as he raised the hand impulsively to his lips. "What have I to forgive? And never fear, Mademoiselle shall be safe; no harm shall come to her while I am alive to guard her, Monsieur."

Then Madame de Saxe descended the stairs, followed by Marguerite, both ready for their journey. Crossing the hall, Madame came over to Rupert, taking his hand in both of hers.

"M. de Vrieac," she said, a very soft light in her eyes, "if the gratitude of an old woman is any help to you, you know you have it unfailingly, do you not? But there! What is the use of words? They are easily spoken. I will try and prove what I have just said. Do not feel anxious for Marguerite. Martin and I between us will see that she suffers no harm, and when you come for her you will find that we have taken good care of the child. The time will pass, not quickly I know, but it *will* pass, and you will be surprised that five such years could seem so short. Marguerite is little more than a child, but she loves you very dearly, M. de Vrieac, never doubt she loves you."

And leaving him with this little ray of comfort, she turned coldly to the Comte and allowed him to lead her down to the coach.

The parting with Marguerite was not so easy. Now that the actual leave-taking had come she clung to Rupert, weeping bitterly. To the young, five years seem like fifty, and they stretched out before her as a boundless desert of interminable loneliness and sorrow.

"It is 'Good-by' for always," she cried. "I will not leave you behind. M. de La Roche cannot make me. You must come to the Arsenal or I shall stay here." And her hands fastened round his neck, refusing to let go.

Finally, with white, set face, Rupert gathered her in his arms and carried her out to the coach, where Madame and the others were waiting. With gentle firmness he loosened her clasp and laid her half fainting in Madame's arms.

"Be brave, my dear heart," he whispered; "be brave, it is only for a time."

But Marguerite hid her face against Madame's shoulder with a moan.

"It is forever," she sobbed. "I shall never see him again."

Then Rupert stood back, Carlote closed the door, the soldiers fell into their places and the coach rolled slowly away.

Like one in a dream Rupert followed the Comte and Paul de Voes back to the room, whilst Carlote went upstairs, extinguishing the lights.

Bringing out some dice, de Voes suggested to the Comte that they should play.

"I suppose you will not care to join us, de Vrieac?" asked the latter. "De Biron's letter cannot be here for half an hour, so, as your promise does not hold till it comes, there is still time for you to go out if you wish." And he gave the Huguenot a very sharp, keen glance.

Rupert did not, however, reply, but crossing once more to the fireplace, stood with averted face, and the Comte, shrugging his shoulders, joined de Voes at the table.

A great silence seemed to fall over the house, broken only by Carlote's heavy tread on the stairs and the ceaseless clatter of the dice. Outside the soldiers stood with crossed pikes. Several times bands of the rabble, looking for fresh victims, went up the street, but the guard made them disinclined to meddle with the house, and they passed on, singing and shouting.   The gray light of the day crept in through chinks in the shutters; several of the candles had guttered and their grease trickled over the sconces; a small table had been upset, scattering the contents of a workbox on the floor; the whole room looked deserted and comfortless.

Suddenly there was a sound of horses trotting up the street, and coming gradually nearer, until they finally stopped outside.   A moment later Carlote knocked at the door, and entering, brought the Comte a letter.   Breaking the seal he read it, then turned to Rupert, who had moved forward with a quick intake of his breath.

"They have got there safely," said the Comte.   "Here, read it for yourself.   That is de Biron's writing, I think?"

With a hand that never trembled, Rupert took the letter.

It was a formal acknowledgment of the safe arrival at the Arsenal of Madame de Saxe, her niece Mlle. de Vainçeoire and seven servants, in the Grand Master's hand and sealed with his signet.

"Yes," said Rupert quietly, "that is his writing without doubt," and raising his head he looked his enemy unflinchingly in the face.

"Very well," replied the Comte, meeting his eyes as steadily.   "Then I have done my part of the bargain.   It remains for you to take your oath and do yours.   Give me your sword," he added, a peremptory note of command in his voice.

For a second Rupert hesitated.   They were at the Arsenal now, safe from all harm or the power of the Comte's revenge.   Carlote stood at the end of the room, de Voes at the other side of the table, and he had not yet given his word.   What was to prevent him, instead of handing up his sword, from running it through the Comte's body and having de Voes' or Carlote's through his own?   It would be an easy thing to die and what should stop him?

Then his lips set hard and without a word he handed

the sword, hilt forwards, to his enemy. The chain of
honor still held firmly. What Vrieac owed Vrieac would
pay to the full, and, his hands on the naked sword, as a
man swears to his over-lord, so Rupert gave his oath to
the Comte, swore to serve him faithfully for five years
and never, knowingly, to let either death or injury come
near him during that time.

When he had sworn the Comte stood silent, turning the
sword in his hands; then with a quick movement he bent
the blade across his knee, snapping it in two, and flung
the pieces on the floor.

"Only my soldiers wear swords, not the servants," he
said, eyeing the Huguenot coldly.

It was a dramatic touch of cruelty, and the flush that
crept into Rupert's cheeks showed that it had hurt. The
Comte watched him for a second, then turned to de Voes.

"You have now, Paul," he said, "the story of M. de
Vrieac's revenge—and mine. I am sure your friends will
find it both amusing and interesting. I hope you will tell
it to them as soon as may be. Now, if you are ready, let
us go. I wish to be out of Paris in an hour. Carlote,
you can leave the door open behind you, there will be
plenty of wolves ready to pillage the house as soon as we are
safely gone."

Outside, the Comte gave a few instructions, and the order
to mount; then he and de Voes moved off, followed by
Rupert and Carlote riding together, the rest of the troop
bringing up the rear, whilst de Guise's pikemen marched
away in the opposite direction. Hardly had they disappeared when, apparently from nowhere, figures came creeping stealthily, and, with a swift rush, crossed the street to
the empty house. If they could not have the heretics,
they would have what they could get of their possessions.

It was seldom that the dregs of the city found themselves
encouraged to rob and murder with a King's order to
support them, and they meant to make the most of their
time.

CHAPTER V

A N hour later, the Comte de La Roche and his company rode out of Paris by the Porte St. Louis, taking the great high road which led to the southeast.

The King's orders had been that none were to leave Paris and they found the great gates closed against them; but the Comte showed the captain-in-charge a pass signed by His Majesty, also—more important still—cross-signed by Henri de Guise, and after one glance at it, the guard had received instructions to let them through. So they rode forward, the Comte in front, then Rupert with Carlote two lengths behind, the sixteen troopers following.

With only a short halt at noon they rode all day, hard at first, but more leisurely, once Paris was left behind. The Comte, keeping aloof, did not speak or even seem to notice Rupert, whilst Carlote, riding alongside, was equally silent. Only when Rupert's horse picked up a stone, and Carlote, brusquely preventing Rupert from doing so, got down to take it out, did he speak. Then as the soldier swung himself into his saddle again, Rupert, moved by a sudden impulse, asked their destination.

"La Roche," Carlote answered gruffly. "My lord's castle there, four leagues from Beaunais, three days' ride from here."

Rupert, although he had already guessed the answer, shuddered, and lapsed once more into silence. Truly, he was to pay the fullest price, for in the heart of the enemy's country what hope could be left to him?

As the dusk began to fall, the Comte, avoiding the town of Montmai, rode to a little village beyond and there called a halt. In the bustle and confusion of arrival he turned to Rupert, speaking to him for the first time since they had left Paris.

"Come with me," he said harshly. "Carlote will see to the horse. I do not please that you should eat or sleep with the soldiers."

Then he entered the inn, the host, overjoyed at the unexpected amount of custom, bustling on before, Rupert, silent and miserable, following him.

A wood fire crackled on the wide hearth and the room looked bright and cheerful after the darkness without. The hostess, having brought water, hurried off to see to the supper, and the Comte, drying his hands leisurely, placed one foot upon a chair.

"Unfasten my spur-leathers," he said, turning to Rupert.

Then as the Huguenot took a step forward with angry eyes, the Comte held up his hand.

"Do not look at me like that," he cried sternly. "I said I would have no scowls from you and I mean what I say. The sooner you learn that the better, do you understand? Obey your orders."

His gauntlets lay near, and picking one up, he struck Rupert sharply with it on the shoulder. They were alone in the room, and for a moment it seemed that Rupert would attack his enemy, but the Comte smiled coolly into the blazing eyes and made no movement to defend himself.

Rupert stooped down in silence and unbuckled the straps, a flush of impotent anger burning his face. And the Comte, as he watched him, flushed slightly too.

When the supper was brought, he ordered Rupert sharply to be seated, and, one at each end of the table, they sat down in silence. The Comte ate and drank heartily, but Rupert, choked with a passion of hate he could hardly control, sat still, staring at the blazing logs, his hands clenched fiercely before him. The Comte, having finished his meal, watched him under narrowed lids.

"You are devilish poor company, and you had better eat

some food," he said at last. "I noticed you had little when we halted."

But neither by word nor movement did Rupert show that he had heard. The Comte waited for a moment, then he rose, an angry sparkle in his eyes, and putting some meat on a plate he set it down before Rupert, filling his glass with wine.

"Take that and let me have no nonsense," he said sternly. "I will not have you ill, so do not try any tricks of that kind." Then, as Rupert sat obstinately still, he added sneeringly, "I was not aware that any exceptions were mentioned when you took your oath. When I give an order, *any* order, you will obey, the sooner the better for you. I am not used to disobedience from my servants. If I tell you to cut off your finger you will do so, and when I tell you to eat you will do so also, M. Rupert de Vrieac."

And with a sweeping bow he walked out of the room, leaving Rupert to eat his supper in silent fury.

They made an early start the next morning, stopping at noon in a little wood where the Comte gave orders for a several hours' halt. The horses having been hobbled and turned loose to graze, the men, hot and dusty with their long ride, were glad to fling themselves down under the shade of the trees, some sleeping, others playing cards.

It was a brilliantly hot day, and Rupert, fearing that the Comte was observing him and dreading a repetition of the previous evening's scene before the soldiers, forced himself to take some food, and then went away further amongst the trees where he could escape the sound of the men's voices. With the instinct of a suffering animal he longed to be alone. Much more of his enemies' company would sap his self-control, and he would either give way to an hysterical outburst of anger, or snatching up a weapon, make a murderous attack on some of them.

A little stream ran through the wood and, following it down, he came to a bed of soft moss spread at the feet of two giant oaks. Lying on his back, Rupert stared up at the blue sky between the branches and wished that life could end for him there. The next day, within twenty-four hours or less, they would reach the Castle of La Roche, and it would be there that the real humiliation of his position would begin. Up to now his relations with the Comte had been just bearable; indeed, before the soldiers, the Comte had always been coldly civil to him; but once at the castle what would happen? Rupert shuddered, and closed his eyes quickly, as though to shut out the visions which crossed his mind.

Lying thus, soothed by the running water, the birds' songs, the soft stirring of the leaves, his mood grew calmer and he began to doze.

Suddenly a slight sound disturbed him, and he sat up abruptly, looking at the opposite bank. Then he shrank back, drawing himself more behind the shelter of the trees, for just across the stream, a short stone's-throw away, lay the Comte de La Roche, his head pillowed on a fallen branch and his whole attitude denoting profound slumber. So absorbed had Rupert been in his own thoughts that he had never observed his enemy's approach, and it was only when a loud snore attracted his attention that he became aware of his proximity.

Rupert's instant thought was to move away before the Comte, who had, apparently, not observed his presence, should wake and discover him, and he was just about to quickly do so when there was a rustle in a thicket on his left, and he heard his name called in an urgent whisper. Softly a hand pushed the leaves aside, then a man's head appeared, slowly followed by his body.

Stealthily he crawled forward, keeping a keen watch on the Comte; then, having put a thick tree trunk between himself and the sleeper, he sat down, nodding to Rupert with a friendly smile. Rupert, who had watched him in silence, caught his hand eagerly, for he recognized him as one of five Huguenot brothers in the service of Teligny.

The Comte De La Roche and his company left the bloody streets o. Paris for the south.

"De Maublas! What in heaven's name are you doing here?"

The newcomer laughed grimly.

"I came to see you," he said, laying his hand on Rupert's shoulder. "François, Gil and Marc are dead," he continued, passion blazing in his eyes; "they were butchered by those devils, killed in the street like rats, but Hugo and I fought our way through and got to the Arsenal. Then Mme. de Saxe with Mlle. de Vainçeoire came and told us what had happened to you. So Hugo and I thought we saw a way to revenge the others. It was useless to try in Paris. One could, of course, kill some of the scum, but it was impossible to get at any of the leaders. Out in the country, however, we should have more chance. La Roche is Guise's friend, and we could make him pay for that friendship. De Biron got us a pass out, and we have been following you close ever since, but La Roche kept such a guard that we have not had an opportunity to show ourselves before. Now, however, nothing could be better. The soldiers are off guard; we heard that no start will be made for a couple of hours, and La Roche is asleep. Hugo is with the horses at the bottom of that ride. We have a spare one for you; the Loire is only twenty leagues away, and once across that we are safe. All you have to do is to slip quietly away with us and by the time your escape is discovered we will have a good start. Besides, they will never think we have taken their road, so they will waste some time hunting the woods and the other tracks. Come. The sooner we start the better, but first we will leave de Guise's friend a little present of this through his throat." He drew out a poniard, putting it into Rupert's hand. "Strike quickly, and he will never make a sound. I would like to have the killing of him, but you have the bigger debt to repay. Be quick."

He had been speaking in an urgent whisper, giving no chance to interrupt him. Now, however, Rupert shook his head, his face very drawn and white.

"I cannot, de Maublas," he muttered; "God help me, I cannot. I swore I would not kill him or try to escape. You must ride on and leave me. I gave him my oath."

But de Maublas shrugged his shoulders impatiently.

"And you think of keeping it—to a Catholic after St. Bartholomew! What of the King's oath to Coligny? His promise to us Huguenots? You are a fool, de Vrieac. But if you will not do it, then give me the dagger. I never promised anything, and I suppose you did not swear to kill yourself at his death or keep a vigil over his corpse? Very well," he added grimly, as Rupert's face set obstinately, "then I will kill him with my sword, 'twill serve as well."

But with a quick movement Rupert stood in front of him, catching his wrist.

"No! I swore that too, de Maublas—to guard him. 'What Vrieac owes Vrieac pays,' and he saved Mlle. de Vain-çeoire. For God's sake ride on and leave him!"

De Maublas' eyes blazed with anger and he made a sudden swift movement, but Rupert was on the alert and, eluding his grip, jumped quickly back across the stream, standing almost beside the still-sleeping Comte.

"Go," he whispered sharply to de Maublas, "or, God's death, man, I will raise the alarm."

They stood thus for a second, facing each other across the stream, de Maublas flushed with passion. Then as Rupert's face showed no signs of yielding, he shrugged his shoulders.

A sour smile twisted his lips and he made a little ironical bow to the man waiting on the other bank.

"My very hearty congratulations, M. de Vrieac," he said in a clear whisper, every word of which cut like a lash. "I think I understand you now. Having a pref-erence to be on the winning side you will of course make every effort to gain La Roche's friendship, for you are certainly aware that he has great influence with de Guise. To do this you must naturally keep M. le Comte alive. You will no doubt have to change your religion also. But perhaps you have already done that? You traitor! And I came to save you! Ugh!"

Turning abruptly away he hurried down the glade to his brother, while Rupert watched him in silence with miserable eyes.

When de Maublas had disappeared, Rupert looked down at the Comte, who was still sleeping soundly.

"You devil!" he said, a sob of rage in his voice. "You devil!"

He still held the poniard in his hand. One quick downward stab and the Comte would be a dead man. The blade was very bright and sharp, it needed only the smallest thrust of his wrist. Then he realized the danger of such thoughts, the misery deepened in his eyes, and with a jerk of his arm he threw the weapon away across the stream. He watched it flash through the sunlight and fall into a hazel thicket, then with bowed head he walked away.

When he was gone, the Comte opened his eyes cautiously and, sitting up, looked around him, smiling in quiet amusement.

"I think I have had a narrow escape of being stabbed," he said to himself. "Ciel! I thought once I should have to wake up and help de Vrieac. He stood against the fellow well, though I am not sure he did not feel more tempted to kill me after the other had gone. Upon my soul I felt quite relieved when he threw that thing away. Where has it gone?"

Crossing to the thicket he hunted about till he found the poniard. And slipping it into his belt, the Comte walked back to his men, a thoughtful look on his face.

The sun was shining gloriously in the first freshness of the young day when the Comte, having left the soldiers to follow on more slowly with the pack animals, rode with Carlote and Rupert out of the beech woods and saw the Castle of La Roche two miles away across the valley.

The original castle had been built by that fierce Roland

des Roches who had fought so gloriously for Charlemagne
and had received the surrounding country as a reward.
It had been added to from time to time by his descendants,
and now stood, a grim, gray pile, strongly walled and
towered, frowning down from its commanding height on
the woods and village, river, fields and vineyards, spread
around its feet.

The Comte's eyes brightened as he saw it all, and he
quickened his horse's pace. Unlike many of the younger
nobles of his time, he had a deep affection for his in-
heritance; life in Paris was merely an interlude from
which he was always glad to escape back to his country.
Wherever he might look the land was his, and from early
childhood he had known and loved each acre. No ranger
could tell better than he the spot in that marshy ground
beyond the causeway where the herons would be found;
into those steep pinewoods beyond the river—in whose
depths the wolves still lingered, coming stealthily down
in the winter sometimes to the very doorways of the houses
to find food—he had gone hunting alone after boar and
wild cat.

The clock on the west tower of the castle struck nine
as they rode through the great gates. To Rupert the
deep, slow notes were a knell tolling for freedom, happiness and love, lost by him for five long years.

He looked around and felt a chill of misery. The place
appeared so somber and prison-like that his courage faltered
for a moment, and it was pride alone which kept his manner
calm and apparently indifferent to his surroundings. What
Vrieac owed Vrieac would pay, but his enemy should never
guess what the payment of that debt cost him.

In the courtyard the Comte dismounted, and two great
hounds which had been baying round a wolf, newly captured and chained to a staple in the wall, bounded up to
greet him, whilst several men who had been looking on
came forward quickly to take the horses.

"Where is your mistress, Perron?" the Comte asked

the old steward, who had hurried out with evident pleasure to welcome him.

"Mademoiselle is in the new garden, Monsieur; she does not know you have arrived."

"Very well, we will go to her there and announce the fact. Carlote, give me those packages," and taking from the trooper two bundles sewn in linen which had been divided from the baggage at that morning's start, and carefully carried by Carlote, the Comte handed them to Rupert.

"Come with me, de Vrieac, and bring these."

They went through an archway to a long terrace on the south side of the castle, whence there was a glorious view over the whole countryside, reaching away to where the spire of Beaunais Cathedral pierced the blue heat haze, down some stone steps and across a lawn to a high yew hedge in which there was a little wicket gate.

Unlatching it softly, the Comte passed in, followed by Rupert. Within the garden were many flowers growing in glorious profusion—roses, pansies, regal white lilies. A smooth green lawn sloped down to a bubbling fountain, beside which, his magnificence duplicated in the water, a peacock was displaying the glories of his tail.

At the far end of the garden was an old stone seat, overhung by honeysuckle, and here, her back turned to them, her hands full of trailing sprays, stood a tall, dark-haired girl. She had not observed their presence, and for a second the Comte stood watching her, smiling quietly to himself, then he gave a clear, soft whistle. Instantly she turned, the flowers fell from her hands, and she came towards him with shining eyes.

"Charles!" she cried. "When did you come? Perron never told me."

"I thought I could better bring the news myself. Perron is getting old and slow," the Comte answered laughing, as he kissed her.

And then across his shoulder, the girl's eyes met those

of Rupert de Vrieac, who stood ten paces away watching her. Instantly the soft light died out of her face, changing to a cold disdain. Catching her glance, the Comte turned.

"Ah! I had forgotten," he said. "You had the letter I sent to you by Pierre on Thursday, Yoeland? Well, this is —our new servant. De Vrieac, I present you to Mlle. de Breux, my sister and your mistress. You will take your orders from her as you would from me."

With a slight inclination of her head the girl extended her fingers, and Rupert, a flush creeping into his face at the scarcely-veiled contempt in her manner, stepped forward quietly and kissed her hand.

He concealed his feelings well. Outwardly calm, within he was seething with anger and a longing to crush the fingers which he had raised so gently with his own. Love is not the only emotion which may come to a man at first sight, and in Yoeland de Breux Rupert instinctively knew that he had met a woman who could hate and be hated by him very passionately. He had completely forgotten that the Comte had any sisters. Now in this beautiful, cold-mannered girl he divined an enemy, who would be more exacting, more subtly cruel, than a dozen Comtes. Gently releasing her hand he bowed and stepped back to his former position.

The Comte had watched in silence, looking from one to the other with his quiet, whimsical smile. Now he took the bigger package from Rupert, and having cut the fastenings with his poniard, presented it to his sister with an elaborate obeisance.

"From Paris, for the acceptance of Mlle. de Breux," he said.

As she unwound it, the girl gave a low exclamation of pleasure, and drew out a long, black velvet cloak with a deep collar of splendid ermine.

"Charles!" she cried with shining eyes, "how beautiful."

"Then 'tis fitting you should wear it," he replied, slipping it on her shoulders. "Why, you look like a queen indeed, ma mie. I thought," he added more quietly, "that when you sat with Anne and the nights were cold, you would like it. How is she, Yoeland?"

A deep shadow of anxiety fell across the girl's face.

"Oh, Charles, let us go and tell her you have come. She will be so glad. I—I do not think she is so well, her sleep is broken and she has been very fretful lately."

"Let us go to her now, then," said the Comte, taking his sister's arm and hurrying her across the garden. "I have got a little thing which may amuse her. Perhaps it is only the heat which makes her restless."

They went out of the garden gate, over the terrace, and into the castle, through the great hall, and up the staircase, Rupert, carrying the remaining bundle and wondering what was expected of him, following quietly. At the head of the staircase ran a long corridor, and they stopped at a door half-way down it.

Turning the handle softly, Mlle. de Breux peeped into the room, then pushed the door wider.

"Anne," she called softly, "Charles has come back."

Some one gave a cry of pleasure, and the Comte and his sister went quickly into the room, whilst Rupert waited outside in the passage. From beyond the half-closed door he could hear the Comte speaking very gently, and the sound of a clear soft laugh. Then the Comte called him.

"De Vrieac! Are you there? Where is that parcel? Bring it in here."

Entering, Rupert shut the door behind him and moved forward. At the far end of the room, on a low bed, supported by many pillows, lay a little girl, with straight golden hair and beautiful wide blue eyes. Beside her sat Mlle. de Breux holding one of the child's thin hands, all the cold disdain gone from her face and replaced by a very tender smile. Opposite, on the other side of the bed, knelt M. le

Comte de La Roche, his arm round the little figure, the golden head lying contentedly against his shoulder.

It was quite obvious that to these two there was nothing so precious as the little ten-year-old sister, crippled by a nurse's carelessness from babyhood, and whose life could only be made bearable by their love and a service which each vied with the other in rendering untiringly.

As he looked at the child Rupert thought he knew the reason why the Comte had saved the Huguenot girl. She had had the same intense blue eyes, the straight gold hair, and bore a general resemblance to the little cripple sister at La Roche.

Having signed to Rupert to undo the fastenings, the Comte put the package in the eager, outstretched hands, which trembled so much with excitement that Mlle. de Breux came to their assistance. Then, a flush of pleased surprise burning in the white cheeks, the child looked up quickly from one to the other of the smiling faces bending over her.

"O-oh!" she said, with a little gasp.

Within the linen wrappings was a wax model of La Belle Valois, dressed in an exact copy of the splendid robes in which she had been married to Henri de Navarre, who was also there, in a dashing costume of black and silver. By an ingenious arrangement of clockwork, the two figures would stand up and gravely bow, then the queen slowly extended her hand, and Navarre, bending stiffly from the waist, leant forward and kissed the out-stretched fingers.

With sparkling eyes the child watched the evolutions, clapping her hands in spontaneous delight; whilst Mlle. de Breux, laughing softly, laid her cheek against the golden hair, and the Comte, pleased at her pleasure, wound up the toy again and again for her amusement. Then suddenly the laughing blue eyes encountered those of Rupert de Vrieac, who stood at the end of the bed, noticing him for the first time. With grave interest they scanned him, taking stock of the stranger, then the smile returned, approvingly friendly.

"How do you do?" she said, putting out her hand. Coming forward, Rupert knelt by the bed, and with very different feelings from those with which he had taken her sister's raised the child's fingers to his lips.

"My name is Anne," she said gravely. "What is yours? I like you, Monsieur."

Before he could reply, however, Mlle. de Breux took the child's hands quickly in hers and rose, standing tall and straight by the bed. The smile had faded from her face, leaving it cold and scornful.

"He is no one, Anne dear," she said, "only a new servant of Charles'. Vrieac, wait for M. le Comte in the passage."

Without the slightest change of expression Rupert rose and having bowed quietly, left the room, putting the crown to his self-control by closing the door very gently behind him, though once in the passage, out of her sight, he stood with clenched hands, cursing Mlle. de Breux fiercely under his breath.

CHAPTER VI

RUPERT had been given a little room at the top of the east tower of the castle. Except for Carlote, who slept in a kind of large cupboard at the bottom of the stairs, he was here away from the rest of the household, a fact for which he was duly grateful. Rather to his surprise he was also allowed to have his meals alone and undisturbed. He had fully expected to be quartered with the servants, and had prepared himself to bear their insults without betraying his feelings. This, however, had evidently not been part of the Comte's plan. With the exception of Carlote, for whom, in spite of his gruff, blunt manner, Rupert began to entertain a quiet liking, he had nothing whatever to do with any of the household save the Comte and Mlle. de Breux. But these two—and especially the latter, as he had foreseen—contrived to make his days a burden from which the nights in the quiet of his little turret room were all too short a respite.

Of Mlle. Anne he saw nothing since his ignominious repulsion from her room until, on the second afternoon after his arrival, he was sent by the Comte with a message to Mlle. de Breux, who was with the child on the south terrace. For on fine warm days the little invalid was often carried down to a couch placed in a sheltered spot in front of the castle, where she would lie for hours watching the birds and trailing clouds with Mlle. de Breux or old Jeanne, her nurse, sitting beside her. This afternoon Mlle. Anne lay busily engaged in putting La Belle Valois and Navarre through their clockwork evolutions, and Rupert's eyes softened suddenly as, coming across the lawn from the yew garden, he looked up to the terrace and saw

the child's grave, absorbed face. Beside her sat Mlle. de
Breux bending over some work, her hair turned by the
sunlight into shining darkest silk and the whiteness of her
skin accentuated by the black velvet cloak the Comte had
brought her, which in case the child should feel cold, had
been placed on the back of her chair.

Suddenly Rupert saw Mademoiselle raise her head and
look along the terrace, then with a cry she sprang to
her feet and placed herself before the couch with arms out-
spread, in an attitude of fierce protection. Following her
horrified gaze Rupert gave a startled cry also and began to
run swiftly towards her. From under the archway leading
to the courtyard, its eyes red and cruel, foam dropping from
the great jaws which snapped fiercely at the air, and part
of the chain that had held it still hanging around its neck,
came the great wolf which Rupert remembered having seen
fastened to the wall when they had arrived the previous
morning, and which, driven mad by its captivity, had broken
loose and was now coming down the terrace straight towards
Mlle. de Breux and the helpless child behind her.

Rupert ran swiftly, yet it seemed to him that his feet
were leaden and would hardly move. The steps to the
terrace were a little behind Mademoiselle, in the opposite
direction to the way the wolf was coming, and as Rupert
sprang up them, she turned her head slightly towards him.
He had a glimpse of her eyes, anxious yet unafraid, looking at him from a white set face, then he ran past her,
catching up the velvet cloak as he did so. At the same
moment the wolf sprang. Holding the cloak before him,
Rupert received the brute's charge, and managed to fling
the thick folds over its head; then both rolled on the ground
together, as the archway at the far end of the terrace was
filled with a hurrying crowd of men armed with various
weapons who ran towards them, shouting loudly.

Fortunately for Rupert he had fallen uppermost, and
with his knees on its side, his hands grasping the great

throat, he strained every muscle to keep the wolf down and the cloak over its fiercely biting jaws, whilst the maddened brute struggled violently to fling him off and escape from the darkness which enveloped it. The strain was tremendous and slowly Rupert felt his strength giving way. If help did not come very speedily, he would never be able to keep the wolf down. Then, as he gathered all his power in one last effort, some one was beside him, a hand pulled him slightly backwards, and leaning across him, the Comte put the muzzle of a pistol against the cloak and fired both barrels into the wolf's head. There was one horrible convulsion, a grim snap as of a steel trap shutting, and the brute lay still.

The struggle, which had really only lasted a few seconds, was over, but for a little time no one moved or spoke. Then the Comte laid his hand on Rupert's shoulder.

"You are not hurt, de Vrieac? The brute did not touch you?" he asked rather breathlessly.

Rupert rose stiffly. His arms and knees were trembling from the strain and perspiration trickled down his forehead.

"No, Monsieur," he replied quietly. "He did not bite me. There will be no need for you to have me killed too." And he laughed sourly. "His teeth could not get through Mademoiselle's cloak, which, I am afraid, is ruined. I am very sorry," he added, turning to her apologetically, "I had to have some shield and caught up the first possible thing."

Mlle. de Breux had risen and was standing by the couch, her hands clasping the child's. And as he met her gaze Rupert felt a sharp surprise: he had not believed that the proud, dark eyes could look so kindlily upon him.

"You have saved Anne's life—and mine," she said, shuddering.

Rupert flushed hotly.

"What did you expect me to do, Mademoiselle?" he

asked rather bitterly. "Climb the nearest tree and let the brute come on unchecked? There was no danger once the cloak was over his head."

Yoeland de Breux came a step nearer.

"And before?" she asked. "Or if you had failed to get or keep it over?"

Then, as he did not answer, her eyes dropped and suddenly she gave a little cry. "But you *are* hurt," she said. "Your knee!" And looking down Rupert saw that the hose was torn and a thin stream of blood was trickling into his shoe. He shrugged his shoulders.

"It is nothing," he said; "one of the brute's legs got loose from the cloak and his claws scratched me. It cannot carry the poison, but I will put on some caustic in case. With your permission, Mademoiselle." And, having bowed, he walked away. Yoeland watched him go in silence; then as the men, at an order from the Comte, began to remove the wolf's body, she bent over Anne that the child might not see, and one or two tears fell on the golden hair.

"It is all right," said her brother's voice behind her. "They have taken it away. Ciel! but de Vrieac did well. He saved both your lives."

Yoeland, standing up quickly, faced him with eyes which flashed angrily.

"Yes," she said, "and placed us under a horrible obligation. I wish you had never brought him here, Charles. I hate Huguenots, and M. de Vrieac most of all."

"But—but it is just as well I did bring him," cried the Comte. "If he had not been here, who would have stopped the wolf?"

"I know," she answered; "but I wish you had not brought him, nevertheless. You had better go and see if he is all right, Charles—and thank him. He will not take thanks from me, it appears."

She turned her back decisively, whilst the Comte, marveling greatly at the ingratitude of women, went to find

Rupert de Vrieac. When her brother was out of sight Yoeland knelt down by the couch, laying her face on the pillow beside the child's.

"Anne, Anne," she whispered, "he saved our lives, and —and—I think he hates me—as much as I hate him," she added, a slight tremble in her voice.

Meanwhile the Comte, going to the little room in the east turret, found Rupert submitting to the ministrations of Carlote. The wolf, in his desperate struggles, had struck out strongly, tearing the leg from knee to ankle. Carlote, who, like most soldiers, had a rough knowledge of surgery, having washed the wound and applied the caustic with a liberal hand, was bandaging the leg with skillful care, whilst Rupert sat with set teeth, enduring the process in silence. The Comte crossed to the window and stood looking out until Carlote, having finished and gathered together his appliances, left the room and clattered downstairs. Then he turned and went over to Rupert.

"De Vrieac," he said, standing before him, a certain hesitation in his voice. "No, do not get up, sit where you are. You saved their lives. If it had not been for you that brute would have got them both. Mlle. de Breux could have done nothing and Anne—Anne——" He paused for a second, then continued: "But for you they would both have been killed, or horribly mangled. I came to try and thank——"

But at the word Rupert cut him short.

"No thanks are needed from you to me, Monsieur. As your—servant I could not do less. It was obviously my duty to save—my mistress and Mlle. Anne."

And shutting his lips firmly he looked at the Comte in angry defiance.

In spite of his refusal to accept the gratitude of either the Comte or Mlle. de Breux, Rupert had, however, quite unwittingly, gained for himself a very pleasant reward and one which made his life considerably more bearable. To Mlle. Anne he was a mighty hero of whom she wished to see a great deal, and as the child's slightest wish was law to the whole castle, Rupert spent many hours talking to and amusing her, in spite of the opposition of Yoeland de Breux. The Comte, after watching Rupert with the child, had shrugged his shoulders tolerantly when his sister protested that the Huguenot was not a fit person to associate with little Mlle. Anne.

"He will do her no harm," he said. "His religion is not of the fanatical kind; I imagine he is only what he is for political reasons and a cursed hereditary obstinacy. You need not be afraid that he will try to convert Anne. That he will protect her from danger we have proved. As for her mind——De Vrieac is a gentleman, let us give the devil his due. He will do her no harm in that way either. Besides, you know what Anne is. If you forbid him to go near her, you will only have the child more anxious for his company than ever. Let him amuse her if she wants him, she has little enough, heaven knows."

So Rupert was allowed to be with her and gradually developed into her constant companion. With that protective affection for anything weak and helpless so often noticeable in strong and active people, Rupert found a strange pleasure in doing what he could to help this crippled child. And gradually the loving, clinging nature caught hold of him and he grew to return very heartily the devotion which Mlle. Anne openly accorded him. It was such an innocent childish heart which she laid bare, so unsuspecting of any evil, and incapable of thinking harm. That Rupert should have come to La Roche from any motive other than his own free desire to do so, or that he entertained anything but the highest regard for her two beloveds, M. le Comte and Mlle. de Breux, never occurred to her for a moment, and the severest torture would not have dragged the truth from him or have led him to give her the slightest hint that they were not both perfect and charming to his mind in every way.

He was very glad that no one had given her an idea of the

real state of affairs or instilled any poison into her mind concerning him, though he frequently found the situations which arose from the child's conviction that he was on the friendliest terms with her brother and sister very embarrassing. With the Comte matters were not so difficult to manage, for having grasped the state of affairs and been secretly amused by it, he took up his allotted rôle of de Vrieac's friend with quiet good humor, a whimsical smile twisting his lips.

But with Mlle. de Breux things were harder. It took all her tact, de Vrieac's self-control and their combined love for the child to prevent Anne from guessing that all was not peace between them, to keep her from the track of knowledge which would deal a bitter blow to her belief in them both and bring a shocked, horrified surprise into the big blue eyes. Being convinced that they were friends and must therefore appreciate each other's company Anne demanded that they should spend long afternoons together, one on each side of her couch, participants in the wonderful games of make-believe which were to her such an unfailing delight. Only his affection for Anne and a firm determination to stay upon the pedestal, very little lower than those of M. le Comte and Mlle. de Breux, to which she had exalted him kept Rupert at his post and prevented him from hotly repudiating the parts assigned to him, especially when, looking up suddenly, he would sometimes surprise a gleam of malicious amusement in the eyes of Mademoiselle.

It was a profound relief to one at least of the actors when the plays were over and Rupert was permitted to leave the room; for although Yoeland de Breux no longer voiced her opposition to Rupert's companionship with Anne, she had by no means abandoned it and kept him perfectly aware of the fact.

The hot weather tried the child, making her tired and fretful, and one day Rupert, returning to the castle from a long ride in attendance on the Comte, was met by

"This, Yoeland, is our new servant, De Vrieac."

Carlote with a peremptory order that he was to go at once
to Mlle. Anne's room.   Here he found Jeanne, the old
nurse, vainly trying to persuade the child to take some
soup, a thing that she had quite made up her mind not to
do.

"Where have you been?" she cried petulantly as Rupert
entered. "I have wanted you all day. You are a silly
old woman, Jeanne, and I will not take your nasty broth.
So there! Go away, and do not bother me any more.
Now, M. Rupert, tell me a story."

At the times when he was alone with her, Rupert, drawing on a little classic learning acquired in boyhood from
an old monk, would reconstruct for the child's pleasure
the stories of Greece and Rome. Many of the details
had slipped his memory and were replaced in a way which
would have shocked his venerable teacher could he have
heard him, but Anne detected no errors, and even if a
Roman hero appeared on a Greek stage or Jason was un-
blushingly proclaimed King of Troy she thought it all
very wonderful and listened enraptured.

The child's delicacy and her maimed, unnatural life had
made those around her disinclined to cross her desires, and
the slightest whim of Mlle. Anne became an imperative
law to the whole castle.   As he caught the imperious tone in
the child's voice and noticed the willful curve of her mouth,
Rupert was moved by a sudden desire to know how strong
an influence he had with her.

"Certainly I will, with pleasure, Mlle. Anne," he said,
"a splendid new one I have just remembered, when you
have taken your broth. Not before."

Unaccustomed to any conditions being attached to the
fulfillment of her orders, the child looked at him in quick
surprise, a slight frown gathering between her eyes; and Rupert returned her gaze steadily.

"I do not want to take my broth," she said slowly.

Without replying Rupert crossed over to the window
and stood looking out into the gathering twilight, hum-

ming a song softly to himself. Anne surveyed his back with resentment for a moment, her mouth set obstinately, then she turned and, taking the cup from old Jeanne, swallowed its contents with a little *moue* of disapproval.

"It was very nasty, but I have drunk it," she announced to the unrelenting figure before the window. "Now tell me the story, M. Rupert. What is it about?"

With a quiet smile Rupert came and sat down beside her, whilst the old nurse, marveling that he should have dared to take such an attitude with Mlle. Anne and be victorious, left the room to report the matter to Mlle. de Breux. Then, having straightened the pillows, Rupert began to tell the child of the Labors of Hercules.

CHAPTER VII

THE autumn was beginning to close in. The harvest had been carried and stored, the swallows had long gone, and in the beech woods the leaves had turned to flaming golds and browns.

With the change of the weather Anne seemed to grow weaker. To the eyes watching her so anxiously it was evident that the cold, damp days affected her, and though they strove, by heaping the fires and closing all windows firmly, to keep out the menace, yet the thin face grew whiter; her sleep more broken, and, always a sign that things were not well, the child was fretful and unkind. It was then that Rupert came into serious conflict with Mlle. de Breux.

One afternoon, when Anne, after an almost sleepless night, lay tossing restlessly, refusing all food and exceedingly difficult to manage, she demanded Rupert's presence imperiously. Mlle. de Breux, who had been up with her all the previous night, had gone to rest in her room, and only old Jeanne sat with the child.

Very cautiously and with great tact, Rupert persuaded the nurse to leave him alone with her charge, and Jeanne, who had a certain respect for the man, heretic or not, who could wield such an influence over her Mlle. Anne, agreed with little demur, and having filled a cup with some heated broth and begged him in an urgent whisper to get the child to take it, stole softly out of the room.

Alone with Anne, Rupert was always at his ease, and now with gentle insistence, and by diverting her mind to other things, he persuaded her to take the broth. Then as a reward he sat down to tell a story of his own invention, of a beautiful princess who, turned by an evil magician

61

into a white wolf, passed through exciting vicissitudes until
she was finally rescued by a charming and gallant prince.

Having caught the child's attention, Rupert strove to keep
it by a strenuous use of his imagination, and Anne listened
wide-eyed and breathless. So absorbed were they both that
neither noticed the entrance of Mlle. de Breux, or were
aware of her presence until she stood by the child's bed. ..

She gave one look at the hot cheeks and burning eyes,
felt Anne's hands, and then her wrath fell on Rupert like
an avalanche.

With a man's ignorance he had mistaken the flush of
fever for mere excitement, and had never dreamt that he
was doing the child harm.

That night in her moments of fitful sleep Anne saw
many white wolves from which she vainly tried to escape,
and as Yoeland de Breux held the little shrinking figure
in her arms, pouring assurances of safety into unheeding
ears, she vowed to herself that Rupert de Vrieac should
never enter the child's room again.

For two days Anne was seriously ill, and they were
amongst the most miserable that Rupert had ever spent.
Of Mlle. de Breux he saw nothing, for she was always with
the child. Once he managed to stop old Jeanne, but with
a bitter self-censure that she had ever allowed him to be
alone with her little Mademoiselle, she hurried on, leaving
him miserably conscious of the justice of her reproach.
The Comte spent many hours pacing up and down the
stretch of grass beneath the sick child's window, and when
Rupert begged news of her, had turned on him angrily, ordering him to his room.

Only Carlote, with rough kindness, would sometimes
bring him tidings, and they were of the worst. Mlle. Anne
was very ill, she might die, and at that a wave of desolation
swept over Rupert's heart. She had not wanted him or
he would most certainly have been sent for. It was he
who had made her ill, and now perhaps he would never
see her again. Very quietly he crept down the passage

outside Anne's door, and it was here that Yoeland de Breux,
coming suddenly out of the room, found him. Her face
was white and very weary, and dark shadows lay under her
eyes. She looked at him in angry astonishment.

"Ah, Mademoiselle!" he cried softly, reading her expression and humbling his pride. "I beg of you to tell
me how she is."

Yoeland shut the door and her eyes darkened.

"I think she is—not going to get better," she answered
with quivering lips. Then, all sense of justice deadened by
anxiety and a great fatigue, she turned on him fiercely.

"What are you doing here? Go back to your room at
once," she said in a clear, low whisper. "It is your fault.
You excited her and brought on the fever. If Anne dies,
you will have killed her."

Like a stricken animal Rupert shrank back.

Stumbling up to his room, he knelt by the open window,
staring out into the darkness. It was a still, cloudless
night. Overhead the stars twinkled and shone, and looking
up at them, Rupert thought of Marguerite's eyes watching
for him, far away in Vainçeoire. His thoughts were constantly of her, and now in his misery he wondered if she
could know, if across the wide spaces between them, her
soul could feel his desolation.

Suddenly he raised his head, listening. Footsteps were
hurrying up the stairs, there was an urgent knock at the
door, it was flung open and Carlote, breathless with haste,
stood on the threshold.

"For God's sake, come, M. de Vrieac," he gasped.
"Mlle. Anne is asking for you and Mlle. de Breux begs that
you will make haste."

Hardly waiting to hear what Carlote said, Rupert ran
past him, down the stairs and along the corridor. Outside
the child's door, Yoeland de Breux was waiting for him.
Her eyes were dark with a great anxiety.

"Anne wants you. Nothing else will quieten her. You
will not——"

Very swiftly he cut her short.

"Do not be afraid, Mademoiselle," he said coldly. "I will do her no harm."

Then he went softly into the room.

The child lay supported by many pillows, the thin, pinched face flushed with fever, her eyes, burning luminously, had sunk into her head and the hands which clutched Rupert's were hot and dry.

"Oh, you have come at last!" she cried in a weak whisper. "I have wanted you so badly. Why did you not come before? Yoeland said you would not, that you did not care that I was ill."

Rupert knelt down by the bed, drawing the child into his arms.

"That I did not care, Mademoiselle?" he said slowly.

"Yes, but you did, didn't you?" she murmured, nestling against him trustingly. "I told Yoeland that she had made a mistake, because you cared so much the day I cut my finger. Do you remember? When you made me a cage for my blackbird? But perhaps they did not tell you how much I wanted you to come, you did not understand it was ever so much," she added drowsily, her hot little hands clasping his sleeve tightly to prevent his leaving her.

Without replying, Rupert turned his head slowly and looked at Yoeland de Breux, who had followed him into the room and was standing before the fire, staring down at the blazing logs. Her lips were tightly drawn and her whole attitude told of an intense strain. For a moment his face hardened, then he looked at the golden head lying against his shoulder and his eyes lighted with triumph.

Jealous that in her sickness she should want him, they had tried to put the child against him, to keep him from her, but they had failed. Anne still wanted him, and her trust in him had never faltered.

"It is not—not true, Mademoiselle, that I did not care," he said in a voice that shook slightly. "And had I known you wanted me so much I should have come—in spite of everything."

The child raised her head a little from his shoulder, looking at her sister,

"You see, Yoeland, you *were* mistaken. M. Rupert *did* care, and he did not know I wanted him so badly. Jeanne must have forgotten to give him my messages."

Slowly Yoeland de Breux turned from the fire and her eyes met Rupert's over the golden hair. It was in his power to tell the child the real reason why he had not come, to deal her love for her sister a very bitter blow. Would he strike or would he forbear? The child leaning against his shoulder nestled more closely in his arms.

"I am so glad you have come at last," she murmured.

For a moment Rupert did not reply. He was watching Yoeland very intently. Then he looked down at the little face, leaning so•confidently against him, and with a sudden smile, his hand closed over the child's.

"Now I *am* here, what would you like me to do, Mlle. Anne?" he asked softly, and Yoeland, turning back to the fire, sat down with a deep sigh, as though some great burden had been lifted from her shoulders.

"I should like you to tell me a story. And will you please hold me up in your arms, M. Rupert? My bed is so hot and lumpy."

"Shall I carry you for a little? I could tell you a story just the same," he suggested. And the child smiled.

"I should like that," she said.

So, having wrapped her in a cloak, he lifted her very gently in his arms, and began to pace slowly up and down the room, whilst he told her a story of shepherds and shepherdesses in Arcady. It was a very long, dull story, the ramifications of whose plot no one could be expected to follow.

Gradually the child grew less restless, her eyes began to close and her head sank lower against his shoulder. The Comte slipped softly into the room, but Rupert took no

notice of him. With arms which ached agonizingly, he
paced up and down, whilst the story grew duller and more
involved, and his voice more sleep-inducing. The child's
eyes closed tighter and tighter, until at last they refused
to open any more.

". . . and the first shepherd called the second, the second
called the third, the third shepherd called the fourth, and
so on, until all the two hundred and forty shepherds, each
piping before his hundred and twenty sheep, had come down
from the mountains into the valley," said Rupert in a slow,
monotonous voice, adding, without any change in his tone,
as he passed Yoeland's chair, "She is fast asleep, Mademoiselle."

For a little while he continued to carry the child, and
then, when his arms refused to hold her any longer, laid
her gently down in the bed.

She was sleeping very peacefully and already the pinched
look was fading from her face. One hand still held his
sleeve, and kneeling down, Rupert made no effort to un-
clasp her fingers. Yoeland came softly across the room to
the bedside.

"I think she will sleep so for some time, Mademoiselle,"
whispered Rupert, looking up at her. "If she grows restless I will carry her again."

Yoeland laid her fingers softly on the child's forehead.

"Her head is cooler. If you will stay with her I think
I will go and lie down, M. de Vrieac," she said softly.

For a moment she hesitated as though about to say
something further, whilst a sudden color crept into her
cheeks. Then, as he met her eyes, Rupert's suddenly
hardened and his mouth set in stern lines.

"Good-night, Mademoiselle," he murmured coldly.
"That is, if you are not afraid to leave me with Mlle.
Anne?"

Their eyes met and clashed like swords. Without replying, Yoeland turned and, crossing to the door, slipped out
of the room. The Comte, having softly replenished the

fire, followed her, and Rupert was left alone with the sleeping child.

Slowly the hours dragged on. Kneeling beside the bed, afraid to move lest he should arouse Anne, Rupert grew cold and stiff. The fire died down, deep shadows crept over the room, and still she slept. Very cautiously he moved his position, easing his cramped limbs. Gradually sleep stole upon him.

So Yoeland de Breux, coming in softly in the early morning, found them; both asleep, the man's dark head lying on the pillow beside the child's golden one. And as she stood looking down at them, a curious little smile hovered round her lips.

The consciousness that some one was watching him aroused Rupert, and he started up, flushing hotly when he saw who it was.

"I have slept at my post, Mademoiselle! But Mlle. Anne has not stirred or I should have heard her. The fever seems to have died down."

Very tenderly Yoeland bent over the child, who was sleeping with soft regular breathing, the burning flush gone from her cheeks. Then she looked across at Rupert with eyes that were no longer proud or angry.

"I did not believe that she would live through last night," she said in a voice which shook in spite of herself. "Nothing would pacify her and—and then you came and she slept. I think you saved her life, for the second time. She would not go to sleep for Jeanne or me. It was you she wanted and—— You were very generous, M. de Vrieac."

Looking up at her Rupert realized that tears were not very far from her eyes; noticing also, with a sudden surprise, how soft and beautiful those eyes were. He rose to his feet, a faint flush creeping into his cheeks.

"To whom, Mademoiselle?" he asked coldly.

And lifting her head proudly, Yoeland de Breux met his glance with steady eyes.

"To me," she replied.

Worn out by long watching and anxiety for the child, she was losing grip of her self-control, and Rupert knew that she was on the verge of an hysterical outburst. He stood very still, his face suddenly grown hard.

"And Mlle. Anne?" he asked, a deep under-note of anger in his voice. "You have forgotten her, I think, Mademoiselle. What if I had told her the truth, that you would not let me come, that, until Carlote called me, I had no notion that she wanted me?—Was that why you sent me from the passage, Mademoiselle, lest I should hear her calling me?—If I had told her that, do you think it would have made her better? She believes in you utterly. Would the shock of what she would have understood then have been so good for her? Do you really believe that I do not care for Mlle. Anne? I thought that was only what you told her."

She had listened to him without any movement or protest, now she raised her head and faced him with a glance as antagonistic as his own.

"You make the most of your victory, M. de Vrieac," she said quietly.

Autumn had drawn into winter, and the short, bleak days of January were upon them. Anne seemed to have completely recovered, and in the paradoxical manner often shown by delicate people, to have gathered increased strength from her illness. Rupert, with an apparently unending fund of stories and a certain dexterity in making rough wooden toys for her amusement, was very constantly with her. In fact, he had been rather surprised by the freedom with which he was allowed to be her companion. The Comte would only laugh and shrug his shoulders when, commanding Rupert's presence, he frequently learnt that Anne had already laid claim to it, and watching the Huguenot with a whimsical smile, would send him back again to the child's room, with an order to remain so long as she required him. And Yoeland de Breux, although she neither laughed nor shrugged her shoulders, made no effort to keep him away from the child, although Rupert was perfectly aware that she resented Anne's need of him intensely.

The weather for some weeks had been very severe, and up in the pine woods the wolves were feeling the pinch of hunger. Peasants had lately reported the presence of several of the brutes, slinking round the houses at night, searching for food, and the Comte, who was passionately fond of all forms of sport, had speedily organized several hunts which had successfully accounted for some of the wolves.

Rupert, to his great chagrin, had not been permitted to join these expeditions, possibly, he guessed, because he had shown too much eagerness to do so. The dull monotony of his life at La Roche was driving him to desperation, and as he listened to the men sitting round the fires and talking over the hunts, he felt he would have given or risked anything to have been with them.

There was one wolf of which they spoke with a grudging admiration—a huge, gray king of the pack, lean, swift, full of cunning and, strange in the wolf breed, a fierce courage. Several times they had got him at bay, but his desperate defense had cowed even the great hounds and he had managed to fight his way out from death.

It was on the capture of this wolf, if possible alive, that the Comte had set his mind, and all the men their hopes. But it was no easy matter. In vain they set traps, the gray wolf was too cunning to be deceived. Night after night the Comte and his men lay in wait for him, but not a sign of the great shaggy form, slipping silently over the ground, rewarded them. Yet in the morning there would be the marks of his pads on the snow, and a peasant would come with a bitter tale of something carried off in the darkness by this prince of thieves.

His ill success made the Comte more determined, and he laid his plans with great thought. In three nights the moon would be full, shining on the frozen, snow-covered ground

and making field and village as light as day. For this night
the Comte had organized a hunt; and great efforts were to
be made to capture alive the huge, gray wolf.

Rupert, as he listened to the men's eager talk and preparations, grew restless and miserable. He guessed that he
would not be allowed to go, yet felt that go he must. In
desperation he went to the Comte and with a queer mixture
of pride and humbleness, asked permission to join the hunt,
but Charles de La Roche shook his head with a slow smile.

At sight of that smile Rupert lost his self-control. The
life which he had been compelled to lead under his enemy's
authority had tried his temper more than even he himself
guessed, and in an instant all his dislike, despair, and irrita-
tion boiled over in a tremendous burst of passion.

The smile died out of the Comte's eyes and his face grew
stern as he raised his hand imperiously for silence. But
for a moment or two Rupert paid no heed. His words
poured out in an angry torrent, whilst his eyes blazed like
those of a trapped tiger. Then, gradually, the calmness of
the man who watched him and the knowledge of how satis-
fying to the Comte's hatred this open betrayal of his
enemy's sufferings must be, cooled Rupert's temper, and
with a fierce effort of self-control he stood silent, breathing
hard, with clenched hands and eyes which smoldered with
hate.

The Comte waited for a few seconds, then he nodded his
head gravely, whilst his eyes lit with a cruel amusement.

"So," he said, "you have not been enjoying yourself
here at La Roche, de Vrieac? How strange," and he
laughed sneeringly. "You have been dull, and you wish to
go hunting, and when I say 'No,' you challenge me to fight
you with swords for permission to go on this hunt to-night.

"Now listen to me," he continued harshly, his whole manner grown very stern as he came a step closer to the Huguenot. "I do not fight with a—servant. No! Be silent!
That is what you are to me by your own oath.

"You find life here at La Roche almost intolerable, and

you wish to relieve your ennui by joining this wolf-hunt to-night. I decline to allow you to do so, and immediately you lose your temper. My dear de Vrieac, you are most unreasonable. How could you expect your life in my house to be anything but difficult? That is why you are here. When I proposed my condition for the safety of your friends and you accepted it, no one, I think, entertained the idea that you would enjoy your sojourn with me, and the fact that you have found it even more unbearable than you imagined, is, I take it, a compliment to my powers of invention. You gave way just now, de Vrieac, to an exhibition of temper, which I do not permit in my servants. I shall not punish you for it, however, as I must confess that it was most gratifying to me. You are very proud, and since your arrival at La Roche have managed to conceal your feelings with considerable success. It is only by such outbreaks as you have just indulged in that I can know you are suffering, and that my efforts in that direction are, therefore, being crowned with success. You may go to your room and remain there until I send for you."

Without a word, his head held high and the mask of indifference once more upon his face, Rupert moved quietly towards the door. Leaning forward slightly, his legs swinging from the table, the Comte surveyed him with amused eyes.

Mounting the stairs quickly to his room, Rupert shut the door and then leant against it, shaking with passion.

"The devil," he muttered hoarsely. "My God, if I could only kill him! I *will* go to the hunt to-night, I *will* go, whatever befalls, even if—if," and he paused, struck by a sudden idea, "even if he kills me for it," he added more quietly.

CHAPTER VIII

THE moon was shining gloriously in a star-lit, cloudless sky as a group of men stood ready that evening in the courtyard to start on the hunt of the great gray wolf. They were armed with short boar spears and several of them held fierce-looking, shaggy-coated hounds in leash. The men wore short woolen cloaks with deep hoods which completely covered their heads and necks, keeping out a good deal of the biting cold of the night, whilst most of them had roughly-shaped gauntlets made of sheepskin.

Presently the Comte came out of the castle, walking quickly down the stone steps into the courtyard. He was armed with a heavily-fashioned sword and his eyes flashed with excitement. He glanced at the men before him keenly.

"Where is Hugues?" he asked. "Ah, there," as a hooded figure, leading one of the hounds, moved forward from the back of the group. "You stay close to me, Hugues, with Pascal," he ordered, laying his hand caressingly on the great hound's head.

"Yes, M. le Comte," the man replied in a low voice, stepping up beside him. And then the Comte gave the word to start.

Down the hill, about a quarter of a mile to the north of the village, on the side where the pinewoods lay, the Comte had had a large pit, similar to those used for trapping deer, very carefully dug, with smooth straight sides and deeper than any beast, even the great gray wolf, could spring from. Over this light branches and scattered snow had been laid so that it was almost impossible to tell the covered pit from the solid ground around. Then, for a mile in the forest beyond, a sheep with its throat cut, had been trailed

72

up to the pit, and here the carcass had been divided, portions being scattered round and some, too small to bear down the covering, but large enough to tempt a hungry wolf, had been flung upon the concealing boughs. Woe betide the wolf which went after them, for down he would go, through the light branches into the pit below, with little chance of escaping from it.

Around the pit in a rough horseshoe some three hundred yards across, the Comte had concealed his men and hounds behind bushes and tree trunks, the open end of the shoe being towards the forest from which the wolves would come and in which direction also the wind lay, so that no scent of their enemies might carry warning of danger to the pack. The Comte's plan was for all to wait concealed until the wolves, drawn by the dead sheep's trail, should be within the horseshoe and then it would be "the King of Israel only." Each man was to mark the great gray wolf and all springing up from their hiding-places at a given signal from the Comte, were to close in upon the leader of the pack and endeavor to drive him on to the concealed pit. The other wolves were to go as they chose, though no doubt several of them, terrified by the sudden shouting and the flare of the torches which some of the men carried concealed in earthen jars, would also crash into the pit. From it none of them could escape, and it would be an easy thing when daylight came, to spear the other wolves, whilst the great gray king would be hauled up by ropes and nets to the castle, where a strong cage was ready for him.

At the end of the horseshoe nearest the pinewood the Comte, with Hugues and the great hound, Pascal, crouched behind a thicket of hazel bushes.

The moon rose majestically overhead, throwing deep shadows of tree and bush on the snow, the wind blew in cold gusts from the forest, the silence grew more intense. Suddenly, very faintly, from far up amongst the pines, came a long wailing cry—the howl of a hunting wolf. Then the silence fell again and all waited in breathless expectation. Once more the call came, nearer this time, and answered by several others. Hugues, lifting up the edge of his woolen cloak, slipped it over Pascal's head and drew the hound closer to him, feeling the hair on the great brute's back bristle with rage at the sound. And then, from within the forest, very far off and indistinct at first, but growing rapidly nearer and louder, came a discordant clamor rising to a sudden fierce note, then sinking suddenly to silence. The pack had found the sheep's trail, and with their swift, tireless strides were rapidly hunting it down to where the men lay in wait for them. What wind there was had died away. Not a twig stirred, not a sound broke the deep silence, as the men crouched breathlessly expectant, holding the hounds' heads tightly, lest, in their excitement, they might give a betraying growl.

Then, from the edge of the pinewoods, startling in its nearness, came a loud wailing cry, and across the strip of open snow between the forest and the trees where the Comte's men were, swept gray, shaggy forms, moving noiselessly over the ground, their fierce, bloodshot eyes and open mouths eager for food. In another second the foremost wolves had found some portions of the sheep and there was silence no longer. Snarling, snapping, each fighting furiously to rend the spoil from the others, they struggled in fierce groups, all ideas of danger or a trap completely overlooked. By all but one. The great gray wolf stood not thirty yards from where the Comte and Hugues were hiding. In the moonlight his eyes gleamed fiercely as he raised his head in the air, sniffing suspiciously. It was plain that he was not at ease, that he feared some hidden danger.

The other wolves had passed on well within the horseshoe of waiting men, as they found fresh pieces of spoil, some of them almost on the hidden pit which lay at the far end. Only their leader hesitated, seeming to scent that all was not well. Then as some of the wolves found another large piece of the sheep and fell upon it with proclaiming snarls, the gray wolf appeared to be satisfied and moved swiftly forward. At that second the foremost wolf sprang at a piece of meat placed over the pit, the thin branches gave way beneath him and he crashed down with a terrified howl. The gray wolf paused, flinging up his head to listen, and as he caught the warning note of danger, flashed round and sped back towards the forest. Instantly the Comte leaped from his hiding-place, hurling his sword at the wolf as it dashed by. The blade gashed the brute's flank, but it never broke its stride, leaping forward amongst the pines with a snarl of rage and pain. The Comte, calling an order sharply to his men and scarcely making his voice heard above the clamor, caught up his weapon and ran forward on the track which the gray wolf, closely followed by Hugues, with the great hound, Pascal, straining fiercely at his leash, had taken.

On they went, in and out amongst the trees, Pascal dashing along and pulling Hugues after him; across several frozen streams and open glades where the moonlight made all as clear as day, whilst a quarter of a mile behind the Comte followed swiftly, followed again by a few of his men, the rest of whom had not heard his order and were still dealing with the wolves round the covered pit. In one of the glades a fallen pine lay across the trail. The wolf had evidently tried to leap it, missed his spring and had scrambled over as best he could. There were red stains on the snow, whilst the impress of the brute's pads were more deeply marked, showing that his pace was slackening. Weakened by loss of blood the gray wolf could not go much further.

Hugues softly cheered Pascal on, although the great hound needed no encouragement, pressing forward with open, foaming jaws on the trail. As they reached the next glade they were just in time to see the gray wolf leap into the trees on the other side, not a hundred yards in front of them. With a fierce effort man and hound increased their pace, dashing after him; a sharp howl from the wolf sounding close before them. And then it seemed to Hugues that Pascal gave a sudden lunge forward, the ground opened beneath his feet, and man and hound went crashing down, down into space, till they hit hard ground with a thud.

For a moment the man lay still, then raising his head slowly he gazed round him, dazed by the fall and an agonizing pain in his right leg. It was a common practice of the foresters to dig pits similar to the one prepared by the Comte for the wolves, and, having concealed them under lightly strewn branches and leaves, trust to some deer or other animal trying to cross and so being captured. It was obviously into one of these traps that Hugues and the hound had fallen. The moon coming through a rift in the trees shone full on the man as he lay in. the middle of the pit, but threw deep shadows round the sides. With a desperate effort he raised himself on one elbow. From the darkness before him two vivid green eyes stared unwinkingly.

"Pascal!" he called faintly, but the eyes did not move, and as he fell back once more the man was startled to see the great hound lying just beside him, perfectly still, its neck broken by the fall. For a moment he lay quiet, whilst his heart beat in great, leaping throbs, and the sharp, startled cry of a wolf which had sounded just as he and Pascal crossed the glade rang in his ears. Then he slowly raised his head once more. The eyes had come closer, and the next second the great gray wolf moved noiselessly out of the shadows, its bloodshot eyes gleaming evilly, whilst its teeth were bared in a savage snarl. The man had no weapon, the sudden fall having jerked the spear out of his hand; there was only his woolen cloak to keep the brute's fangs from his throat, for after one agonizing effort he had not tried to rise, his right leg having been broken by the fall.

Slowly, silently, the great brute crept forward, the hair on its back bristling like an angry dog's; then with a fierce, deep snarl it was upon him. Blindly the man struggled, gripping the wolf's shaggy throat, trying to hold the snapping jaws with his gauntleted hands, but it was a futile effort. The strong teeth were buried in the folds of his cloak, shaking him backwards and forwards like a helpless rat, and were swiftly biting through to the unprotected throat beneath. At that second a shout came from the ground above and a man's face looked into the pit, then the Comte de La Roche swung himself down to the struggling heap below. The man beneath the wolf caught the gleaming flash of a sword, felt the brute's teeth suddenly relax, saw death cloud its eyes, and then it lurched forward over his face and chest. Very quickly it was dragged aside, and he found himself looking up into the Comte's face, bending close above him. The Comte said something, but he could neither hear nor answer, and a great darkness seemed to fall upon him.

In a few minutes, which might have been years, he struggled back to the light. The Comte was still beside him, supporting his head against his knee, whilst he urged him to drink from the flask held to his lips. Unresistingly the man obeyed, and as the wine revived him his brain grew clearer and he looked round. At a little distance lay the wolf, dead, with the Comte's sword through its body. Slowly the injured man lifted his eyes to the Comte's face, and for a second they gazed at each other in silence. Then the Comte bent a little lower.

"Well, de Vrieac," he said, his lips twitching with a whimsical smile, "I hope you have enjoyed your wolf-hunt?"

Rupert de Vrieac, for it was he who, having bribed the man Hugues, had taken his place and, with Pascal, had hunted the great gray wolf, flushed hotly and then looked once more at the dead, shaggy body.

"You saved my life at the risk of your own, Monsieur," he murmured.

The Comte shrugged his shoulders.

"At the cost of the wolf's," he replied.

Rupert's eyes, puzzled and very weary, came back to the Comte's face.

"If you had let him kill me you could have taken him alive, he would never have jumped out of this place."

He was barely conscious of what he was saying, only the confused thoughts of his brain seemed to slip out on his tongue.

The Comte looked down at Rupert sharply, then held the flask once more to his mouth.

"I preferred losing his life to yours," he said. "Here, drink some more of this and stay quiet. I suppose those slow fellows will find us in time." And putting the cloak under Rupert's head he laid him down; then, taking his silver hunting-horn, stood in the middle of the pit and sent a loud call echoing up through the forest.

Rupert lay still with closed eyes, almost stupefied by pain, but he started up with a sharp exclamation as the Comte gently felt his injured leg, then sank back once more with an exhausted sigh. For a moment the Comte stood gazing down at his enemy's white, drawn face. The moonlight made it look ghastly, showing up the deep lines of pain and the piteous quiver at the corners of the tightly closed lips. Then, with an impatient movement of his shoulders, the Comte knelt down and, moistening his fingers with the wine flask, drew them gently across Rupert's temples. For a second the dark, pain-filled eyes looked up at him in surprise, then they closed and the strained look on the injured man's face relaxed a little. A few moments later some of the Comte's men, guided to the spot by another call from his horn, arrived.

Having improvised a rough stretcher from cloaks and branches, they lifted Rupert, now completely unconscious, on to it and bore him back to the castle. Here Carlote took charge of him, and having set the broken leg and bound it in rough splints, put his still unconscious patient to bed, assuring the Comte that all he needed was rest and quiet.

One morning, more than a week later, Rupert lay in bed in his little turret room gazing up at a patch of blue sky. It was just the color of Marguerite's eyes, those big innocent eyes which even now might be looking out for him. He could picture her, sitting in the tower of the old castle at Vainçeoire, working at some wonderful piece of embroidery and turning every now and again to gaze longingly down the road which led north over the Loire to La Roche. He closed his eyes that he might the better picture her face, and then his forehead wrinkled in surprise, for it was not the big blue eyes, the golden hair, the flower-like, childish face of Marguerite which rose before his mind. Eyes, dark as purple pansies and full of a great compassion, looked down into his, a soft hand brushed the damp hair back from his forehead, whilst Yoeland de Breux stooped gently over him. He opened his eyes, looking round the room with a restless sigh.

In the night that they had carried him back to the castle he had had a strange dream, so vivid that it seemed almost like a seen reality. He thought that as he lay, tossing restlessly on the bed, pain-racked and feverish, the door had opened and Mlle. de Breux accompanied by old Jeanne came softly into the room. Not the Mlle. de Breux with cold, proud eyes and disdainful manner, but a girl whose face was full of pity and who, bending down, slipped an arm beneath his pillow, raising him, as she gave him a cool, delicious drink. Then as she laid him back he had tried brokenly to thank her and she had smiled, a smile of great gentleness, as she knelt beside him, drawing her fingers lightly across his burning forehead, until, soothed and contented, he fell asleep. Awakening the next morning he had laughed grimly at his impossible dream, yet with a wistful hope that it might come again. Her fingers had been so soft and cool, her eyes so kind and beautiful. He shut his own in an effort to conjure up the face of this dream lady, opening them a few moments later with a slight start, for the Comte de La Roche stood at his bedside.

"I woke you, I fear," said the Comte; "are you in pain?"

"No, Monsieur, thank you," Rupert replied quietly.

The Comte smiled to himself as he drew forward a stool and sat down by the bed.

"And do you consider the hunt was worth the consequences? That the value of the tune matched the piper's bill," he asked, "though you do not know all the price yet, do you?

"I think," he continued, as Rupert remained silent, "that you are a poor plotter, de Vrieac. You lack judgment. To begin with, you chose the wrong man for your purpose. One who could be bribed as easily as Hugues is obviously a traitor at heart, and would in turn betray you without hesitation, to serve his own ends. In fact he did so—to me. Hugues wanted your money, but he was also as eager as any to be in the hunt. So, having made you think that all was safe, and received his pay, he came straight to me with the whole story. He felt no shame. I think, indeed, that he considered himself a clever fellow and expected me to praise him. As a matter of fact, I ordered him three days in chains for daring to plot against my orders and three more for taking your bribe, which, by the way, I confiscated. Here it is, do not use it again to corrupt my servants." And taking out a small bag of money the Comte laid it down beside the bed.

Rupert looked at him with curious eyes.

There was silence in the room for several minutes. The smile had died out of the Comte's eyes and they grew very stern. Instinctively Rupert knew that the storm was gathering and set his face to meet it.

"When you took your oath to me in Paris, de Vrieac," said the Comte, looking at him with frowning brows, "you swore to obey my orders implicitly. I had no intention that you should join the hunt, and this you knew perfectly well. You deliberately went against my order. You broke your oath and openly defied me. Do you know how I punish a disobedient servant? Sometimes, I hang him. Oh, no," raising his hand with a quick gesture as he caught the expression in Rupert's eyes. "I shall not do that to

you. Under present conditions and the state of your feelings you might be rather glad to die. Besides, I do not often
hang my servants. As a general rule, if one disobeys me
as you have done, I hand him over to my men-at-arms and
have him flogged—like a dog. Can you give me any reason,
Rupert de Vrieac, why I should not deal so with you?"

Tilting his head back a little, Rupert looked up with
steady eyes into the Comte's face.

"No, Monsieur," he replied quietly, "I can conceive no
reason whatever."

The Comte nodded.

"Good. I did you the credit to believe that you would
give me none. And yet," he continued, the harshness dying
from his voice as his eyes grew almost friendly, "there
are two very excellent ones why I shall not order that to
be done to you. Since you came to La Roche, you have
rendered me services, the value of which are not to be
estimated. You have twice saved the life of Mlle. Anne.
And you have done more, you have amused and helped
her through many long days. I am not blind. The child
is fond of you, and I know that what you did was quite
without thought of thanks or reward. You did it for
Mlle. Anne's own sake because you also are fond of her.
But I like to be just. If a man does me an injury, I do
not forget to repay him; and if one does me a service, I remember to repay him also. So I shall overlook your disobedience this time. But do not let it occur again," he
added, the harshness returning to his voice, "for I shall
not let it pass twice. The next time I shall punish you,
Mlle. Anne or no. So remember, for I mean what I say."

And rising, he struck Rupert across the cheek with the
back of his fingers, then turned without another look or
word and left the room.

CHAPTER IX

ONE evening, some five weeks later, a horseman, bearing the stains of many leagues' travel, rode up to the castle and announced to the Comte and Mlle. de Breux the near approach of their uncle, M. le Vicomte de Briege.

Immediately the whole castle was stirred with activity, for the Vicomte was a great personage for whom great preparations had to be made. Men were sent to light fires in the guest room, move the heavy furniture and spread fresh rushes on the floors; Mademoiselle's women, their arms full of lavender-scented linen, rugs and tapestries, hurried along the passages, whilst Mademoiselle herself, calm amidst the general bustle, was busily preparing her choicest dainties in the great kitchen.

At noon the next day, M. le Vicomte de Briege, attended by a score of troopers, rode through the castle gateway. Swinging himself from his horse, he nodded brusquely to the Comte, who had hastened out to greet him, kissed Mademoiselle, with a rough compliment on her looks, and allowed himself to be conducted to his room.

He was a short, squarely-built man with a black, bristling beard and a harsh, imperious voice. His dark, watchful eyes seemed to take note of everything, and it was not long before they fell upon Rupert de Vrieac. In loud tones he demanded who the Huguenot was and the reason of his presence at La Roche, and his roar of laughter, when the Comte explained the situation, rang through the room like the discharge of a cannon.

"Magnificent! Magnificent!" he shouted, banging his fist down on the table till jugs and plates danced as though bewitched. "St. Denis, you have a most excellent wit, Charles.

Who would have thought of that plan but yourself! And for five years too! Blessed Mother, but he will murder you long before then, in spite of all his vows."

"I think not," replied the Comte, smiling quietly.

"Ha! ha!" laughed the Vicomte, unable to contain his mirth. "A Daniel in the lion's den, or, rather, Daniel with a lion in leash—for five years. You should take him round the country on a chain and make him dance, as they do the bears, Charles. Where is the fellow? I should like to see you put him through some of his tricks. It would really oblige me immensely if you would send Carlote to fetch him."

But the Comte shook his head.

"I regret I cannot to-night," he replied firmly. "De Vrieac had the carelessness to break his leg some little time ago and has scarcely recovered. It would not be wise to work him into another fever. Besides, he never swore not to kill you and might do so before I could prevent him, for he has a fierce temper when roused. He can move quickly, too."

And then, with the object of diverting the Vicomte's mind from his desire to bait the Huguenot, the Comte told him the story of the hunt of the great gray wolf; omitting, however, any mention of the two interviews which he had had with Rupert, before and after that momentous night.

So for the time the matter was dropped, but in the days which followed the Vicomte made many efforts to drive Rupert into a corner, intending, by a coarse display of humor, to test the strength of the Huguenot's self-control, and it afforded the Comte considerable amusement to observe the adroit way in which Rupert, who was perfectly aware of the Vicomte's intentions, contrived to frustrate them.

One evening, about two days after the Vicomte's arrival, Rupert was entertaining Anne with a story of high adventure, when Carlote brought a message from the Comte ordering Rupert to go to him immediately. Somewhat surprised, for it was seldom now that he was ordered away when Anne desired his company, and filled with a strange foreboding of evil, Rupert rose to obey.

The Comte had a room in the west tower which he used as an office and general private sanctum of his own; no one, even Mlle. de Breux, went there without his knowledge and permission. Mounting the rough stone stairs to this room, Rupert raised the heavy curtain across the doorway and entered.

"You sent for me, Monsieur?"

Then he paused with a startled exclamation, his face gone suddenly pale, for a man to whom the Comte had been speaking turned, and springing forward, sank on his knees before Rupert, kissing his hands passionately. Looking down at him with anxious eyes, Rupert felt a horrible dread seize hold of him.

"Martin!" he cried. "My God, what brings you here?"

"He bears you a message from Mlle. de Vainçeoire," the Comte answered in his quiet drawl. "Unless I mistake, 'tis the same fellow who offered me his life for yours that night in Paris. A good lad! When he has given his message, send him to Carlote, who will see that he is fed and housed." He turned to leave the room, but in the doorway he paused. "I shall not require you any more to-night, de Vrieac," he added. "You may stay here if you wish, 'tis warmer and you will not be disturbed."

Then the curtain fell to behind him, and laying his hands on Martin's shoulders, Rupert stared into the servant's face.

"What is it?" he asked hoarsely. "Mademoiselle is not——"

But Martin shook his head reassuringly.

"Have no fear, Monsieur, Mademoiselle is well. 'Twas she, herself, gave me the message. She bade me say—that is—I was to give you this, Monsieur."

And he held out his hand, on the open palm of which lay a gold ring. Rupert looked at it with a start of surprise, whilst the color flooded back hotly into his face.

"My signet ring! Why, Martin, what does that mean? I gave it to Mademoiselle."

"And she needs it no longer, Monsieur," replied the servant in a low voice. "She bade me bring it back to you and say that with it she sent also—your heart! Mlle. de Vainçeoire requires neither any more, Monsieur."

For a moment there was silence, whilst Martin watched his master with troubled eyes as he stood, staring before him blankly into space. The blow had been so utterly unexpected that Rupert was too surprised at first to realize exactly what Martin was trying to tell him. Then he raised his head with a sudden characteristic squaring of his shoulders.

"Did Mademoiselle not send any letter?"

"No, Monsieur. She said she had no fancy for writing, that it wearied her, and that my tongue would tell you her message well enough. So she gave me the ring, Monsieur, and bade me come to you at La Roche."

"And what was the message? God's death, man, cannot you speak plainly," Rupert flared out suddenly, passionate with misery and apprehension.

"Mademoiselle bade me say, Monsieur," replied Martin in the tones of one repeating a well-learnt lesson, "that she found five years too long, that she could not wait until M. le Comte de La Roche should release you, for by then she would be an old woman, no longer beautiful, and you would not wish to marry her. Mademoiselle bade me say she felt it would be wrong to wait so long and then, when at last you came, that you should be compelled to marry a woman you wanted no more, simply from gratitude for her constancy. Mademoiselle did not wish you to make such a great sacrifice for her. Therefore, Monsieur, Mademoiselle de Vainçeoire bids you 'Adieu,' and begs to remind you that it is foolish to give way to inconsolable grief and that there will be many a charming lady in France, five years hence, who will make you a most admirable wife. Mademoiselle wishes you all happiness, Monsieur, and is sure that you, too, will wish her the same with M. de St. Caux."

"With M. de St. Caux! What do you mean?" asked Rupert with a start.

"Mlle. de Vainçeoire is betrothed to M. de St. Caux," Martin replied slowly.

"Betrothed to M. de St. Caux!"

Rupert remembered Ambroise de St. Caux, a dark, evil-faced young man in the service of M. d'Anjou. Immensely rich, he was equally dissolute, and even in those lax times, a notorious libertine. And Marguerite was betrothed to him. Then Rupert lifted his head, struck by a sudden thought.

"But M. de St. Caux is a Catholic, Martin!"

The servant drew in his breath like a man on whom some long-dreaded torture is at last inflicted, as he answered in a voice so low that Rupert could hardly catch the words:

"Mademoiselle is also a Catholic now, Monsieur. She is no longer of the Religion. M. de St. Caux has converted her."

Marguerite a Catholic! Marguerite a traitress, gone over to the enemy! A deep flush of passion swept over Rupert's face as, striding forward, he seized Martin by the collar, shaking him roughly.

"You dog!" he cried hoarsely. "How dare you speak such lies of Mlle. de Vainçeoire? For that is a lie."

Very steadily Martin looked up in his master's face making no effort to release himself.

"It is God's own truth, Monsieur," he replied, "and Mademoiselle herself bade me tell it to you. M. de St. Caux made it the condition for their marriage, and Mlle. de Vainçeoire agreed immediately."

Letting his hand fall heavily, Rupert turned away, and leaning against the stone mantel, stared into the fire.

It was most certainly true, he had known that in the bottom of his heart all the time. Untrue to him, Marguerite had been untrue to her faith also—at the bidding of a rich libertine.

He raised a face which had suddenly grown very white and haggard to the servant.

"Tell me, Martin," he said in a voice which shook despite all his efforts to keep it steady, "tell me—this marriage? There was no coercion—Mademoiselle consented to it of her own free will?"

"Oh, yes, Monsieur, Mademoiselle was very glad when she was betrothed to M. de St. Caux. Every one knew she wished to marry him."

"But how, in God's name, did she meet him at Vainçeoire?" cried Rupert. "M. le Vidame would not have such a man inside his gates."

"It was not at Vainçeoire, Monsieur. After the King had recalled his edict and Paris was once more safe for those of the Religion, Mlle. de Vainçeoire did not wish to return immediately to M. le Vidame, although Mme. de Saxe urged her to do so. She went to stay with a lady of M. de Biron's acquaintance, who introduced her to Mme. la Duchesse de Lorraine, and it was Mme. la Duchesse, who, in turn, introduced Mademoiselle to M. de St. Caux. Monsieur admired her from the first, and they have been betrothed this month back. Mademoiselle consented gladly enough, there was no need of coercion, Monsieur."

Consented gladly! How could she, to marry a vicious profligate, whose name was a byword even in Paris! And yet deep down in the bitterness of his soul he knew her reasons. Married to St. Caux she would have a position at the Court, and vast wealth; she could, as a lady of Paris, indulge in the frivolities, the flirtations, the petty intrigues in which she delighted, and from which she would, in the old castle of Vainçeoire, have been utterly debarred, had she gone back there to wait five long years for her Huguenot lover. Staring down into the fire Rupert gave a sudden bitter laugh as he recalled her vows made that night at Paris, that night when they had waited safely in Mme. de Saxe's house whilst in the streets outside, in the houses, even in the churches, men, women and children of their religion were being hunted down and murdered.

Martin, who had been hovering anxiously behind him, watching his master with troubled eyes, came nearer at that sound and, stooping down, took Rupert's hand, raising it softly to his lips.

"Ah, Monsieur, Monsieur," he murmured. "If I had never had to give you such a message."

At his touch, Rupert turned with a slight start, looking at him with eyes grown suddenly soft. Then withdrawing his hand gently, he laid it on Martin's shoulder, smiling bravely into the servant's eyes.

"There, there," he said. "It is no use to fret ourselves over what cannot be helped. Mlle. de Vainçeoire is quite right, there are as good fish in the sea as ever came out of it, and will still be in five years' time. You, at any rate, are faithful, lad. Thank God for it. There may be plenty of charming ladies, but there are not many Martins, I fancy. There, there," he repeated good-humoredly, as Martin caught and kissed his hand with a sudden passionate movement. "You must go and get some food and rest now. I shall have to send you to Vrieac to-morrow. Would to God I could go with you."

He put his hand on Martin's shoulder and walked with him to the doorway.

"Now go down the passage on the right at the bottom of the stairs and ask for Carlote. He will see after you. And do not look so troubled, lad. 'Twill not be long before you and Mamette have me back at Vrieac again. Then I shall have to see about catching one of those charming fishes."

And he laughed quickly. But when the curtain fell behind Martin, all mirth died out of his face, leaving it very cold and bitter, as he turned once more to the fire.

"No, no! No more fishing for me," he muttered to himself, staring into the leaping flames. "One woman is enough to last any man's life. I'll leave the charming ladies to others, more daring than I. For I think women are something like the wolves, safe in cages and given all they want, very treacherous otherwise. Ah, Marguerite, you had a fine loyal heart, and what a constancy was yours! Well, I might have known perhaps, and in future I'll be warned. I thank you for the lesson you have taught me, Mademoiselle, I will not quickly trust a member of your charming sex again—except Mamette, God bless the dear old soul. She's loyal."

His eyes grew very soft as he thought of his old nurse at Vrieac, who was, he knew, thinking and waiting patiently for the man who to her would always be the little motherless boy she had loved and looked after from childhood.

Rupert's was not a subtle nature, and he was always perfectly frank with himself. As he stood pondering over Marguerite's message he was quite conscious that it was pride as well as love which had been hurt. It was bitter knowledge that this girl to whom he would have given his fine and honored name should have chosen such a man as Ambroise de St. Caux to succeed him in her affections. And it was more bitter that she could not remain true, that his love could not keep its throne in her heart, for five months, much less as many years. Well, he had been foolish to expect constancy from her. The foolishness of a love-blinded man, he told himself bitterly. Well, he could see now clearly enough. As soon expect the strength of steel from a silken thread, or the endurance of an eagle from a butterfly. And he smiled sourly to himself, wondering how the butterfly would fare with M. de St. Caux.

Then, after a second's hesitation, he slipped his hand inside his doublet and drew out the knot of ribbons she had given him. There it lay on his open palm, a little faded and crumpled, but the same which she had kissed when she promised so ardently to be true to him. And now——? He shrugged his shoulders cynically. A woman's promise. He had not much experience of women. His mother had died when he was born and he had had no sister. Mamette, dear simple old Mamette, although he loved her devotedly, was only a servant. In his life he had only met two women of his own rank, who had been more than the merest acquaintances. The first, Marguerite de Vainçeoire, had attracted him by her beauty, her childish gayety of spirits, her helplessness. He had loved her, not perhaps with the deepest strength of his soul, but very tenderly for all that, and he would gladly have made her mistress of Vrieac. Then fate and M. le Comte intervened. "But I will wait for you always, always," she had said. And now, five short months after that promise, she was betrothed to Ambroise de St. Caux. And a double traitress, false to her religion as well as to her love.

The other woman was Yoeland de Breux. Yoeland de Breux, with her cold, proud manner and scornful little smile. Well, at any rate, there had never been any pretense at friendship with her. Hating him fiercely, she had never failed to keep him aware of that fact. Only once, the morning after Anne's illness, on an impulse born of overwrought nerves and a great relief, had she shown him a little glimpse of how charming she could be to those who had her friendship, and that impulse had been speedily checked by his own pride and cold repulse. Since then her dislike had never wavered.

These were the only two women he had ever really known. The one a faithless lover; the other a constant enemy. Truly, he had cause to think well of the sex, Rupert told himself with a bitter laugh, as, stooping down, he dropped the ribbon into the fire.

It fell upon one of the logs and rested there a few seconds, curling with heat, but untouched; then a little tongue of flame leapt up and caught one of the loops of the knot. Involuntarily, Rupert put out his hand, then drew quickly back and stood perfectly still, watching the fire consume it. So it had perished, perished like Marguerite's promise, like his own love and power ever again to trust a woman. And then from out of the ashes of the burnt ribbon and the dancing flames a vision rose before his eyes.

Soft eyes like purple pansies, a slow voice murmuring encouragement as a woman with the features of Yoeland de Breux and the touch of an angel, had raised him up, holding a cooling drink to his burning lips. Ah! he had never known that dream-woman, she was only the product of a fevered brain. But had she been something more, had he really seen her, heard her voice, why then perhaps—— And he stared down into the blazing logs, whilst around his mouth the bitter lines faded and died away.

CHAPTER X

THE Vicomte de Briege had married a sister of the late Comtesse de La Roche, who had died four years after their marriage, leaving one child, a girl Denise. It was this daughter who had been the principal reason for the Vicomte's coming to La Roche. For Denise was, to her father's satisfaction, betrothed to the Duc de Tours and their marriage was shortly to take place.

Not having seen his niece and nephew since they were children, before Anne was born, he had wished to discover into what they had developed, and, approving highly of what he found, had pressed them urgently to return with him to Briege.

Both Yoeland and her brother, however, had found an excuse for refusing, and the Comte's had been accepted with polite regret. But from his niece the Vicomte would take no refusal. He had determined that she should return with him, and when M. le Vicomte set his mind upon anything he generally got his way.

"Denise is young," he said to Yoeland one day, "and has all the romantic ideas of her age. She has no experience of life and is therefore unable to judge the uselessness and instability of the things which she now considers so important. And my sister, Mme. Charlotte, who looks after my house, is a fool. She had a very unsuitable and fortunately brief affair of love in her youth, which has ever since, I believe, filled her mind with foolish ideas of sentiment, which she has also instilled into Denise. 'Tis well for my daughter that I am there to watch over her interests and choose what is certainly best for her. Otherwise she would marry the first penniless rascal with a good-looking face who took her fancy. This marriage with Henri de Tours is most suitable and excellent in every way, and Denise herself will, in a few years' time, be able to see that. Now, of course, her head is full of nonsense about love. So I wish you, Yoeland, to return with me to Briege. You are a good girl with a sensible head, I can see, and Denise will be more inclined to accept the advice of one of her own sex, who is also her cousin. You can point out to her what an estimable husband M. de Tours will make, and how fortunate she is to have caught his fancy."

Yoeland, who had gathered from these remarks that the marriage considered so excellent by the Vicomte was not viewed with equal pleasure by his daughter and sister, and that Denise had some other lover, a marriage with whom was more to her mind, inquired what the Duc was like. Whereupon the Vicomte broke into graphic descriptions of his wealth, his estates, his position; the magnificence which surrounded him, the servants and gentlemen who lived to do his bidding, as though he were a king. But when it came to describing the man himself the Vicomte's eloquence weakened.

"He is short and dark, with a thin, pale face. An unfortunate accident in childhood made him blind in the left eye, but he can see remarkably well with the one remaining. He is a widower, whose wife died some twelve years ago, and is in the prime of life, about forty, I believe."

And his future bride was, Yoeland reflected, a beautiful girl of eighteen, filled with ideas of romance!

"And does Denise love him?" she asked.

"She likes him fairly well," he replied roughly, "and will be glad enough once she is married to him. At present, as I told you, her head is full of silly notions. She thinks that a lover should be tall and young and handsome, able to string rhymes together, to his lady's elbow, or her hair, and ride to the wars on a big black horse. But she will grow out of such ideas in a few years. And I will watch that she does nothing foolish, though the sooner she is married to de

Tours the better," he added in a low voice, more to himself than his listener.

It was at this point that Yoeland decided that she would return with the Vicomte to Briege. Anne was well and would be quite safe with her brother and old Jeanne, and it seemed to Yoeland that this unknown motherless cousin, her pretty, innocent head filled with ideas on which her father had poured such scorn, whilst he made plans to hasten on her marriage with M. de Tours, had need, urgent need, of her help.

Rupert was with the child when Yoeland came to Anne with the news that next day she was going to Briege with their uncle, and when he heard it he gave a great and only partly stifled sigh of thankfulness. For since his recovery from his accident at the wolf hunt, her dislike towards him seemed to have burned more fiercely than ever. She lost no opportunity of irritating and annoying him, and whilst the Comte was just and treated him with cold civility before the servants, she made no effort to conceal her dislike and distrust of him at all times. Without Mademoiselle his life at La Roche would be very much more bearable, and the news of her going was to him a great relief.

Yoeland caught the sigh and, understanding the cause, flushed with sudden anger, but she made no comment. As for Anne, the child was utterly dismayed at the thought of her beloved Yoeland leaving her, even for only a few weeks. Finally, however, she became reconciled to the idea, her sister having promised that her absence should be very brief, and hinting at all the wonderful things she would have to tell on her return.

Anne smiled wistfully.

"If you promise not to be away long, I will try not to mind, Yoeland. Besides," she added, brightening suddenly, "I shall have M. Rupert, so I shall be all right. He will look after me."

At that the intense jealousy which Yoeland's pride had always carefully concealed flared up in a bitter flame, sweeping aside, for the moment, all sense of reason and justice. So long as Anne had this Huguenot she would not miss her, or Charles, or any of them much, she thought, and determined that he should pay hardly for the child's love of him, even if Anne had to be hurt a little too.

"Anne, dear, I am so sorry if it will distress you," she said, holding the child tightly in her arms, "but I am afraid that M. de Vrieac will not be here. I shall have to take some—some people with me to Briege, and I hope M. de Vrieac will be one of them. If he will be so kind as to come and take care of me," she added, looking up at him with a malicious smile.

It was not Anne, although she greeted it with a wail of dissent, who was most concerned at this intelligence. Rupert was absolutely speechless with dismay and anger, which he had some ado to control and conceal.

The news that Yoeland wished Rupert de Vrieac to be one of those accompanying her to Briege, surprised the Comte as much as it had done its first recipients. He never guessed the bitter jealousy, born out of her great love for Anne, which had prompted the idea, or her fierce determination that Rupert should have no chance to get even a stronger hold upon the child's affections when his way would be cleared by her own absence. She was determined on her plan and so, although both Anne and the Comte offered considerable opposition, it was at length settled that Rupert should go to Briege.

They were to start for Briege early the following morning, so that night, before old Jeanne put her to sleep, Rupert went in to say good-by to Anne.

She was sitting propped up by many pillows, eagerly waiting for him, though her face bore the traces of recent tears. No one else was in the room, and, crossing to the bed, Rupert knelt beside it, slipping an arm round the child. She looked up at him with quivering lips.

"Oh, M. Rupert, I do wish that you and Yoeland would not go away. It is bad enough if it were only Yoeland, but I shall miss you *both* ever so much more, and there will be no one to tell me stories when you are gone. Old Jeanne does not know *any*."

And hiding her face against his shoulder she began to weep bitterly.

"There, there, Mlle. Anne," he murmured, stroking her hair in an awkward attempt to console her. "Why you will hardly have time to miss us, we shall be back so soon. And as for the stories—there is the old chronicle, and I shall expect you to be able to tell me a lot of that when I come back."

For he had been teaching the child to read, a process necessarily slow, as much exertion made Anne's head ache, but she was eager to learn and was doing well. The Comte had brought her one day an old book, with large print and curious illustrations, full of stories of saints and heroes and deeds of great renown, and Rupert hoped that the laborious deciphering of this might give her occupation during his and Mlle. de Breux's absence.

The child caught at the idea, and faithfully promised to be able to recount several of the tales when he came back.

"You can pretend you are a knight's lady, waiting for him to return, only instead of embroidering a cover for his shield you have to read a story out of the chronicle instead," Rupert suggested, appealing to her imagination.

"Yes, yes," she cried eagerly. "And you will be the knight who is going to protect a beautiful lady through a country where there are dragons and witches. And when you come back safely you are going to live in a castle made of gold and mother-of-pearl, with your own lady. I am your own lady," looking up at him earnestly, "not Yoeland. She is another knight's lady, though she likes you very much. She must like you very, very much," she added, holding his arm tightly and pulling herself forward in her eagerness, "because she chose you out of every one to take care of her. Charles would have gone if she had wanted him, or Carlote. There is M. le Vicomte, too, but she felt safest with you."

And Rupert, who knew the real reason for Mademoiselle de Breux's decision perfectly well, stooped down and kissed the child with a sudden laugh.

"God bless you, Mlle. Anne," he said softly. "I do believe you would give the Devil credit for good intentions."

And shortly afterwards he left her.

Outside the door a servant was waiting to announce the Comte's desire to see him, and with foreboding of more unpleasant things to come, Rupert obeyed the summons. He found the Comte standing before the fire, intently examining a sword which he held in his hands.

"I think, de Vrieac," he said quietly, "that as you are going to Briege with the object of guarding Mlle. de Breux, it is well you should be armed. A protector without a weapon is not much use in these days. So take this sword, and there is the sheath. At La Roche you do not require arms, but it is different when you escort Mademoiselle through the country. You will give me the sword again when you return. Do not use it to pick quarrels of your own, but in the defense of Mlle. de Breux only."

After Rupert had gone the Comte stood for a few moments in grave thought, then laughed quietly, struck by a sudden idea.

"I do most sincerely trust that he will not use it on Yoeland," he said to himself. "He hates her enough, in all conscience. And why she should want to take him with her passes my comprehension. Truly, women are the very devil, one can never understand their reason."

It was a glorious morning when the Vicomte and Mlle. de Breux, accompanied by the Vicomte's troopers and Mademoiselle's little company of two serving-women, Carlote, four soldiers of La Roche, and Rupert de Vrieac, together with a couple of pack-horses, set out, and a still more glorious evening when, three days later, they rode into the courtyard at Briege.

On the gray steps of the castle Mademoiselle Denise, a pretty girl in white, stood to greet them, and behind her was a gray-haired lady, Mme. Charlotte, whose sad, nervous face bore the faded remnants of beauty, whilst further back the servants were grouped to do honor to their master and his guests' coming.

The Vicomte, without a thought of Yoeland or greeting to his daughter, swung himself out of the saddle and stood giving orders to his men, so Rupert, seeing that Carlote, who had gone to her horse's head, obviously expected him to take the honor, approached Yoeland to assist her to alight. A faint flush crept into her cheeks as, with a low word of thanks, she took his proffered hands, then turned to greet Mlle. Denise, who had come shyly forward.

Yoeland de Breux was, as a rule, coldly reserved to strangers, but as she felt the girl's soft, timid kiss on her cheek, the maternal instinct, which the early loss of her own mother and the consequent care of Anne had developed, stirred in quick response, and putting her arms round her cousin, she returned the greeting warmly.

"I was very glad to come to Briege," she said softly, "for I wished to know you so much, Denise."

"And I am so glad you have come," the girl replied quickly, flushing in pleased surprise, "and I hope you will like me as much as I am sure I shall like you, Yoeland."

As Yoeland turned to greet Mme. Charlotte, she looked back and hesitated. Then with a slight lifting of her chin, "Denise," she said rather hurriedly, "you must allow me to present to you M. Rupert de Vrieac, a—a—who is staying with us at La Roche."

An explanation which was greeted by the Vicomte, who had just come up the steps, with a loud roar of laughter, and which made Rupert's eyes flash curiously as he bent over Mlle. Denise's hand.

It did not take very long for Yoeland to discover that the Vicomte was an absolute despot towards his household, and that every one, from his daughter to the youngest scul-

For little invalid Anne, La Roche and Yoeland would have sacrificed everything.

lion in the kitchens, lived in awe, if not in positive dread, of him. As to Mme. Charlotte, there was no doubt at all that she regarded him with absolute fear. Brought up from earliest childhood, by a father who had never forgiven her for being a girl, to consider herself a useless encumbrance, she had, when seventeen, had the one bright time of her life, the brief affair of love which the Vicomte had mentioned to Yoeland. In her father's house there had lived a poor cousin, without wealth, position, or any hopes of either, with no endowment save a God-given sense of music and the great innocent heart of a child. And this man, with his power of song, brought joy and visions of happiness to poor Mme. Charlotte's lonely heart, of which she had never dreamt.

So they loved each other, these two friendless, down-trodden souls, and for a little time held their secret secure from prying eyes. Then one day all had been discovered. Mme. Charlotte, after a terrible scene which seemed to have taken the power of happiness from her for ever, had seen her lover, with nothing but his lute and empty pockets, thrust from the castle, whilst she herself was hurried off to the security of a convent, from which she was recalled a month later to marry a wealthy friend of her father's, thirty years her senior, who wanted a young and pretty wife who was also meek and yielding. And for twelve years she had endured his tyranny uncomplainingly, until his death at the battle of Jarnac had set her free. But through the villainy of his brother she was both homeless and desperately poor. Having no children to help her or friends to whom she could appeal, she had been glad to accept the Vicomte's offer to come to Briege, only to find that the tyranny of father and husband was as nothing to the new yoke under which she had bent her neck.

There was, however, one joy left to her—Denise. All the starved power of loving in Mme. Charlotte's poor crushed heart was showered upon the girl, and the young, motherless heart had leaped to meet it. Deep down in her inmost soul, hidden securely, Mme. Charlotte kept the shrine of her poor musician, and so neither her loveless marriage nor her lonely life had had power to break her heart or make it anything but sweet and kind.

It was not long before Yoeland found the way into Mme. Charlotte's heart also, and learnt with what horror the poor lady saw her own life's tragedy about to be repeated in that of the girl she loved so deeply. For Yoeland's surmise had been correct and Denise not only disliked M. de Tours, but loved and was loved by Philibert de Vois, whose estates joined those of Briege on the north.

Now Philibert de Vois was young and brave and handsome, but he was poor, indeed; compared to M. de Tours, he was a beggar, so the Vicomte had utterly set his face against such a marriage. In vain Mme. Charlotte, made brave by her love for Denise, had begged the Vicomte to think of his daughter's happiness before wealth and position, quoting the misery of her own loveless marriage. He had answered her with a cruel sneer which sent her from the room with quivering lips and an aching heart. In vain Denise had implored him not to force her into such a marriage. M. le Vicomte, firmly convinced that his sole object was his daughter's good, refused to listen, and hastened on preparations lest Philibert de Vois, who had boldly asked for Denise's hand, only to be met with an insulting refusal, should carry her off by force.

It was for this reason the Vicomte had wished Yoeland to come to Briege, for considering her possessed of great common sense, he felt that she, at any rate, could not fail to impress upon Denise the desirability of M. de Tours as a husband and the utter unsuitability of Philibert de Vois for the same position.

Intelligent, sympathetic, and a good judge of character, Yoeland soon made herself very popular at Briege. The Vicomte treated her with a respect which he had never before accorded to any woman. Denise and Mme. Charlotte were devoted to her, and Father Paul, the silver-haired, gentle-faced old priest, continually the object of sneers and coarse jests from the Vicomte, and whom only a solemn promise made to the dying Vicomtesse that he would stay and watch over her child kept at Briege, when he saw Mlle. de Breux thanked God simply for a good and beautiful woman.

To Rupert her manner had changed since they came to Briege. No longer irritated by the constant reminder of Anne's love and need of him, she showed her antagonism less plainly, treating him with a courtesy as cold and scrupulous as his towards her, and once or twice had surprised him by asking some small service with a quiet, almost friendly smile.

CHAPTER XI

I T was not until four days after her arrival at Briege that Yoeland met M. le Duc de Tours.

He rode into the castle yard very splendidly attired and mounted upon a superb gray horse, with a veritable army of troopers and servants behind him, for he had, at the Vicomte's suggestion, come to stay a few days at Briege, that he might win Denise's liking by giving her a foreshadowing of some of the splendors which, as Duchesse de Tours, would be hers, and also that he might make the acquaintance of the Vicomte's beautiful and accomplished niece, Mlle. de Breux. Yoeland, when he was presented, thought of a snake, a pale, silent-crawling snake, whose bite meant death.

That night as she went as usual into her cousin's room to bid her "Good-night," she held the girl very tightly in her arms.

"Denise, dear heart," she said, "you must certainly not marry M. de Tours, for you could never be happy with such a man as that."

Denise, clinging to her, shuddered.

"I—I hate him," she cried, "but what can I do? My father says I must marry M. de Tours, for he is so rich and great."

"And *good?*" added Yoeland with a little scornful laugh. "Why, what is your M. Philibert de Vois thinking of that he does not come and carry you off and marry you in spite of every one, as Raoul de Vrieac did with Yvonne de Marbleu long ago?"

Lifting her head, Denise looked at her with wide eyes of fear.

"Oh, Yoeland, I—I dare not. My father——"

And Yoeland, although she could not herself understand being cowed by such a power of terror as the Vicomte held over his daughter, kissed the tear-stained face very gently.

"There, there, dear," she murmured, "you must not spoil your eyes crying over M. de Tours, he is not worthy. And, Denise, never fear. You shall not marry him, so go to sleep and dream of your M. Philibert. It will be a poor thing if, between us all, we cannot find some way to foil M. le Duc's plans."

The next afternoon, Yoeland, Denise, Mme. Charlotte and the Duc de Tours, with Carlote and a couple of troopers for escort, went riding.

It was one of the first glorious days of spring. Overhead the sun shone brightly from a sky as blue as the speedwells, whilst from every tree and thicket, where the young budding green showed boldly, came the glad song of birds. Everything around them seemed to tell of joy and hope. Even Marcus, the Duc's great wolf-hound, forgot his dignity, bounding along beside the horses, baying excitedly, and dashing away every now and then in pursuit of imaginary enemies.

They were riding up a wide grassy glade when from a thicket ahead of them came fierce baying from Marcus, followed by a sharp, shrill cry. Quickening their horses' pace they went towards the spot. In a small clearing amongst the trees stood a rude hut, at the door of which was a woman, her black, unkempt hair falling over her face, from which her eyes gleamed fiercely. She was dressed in rough sacking, and one bare arm clasped a baby to her breast, whilst the other was thrust out before her, keeping back Marcus, who was leaping up wildly at the child.

As the riders reached the clearing, a boy of three or four ran from the hut to help his mother, flinging a stone at the great hound. Marcus turned howling, and seeing his master, limped up to him, blood running from a cut on one of his fore-legs. With an oath the Duc sprang from his horse and strode forward, his face dark with passion.

Snatching up the boy he held him by the arm whilst he raised his whip threateningly.

But before he could strike the child there was a sharp exclamation, a horse moved up beside him, and Yoeland de Breux's voice, low and vibrating with anger, cried, "You coward, oh, you coward!" whilst her riding-switch fell sharply twice across the Duc's shoulders.

With a start he dropped the child and stared up at her, silent with rage and amazement. Then his expression changed, giving place to a look of admiration. Never had Yoeland looked more beautiful. For a few seconds he gazed at her, then, with a rueful laugh, rubbed his shoulder.

"Parbleu, Mademoiselle!" he said. "You strike hard."

And Yoeland, the heat of her anger changed into a more dangerous calm by his obvious admiration, replied coldly:

"I am glad to think so, Monseigneur."

Then slipping from her horse, she gathered up the sobbing, terrified child in her arms and carried him into the hut to his mother.

"I am very sorry that the dog was so rough, though he meant no harm," she said and laid some money on the table, adding as the woman thanked her awkwardly, "I will come and see you again to-morrow, so look out for me, little boy," and smiling, left the hut.

Outside, the others were waiting, and though Carlote held her horse, it was the Duc who helped her very carefully into the saddle, Yoeland thanking him curtly.

The ride back to Briege was a silent one. Many times the Duc glanced at Yoeland, and there was both admiration and wonder in his face. Never before had he met a woman with her spirit, always having been courted and cringed to by them, however much they might fear or dislike him. Yoeland de Breux was the first who had not troubled to conceal her scorn, who had gone further, and actually struck him. The novelty pleased M. le Duc's jaded fancy, and he had a great desire to test the strength of Mlle. de Breux's courage. Then, leaning back in his saddle, he glanced at Denise, riding on Yoeland's other side, and his lips twitched contemptuously.

"The tigress—and the dove," he muttered to himself.

Meanwhile, Rupert, having watched the riders off, and knowing he was free for the afternoon, betook himself through the woods to a little hill on which was an old ivy-covered tower. Here, lying on his back in the shade of its ruined, roofless walls, he could watch the clouds sailing overhead and think his thoughts, disturbed by no one but the birds. To-day, however, there were other intruders, for coming quickly round the tower, Rupert stopped short with a startled exclamation. On a heap of fallen stones sat Father Paul, whilst beside him was a tall, good-looking man about Rupert's own age mounted on a black horse.

At sight of Rupert the priest's companion half drew his sword, but Father Paul held up a detaining hand.

"That is not necessary, my son. Gentlemen, allow me to present you—M. Rupert de Vrieac—M. Philibert de Vois."

And Philibert de Vois, slipping back his sword, leant from the saddle, holding out his hand with a smile.

"I am glad to meet you, M. de Vrieac, for I have often heard of you from an old soldier of mine who was with you at Jarnac."

And Rupert, answering the friendly note in the other's voice, laughed.

"Why, the pleasure is mine, for I have heard of M. de Vois from many people."

Then the deep silence which follows an interruption of very confidential talk fell upon them, and Rupert, knowing himself to be an intruder, was about to leave the other two with a murmured apology, when Philibert de Vois made a detaining gesture, and looked across at Father Paul with questioning eyes.

The old priest shook his head, smiling gently.

"You need have no fear, my son, but still if you would——"

Moving his horse forward, de Vois looked down very steadily into Rupert's eyes.

"M. de Vrieac, since you have heard of me from many people, some of them at least will not have failed to tell you that the Vicomte is—shall we say, is not my friend. Indeed, I think I am right in believing that should he find me here now upon his land he would make every effort to catch and hang me. Also, he would not be pleased to know that Father Paul had been with me. So you——"

But Rupert, seeing his meaning, stopped him.

"M. de Vois," he said, meeting the other's gaze frankly, "you need have no fear. Be very sure that I should never, either by accident or design, let M. le Vicomte know anything which could lead to unhappiness for Mlle. Denise. As far as I am concerned our meeting this afternoon is forgotten."

And Philibert de Vois, with a quick smile, took his proffered hand in a grip that hurt. Then he sighed.

"Ah, M. de Vrieac, you can see her, but I—— Tell me, where is she this afternoon?"

"She has gone riding with Mlle. de Breux and Mme. Charlotte," Rupert answered diplomatically.

But de Vois' eyes flashed.

"And M. le Duc de Tours," he cried fiercely. "Holy Mother! when I think of that beast, that villain who all the world knows poisoned his first wife, that snake beside her, when I know that they will try and sell her to him, I—I—— The devil take him to hell," he stammered, with a helpless sob of rage.

Father Paul, who had been standing unnoticed by them, laid his hand soothingly on de Vois' arm.

"Yet the good God made him, my son," he said gently.

But Philibert turned on him hotly.

"Yes, and He made the snakes and wolves too; but would you have me, for that, leave them to bite and tear and spread death, and not—kill them?" he asked.

The old priest looked up at him with troubled eyes.

"God will judge him, my son. You can safely leave the punishment of M. le Duc in His hands."

"Yes, father, that no doubt is so," Rupert interposed; "but it seems to me that the justice of heaven is—er—unnecessarily delayed. If therefore one should take steps to accelerate the punishment of these wolves and snakes—and other things, may not such assistance rendered to the holy powers be acceptable and even a sacred duty?"

With a quick laugh Philibert de Vois reached down and caught Rupert's hand.

"M. de Vrieac," he said in a voice trembling with eagerness, "may I take that as a promise of help if ever I should require it in the performance of my—sacred duty?"

Rupert looked at him with very grave eyes.

"Most certainly, M. de Vois," he replied earnestly. "If ever you should require assistance when carrying out the justice of heaven on M. le Duc de Tours and I can render it, be very sure that I shall not fail to do so."

But Father Paul, the trouble deepening in his eyes, shook his head with a sigh.

"Leave him in the hands of God, my sons. He will give M. le Duc justice at the right time," he said softly.

The next day Yoeland, a basket of provisions on her arm, left the castle and passed into the woods on her way to the poor woman's hut. But though her going had been unobtrusive, two people saw her—the Duc le Tours and Rupert de Vrieac. The Duc, knowing her errand, smiled sourly, and after a little time, calling up two of his men, disappeared also in the direction taken by Mlle. de Breux. Across the way she must return ran a stream traversed by high, flat stepping-stones. Crossing the stream, the Duc sat down, watching complacently whilst the two men, acting under his directions, waded into the water and carefully removed the stepping-stones, laying them on the bank nearest Briege.

"Now go beyond those trees," he said, pointing to a little hillock, "and stay there until you hear me blow this whistle, then come quickly."

And seating himself upon a bank of grass in the shade of a large beech, he prepared to await the return of Yoeland de Breux.

Yoeland, having emptied the goodly contents of her basket into the surprised woman's arms, departed, waving aside the woman's awkward thanks with a smile. She was rather surprised when coming down the hill towards the stream to see a man lying on the grass, and wished, a second later, that she had brought Carlote with her, for she recognized the Duc le Tours, and it was plain from the way he greeted her that he had been awaiting her.

"I trust you have had a pleasant walk, Mademoiselle," he said, doffing his hat with a low bow. "But, may I venture to say it?—is it wise for a lady with the appearance of Mlle. de Breux to go about unattended, even at Briege?" And without asking her leave, he turned to accompany her.

"I thank you, M. le Duc, for your kind consideration," she replied rather haughtily; "I believe it to be perfectly safe, otherwise I should have brought Carlote or——"

She ceased abruptly, for she knew now the reason of the Duc's presence. Before her, swift and wide, ran the stream, and on the far bank, neatly stacked, lay the stepping-stones. Very coldly she looked at the man beside her, who was vainly trying to appear surprised.

"Why, Mademoiselle, what can have happened? The stones were in their places when I crossed over. Who can have moved them? Perhaps the Fairy Queen who, the peasants say, lives in that old oak?"

"No doubt," Yoeland replied in cold tones; "but as she has omitted to replace them, perhaps you would kindly do so instead, Monseigneur."

"Certainly, Mademoiselle," he replied blandly. "If it were in my power I would deem it the greatest honor to serve Mlle. de Breux in any way. But unfortunately I am a small man and the stones are large. It would take three men such as I to move them."

"Then could you not, with that whistle, summon two

more?" she asked quickly, for she guessed that he had men hidden not far away, and knew that she could not keep down her rising anger many minutes, though she felt to show it just then might be dangerous.

"Yes, Mademoiselle, perhaps I could," he agreed; "but surely there is no need for haste. Will you not be kind and give me a few seconds of Paradise, Mademoiselle? Will you sit down on this bank and permit me to talk to you? The moss here is soft and dry."

And Yoeland, although her heart was beating quickly as she realized that she had little chance of escape from him, and longed desperately for her brother, or Carlote, or even Rupert de Vrieac, forced herself to answer gayly:

"I am sorry that I cannot grant a request made so gallantly, Monseigneur, but I must return to Briege at once. And since you cannot replace the stones I will wade across. Adieu, M. le Duc."

She started resolutely down the bank and had reached the water's edge, when Rupert de Vrieac stepped quietly from the trees on the opposite bank. Without stopping to take off his shoes, he walked unconcernedly through the water to Yoeland's side, looking at her with eyes which showed no signs of having seen anything unusual.

"Do you wish to cross the stream, Mademoiselle?" he asked. "M. le Duc and I can easily replace those stones for you. Though would it not be quicker," he added, as though struck by a sudden thought, "if you would permit us to carry you over and then we could send some men from Briege to put the stones back?"

And Yoeland, inwardly rejoicing at such a task for the Duc, replied gravely that it was an excellent plan.

Turning, they both looked expectantly at the Duc, but for a second it seemed that he was not only going to refuse to do any such thing, but that he also had thoughts of springing at Rupert's throat. Rupert, waiting, hoped that he would, fully intending to place him in the stream as a stepping-stone for Mademoiselle.

No doubt something of his determination showed in his face, for shrugging his shoulders, the Duc stepped forward, saying it was always a pleasure to serve Mlle. de Breux. Then he joined his hands to Rupert's, and Yoeland mounted on the seat thus formed, holding the basket on her lap with one hand, whilst she rested the other on Rupert's shoulder. The stream was not very wide, and they crossed it safely, the Duc, if he had had any idea of loosening his hold and dropping Yoeland into the water, being prevented by the strong grip of Rupert's fingers.

Putting Yoeland down on the other side, Rupert took her basket and showed every intention of accompanying her back to Briege, whilst the Duc sat down on a stone and began to remove his water-filled shoes, looking at the others with a maliciousness which he made no effort to conceal. And Yoeland, moved by his scowl and the protection of Rupert's presence to sudden mischief, made him a deep curtsey, as she cried:

"Adieu, M. le Duc. A thousand thanks for your kind assistance across the stream," and turned away with a gay, mocking laugh.

Yoeland, walking in front of Rupert, did not speak, though her eyes, unseen by him, were shining, and once he heard her laugh softly. But when they reached the castle and Rupert, opening the wicket-gate, stood aside to let her pass, she paused, holding out her hand in silence.

Very gravely he handed her the basket; but taking that in her left hand, she still held out her right to him, and looking up at her, Rupert flushed with sudden surprise, for in her eyes he saw a faint likeness to his dream lady.

"Thank you, M. de Vrieac," she said, "for your very timely presence and your help."

And Rupert, his heart beating strangely, raised her fingers to his lips.

"My help was a pleasure to give, Mademoiselle," he replied in a low voice, "and I am glad my presence was not distasteful to you."

Then he released her fingers, turning, with a deep bow, abruptly away. But Yoeland, sitting in the low window seat of her room a few moments later, laughed as she thought of the Duc's wet shoes; then the laughter faded and her eyes grew soft and dreamy as she looked intently at the fingers of her right hand.

"Is that what made it a pleasure?" she whispered, as though to some one near, "only that? Ah! what a foolish girl I am." And raising her fingers with a little laugh she laid them against her lips.

That evening there was a tragedy at the castle. One of Denise's women, a young and pretty girl named Lucile Boron, waiting in the dusk for her lover, met M. le Duc de Tours as he returned in no pleasant temper from the stream. What happened none might ever know. There was a stifled scream from the girl and cruel laughter from the Duc. Then Jacques Gallon, the girl's lover, who was a soldier in the Duc's troop, came running up, and in the twilight there sounded fierce oaths, a sharp struggle, a groan and the thud of a falling body, followed by silence.

When the Vicomte, with Rupert and some servants carrying torches, came, they found Lucile Boron in a swoon, Jacques Gallon dead, stabbed in the chest, and the Duc calmly wiping his poniard on the fallen man's tunic.

"The girl thought I was a ghost and screamed, and this insolent fool rushed up and attacked me, so I killed him," was the Duc's haughty explanation to the Vicomte. And there seemed nothing more to be said, since the Duc was a great gentleman and Jacques Gallon but a poor soldier in his service, who should have known better than to resent any action of his master's.

So Lucile was carried to the castle, his comrades buried Jacques Gallon, and although Denise shuddered and turned very pale when next she saw the Duc, and Yoeland surveyed him with scornful eyes, the affair seemed very soon to be quite forgotten.

But Lucile Boron did not forget; neither did Pierre Gallon, the dead man's brother, who was also in the Duc's troop.

CHAPTER XII

ONE morning a fortnight later, M. le Vicomte de Briege with most of his men-at-arms clattered out under the castle gateway and took the road to Valdante. There had been serious fighting there lately amongst the Huguenots and Catholics in the town, and the Vicomte, as overlord, felt himself called upon to go and quell the disturbances. He had invited the Duc to accompany him, but Henri de Tours never took any risk of fighting if he could help it, and had decided to remain at Briege; to take care of the ladies, he explained. So the Vicomte, who knew the real reason of his future son-in-law's refusal perfectly well, shrugged his shoulders and, saying that he would return in a couple of days, rode away.

That night Yoeland retired early, but it was with no thought of sleep, for the heat of her room made that impossible. So having let down her hair, she sat on the broad seat by her window, looking out into the dark, starless night.

The atmosphere was oppressive, not a leaf stirred, not a sound broke the intense silence. Everything seemed to be waiting breathlessly. Then, away over towards the Loire came a faint flash, followed slowly by the first muttering rumble of the storm which was gathering. And sitting at her window Yoeland watched it creeping up gradually nearer and nearer. The lightning became more vividly blue, the crash of the thunder louder, whilst the pause between them grew briefer. One or two large drops of rain fell heavily. Then they ceased. And then, as though it had been gathering its forces together, down came the rain in a rushing sheet of water, driving through the trees, beating fiercely into the ground and swishing over the roof. At that

113

moment there was a tremendous flash of lightning, blindingly vivid, followed instantly by a crash of thunder which seemed to shake the whole castle and, peals following flashes almost simultaneously, the storm broke overhead.

Closing the window, Yoeland moved back into the room. The blue glare of the lightning made everything clear as day, and as she turned towards the door her heart gave a sudden leap. For the latch was moving as though some one outside the door were trying to open it. She had shot the bolt when coming to bed, so stood for a moment watching more surprised than frightened; then, with a caution rendered unnecessary by the noise overhead, she stole softly to the door, and leant her ear against it. From outside came knocking and a voice, which with a smile of relief she recognized as Father Paul's, called to her. Putting up her hand quickly she drew back the bolt and flung the door open.

In the passage stood Rupert de Vrieac, fully dressed and armed, beside him Father Paul. She stared at them in surprise, glancing questioningly from one to the other, her instinct warning her that something was wrong.

"What has happened, Father Paul?" she cried, apprehensively.

But it was Rupert, stepping closer and speaking very loudly to make himself heard above the uproar, who answered.

"We are sorry to disturb you, Mademoiselle, but it was necessary and urgent. Will you, as quickly as possible, go to the turret where Carlote is lodged. Father Paul will bring Madame Charlotte and Mademoiselle Denise to you there. I hope that we are mistaken and are taking unnecessary precautions, but we—Father Paul, Carlote and I —think that M. de Tours' soldiers and the half-dozen the Vicomte left behind are planning some mischief. If that is so, it is against the Duc only. They mean no harm to you ladies, but once they have started their devilment, who knows where they might end, or what you might see and hear? I beg of you, Mademoiselle," he added earnestly, mis-reading her expression, "to do as we ask. And you, Father, will you fetch the others?"

"Why should we go to the tower?" Yoeland asked, as Father Paul hurried away.

"Because the stairs to Carlote's room are steep and narrow and he can hold them should any of the soldiers attempt to reach you, Mademoiselle. We are only six to their thirty-two, for Father Paul cannot fight. If you wished to remain in your rooms we could, of course, keep the door-ways for a time, but it could not be very long if they really meant mischief. And it does not take much, when there are so many of them together, to turn men into devils, Made-moiselle. It would be better to stay out of their way in the turret and then, if any of them should go mad and try to reach you, we shall have the advantage of a good position."

"Do you mean—do you really believe that they are planning to harm M. le Duc?" she asked with horrified eyes.

"Yes, Mademoiselle, I do, and God knows they have just cause," Rupert answered gravely. And Yoeland, re-membering the death of Jacques Gallon and a look which she had sometimes surprised in the eyes of the Duc's sol-diers as they watched their master, shuddered. Taking ad-vantage of the Vicomte's absence with most of his men, they had won over the few soldiers of Briege remaining. Carlote and the four men of La Roche were away in the west turret; the servants all slept in a different part of the castle; M. de Vrieac, Father Paul and the ladies were safely in their rooms suspecting nothing, and the Duc was practi-cally defenseless. What more easy than, relying upon the storm to drown any noise which they might make, for them to steal up to the Duc's room. Here they could either murder him quickly or, muffling his cries for help, bear him back to their quarters and there wreak their vengeance upon him more slowly. And Yoeland, the whole ghastly scene pictured in her imagination, closed her eyes, shuddering again.

"Where are Carlote and our men of La Roche?" she asked.

"They are getting the room in the tower ready for you and making other preparations, Mademoiselle."

"And M. le Duc?"

Rupert shrugged his shoulders.

"He is a man and must fend for himself, Mademoiselle," he replied coldly. "When you ladies are safely in the tower I will warn him, and he can then barricade his room or make what preparations he thinks best."

Yoeland looked at him intently, her face gone suddenly white.

"You said just now, M. de Vrieac, that six against thirty-two could not hold their own for long. The Duc is only one."

Again Rupert shrugged his shoulders.

"I cannot help that, Mademoiselle. If there is trouble he will have caused it, and for my part, I sympathize with his men. To have him in the turret room would be sheer madness. As it is, the soldiers may attack us too, but if they knew that M. le Duc were there they would certainly come, the whole band like devils, and murder us all to reach him. No, no, Mademoiselle. M. le Comte told me to guard you, and I will do all I can, but I will not give my life and Carlote's and perhaps yours, for the Duc de Tours."

"He will be another sword, one more to fight," she said slowly.

Rupert did not answer, but his laugh was eloquent, and Yoeland knew that he was right, that neither the Duc's help nor his courage were to be relied upon. Yet she raised her head proudly, looking Rupert very steadily in the eyes.

"M. le Duc is a guest in my uncle's house, and as such we cannot leave him. He *must* come to the tower, even if it means danger to the rest of us. Therefore, M. de Vrieac, you will please fetch him—now."

But Rupert made no movement to obey her.

"I order you to do so," she cried hotly.

"Then I will not take your orders, Mademoiselle," he replied, and his mouth set as firmly as her own.

For a second she stared at him with flashing eyes, then moved swiftly towards the Duc's door. But Rupert was before her, barring her way.

"This is folly, Mademoiselle," he said, in low, angry tones.

She drew herself up haughtily.

"Have the goodness to obey your orders or stand aside, M. de Vrieac."

But he shook his head.

"Your pardon, Mademoiselle. I had M. le Comte's orders first, and they were that I should protect you from danger as much as possible."

"And yourself too?" she retorted quickly, trying to move him with a sneer. But though he flushed hotly, he did not give way.

It was at this second, when Yoeland was thinking desperately of some way by which she might overcome his opposition, that the door behind Rupert opened very cautiously and the Duc's face, white and nervous, peered out.

He gave a sigh of relief at sight of them, and slipping the sword which he held before him back into its sheath, stepped into the passage. He was still fully dressed, and Yoeland noticed that he was shivering, as though the night were very cold.

"Ah! Mlle. de Breux," he said, bowing to her, whilst his eyes surveyed Rupert with an insolent stare, "so you are awake also. Small wonder! Who could sleep in such a storm? It seems as if all the devils from hell were holding carnival on the roof. I am glad I am not in the woods, 'twould be vastly dangerous under those trees to-night."

"It may be equally dangerous for us to be under this castle roof to-night, Monseigneur," Yoeland said, moving forward. "For M. de Vrieac believes that the soldiers are hatching some plot, that they mean mischief. We—Denise, Mme. Charlotte and I, with M. de Vrieac, Carlote, and my four soldiers from La Roche—are going to the west turret. M. de Vrieac thinks that, should the soldiers attack us, that would be the best position to hold. You had better fetch all your weapons, Monseigneur, and join us there."

For a second the Duc stared at her, whilst his face turned slowly from white to a sickly green.

"The soldiers plotting, Mademoiselle," he stammered. "Is there danger? Why, what——"

Rupert took his arm quietly.

"M. le Duc," he said, holding the other's eyes with his own and speaking very distinctly, "your soldiers are plotting to revenge the murder of Jacques Gallon. I am going to take Mlle. de Breux, with Mme. Charlotte and Mlle. Denise, to the west turret. The soldiers mean no harm to them— it is you they want—and should a few, madder than the rest, attack the turret, Carlote and his four men will be able to hold the stairs against them. When I have seen the ladies safely there and arranged with Carlote, I will return to you.—There is time enough, for the soldiers are at present enjoying some of M. le Vicomte's wine, they will not start business yet, till they think we are all in bed.—We will then barricade your room and do what we can together to hold them off. You had better go now, Monseigneur, and begin to move some of the furniture near the door. I will be with you in a few minutes."

The Duc neither moved nor answered. He stood perfectly still, the terror in his eyes horrible to see. Once or twice he swallowed hardly and his lips moved, though no sound came. But Yoeland, with a low cry, caught Rupert's arm.

"No, no, M. de Vrieac! No, no! Two against thirty-two! It is certain death in that room."

He looked down at her, smiling quietly.

"Perhaps, Mademoiselle," he replied, shrugging his shoulders. "It does not greatly matter. Better they should attack us there and possibly kill us two, than that they should all storm the turret. For six might not hold the stairs till morning against the whole thirty-two, and once they got amongst you ladies, God knows what would happen. By then their blood would be up and they would be like devils. Therefore,

Mademoiselle, I beg that you will go to the turret quickly. I will return to you in a few minutes, Monseigneur."

But Yoeland stood perfectly still.

"I shall remain here, just where I am, soldiers or no, unless you also come to the turret, M. de Vrieac," she said firmly.

With a gesture of protest and entreaty he turned to her, but before he could speak the Duc gave a shrill scream like a frightened girl's, and flinging himself upon his knees before Yoeland, clutched her dress with trembling fingers.

"Mademoiselle! Mademoiselle!" he cried wildly. "Do not let him leave me to those devils. They mean to murder me, I know. I cannot be left. I—I will not. Take me with you to the turret, Mademoiselle, for the pity of God."

With a low exclamation of anger, Rupert leaned forward, but Yoeland held out a restraining hand, whilst she looked down at the cringing figure before her with scornful eyes.

"You need have no fear, M. le Duc," she said coldly. "As a guest under my uncle's roof we owe you all the protection we can give, even though it is from your own servants that you require it. So release my dress, Monseigneur, if you please, and go to the turret."

But Rupert interposed.

"Mademoiselle, this is rank folly. If you will not think of yourself, consider the others—Mme. Charlotte, Mlle. Denise. Would you have them murdered to save—that? For the soldiers will show scant mercy to any one trying to help M. le Duc. He has given them too good cause to hate him, and they mean to pay their debts to-night. I will stay and give him what assistance I can, but I beg that you will go to the turret quickly. You should all be safe there, for once they have found M. le Duc the soldiers will, I think, be content. And you," he added, catching the Duc by the shoulder and shaking him roughly, "pull yourself together, man, and do as I bid you. See to the defense of your room and release Mademoiselle's dress instantly."

It was at this moment that Father Paul returned with

Madame Charlotte and Denise. Madame was perfectly calm and held Denise's hand protectingly in hers, for the girl was very pale and her eyes looked apprehensive, although she was quiet and self-controlled.

At sight of his betrothed the Duc rose, and catching her hands, kissed them passionately, whilst he poured out incoherent protests of affection and promises of future kindness, mingled with agonized pleading for protection.

At his touch Denise drew back with a slight shudder, trying to release her hands, but he clung to them like a terrified child. Desperately he turned from one to the other as they stood watching him in amazement. Pleading, he knelt before them; all his haughty magnificence fallen away, leaving a shuddering wretch, utterly cowed by the fear of death. It was a sight to fill the heart with disgust.

Finally to end it and save precious time, Rupert reluctantly gave way, and, fear having robbed the Duc of all power to think or act, picked him up in his arms and carried him, limp and unresisting, to the turret. Here Carlote and his four men had been busy, lighting a fire in the little room, for the rain had made the air colder, and getting ready for an attack.

The top of the turret was reached by a steep flight of thirty-five or forty steps, in which, about two-thirds up, there was a turn, so that those in the room would be unable to see what was happening on the stairs. A few steps below this turn was a flat slab of stone, a tiny landing, large enough for two men to stand on it abreast. Here Rupert meant to station himself with Carlote, whilst on the stairs a little above the four soldiers in two pairs would stand, ready to relieve those in front or fill their places should one or both fall. At the bottom of the stairs Carlote had fixed torches on either wall, so that the Duc's troopers could not take them by surprise, and their movements would be plain to the men of La Roche, who in the darkness above could themselves be hardly seen.

Following the ladies and Father Paul to the room at
the top of the turret Rupert dropped the Duc, none too
gently, into a corner, and with a quick glance round to
see that all was as comfortable as possible, went down to join
his men, for the other five had, from the first, proclaimed
him leader.

In front of the little landing they firmly wedged a table
on its side between the two walls, to prevent the soldiers
below from rushing their position. This and a few other
preparations being completed, the defense sat down to wait.

An hour passed slowly. The storm had rolled further
away, and the mutter of the thunder came to them sullenly
in the silence, whilst a blue flicker of lightning lit the room
dimly every few minutes.

Then, suddenly and noiselessly, four of de Tours' troopers
appeared at the foot of the stairs, peering up into the darkness above. Not a sound greeted them. The unseen
watchers above remained motionless, holding their breath lest
it should betray them. Then one of the troopers ran softly
up the stairs and, leaning across the barrier, held a torch
above his head. Its flickering light showed him the six
armed men standing above.

"Varten," he called down to one of his comrades,
"go and tell Pierre that M. de Vrieac and the men of La
Roche are here."

A few seconds later Pierre Gallon, the men's leader,
with the rest of the troopers at his heels, appeared. Telling
the others to stay where they were at the foot of the stairs,
he joined the soldier by the barrier.

"Ah! so you are there, M. de Vrieac," he said, saluting
Rupert, who, with Carlote, stood ready in his place. "And
it seems you have made some preparations to receive us.
Well, you might have spared your trouble and stayed quietly
in your beds. We should not have disturbed any of you—
save one. Father Paul and the ladies are in the room above
perhaps?"

"They are, Gallon," Rupert replied quietly.

The smile left Pierre Gallon's face and his eyes gleamed. "And M. le Duc also?" he asked fiercely.

"M. le Duc also." For a second Gallon stood with narrowed eyes, then he cried:

"Come, M. de Vrieac, what is the use of playing with words. You know quite well whom we want and mean to have. This is no quarrel of yours, why meddle in it? Give M. le Duc up to us and you may all go back to your rooms; no one will molest or harm any of you. The ladies will be perfectly safe. I promise you also that they shall hear or see nothing which will alarm them. Be reasonable, M. de Vrieac, hand out that fox. That is all we want."

Rupert leant forward, touching Gallon's hands with the point of his sword.

"You will oblige me by standing a little further back, Gallon," he said, "and I should advise you and your men to return to your quarters immediately. As for M. le Duc," he added with a careless laugh, "if you want him you will have to come and get him."

Pierre Gallon's eyes flashed dangerously as he stepped back a couple of stairs, though he controlled his temper with an obvious effort and still spoke respectfully.

"But this is folly, M. de Vrieac. We are thirty-two to your six. If we fight it is obvious that in time we must tire you out by force of numbers. Come, Monsieur, do not be foolish. Give us M. le Duc and save yourselves a great deal of useless trouble. For be very sure that we mean to have him."

And again Rupert answered quietly:

"If you want M. le Duc you will have to come and fetch him—if you can."

Pierre Gallon gave an impatient movement, though he still kept his temper.

"Your pardon, Monsieur," he said brusquely, "but you are not master here, nor has M. le Vicomte made you his deputy, I fancy. Will not Mlle. Denise speak to me? Perhaps I can make her see reason."

Every word of this parley had been plainly heard by those in the room above, and now, in the second's pause which followed Gallon's request, the Duc, waking from his torpor of fear, sprang to Denise's side and caught her hands convulsively.

"Denise! Denise!" he cried, shuddering. "Do not give me up to those devils! For the pity of God save me from them!"

At the sound of his voice a low, dangerous murmur ran through the group of soldiers gathered at the foot of the stairs, whilst Gallon looked up at Rupert with an unpleasant laugh.

"M. le Duc seems to be alarmed," he said, "but I hope, for her own sake, that Mlle. Denise will not let that weigh with her. We will soon still his fears."

And a deep assent, like the growl of angry beasts, came from the men below.

A second later Denise, a slight girlish figure with her head held high, stood on the stairs above them.

"What you ask is impossible, Gallon," she said in a low but steady voice. "M. le Duc is our guest, and in my father's absence we must do what we can to protect him. Go back to your quarters, men of Tours, and I promise you that, when M. le Vicomte returns, you shall not be punished for what you have tried to do to-night."

But Pierre Gallon, moving forward, held out protesting hands to her over the barrier.

"What you ask is also impossible for us, Mademoiselle," he cried. "M. le Duc we must and will have. The saints know we have endured enough at his hands. Have you forgotten what happened to Lucile Boron, Mademoiselle? And how Monseigneur murdered my own brother Jacques? There is not a man amongst us that he has not ground down and treated worse than beasts. But it is to be our turn to-night. We are going to pay our debts to M. le Duc."

Denise came a few steps lower, looking at him very steadily.

"I know, Gallon," she replied in soft, troubled tones, "I know you have all suffered, but oh! a wrong will not cure a wrong or one man's death bring another to life. Trust your cause to the good God, He will judge what is just, never fear. Go back to your quarters, and leave M. le Duc to God's justice."

But Gallon shook his head with a low, rough laugh.

"No, no, Mademoiselle. We shall be the good God's justice—to-night. And it will be useless for you to try and protect M. le Duc. Better to save the lives of the others with you, and let us have him now. For we mean to have him, and if you will not give him up, why, we shall fetch him."

Then the good blood which flowed in Mlle. Denise's veins showed itself plainly.

"Very well," she cried, courage ringing in her voice, "if that is so then my answer is the same which M. de Vrieac has already given. If you want M. le Duc you must come and fetch him—if you can."

For a second she and Gallon watched each other in silence. Then the man shrugged his shoulders.

"As you choose, Mademoiselle," he said.

And he turned, clattering down to the bottom of the stairs, where he stood in whispered consultation with his comrades, whilst Mlle. Denise, her head held high and a grave determination in her eyes, went slowly back to the room above.

CHAPTER XIII

IT seemed to Yoeland that she had been listening to the clash of swords, to the low cries and heavy breathing of fighting men, for hours, although it was really not twenty minutes since Gallon and the men of Tours had begun their attack. Prevented by the turn from seeing what was passing on the stairs, those in the room above could only wait and hope for the best.

And that seemed to Yoeland the very hardest thing to do just then, to be unable to give any help to those brave men who were risking wounds and perhaps death itself in their defense—simply to wait and hope. There had been a few seconds' silence, whilst the attackers had drawn off to give way to some fresh fighters. Then came a warning in Rupert de Vrieac's voice, a rush of feet on the stairs; and another bout, more desperate than those before, had begun. Father Paul, his prayers finished, had gone to see if there were any wounds amongst the defenders which required his attention.

As the sounds of conflict grew fiercer, Yoeland left the window and, turning, walked slowly across the room, for she felt that she could bear the suspense no longer, that she must see how they fared on the stairs. She had almost reached the door when there was a sudden hoarse shout, the clash of arms grew fiercer, and Rupert cried clear above the tumult:

"Quick, Carlote, into his place! Take Jules back to Father Paul, two of you others behind."

And Yoeland knew that one of the defenders was down and that the men of Tours were pressing them hard. The next second, Jules, a soldier of La Roche, was carried by two of his comrades into the room, and, under Father Paul's direction, laid gently down on Carlote's bed.

But it was little enough any of them could do for him. A sword-thrust had pierced his right lung and death was already glazing his eyes. With a sob Yoeland knelt down, taking the poor fellow's head against her shoulder, whilst Father Paul, after a brief examination, shook his head sadly, and in clear, gentle tones, gave the last rites to the dying man. Then after a brave attempt to smile up at Yoeland bending over him, Jules' eyes closed quietly, and the defense numbered only five.

A few moments later Carlote came to the door to ask Father Paul's assistance in tying up a severe gash in his left arm. It was Yoeland, however, who attended to it, and as she bandaged the wound with skillful fingers, asked anxiously how things went.

"And M. de Vrieac, Carlote? He is not wounded at all?" she added. But Carlote caught an anxious look in her eyes as they searched his face.

"No, Mademoiselle, he has not been touched yet; they cannot get under his guard. Ah! Monsieur can fight!" he cried, his eyes kindling with enthusiasm. "Never have I seen such a swordsman. There is not a feint he cannot meet, a trick he does not know. They would have been through us long ago but for him. I wish M. le Comte could see him, it is a fine sight, Mademoiselle."

He hurried back to his place, and Yoeland, her eyes shining, stood looking out into the night. The storm had rolled away and the rain ceased. Overhead a crescent moon shone dimly, whilst from far down in the valley came the hooting of an owl. Was there nothing she could do, no help she could give? Jules was dead, and Carlote wounded. Rupert de Vrieac was as yet untouched, but for how long could he keep up his splendid fight? When one of the attackers tired, there were thirty fresh men to take his place, but who was there to relieve M. de Vrieac? Soon his arm must tire, his defense weaken, and then their swords would be beneath his guard.

Yoeland closed her eyes with a whispered prayer. Was there nothing to be done but wait and hope? Out there, over the forest, only seven leagues away, were the Vicomte and his men-at-arms. Ah! if she could only fetch him before that brave defense slackened, before Rupert de Vrieac would be hurt like Carlote, or perhaps—perhaps lying still like Jules. If she could only fly over the trees to Valdante. But no, that would not be quite the direction, Valdante lay more to the east. Straight in front, the way she was looking, must be Vois—Vois and M. Philibert, who also had men-at-arms. And she caught her breath suddenly. Valdante was seven leagues away but Vois was barely one. If she could only get out of the tower, there might be time to go to Vois and bring back help before—before——

Yoeland closed her teeth fiercely to keep back the sob which rose in her throat as a vision of that gallant defender, too weary to fight any more, lying still and conquered, rose before her.

There was no way of opening the little window, and for a second she stood at a loss, then, turning, picked up a chair and thrust a leg of it again and again through the glass.

At sound of the smash, the Duc started up with a sharp cry and Mme. Charlotte caught Denise to her tightly, but reassuring them by a silent nod, Yoeland continued her efforts. Having broken as much glass as she could, she placed the chair beneath the window and stood upon it. The frame was wide enough to put her head and shoulders through, and leaning out as far as she dared, Yoeland looked anxiously down the wall of the tower.

By the dim light of the moon she could just discern a small ledge some thirty or forty feet below, and remembered that at the foot of the stairs there was a room, the window of which would be about where she saw the ledge. It was heavily barred, she remembered, but directly below it was a big window belonging to one of the lower rooms of the castle. If she could once reach that lowest window it would be easy to enter the room, slip through the castle unseen by the men of Tours, who were all gathered on the turret stairs, out to the stables for a horse and then away to Philibert de Vois and his men-at-arms.

But how to reach it? That was the question and precious time was being wasted. Once solve that point and the plan seemed workable.

She turned back into the room, looking round with anxious, desperate eyes. There was no rope or anything that would serve. Father Paul had covered Jules' silent figure with a blanket and now knelt by the bed praying for the dead man's soul. As Yoeland looked at him she started with a sudden inspiration. The rugs on the bed, if torn into strips and knotted together, might make a rope long enough to reach the first window. But what to do then?

Unable to solve the question by herself she went softly over to the old priest and told him her plan and difficulty. He listened to her intently, then, going to the window, gazed thoughtfully down at the ledge below. Withdrawing his head, he gave a satisfied nod.

"It might be worked, my child, I think," he said, "if we could get enough rope to reach even that first window. Let us tear up the blankets and see what length they make first, and in the meantime we may think of some way to manage the rest."

So Mme. Charlotte, Denise, Yoeland and Father Paul set to work, and, anxiety for the living overcoming all shrinking from the dead, removed the blankets from under Jules, and, tearing them into strips, knotted them firmly together.

The Duc watched them in silence, offering no assistance. Yoeland had at first urged him to help them, but soon desisted, seeing that his hands were trembling so much as to render them powerless to be of use.

They had just finished the rope, and were making sure

of the knots, when there came loud shouting from the stairs, followed by the clash of steel and sounds of a fierce struggle, then—sudden silence. A second later Rupert de Vrieac and Carlote staggered into the room, carrying the body of yet another man of La Roche, which they laid down beside Jules.

"I am sorry to bring him in here, ladies, but we cannot have him blocking the stairs," said Rupert, in a voice strained with fatigue. Blood-stained, hot, unutterably weary, yet he looked at them with eyes bravely, unflinchingly determined, as he added:

"There is no need for apprehension. We can, I think, hold them off successfully."

He turned to go back to his post, but Yoeland caught his arm and thrust a wine flask, which she had remembered to bring with her, into his hand.

"Take some of that, M. de Vrieac," she said, whilst her eyes traveled anxiously over him, searching for signs of any wound.

Eagerly, thirstily, he drank, but stopped with quick restraint, remembering his men on the stairs.

"Thank you, Mademoiselle," he said gratefully. "I do not think you can ever know how good that was. I will take the rest to the others. And, Mademoiselle, do not be alarmed. They have not got past us yet, and never will if I can stop them. They are getting discouraged, too, for Gallon is down. I gave him a thrust just now that will prevent him causing any more trouble, but he killed poor Lenoit before I could prevent him."

"Oh, Monsieur, thank you for your gallant fight," she cried softly. "It is magnificent, it—— Oh, you *are* wounded," she exclaimed with quick apprehension, for he had winced sharply. "Monsieur de Vrieac, let me see your hurt at once."

But he moved from her, flushing.

"I thank you, I am not at all hurt, Mademoiselle, only a few scratches, nothing to count. And you must not thank me. All I have done has been my duty, and if I can keep those devils from you I will go on fighting till to-morrow night, if need be."

With an impulsive gesture she held out both her hands, and as he bent over them, she put them hurriedly, almost eagerly, to his lips, looking at him with eyes which were very soft and shining. Just then Carlote's voice sounded from the stairs.

"Quick, M. de Vrieac," he called urgently. "They are coming back."

With a sharp exclamation Rupert released her hands, dashing back to his post, whilst Yoeland, a tender little smile on her lips, turned once more to her plan of help.

Father Paul had not been idle. Having fixed the improvised rope firmly to one of the beams of the roof, he let it out of the window, watching its descent anxiously from above. He drew in his head as Yoeland came beside him.

"It reaches! It reaches!" he whispered excitedly. "To the first window."

Yoeland's eyes clouded with disappointment.

"But, Father, what use is that?" she cried. "It must reach to the lowest window to be any help."

Father Paul laid his hand on her arm.

"Not necessarily. This will do," he said, "for I have thought of a plan. You see I have put a loop on that bottom end? Well, I will climb down the rope until I get to the next window. The bars across that must be strong, strong enough for me to hold to. Be watching, and when you see me jerk the rope, unsling it from the beam and let it down quickly. I think I can then slip the rope around the bars and draw it through the loop with one hand, whilst I hold on with the other. Only let it down to me very quickly. I shall have hold of the loop and put it over the bars as soon as I reach them. That is the only way I can see. If it fails, we shall at least have tried to help."

Yoeland held his arm tightly, the longing to do something,

not to play the woman's weary part of waiting, was strong upon her.

"Let me go, Father," she pleaded, "I thought of it first and I know the way to Vois."

But he shook his head gently.

"It is better for me to go, my child. I am as light and smaller than you, and whereas you only know the road to Vois, I can take a dozen short cuts through the woods, and so save valuable time. And you will be doing something to help, something on which depends the success of my venture, if you let down that rope to me."

She saw that he was right and gave way, watching intently whilst he drew in the rope and slipped the loop at the end over his wrist. Then he played it out again, and with a word of encouragement to Yoeland, prepared to climb out of the window. But at the last second she stopped him, and catching up a cushion, thrust it under the rope where it ran over the sill.

"The stone there is rough and might fray it," she explained, and he nodded with appreciation of her forethought.

Then grasping the rope tightly, he climbed with some difficulty out of the window, and Yoeland saw the rope grew taut, showing that his weight was upon it and that he was descending.

Breathlessly she watched it, standing on a chair beneath the beam, ready to untie the rope the moment the signal came. The seconds of waiting seemed like hours. The rope prevented her leaning from the window to watch him, she could only wait and hope—and pray. Would he never give the signal?

At last, just as she had begun to think he had stopped or fallen, the rope slackened. The next second, the signal came. With fingers which worked feverishly, though they were trembling with excitement, she untied the rope and, holding the end, ran to the window, leaning out so that she could see Father Paul.

He was clinging to the bars of the window below by his right hand, whilst with the left he was pulling the rope quickly over the bars and through the loop. Yoeland let the end go gently, and it fell upon his arm. The next moment he had all secure, and Yoeland caught her breath sharply as she saw him preparing to descend. Just then a cloud sailed over the moon, and for what seemed hours she waited, unable to see, straining her ears to catch any sound which might tell that he had fallen or the rope given way. Then the moon shone out once more, and she saw him climbing down, down, until he swung himself on to the ledge of the lowest window. Holding the rope with one hand, he took out a poniard which Yoeland had given him, and with the pummel began smashing in the glass. Then, letting go the rope, he looked up at her, waved his hand, and disappeared inside the room.

With a deep sigh Yoeland turned from the window. Mme. Charlotte and Denise had been tearing their linen scarves into strips, ready should any more bandages be required, and that finished, sat before the fire, clasped in each other's arms, waiting. The Duc still crouched in the corner, his face white as a dead man's, full of a nightmare of terror; shuddering, powerless, he waited also. And looking around, Yoeland realized that she, too, must wait.

For a few moments she stood very still, following Father Paul in her mind as he slipped out to the stables for a horse, and, mounting it, dashed away along the woodland track. Would he bring help in time? Would he even reach Vois? Perhaps in the uncertain light he might miss his way, or his horse, stumbling, would fling him and break his neck! Then the relief would never come. And she shuddered at the scene her imagination painted. She could see it all. The defense getting weaker and weaker, until at last, Carlote down, his men down, Rupert de Vrieac would stand alone, wounded and exhausted. Thirty blades to one! He could not possibly keep them off. Then they would be over the barrier. A second's struggle, the flash of

a poniard and Rupert would be down also. She could hear
the men of Tours' yell of victory, see them surge over the
defenders' prostrate bodies, trampling underfoot, as they
swept forward up the stairway, to their revenge.

For a moment she closed her eyes, trembling. Supposing Philibert de Vois' men came even a minute too late!
Came even as that last gallant defender fell! Rupert de
Vrieac would be down, crushed by his assailants' conquering
feet, and she could do nothing, nothing but wait—and pray.
Suddenly she opened her eyes, and with a quick lift of
her head crossed to the Duc's side.

"Give me your sword, Monseigneur," she said sharply,
"for since you seem unable to use it, perhaps I will."

At that he looked up at her in wild panic.

"Are they coming, Mademoiselle?" he cried. "Have
our men on the stairs given way? What shall we do?"

"Do!" she replied, her eyes flashing with scorn.
"Since you have already done so much, I should advise
you to stay quiet and let M. de Vrieac and *my* men on
the stairs, who have been doing nothing, give their lives
to protect you. No, Monseigneur, your men of Tours
are not through yet, thanks to a brave and gallant gentleman. But they may be up here any second," she added,
noting with malicious pleasure the terror her words
caused him, "for we have lost two men and the others
are getting tired. So, since you are afraid to use it,
give me your sword and let me see if, at the last, I cannot
help M. de Vrieac."

With a convulsive shudder he gave it up to her, his
one eye gleaming malignantly as he watched her walk
quietly to the door and disappear on to the stairs. The
Comte had taught her to fence, and although she had
never fought with anything but a foil or any one but her
brother, she was determined now to use what knowledge
she possessed in deadly earnest, and should their position
be forced before help arrived, and all else failed, to put
up a last defense with the Duc's sword.

Meanwhile, on the stairs, Rupert was waging the fiercest fight of his life. Again and again the attackers came on, fresh men constantly taking the place of those who were tired, hurling themselves savagely against the barrier, behind which stood the little band of defenders. The table, although it hampered Rupert and his men somewhat in their reach, protected the lower part of their bodies and prevented the attackers from rushing the stairs and beating the men of La Roche back by force of numbers. For all that, it took every advantage which their position gave them and their most strenuous efforts for the besieged to hold their own.

And gradually, although his defense never slackened and he gave his men no sign of discouragement, Rupert knew that their position was hopeless, that, without relief, without some rest, his little band could never keep their enemies off until the morning. Even should they succeed so long, would daylight make matters more hopeful? The Vicomte could not return for two days, was there any chance then of relief in the morning? Yet he gave no sign of his thoughts, cheering on his men by word and example, fighting with all the skill and cunning he knew. And the others, inspired by his leadership, responded nobly, giving the men of Tours a far harder task than they had anticipated.

Then came the desperate rush in which Gallon, half over the barrier, killed Lenoit before he fell back himself, severely wounded by Rupert. And for a little time after they had carried their leader away the men of Tours stood off, discouraged, doubtful, and Rupert began to think that, having lost Gallon, they might now desist and give up the attack.

But his hopes were short-lived, for when he returned to his place at Carlote's urgent call, it was to find that their attackers had a new leader.

On the stairs, wild-eyed, with clenched hands and disordered hair, stood a woman haranguing the men below,

urging them on with voice and gesture. Then as they
stood, still irresolute, she snatched a dagger from her belt,
and leaping up the stairs made a savage stab at Rupert
across the barrier, whilst, with a wild cheer, the men of
Tours came on behind her to renew the attack.

At first he did not recognize her or realize why she should
be there. It was only when Carlote called out "Lucile
Boron!" that Rupert understood. Gentle, quiet-mannered
Lucile Boron, driven mad by her lover's death and her
hatred of the Duc, was thirsting for revenge, and seemed
very likely to get it. Her face distorted by madness and
fury into that of a fiend, she leant across the barrier, shriek-
ing, struggling, stabbing viciously at the men of La Roche
beyond.

Had she been a man, Rupert would have run her through
instantly, but he could not bring himself to kill a woman.
Yet something must be done. There were those other
women behind him to be thought of, and in another second
Lucile would be over the barrier.

Hating the act, Rupert leaned forward and, avoiding
her dagger, struck her sharply with the pummel of his
poniard between the eyes. Stunned, she fell back into the
arms of a trooper behind her, and was carried to the bottom of the stairs. But her example had put fresh life into
the attackers, and they pressed the men of La Roche very
hard.

A little later the trooper fighting with Carlote on Rupert's
right turned suddenly, and ignoring Carlote entirely, attacked Rupert savagely. Tired, weakened by several
wounds, Rupert found himself with two assailants, and
although he strove desperately, his new enemy got beneath
his guard, wounding him severely in the right shoulder.
The next instant, Carlote, with a shout of fury, literally
transfixed the trooper with his sword.

Quickly Rabat, of La Roche, took Rupert's place, whilst
he stepped behind, and the remaining soldier hastily attended to his wound.

But this success had greatly encouraged the men of Tours, for from the first they had recognized that Rupert was the leading spirit of the defense, and all had aimed at disabling him.

Cheering wildly, they redoubled their efforts to beat back Carlote and his companion, who with dogged determination kept them off.

Sitting on the stairs with closed eyes, his head leaning against the wall, whilst the soldier clumsily dressed his shoulder, Rupert caught a soft movement, and some one whispered his name. Looking up with a start, he saw Yoeland de Breux, her eyes shining like stars and in her hand a naked sword, standing above him.

At the sight of his face she laid down her weapon, and with a low exclamation of pity and concern, knelt beside him, taking the soldier's place and attending to his wound with soft, skillful fingers.

Feebly he tried to prevent her, but she put aside his protesting hands with gentle firmness, continuing her task whilst he watched her under half-closed lids, well content. For it was his dream come true. Here was his lady with the dark, soft eyes, gentle-handed, gentle-voiced, beside him.

Weakened by loss of blood and the pain of his wound, unutterably weary and barely conscious, he leant his head against her, closing his eyes with a deep, satisfied sigh, and Yoeland, holding him in her arms, looked down with a wonderful smile of happiness.

Then, very gently, she held a flask to his lips. Obediently he drank, the wine revived him, and so the spell was broken.

With a quick flush he sat up, stammering an apology, but for a second longer her arms held him, her eyes looked into his.

"Oh, Mademoiselle!" he cried, bitterly ashamed to find that he was too weak to loose himself from her hold, "I—I beg that you will return to the room above. This is no place for you. Indeed, Mademoiselle, we are getting

on well, they have not conquered us yet, there are still four
of us left to fight, though——" and he checked himself
sharply, urging her to go back.

She looked at him with grave eyes. "If needs be, I
too, can fight, Monsieur," she said. "I have M. le Duc's
sword. See!"

And she held it up before him. He stared at her in
amazement.

"You, Mademoiselle! Ah, never that!" he cried, stumbling to his feet. "I am not such a weak coward that I
cannot fight for you still! That you must defend yourself!
No, Mademoiselle, go back above and give M. le Duc his
sword again. You shall not have to use it. God bless you
for your courage, but indeed it will not be necessary. We
four can fight a long time yet."

She held his arm with a quick smile.

"It need not be for very long now," she whispered.
"Father Paul has gone for help."

"Gone   for   help!   Gone   from   the   turret!   But—
but——"

"We made a rope with blankets and he climbed down,"
she explained briefly. "He has gone to Vois and must
be well there by now. It will not take him long to come
back with help."

Help! A chance of relief! And it was only then that
Rupert realized how hopeless of success, doubtful of
the possibility of keeping their assailants at bay, he had
been. With a low sob of gratitude for such good news
he caught her hands and bent to kiss them, but with a
sudden stiffening of her wrists she prevented him, and
as he glanced up at her quickly, he drew in his breath
with a gasp of incredulous surprise. For her eyes were
shining into his, and what he read there made his heart
leap with great, uneven throbs.

Just for a second, everything around them completely
forgotten, they gazed at each other in silence, her eyes
meeting his steadily and unashamed, whilst he still held

her hands.   Then a shout startled them, and looking round, Rupert saw that Rabat was down, and that one of the attackers was over the barrier and at close grips with Carlote, whilst two more, half over, were being held at bay by the remaining soldier of La Roche.

Rupert caught Yoeland's fingers to his burning lips with an urgent entreaty for her to get back to the room above, then seizing his sword—weakness and pain forgotten in the wild glad hope which had set his heart beating tumultuously and the prospect of help near at hand—he sprang back into the fray. "For the Faith and Vrieac!" he shouted, the battle-cry of his house ringing out clear above the clamor.

To those who watched from below he seemed like a man inspired, his face shining with a great joy, whilst he laid about him with a strength barely credible in a wounded man, whom they had deemed disabled and defeated. The attackers fell back before his fierce onslaught and he followed them up hotly, leaning out over the barrier to get in a final thrust. A great light shone in his eyes; he laughed gayly like a man whose heart is full of some wonderful joy.

And it was just then, as the men of Tours hung back irresolute before him, that Philibert de Vois and his men-at-arms dashed, with a wild cheer, up the stairs and took them in the rear.

CHAPTER XIV

THE struggle that followed was short but desperately fierce. For the men of Tours fought with a reckless courage born of despair. The relief to the besieged had come utterly unexpectedly, and taken between two fires, there was no possibility of escape for them. Yet they hoped, in their moment of defeat, to win their purpose, and overcoming those above, to reach and murder the Duc before they were themselves killed by the stronger, fresher force brought by Philibert de Vois. So, as a few turned to face and keep back those coming from below, the greater number dashed at the men of La Roche, cutting, hacking, stabbing, in a last desperate effort to reach the room above.

And the three men left behind the barrier, weary, wounded and almost beaten, took heart at the nearness of relief and met their rush with a defense as fierce.

Silent, save for the harsh clash of steel and the gasping breath of struggling men, the fight was sharp and bitter. Rupert fought doggedly, thrusting, parrying, heedless that the wound in his shoulder was bleeding quickly and that his enemies had several times touched him with their swords. The stairs were slippery with blood; he saw the fierce faces of the men attacking through a mist of the same deep color. Mechanically he cut or warded off a blow. He had ceased to move consciously, to think, his limbs seemed those of another person, his brain to be dead and senseless. Only in his heart he was aware of some wonderful hope, the knowledge of which he fancied having caught in a girl's dark eyes and for whose consummation he must fight and strive and beat off death, though strength and sight and sense had almost gone.

Then the faces dimly seen before him drew back and the

men across the barrier seemed to be fighting amongst themselves, gripping each other by the throat, striking with fist and dagger. Holding fast to the barrier for support with one hand, Rupert leaned forward, thrusting weakly at the nearest figure. But his sword was swept aside, and he felt himself held in strong arms as he stared up into a man's face which had come close to his own out of the mist, whilst far away some one said: "Saved, M. de Vrieac. We are through at last. Thank God, Denise and the ladies are safe." Then the red mist seemed to close round him once more and he lurched forward limp and senseless into Philibert de Vois' arms.

He came to himself out of a cloud of darkness in which, shining like stars, the eyes of his dream-lady had looked softly into his, whilst, dimly seen, vague forms had come round him, hands had touched him, very gently, but causing sharp pain which drove him down into a deeper night, black and starless. And now once more had come the light. Turning his head, he looked about with vague, wandering eyes, whose expression grew suddenly intent as they encountered another pair, dark and anxious, watching him.

For a moment he gazed at Yoeland in silence, then his eyes wandered off round the room once more, returning to her face with a puzzled smile. Of course it was only a dream. The room seemed to be the one he had at Briege, but it must really be in the tower at La Roche, and he had broken his leg in the pit, hunting the great gray wolf; then the Comte had come and they had taken him back to the castle, and here was his dream-lady bending over him with compassionate eyes, whilst, slipping an arm beneath his pillow, she raised him, holding a cool, delicious drink to his burning lips. With a sigh of content he closed his eyes and sank asleep, his head resting against her shoulder.

When he awoke again, it was to a stronger, fuller knowledge of his surroundings. He had no recollection of going to bed, yet he was in one and there were many bandages tied round him. He looked down in some surprise at a

Jacques Gallon was dead with the Duke's poniard through his breast.

hand, white and thin, which lay on the blanket before him. For a second he eyed it intently, then followed up the arm until, with a slight start, he realized that it joined his own shoulder. He lifted eyes full of a resentful astonishment to Yoeland de Breux's as she bent over him, looking down at the hand and back again to her face.

"Is that really mine?" he asked somewhat disconsolately. "It does not look like mine and it feels—strange."

With a soft laugh she laid her own over it, then touched his bandaged shoulder lightly.

"You have had a sword through there and have lost a great deal of blood. No wonder it feels—strange," she said. "Now, Monsieur, drink this, if you please, and do not think or move or talk. All you must do is to get strong quickly and your hand will soon not feel strange any more."

He drank obediently, watching her intently, whilst the defense of the stairs and the events connected with it returned slowly to his mind.

"They did not get through, or touch you?" he asked, as she put the empty cup away and settled his pillows. "M. de Vois did well to come when he did and Father Paul was a fine fellow to fetch him. I do not think we could have kept those rascals back for many minutes longer, though Carlote and your men of La Roche fought like heroes."

"And M. de Vrieac?" she said. "No thanks are due to him of course? His bravery and skill counted for nothing. We will not give him any thanks or praise?"

He looked up into her laughing eyes with a shy smile, whilst a deep flush swept over his cheeks.

"No, Mademoiselle, we will not, for they are not required," he replied. "Did you expect me to go and shiver in a corner with M. le Duc? I did what I could, what was my duty. But it was a joy too," he added eagerly, "to know that whilst I stood there they could not reach you in the room above."

She looked at him with sudden mock-seriousness, then she rose and swept him a deep curtsey.

"A thousand thanks," she cried; "I have heard it said good soldiers never make good courtiers. You are surely an exception, Monsieur. And yet," she added seriously, "I do not like your compliment, it places too great a weight of gratitude on my one pair of shoulders, a gratitude which I have no way to express. For what can one say, or do, for another, who, not in a sudden heat of excitement, but deliberately, minute after minute, has borne wounds and pain, and risked death, on her behalf? It would be useless to attempt to pay such a debt as that. I can only say, 'Thank you, M. de Vrieac.'"

He put out his hands protestingly.

"Is it not unnecessary to say so much, Mademoiselle? Why should you thank me at all, for a trifling service which I was bound to give, and which was pure joy? I would have risked hell's fire to keep those devils from you, instead of which I got a few slight scratches. Faugh! You make too much of the affair."

There was a look almost of indignation in her eyes as she rose, and, crossing the room, took up a doublet which hung across a chair.

"Do I?" she said, returning to his bedside, "do I indeed make too much of the affair, Monsieur? And did you have but a few scratches? Look!" And turning the doublet over she put her hand through a large slit in the shoulder, marked round with a faded yellow stain. "Does that slight scratch deserve no thanks?"

Flushing quickly, she put down the doublet and turned to him with a charmingly impulsive gesture.

"I am the worst nurse in the world," she laughed, "because I hope that you will not get well for the next few days. If you do you will have to go doubletless. I have had it cleaned, as you see, but the places where you got those 'slight scratches' will take some mending, Monsieur, though I will make it ready for you as soon as I can."

He looked up at her aghast.

"Mend my doublet! Indeed, you must not. I will buy another."

"Will you?" she replied, smiling; "where, I wonder? You forget this is not Paris, there are no shops within ten leagues."

"Then I will borrow one," he persisted. "I beg you not to touch the doublet, Mademoiselle."

But she put aside his protesting hands and made him lie down.

"Indeed, I need not fear that you will get well too soon if you excite yourself like this, M. de Vrieac. You must rest quiet and go to sleep immediately," she said with an attempt at sternness. "And I will mend your doublet, whatever you say. I wish to do so, for—do you not see?—it is the one way I can show my gratitude."

Then, because he was still very weak and even so little talking had exhausted him, he obeyed, lying quiet with closed eyes, and in a very few minutes had dropped asleep, whilst Yoeland, going to the window, sat down on the wide seat, and began to carefully mend the torn doublet.

A quiet smile hovered round her lips as she worked, and several times she looked across at the sick man, a very soft light in her eyes. Steadily all the afternoon she worked at the rent whilst Rupert slept quietly with deep regular breathing. Presently, however, he grew restless, tossing his head from side to side and muttering to himself. Laying down her work, Yoeland crossed to the bed. His face was flushed with fever and, as she raised him gently, holding a cooling drink to his lips, he looked up at her with an unrecognizing stare. Then, as she put down the empty cup, a frown puckered his forehead.

"Doubly false," he gasped hoarsely, "to God and to me. So you are to marry St. Caux, Mademoiselle? Well, I wish you joy of him." And turning away his head he sank back into a deep sleep, which was almost stupor. With thoughtful eyes Yoeland stood looking down at him, a crease between her eyebrows. She knew for whom he had mistaken her, of whom he was dreaming—beautiful, faithless Marguerite de Vainçeoire. And the thought of her was breaking his sleep, making him unhappy and restless. With a quick lift of her head Yoeland returned to the window. She had believed that he had forgotten the Huguenot girl. It seemed that was not so. Had he loved her very deeply, she wondered. Did he—could he love her still?

The evening was drawing in and it grew too dark for her to work any more. Folding up the doublet she laid it on a chair and in so doing caught sight of a tear in the lining which she had not noticed before. It seemed to have been purposely made, for there was no ugly stain around it or corresponding slit on the outer side. Without thinking, she put in her hand and the next second a deep flush spread over her face, for her fingers had found something hidden within. Quickly she drew it out—a square of linen folded small, inside which was a piece of hair tied with a knot of ribbon. Crossing the room she held it in the firelight that she might see the better. There it lay on the palm of her hand, a curl of coarse fair hair with its pale blue tie and it had been hidden over Rupert de Vrieac's heart! A fierce, jealous anger seized her, but for a moment she fought with it. M. de Vrieac had no sister, and his mother had been a famous Spanish beauty, dark-eyed, dark-haired, Anne had fair hair, perhaps—but it was not possible, Anne's hair never curled and Denise's, which was also fair, was fine as silk. The description of Marguerite de Vainçeoire which the Comte had given her recurred very clearly to her mind. "She is petite with big blue eyes and a beautiful complexion. Her hair is beautiful too, fair and curling, but rather coarse." And no doubt Mlle. de Vainçeoire, with her beautiful complexion and fair coloring, would wear ribbon to match her eyes. And how anxious M. de Vrieac had been that she should not mend the doublet, should not touch it!

With a sudden movement Yoeland dropped curl and

ribbon into the heart of the fire. They burnt quickly, and when she could see them no more, she rose, and, turning, looked across at the wounded man. He was sleeping quietly, deeply, a smile on his lips. And as she watched, it seemed to Yoeland that the smile grew into one of derision. Derision from Rupert de Vrieac! A sudden thought came to her, making her heart beat with quick angry throbs. She was the enemy of his house, her brother had imposed a bitter condition upon him. He had not one reason to love, though a thousand to hate her. Might he not have planned a revenge? First he had gained Anne's love and now——She crossed softly to the bed, looking down at him with gleaming eyes. Never that, never that!

"I hate you—do you hear! I hate you!" she whispered. "And I am glad that you love Mlle. de Vainçeoire, for she has married M. de St. Caux and she does not care for you any more. So you will suffer, as you have tried to make me suffer, and I am glad—glad. I thought you brave and generous, and you shall never guess how much I could have loved you, never—never. You shall know instead how I hate and despise you," and turning, she left the room.

In the passage she met the Duc. He seemed in high good-humor and greeted her with a deep bow.

"I trust that M. de Vrieac is stronger this evening, Mademoiselle? I have been to see our other patient. It seems de Vrieac did not wound Pierre Gallon as deeply as he thought. The fellow is still alive, and I am having him nursed, oh, very carefully, till he grows stronger, strong enough to bear pain without losing consciousness too quickly. And then, when M. de Vrieac is well, I have planned a fête in his honor. Have you ever seen bear-baiting, Mademoiselle? No? Well, I will then show you Pierre-Gallon baiting instead. Oh, I made him cringe and turn white just now when I unfolded a little of my future plans for him, I assure you."

He had come upon Yoeland in a dangerous mood. She looked at him with eyes smoldering with passionate scorn.

Yet, when she spoke her voice was cold, with the bitter chill of ice.

"I knew, the other night and before, M. le Duc," she said slowly, "that you were a coward, but that you had such a fiend's heart I never guessed. May God forgive you the thought of such a plan, though carry it out you never shall."

And with head held high she swept past him down the passage.

The Duc watched her in silence, his one eye gleaming evilly. To a nature such as his, anger never came openly, violently. Dangerously still, it worked cunningly, unseen, taking revenge long after the offender had forgotten his deed. To him the unforgivable crime, or rather, since in his whole life he had probably never had the grace to forgive anything, the one which he punished most vindictively, was for those around him to show the contempt or dislike which they felt for him.

And it was this crime which Yoeland, Rupert de Vrieac, Philibert de Vois, and in a smaller measure, Denise also, had all unconcernedly committed, and would, without the smallest hesitation, commit again. But the Duc, although he was intensely careful to give no sign, was lusting for revenge and had already glimmerings of a plan by which he might requite them all in overflowing measure.

Meanwhile Yoeland paused suddenly on the way to her room. Pierre Gallon had been wounded by Rupert de Vrieac, so falling into the Duc's hands. He had, therefore, nearly as much cause to hate the Huguenot as she. And Gallon, weak and suffering, had just been visited by his master! A sudden touch of sympathy made her turn and ascend the stairs to the injured man's room.

At the sound of her entrance, Gallon, tossing restlessly on his hard pallet, lifted his head, looking at her with apprehensive eyes; then with a groan he turned his face to the wall. On his cheeks burned a bright flush of fever, his lips were dry and cracked, the tip of his tongue protruding from between them, betraying a great thirst. A little from the bed, just beyond the sick man's reach, was a cup of cool clear water. And Yoeland guessed whose hand had placed it there, whose brain had thought of such refinement of cruelty.

A great pity filled her eyes. Kneeling down by the low pallet she raised Gallon gently, holding the cup to his lips. But although he was obviously consumed with thirst he jerked back his head.

"Ah, Mademoiselle," he cried brokenly, "is it salt?"

"Salt!" she repeated. "Salt? Why, of course it is not salt. Drink and see, Gallon."

His eyes searched her face.

"If I could be sure," he murmured piteously. "If I could be sure."

"You may be very sure," she replied. "See!" and raising the cup to her lips, she took a drink, then offered it to him again."

He drank eagerly, looking up at her with grateful eyes.

"God bless you for that, Mademoiselle," he whispered when he was satisfied. "I—Monseigneur came here just now," and a convulsive shudder shook him from head to foot; "I was thirsty and he gave me a drink. I did not think, or know it was salt till I had taken half. And then he laughed, God curse him, and put the water where I could not get it. And so when you——"

He broke off with an exhausted sigh and lay silent, staring at the roof with quivering lips. For a second Yoeland watched him, then, very gently, she shook his pillow and made him more comfortable.

"Now, Gallon, listen to me," she said, speaking in a very clear soft voice. "I know something of what M. le Duc said to you just now. Well, try to forget it. You need not be afraid. I promise you most faithfully that he shall not torture you in any way. Just lie quiet and try to get well. Your head is very hot, I will bathe it for you and perhaps that will make you sleep."

So moistening a strip of linen in cold water, she laid it very gently across his burning forehead from temple to temple, softly removing and damping it again as it grew hot. And Pierre Gallon lay and watched her in silence with quivering lips, until at last the soothing application did its work, and he fell asleep.

CHAPTER XV

THE Vicomte de Briege, returning from Valdante three days after the attack on the stairs, was considerably surprised to find the castle practically ungarrisoned. For Philibert de Vois, like a wise man, taking advantage of the opportunity which his relief of the besieged gave him to be near Denise, had left some of his men to guard the castle and, making them an excellent excuse, rode over each morning to Briege. Here he would stay but a short time, to give his men orders for the day and inquire after the ladies' health, but it always happened that Mme. Charlotte or Yoeland would come down to speak with him. And who was to say what letters and tokens their hands might not exchange as he bent from his horse to greet them. Though the Duc, keeping a spiteful watch, never discovered anything, and Denise, mindful of her father's prohibition and the danger to them all should she disregard it, made no effort to speak with her lover.

But when Philibert learnt from one of his men, posted on the northern road for that purpose, that the Vicomte was returning and within three leagues of Briege, he recalled his soldiers to Vois. There was no longer any necessity for them to guard the castle with its master and his troops so near at hand, and he had no wish to receive the Vicomte's thanks.

The Vicomte, reaching Briege, heard of the men of Tours' attack with a violent indignation which was outmatched by a disgusted annoyance when he learnt that it was to Philibert de Vois that Denise and her companions in the turret owed their rescue.

Of the thirty men of Tours, only eight had been taken

prisoners, the rest had died on the stairs, or from their wounds, but the Vicomte worked off a little of his anger by having seven of these hanged outside the castle gate as a warning to his own troopers.

Pierre Gallon, his life slowly fluttering back under Yoeland's careful nursing, would have been dispatched by the same road, but that Yoeland protested firmly, and the Duc, who had no objection to the fate meted out to the seven others, quietly claimed the right to deal with this servant of his as he chose. So his life was spared, much to the Vicomte's disappointment.

But although the Vicomte felt that justice had been done on the rebels, there yet remained a more unpalatable duty before him—the reward of the relieving force. To thank Philibert de Vois' men-at-arms was easy enough, a few gold pieces would do that—but Philibert de Vois himself——!

The day before the Vicomte's return, the Duc de Tours, accompanied by two servants carrying a richly chased sword and some very valuable jewels, had ridden over to Vois. But Philibert, meeting the Duc in the gateway, had invited him neither to enter nor dismount. With a white face from which his eyes blazed ominously, he stood perfectly still, whilst de Tours, making no effort to conceal that he considered them a liberal reward for service rendered, offered his presents. Then, very curtly and definitely, Philibert refused even to look at them, explaining that, for what help he had brought to Briege, he required neither thanks nor payment from the Duc de Tours.

With a sharp laugh, which concealed a furious anger, the Duc shrugged his shoulders.

"I am sorry M. de Vois will take no gifts from me," he said. "I fear there is no other way in which I can display my gratitude except this," and leaning from his saddle he held out his hand.

But putting his own behind his back, Philibert de Vois looked up steadily into the other's face.

"M. le Duc," he said in a dangerously quiet voice, "I

am a blunt man and I dislike hypocrisy. You know full well that my wish to bring relief to Briege was not on your behalf; that had you been alone in the tower I should have made no effort to come. Why then offer me your hand? I will not take it. The only way in which you can thank me is to leave my castle."

The Vicomte knew all about his visit, yet one morning, accompanied by neither servants nor presents, he rode over to Vois. He owed thanks to Philibert and he would pay them, although they were neither welcome nor accepted.

But Philibert de Vois, flushing hotly at sight of his visitor, invited him into the great hall. He did not know the Vicomte's object for coming, and his heart beat wildly with hope. But when the Vicomte, brusque with awkwardness, explained what had brought him, Philibert waved his thanks aside.

"What need of them?" he said. "Why, 'tis I who am grateful to have been of any help to—the ladies."

"Very well," replied the Vicomte, "since you will not take thanks from me, you must come to Briege and the ladies themselves shall thank you."

But Philibert's eyes clouded.

"There is only one condition under which I could come to Briege, Monsieur. I hoped that perhaps you came here to tell me I might claim it. I know that I have neither great wealth nor a grand position, but—— Ah, Monsieur, will you still compel her to marry that one-eyed, craven cur?"

The Vicomte walked slowly down the castle steps and mounted his horse before he answered. Then gathering up his reins, he looked at Philibert standing beside him.

"In that case I fear we shall not see you at Briege, M. de Vois, for I expect my daughter to be Mme. la Duchesse de Tours before this day month."

And with a quick salute, without offering his hand or saying adieu, he rode away.

But on the way back to Briege his forehead grew puckered

with thought, and pulling up his horse to a walk, he rode
forward with bent head. He did not hide from himself
that he despised the Duc de Tours and that Philibert de
Vois' looks and manner appealed to him. Had both the
suitors for his daughter been of equal wealth and position,
he knew perfectly well that he would have favored the
younger. Yet he was determined that Denise should marry
the Duc as soon as might be, mistaking his pride, ambition
and love of power for a desire to seek his daughter's wel-
fare and choose what was best for her.

His contempt for the Duc had greatly increased since he
had heard the accounts of the attack by de Tours' men,
and he had made no effort to conceal his feelings from the
Duc himself, telling him very bluntly what he thought of
his cowardice. The Duc had listened with a quiet interest
which considerably surprised the Vicomte and led him on
to say more than he had intended. But when, with a
final snort of contempt, he strode out of the room, the Duc,
his lips twisted in an ugly smile, bowed deeply to the closed
door.

"A thousand thanks, Monsieur. I shall not forget to
repay you for your good opinion of me and the clearness
with which you have expressed it. I will keep your debt
with that which I owe to Mlle. de Breux, who has also not
hesitated to state her ideas on the same subject. And since
you think so ill of me, M. le Vicomte, it is evident that I
must not marry your daughter, an intention which I have
ceased to have for some time, though you shall not know
that until I choose. You old fool!" he added, his face
livid with rage, as he shook his fist at the door through
which the Vicomte had gone, "I will show you and Mlle.
de Breux, with that Huguenot fellow and the rest, that it
is unwise, even dangerous, to scorn Henri de Tours."

Yet until he could perfect the plan by which he hoped
to be revenged on them all, he hid his dislike very cunningly.

One morning, as Yoeland was sitting with Gallon, who
still lay weak and helpless, the door opened, and she felt

the sick man's hands tighten convulsively on hers as the Duc entered the room.

The Duc, with a smile meant to be agreeable, bowed deeply to Yoeland, giving no sign of resentment that she had risen at his approach and stood protectingly before the sick man.

"Mademoiselle," he said, standing at the bottom of the bed and marking the fear in Gallon's eyes with secret pleasure, "I have never wished to be wounded before, but a sword thrust or two, provided they ensured a visit each day from Mlle. de Breux, could be nothing but happiness— eh, Gallon? There, there, man!" he added with forced good humor, "do not scowl at me like that. I mean you no harm, though no doubt your conscience tells you that you deserve it. I have, Mademoiselle," he continued, catching a little curl of scorn on her lips, "decided to abandon my plans for this fellow's future which I mentioned to you the other day. I agree with you that they were too bloodthirsty, and that a wrong will not cure a wrong. Therefore, when he is strong enough, Gallon may return to my service without misgiving. I shall be content to forget the past, if he will promise to be a more loyal servant in the future."

He paused, looking from one to the other, but neither answered. Yoeland was watching him intently with doubtful eyes, and Gallon made no effort to conceal his dismay at the thought of returning to his master's service. The Duc shrugged his shoulders with a quick laugh.

"You do not believe me, Mademoiselle? You think that once he is back again in my power that I shall take vengeance on him? How can I assure you that my intentions towards Gallon are real, that I freely forgive him? Why, Mademoiselle, as you do not trust him with me, and as he undoubtedly owes his life to your care, will you not take him into your own service, in place of one of those men he helped to kill? Do you understand, Gallon? You are no longer in my service, but belong to Mlle. de Breux."

And without another word he left the room.

Yoeland listened to his retreating footsteps with questioning eyes. What could he mean? What was his scheme? That he meant no good, either to Gallon or herself, she was firmly convinced.

And Gallon, clinging to her hands, shuddered convulsively.

"Oh, Mademoiselle, why did Monseigneur say that?" he whispered. "He is not speaking truth. M. le Duc never forgives, and it is not natural for him to be so kind. Ah, you will take me into your service, you will not give me up to him again?"

In a gentle, soothing voice, as though he were a terrified child, Yoeland reassured him, promising that the Duc should never harm him, although at the bottom of her heart a dread, which she could neither explain nor account for, made her wonder if she were justified in giving such an absolute assurance.

While Yoeland was nursing Gallon back to life and hope, Rupert was finding his convalescence a very unpleasant affair. Awakening from his sleep refreshed and strengthened, he had looked round eagerly for Yoeland, only to see Mme. Charlotte seated in the big window-seat. And in the days that followed, it was always the same. Whatever kind hands and gentle voices could do for him was done, but they belonged to Mme. Charlotte, Mlle. Denise, or one of her women, never to Yoeland de Breux. And gradually he began to realize that his hope and the blessed moments when she had knelt beside his bed were only a dream.

Yet, in his heart, he felt it was not all dream. The expression he had caught in her eyes as she stood by him on the stairs before the men of Tours made their last rush, and the soft touch of her hands on his before he had lost consciousness that night, must have been real. Then what had he done, how had he vexed her, that she never came near him now or seemed to care if he grew well? He had been delirious he knew. Could he then have said too much, have poured out all his devotion and his presumptive hope of its return, making her, afraid in her kind heart of raising expectations which could never be fulfilled, decide not to come near him again?

Apprehensively he questioned Mme. Charlotte as to what he had said during that fevered night of unconsciousness, but her answer only added to his restlessness, for she was unable to give the desired information, explaining that Mlle. de Breux had been with him then.

There was obviously but one thing to be done. Since Yoeland de Breux would not come to him, he must go to her, for he could endure the torturing uncertainty no longer. He must know how he stood with her and if it had all been a dream.

This resolve led to such a speedy recovery that Mme. Charlotte became seriously alarmed. It was absurd that a man as weak as he should get up and walk about. Yet when she refused to allow him to do so, he grew so restless and insistent, that, for fear of a serious relapse, she reluctantly gave her consent.

With Carlote's help Rupert very laboriously dressed himself. His doublet, wonderfully mended, lay ready, and waiting till Carlote's back was turned, Rupert caught the darned, patched garment to his lips; her hands had touched it, she had labored to make it presentable. Then with set teeth and a firm resolve to take no notice of the way in which objects doubled themselves before his eyes, or of the drums which beat within his head, he staggered, rather than walked, downstairs.

But when, in the corridor, he met Yoeland, there was no welcome in her eyes, no pleasure to see him; the barest, coldest acknowledgment answered his bow.

"Oh, M. de Vrieac, so you are about again. How relieved you must feel. But have you not got up too soon?" she added, as her eyes marked his white face and the deep shadows beneath his eyes. And Rupert, seeing two Yoelands, two corridors, two of everything, whilst the drums in his head beat louder than ever, assured her gravely that he was well and strong.

"I am glad you feel so M. de Vrieac, for you do not look that," she replied; and entering her room, closed the door.

In the corridor outside, Rupert leant against the wall and wished that the soldier's sword had pierced his heart instead of his shoulder. Groping his way unsteadily he found a chair and, sinking into it, buried his face in his hands.

So it had been all a dream! She did not care. Why should she? He had been a presumptuous fool even to think such madness—that he, a Huguenot, the enemy of her house and her brother's prisoner, could be loved by Mlle. de Breux. And fools must suffer for their folly. Life would be more intolerable than ever, for hope itself, which had held its blessed image before his eyes, turning the desert into Paradise, even that was dead now. And he had still four long years before his oath to the Comte expired. He did not feel that he could endure them, so very little was left to him—one thing alone.

He slipped his hand inside his doublet, feeling for the slit in the lining. It seemed to have gone, and unfastening the buttons, he looked for it anxiously, but where the slit should have been was a neat patch.

He gave a sharp exclamation and taking off the doublet, passed his hand quickly over the lining, but he could feel nothing inside. With a face grown very grave he drew his poniard and slit the lining, searching quickly.

It was at this moment, when he stood in his shirt, shaking his doublet violently, its lining waving like a torn banner, that Yoeland left her room and came down the corridor towards him. She stopped abruptly, watching him with startled eyes, whilst a flush dyed her cheeks deep crimson.

Rupert, miserable, upset over his loss, very embarrassed, began to thank her haltingly for mending his doublet, but she cut him short with an amused laugh.

"I am afraid you did not approve of the mending, M.

de Vrieac. You appear to have uncut most of it," she said.

He looked at her with troubled eyes.

"There was something in the lining, Mademoiselle, a trifle I—valued—just a curl of hair and a blue ribbon. I was looking for it; I cannot find it now."

She raised her eyebrows.

"Indeed," she said indifferently. "You had better ask my woman Jeanette if she knows aught of it. I found the mending of your doublet too great a labor, Monsieur, so gave it to her to finish. Perhaps she has moved your treasure or can give you news of it."

And she passed on down the stairs, whilst Rupert, summoning all his resolution and choking back his bashfulness, went in search of Jeanette.

But she could give him no news of his token, and he was well aware that his demand for information concerning it aroused much mirth and curiosity within her; also that she would not fail to recount his quest to her fellow-servants amidst laughter later on.

With a heavy heart Rupert climbed once more to his room, and, sitting down on the bed, buried his face in his hands. Love and Hope and all had gone, whilst his oath to the Comte held him for four more years. With a hard, dry sob he lifted his head, staring out across the room, his eyes full of the horror of despair.

The Vicomte had returned to Briege barely a week, when one evening a messenger, his horse utterly spent and himself worn out with the urgency of his mission, rode up to the castle, bearing a dispatch for the Vicomte from the Duc de Guise.

Breaking the seals the Vicomte gave a sharp exclamation as he scanned the contents, for it was both gratifying and yet, at the moment, unwelcome.

Since the August massacres the remaining Huguenots had banded themselves together in their cities south of the Loire, where they had, under Henri de Navarre, resisted all efforts to destroy them.   The Duc de Guise now offered the Vicomte an important command in the great campaign which the League was organizing to exterminate the heretics and their leader, the Bearnese king.

Should he accept the command, however, the Vicomte would be obliged to leave Briege within twenty-four hours to confer with the other leaders at Verdun.   Denise's marriage had been arranged to take place in a month's time with great pomp in Paris, and the Vicomte felt disinclined to go on a long expedition which might mean an absence of many months, leaving his daughter with only Mme. Charlotte to look after her.   Yet to hasten on her marriage for that evening seemed hardly possible.

The Duc hailed de Guise's letter with great but hidden joy, for it supplied alike the delay to his marriage and the absence of the Vicomte which he desired, though he realized that he must act with both cunning and caution if he were to benefit by it.   Accordingly he sought a private interview with the still undecided Vicomte.

"You will pardon me, Monsieur," he began, "if I speak very plainly, without concealing or embroidering anything? You will not, of course, refuse this command?   In fairness to your friends you cannot.   It is not for nothing that de Guise has the reputation of being a judge of character, of choosing just the right man for his purpose.   If you fail him where will he be able to get another commander as able and suitable to take your place?   It is, I gather, only on Mlle. Denise's behalf that you hesitate?   There is no other reason for refusal?   Now I know that the other night when those devils attacked us that I—well, I said I would speak plainly—that I played the craven and that you, Mlle. Denise, M. de Vrieac, all of you, despise me for it.   I do not blame you.   You cannot despise me more than I do myself, and I should like to make reparation for that failure. I never flattered myself that Mlle. Denise loved me, and by my cowardice I feel I have added to her dislike.   Nor do I pretend that Fortune has not given me a great position.

The marriage of a Duchesse de Tours has ever been a grand event, full of pomp and pageantry, dear to women's hearts. Should I marry Mlle. Denise to-night she will have none of the splendor with which I would fain surround her, and she will not—let me be frank—pay her vows gladly. Will you allow me to propose another plan, Monseigneur? Go on this expedition. In a month—two at most—the campaign will be over, you will have crushed the heretics and can return loaded with fame and honors for my marriage to Denise in Paris, which will be celebrated as befits a Duc de Tours and a daughter of M. le Vicomte de Briege.

"Until then," he continued, "let me place a house in Tours at the disposal of Mme. Charlotte, your niece and daughter, and their servants. Mlle. Denise is but a country bird, she has no idea of the power and magnificence which will belong to her as my Duchesse. She will see some of this at Tours. We shall then, I fancy, hear little more of M. Philibert de Vois, and she will be ready enough when you return to marry me. Will you not," he added, as the Vicomte seemed to hesitate, "consult Mlle. de Breux and let us be guided by her decision? She is very clear-headed and has excellent judgment."

So in the end it was arranged that the Vicomte should start next day to meet M. de Guise and that the others should journey to Tours. For Yoeland had, as the Duc guessed she would, welcomed a plan which would put off Denise's marriage and heartily supported the Duc's suggestion. The Vicomte, moved perhaps by the terror which leaped into his daughter's eyes as she learnt that that evening might make her Duchesse de Tours, and having a great opinion of Yoeland's good sense, had consented to delay, having, however, stipulated that his niece should not return to La Roche until Denise's marriage. This promise Yoeland gave readily enough, congratulating herself that he had not specified to whom the marriage must take place.

After the attack and extermination of his thirty men,

the Duc had sent back to Tours for another company of soldiers, and they had reached Briege on the previous evening, their numbers augmented by fifteen troopers, led by a big sunburnt fellow named Blaise Blas, who were in search of employment.

Those were times when each seigneur kept as many soldiers as he could and the Duc, after a few questions, promptly took the fifteen into his service.

Rupert de Vrieac, standing indifferently by, heaved a sudden sigh of deep relief, when the compact was settled. As the strange troopers rode into the courtyard he had flushed hotly, with a smothered, instantly-checked cry of pleasure, and then as the Duc offered his terms had, unseen, nodded to Blaise Blas to accept them. For although they betrayed it by neither look nor sign, each of the stalwart, weather-tanned fifteen had known him since childhood; they were picked men of Vrieac, sent by Martin to be near their master should he need them, and Blaise Blas, their leader, was, Rupert knew, a clever, capable soldier, devoted to his house and absolutely fearless.

With fifteen such men near at hand Rupert felt more secure, for he was perfectly aware that the dislike which the Duc entertained for himself, Philibert de Vois and even Mme. Charlotte, was as nothing compared with that he had for Yoeland de Breux. What his plan was for getting her and Mlle. Denise to Tours he could not fathom, but it was good to feel that, in case of need, there were Blaise Blas and his fourteen men within the enemy's citadel.

CHAPTER XVI

THE next morning at daybreak the Vicomte and his troopers left Briege and two days later the Duc, accompanied by the three ladies and Rupert de Vrieac, with many servants and soldiers, waiting-women and pack-horses, set out for Tours.

In the rear of the cavalcade there was a horse-litter bearing Pierre Gallon, still pitifully weak, his muscles tense in a desperate effort to conceal the torture which each jolt of their progress caused him. For Yoeland, uncertain if she would ever return to Briege, and fearing that Gallon might fall into the Duc's hands, had firmly determined not to leave him out of her reach. So, although the Duc had tried to dissuade her and the sick man was barely strong enough to stand so long a journey, she had taken the risk, and insisted on Gallon being brought with them.

Traveling leisurely, they reached Tours at sundown; and entering by the Porte du Nord, found the town en fête to receive them.

For here the Duc was a veritable king, and had sent on orders for the populace to prepare a welcome for his betrothed. Banners and festoons of flowers decorated the houses, whilst the entire population—priests and soldiers, bourgeois and beggars, men, women and children—all agape, thronged the streets.

As they rode under the archway, past the saluting guard, the Duc turned and, with a gesture to the others to rein in, bowed gravely to Denise.

"Mademoiselle," he said, "will you not ride on before the rest that the people may see you? It is you for whom they wait."

She looked at him with startled eyes, flushing hotly.

"For me, Monseigneur?"

"Why, yes, Mademoiselle, for you, their future Duchesse. This is their welcome. Tours has made itself gay to meet you, and the people will be very pleased if you will ride on beside me and smile at them."

For a second she hesitated, a dark dread of the future and the remembrance of Philibert de Vois holding her; then with a quick little catch of her breath, she nodded consent and alone at the Duc's right hand, the others holding back, she rode on. There was a blush on her cheeks and a shy smile curved her lips as she looked round on the cheering throngs, her blue eyes wide with pleased astonishment. And the people, delighted with her youth and beauty, shouted ecstatically, the Duc riding beside his betrothed being well aware that little of the welcome was for him, and that a good deal of sympathy for the future Duchesse was mixed with their admiration.

In the center of the town was a large square, bounded on one side by the Duc's hotel and the Hall of the City, the remaining sides being occupied by the houses of nobles and more important bourgeois. It was one of these houses which the Duc had allotted to his guests, and as they rode up to its gray frowning walls, massive, barred and loop-holed, Yoeland felt her heart sink. The place seemed to her like a prison, but when they had passed through the heavy iron gates into the courtyard in the center, she gave a cry of pleasure. For here were palms and many flowers, a fountain, whose basin held brilliant gold-fish, and on whose rim cooing doves made a leisurely toilet. It was all very cool and pleasant after the noise and dust without.

The Duc, who, back in his own domain, had developed a new suavity and pride of bearing, shortly took his leave, as it was obvious that his guests wished to rest after their long day's travel, but before returning to his own hotel he invited them to a grand hawking party which he had

planned for the next day, and to which had been bidden
all the important people of Tours, that they might meet
Denise and her friends.

The next morning was fine and beautiful, and Denise,
who evinced a natural and almost childish delight at her
new surroundings, was early astir and aroused Yoeland that
she might hold a grave consultation as to which of her two
riding costumes, both regarded with grave misgivings, she
should put on. For though at Briege they had seemed
smart enough, they appeared hardly adequate to compete
with the grand toilettes of the ladies of Tours. And then
a great surprise came to them.

For the women whom the Duc had appointed to wait
upon them produced wonderful costumes, lovely jewels and
the various glories of a wardrobe which neither Denise nor
her cousin had ever dreamed of possessing, and which removed all fear of their appearing shabby to the curious eyes
of Tours, as presents from the Duc to Denise and her
cousin. Even Mme. Charlotte had not been forgotten, and
Yoeland as she sat on her bed, a critical audience, watching
whilst Denise, who was almost too excited to allow her
waiting woman to put them upon her, tried on the various
costumes, felt something akin to liking for the man whose
thought could give so much pleasure. But in the middle
of it all, when the woman had gone to fetch something from
another room, Denise suddenly came to her cousin's bed and
kneeling beside her, laid her head against Yoeland's shoulder.

"Oh, Yoeland," she whispered, a little catch in her voice,
"if only Philibert were here! It—it spoils everything.
Though I can always see him when I shut my eyes, 'tis not
at all the same thing, especially when he is leagues and
leagues away. And oh, I hope it is not wrong to love all
these beautiful things when I do not want to marry the
Duc and do not even like him. I think I like him less when
he is kind. I—I am afraid, and oh, I do not want to be
Madame la Duchesse, even if I could have every lovely

thing in the whole world. I would rather marry Philibert
and live with him at Vois."

Bending down, Yoeland kissed her warmly.

"Then, Denise dear," she said, "if you are quite sure of
that, you must marry M. de Vois, in spite of every one."

It was a very gay assemblage which gathered in the
great square for the hawking party. The Duc, mounted
on a superb black Arab, rode amongst his guests, talking
and laughing with unusual liveliness. When he saw Denise
approaching with the others, he dismounted and, giving
his horse to a servant, went forward on foot to meet her.
Kissing her hand with elaborate courtesy, he led her jennet
to where a lady in a wonderful costume of blue, her face
shaded by a large hat with sweeping feathers of the same
shade, sat on a white palfrey, chatting gayly with some
friends.

As the Duc approached a great silence fell on those around
as they made way, surveying his betrothed with curious
eyes.

"Denise," said the Duc, stopping her jennet beside the
white palfrey, "allow me to present you to Mme. de St.
Caux, whom the unfortunate absence of her husband, my
cousin, has happily brought to Tours and whom I have
no doubt you will soon learn to love and admire."

Mme. de St. Caux caught Denise's timidly extended hand
with a soft laugh.

"To see Mlle. Denise is to love and admire her," she
said. "I have heard so much of you from M. le Duc,
Mademoiselle. I hope that you will like me and let me
be your friend, my dear," she added, and leaning forward out
of her saddle she took Denise's face between her hands,
kissing it impulsively on both cheeks. Denise, charmed by
her action and kind manner, thought her the most lovely
lady she had ever seen, and heartily reciprocated Mme. de
St. Caux's wish.

But Yoeland, her horse standing a little to one side,
had felt her heart leap with fear as she heard the beauty's

name. Then it seemed to stop beating altogether. Mme. de St. Caux! Swiftly she scanned the other's features, comparing them with her brother's description of Rupert de Vrieac's former betrothed. "Petite, with big blue eyes and a beautiful complexion." And the hair! Oh, yes, it was indeed beautiful too. Curling in riotous profusion, the color of brightest sunlight, round the small, piquant face. But it was coarse, as the Comte had said, coarse as a curl of hair which Yoeland had once seen burning in fire with a bit of blue ribbon.

Yet she greeted Mme. de St. Caux with grave courtesy when the Duc presented them, looking into the big blue eyes without the smallest betrayal of her knowledge.

"De Breux!" Madame murmured, glancing at her searchingly. "I think I met your brother, Mademoiselle, in Paris last summer. M. le Comte de La Roche, is he not?"

"Did you indeed?" Yoeland replied with quiet interest. "I do not recollect his mentioning your name."

Mme. de St. Caux flushed ever so slightly.

"I was Mlle. de Vainçeoire then," she replied somewhat sharply. "It was your brother, Mlle. de Breux, who saved myself, my aunt and our servants from the mob who would have killed us on that terrible night of St. Bartholomew," and she shuddered violently. Then watching Yoeland intently: "He saved my—my betrothed also, M. de Vrieac," she continued carelessly. "You will have met him, Mademoiselle, for it was a condition of Rupert's—M. de Vrieac's —safety that he should return with the Comte to La Roche, I believe. I have since married M. de St. Caux, so that explains why you did not know my name. I trust," she added with slight hesitation, "that Ru—M. de Vrieac is well?"

"Why, yes," Yoeland replied with grave indifference, "I have every reason to believe so. But you can question him for yourself, Madame; he is here."

And moving her horse a little back she beckoned to Rupert, who was standing by Mme. Charlotte, utterly unconscious of the introduction which had just taken place.

"M. de Vrieac, here immediately, if you please," she called.

Leaving his horse, he came to her quickly. Then Yoeland, who was watching him very intently, saw a sudden flush flame over his face and, receding again, leave it as pale as death, whilst his eyes dilated suddenly as he caught sight of the lady on the white palfrey.

For the fraction of a second he paused, then came to Yoeland's side.

"Yes, Mademoiselle?" he asked, looking up at her quietly.

She turned to Mme. de St. Caux, with a quick wave of her hand.

"You do not require presentation to this lady, M. de Vrieac, I fancy. Mme. de St. Caux wishes to know if you are well."

And turning a little to one side she joined Denise, who was talking gayly to some of the Duc's friends. But although Yoeland laughed heartily at their sallies, she was really straining her ears to hear what the two behind her were saying to each other.

A bright flush dyeing her cheeks, Marguerite de St. Caux stooped from her saddle and gave Rupert her hand, which he, apparently entirely unembarrassed, raised gallantly to his lips.

"So you have not forgotten me," she said softly.

He looked up at her with eyes full of genuine surprise.

"Forgotten you? How, or why, should I do so, Madame?"

She sighed quickly.

"Or forgiven?" she whispered, bending a little lower.

He shook his head with a smile which was quite friendly.

"Why, with all my heart, Madame. Though I do not think now that I ever had anything to forgive from you," he added frankly.

She smiled again, though her heart was beating with angry, jealous throbs. It was so obvious that he had

completely recovered from the attachment which he once
felt for her, and an unreasoning bitter resentment against
him filled her, but she still smiled.

"Why 'Madame'? It used to be Marguerite."

Swiftly Rupert glanced round, his eyes wide with mock
apprehension.

"Pardieu! I have but one life, would you wish me
to lose it? M. de St. Caux might not approve and they
say he is a most excellent swordsman," he explained, looking up at her with humorous eyes.

In spite of herself Marguerite laughed.

"You need not be afraid, my cautious gallant. M. de
St. Caux is not here, he has gone on a campaign with M.
d'Anjou and the Guise. That is what brings me to Tours.
For Ambroise is the Duc's first cousin, and we have an
hotel here, where I intend to stay till the campaign is over
and he returns."

In the opinion of most of the Duc's guests, his hawking
party was a magnificent success. Sport was excellent, the
weather glorious, and the company both gay and dis-
tinguished. But to Yoeland it was one of the most miserable days of her life. The presence of Marguerite de St.
Caux at Tours had been an unexpected shock and had
Yoeland known of it beforehand, nothing would have persuaded her to favor their visit to that city. Rupert's manner with his former betrothed did not deceive Yoeland.
She knew from his games with Anne that he was skillful
at make-believe, and feign indifference as he would, she did
not forget that but for her having found and destroyed
it, he would even then have been wearing a love-token
of Marguerite's over his heart.

Consumed by a fierce jealousy, she kept as near to Mme.
de St. Caux as possible, watching her closely. But although
Marguerite several times contrived to bring Rupert to her,
he invariably found something which quickly called him
back to Mme. Charlotte, at whose side he stayed all day.

As they returned in the evening a little incident occurred

which rather pleased and surprised Yoeland, though she would not permit herself to take any comfort from it. Across their way ran a stream, swollen by recent rain into a muddy torrent. The white palfrey, frightened by the rushing water, refused to ford it. Marguerite, her eyes flashing with sudden anger, pulled it round, hitting it sharply with her whip, thus adding to the animal's fear. It backed away from the water, plunging into Yoeland's horse, which was next, and, communicating the alarm to it, made it rear sharply.

A gentleman, riding beside Yoeland, leant forward to catch her mount's bridle, but Rupert, who had already crossed with Mme. Charlotte, his horse splashing unconcernedly through the water, was before him.

"Will you see to Mme. de St. Caux, M. de Loge," he said. "I will take Mlle. de Breux across."

And dismounting, he patted Yoeland's horse, soothing it by voice and touch, then very gently led it forward.

The horse, encouraged by his guiding hand, stepped doubtfully into the stream, and slipping his own reins over his arm, Rupert led it on, the water reaching above his knees and nearly carrying him off his feet.

Safely across, Rupert, without waiting for Yoeland's thanks, bowed gravely and, remounting his horse, rode after Mme. Charlotte, whilst Yoeland, a slight smile curving her lips, waited for Marguerite, who was being slowly piloted over by M. de Loge. Why had not Rupert led the white palfrey, Yoeland wondered. No doubt he had not dared to do so, lest it might betray too plainly his feeling for Mme. de St. Caux.

When they were gathered in the great square at Tours before dispersing, Marguerite rode up to the party from Briege.

"I am having a fête to-morrow," she said gayly, "to which, as it is given in your honor, I hope you will come, Madame and Mesdemoiselles. And you, Monsieur, you will come to my little party also?" she added, turning to

Rupert when the others had signified their pleasure to do
so.

Rather startled at the invitation, he bowed.

"A thousand thanks, Madame, I will come gladly if——"

And he hesitated, looking at Yoeland, who answered
the glance with a careless nod.

"Oh, yes, you may go if you wish," she said, rejoicing
secretly to observe that her power to order Rupert's goings
had brought an angry sparkle to Marguerite de St. Caux's
eyes.

That evening, when Marguerite was alone in her boudoir,
her husband's aunt, Mme. d'Uverte, who lived with her,
having retired early, a gentle tap sounded on the paneled
wall. With a quick laugh Marguerite clapped her hands.

"Entrez!" she cried gayly, a panel slid silently back,
and the Duc de Tours stepped into the room.

"Why this elaborate caution in your entrance, Henri?"
she asked, smiling. "Could you not have allowed my
servants to show you in?"

Slipping off his long black cloak the Duc sank into a
chair. "No," he replied, "I did not want any one to
know that I came to see you to-night. That estimable lady,
Mme. d'Uverte, has, I rejoice to see, had the good sense to
retire. So we can now talk without interruption. Well,"
he continued, "what do you think of my future Duchesse?"

"I think that she is very sweet and pretty, much too
charming to marry you," Marguerite answered, helping
herself to a prune from his comfit box.

The Duc bowed.

"You flatter me, I fear. And Mlle. de Breux? Do
you find her also sweet and pretty and altogether charming?" he asked, with an assumption of carelessness, though
he was watching her intently.

Marguerite faced him with a frank laugh.

"No, I do not, Monseigneur. I think she is beautiful
and dignified and clever, and I would rather be her friend
than her enemy."

For a moment they looked at one another, each striving to read the other's mind, then the Duc laughed.

"So you are jealous of Mlle. de Breux, Margot! Nay, 'tis no use to deny it. I can see you are; you have praised her over much. There, do not get so angry, ma mie. I would not have you be her friend. You saw to-day, what I told you of in my letter from Briege, that the Huguenot fellow—God curse all heretics!—is in love with her? You are not pleased, Margot, that he should have forgotten you and transferred his adoration to Mademoiselle," he added with malicious amusement.

"There you are mistaken," Marguerite replied sharply, with an indignant toss of her head. "It is a matter of no moment to me whom M. de Vrieac honors with his affections."

But the Duc, knowing well that no woman, be she never so fickle or never so unworldly, can bear the thought of a lover's desertion, laughed softly. Then he drew his chair a little nearer, leaning confidentially across the table, whilst he placed a small white-leather case in her hand.

"Permit me to offer a little token of my esteem for Mme. de St. Caux," he said. And Marguerite, as she opened the case, gave a cry of delight. Then slipping the diamond ring within it upon her finger, she moved her hand to and fro, catching the light on the magnificent sparkling gems.

"How beautiful!" she murmured.

"Not more beautiful than your eyes, Margot," the Duc whispered. "And listen, ma mie. There are earrings and brooches and many more rings of better stones than those for your acceptance when this little plan of ours is brought to a successful issue.

"Now attend to me for a few seconds. To-morrow you give your fête at which my betrothed and her cousin, Mlle. de Breux, and that old death's head, Mme. Charlotte, also, I presume, will be present. Very well. I wish you to gain Denise's affection and her confidence. You

will not find it difficult, she is very simple and unsuspecting,
I believe. When you have done so, persuade her to tell
you of her pretty M. de Vois. That will be your cue to
malign me. Take away my character, say what you will,
I shall not charge you with perjury, only strengthen her
dislike to our marriage. Then, if possible, undermine her
affection for Mlle. de Breux. I cannot offer any advice
as to how that may be done, you will know better than I.
You seem to have an admiration for that lady, but for
my sake, I beg you to forget it! Without your help my
plan is unworkable, but with it——! Ah, Margot, it will
not be long before those other diamonds are yours. To sow
suspicion, so that Denise will not confide anything you tell
her to Mlle. de Breux, that is half-way to seeing my little
plot successful. And you can do it to-morrow, Margot.
Your wits will not find that, nor, I believe, would they find
any task, too hard.

"Did you notice," he added, playing on her vanity and
jealousy, to strengthen her wish to assist him, "did you
notice how the Huguenot led Mademoiselle's horse over
the stream, getting a nice wetting and no thanks for his
pains? Now, had I been he, I should have led the white
palfrey and been paid with thanks which would have made
any wetting a pleasure. Or I should have turned my grand
lady's horse back into the stream, to sink or swim as it
could, if she had omitted to thank me."

"He could not," Marguerite replied gravely; "he is her
servant, and she would no doubt have punished him severely
had he shown any resentment."

"H'm! A servant in the position of M. de Vrieac is
ill advised then to love his mistress, even though she is
so beautiful and clever as Mlle. de Breux," said the Duc,
rising to leave.

And he smiled to himself as he caught the jealous flash
which lit Marguerite's eyes at his words.

CHAPTER XVII

THE next morning Yoeland sent for Rupert.

"I am sorry, M. de Vrieac," she said, "that you will be unable to attend Mme. de St. Caux's fête to-day, as there is a very important message which I wish you to take for me."

If she had expected to see dismay or annoyance in his face she was disappointed, for he met her gaze steadily, perfectly at ease.

"Why, yes, certainly, Mademoiselle. When shall I start?"

"When, can you be ready?" she asked. "It is an eleven leagues' ride."

He smiled quietly.

"I can start now, Mademoiselle, if you wish; as soon as the horse is saddled."

His good-tempered readiness pleased her, though she would not show it.

"In an hour will be time enough, Monsieur. I wish you to take a letter from me to M. de Vois. You will stay the night with him and bring back his answer as early to-morrow as possible. The letter is urgent, so waste no time on the road, and you had better change horses at Arc and Luçon, I think. Come to me in an hour's time and I will have the letter ready for you."

Could Yoeland have seen Rupert's face as he went down the passage she would have been considerably surprised and puzzled, possibly rather annoyed. For it was full of a great content. Delighted to have escaped attending Marguerite's fête, he felt like a schoolboy released from some long and arduous task, as he realized that he would soon

be riding away from Tours, away from the thousand
irritations, perplexities, anxieties which chafed him, into
the open country.   He liked Philibert de Vois also, and was
glad to think of spending the night under his roof.   Feeling singularly lighthearted, Rupert hummed a gay little tune
as he went out in search of Carlote.

He found the soldier seated on a rough bench cleaning
his already spotless accoutrements.   Sitting down beside
him, Rupert took up the corselet.

"Listen, Carlote," he said softly, letting the links of the
mail slip through his fingers.   "Appear as though I am
talking to you about this in case any one is watching us.
I am going to Vois for Mlle. de Breux.   I expect to be
back to-morrow about noon, though I think it is very possible that I may be detained on the road.   Should I, however, not return by sunset, you will go to the quarters of
the Duc's soldiers and find Blaise Blas.   You will then
give him this letter, addressed to M. le Comte at La Roche,
which I am slipping inside your corselet.   He will see that
the letter is sent safely and will also tell you where you
will find twenty good men, on all of whom you can rely.
These you will bring here, letting them in at the little door
by the chapel as secretly as possible.   The Comte will
come to Tours as soon as he receives my letter, but until
he arrives, you will keep a very strict guard over Mlle. de
Breux, Mlle. Denise and Mme. Charlotte.   Do not let
them out of your sight, or, at any rate, out of earshot, day
or night.   The twenty men have already received their orders
and they know well how to conceal and disguise themselves,
so always have them near at hand, ready in case of any alarm.
Should you want to consult with any one in my absence,
you can absolutely rely on Blaise Blas.   He and his fourteen are my men, and I have given Blaise very minute orders.   The twenty others he will send you are from Vrieac
also.   Be careful not to mislay my letter to the Comte or
let any one steal it from you, Carlote.   I have an idea that
you and I are at this moment being watched and that every

servant in this house has been set to spy upon us. I would to God that we were safely back at La Roche, for I think this Tours is likely to be an unhealthy place for some of us before long," he added as he rose to make preparations for his journey.

An hour later, well mounted and fully armed, he left Tours by the Porte du Nord, taking the northern road to Vois.

The garden of Mme. de St. Caux's house ran down to a little backwater of the Loire and was full of stately trees and flowering shrubs, between which twisted paths leading to unexpected arbors and shady seats. On the big lawns below the terrace which ran along the south side, Marguerite had provided morris dancers, mummers and other entertainments for her guests, whilst on the water, barges, roofed with gayly-colored awnings and transformed into bowers of flowers, had been moored to the banks, where the guests could sit in comfort and take refreshments. And for those who wished to go further on the river, boats shaped like gondolas, the rowers wearing Venetian costume, were ready.

Many of the guests were already assembled when Denise and her party arrived. Yoeland, watching her hostess keenly, saw a frown of annoyance gather on her forehead when she found that Rupert de Vrieac was not with them, but she made no remark, welcoming them very cordially and presenting them to many of her friends. Waiting her opportunity Yoeland went to Marguerite's side.

"I am sorry, Madame, that M. de Vrieac has been unable to attend this afternoon. I had unfortunately to send him back to Briege on an important message which I could not postpone."

Marguerite's answering smile was apparently full of friendliness as she nodded comprehension.

"You must find it useful to have such a devoted servant ready to obey your commands, Mademoiselle. I did not understand when the Comte, your brother, made his condition, that M. de Vrieac was pledging himself to serve you. I thought it was to be your brother only, and M. de Vrieac believed likewise, I fancy, though, no doubt, he would have acquiesced all the more readily had he known that he was to take his orders from Mlle de Breux."

"Do you really think so?" Yoeland answered naïvely, giving no sign that she had caught the sneer underlying Marguerite's words. "I am glad to believe that M. de Vrieac does not find his bondage irksome, for he has four more years to stay with us. I have always found him a most obedient and trustworthy servant," she added carelessly, as she moved away to join Mme. Charlotte whilst Marguerite looked after her with angry eyes.

"Insolent baggage," she murmured, "but you will wear a more humble air before I have finished with you, my fine lady."

Moving in and out amongst her guests Marguerite at last saw the one for whom she was looking. Denise, with flushed cheeks and eyes sparkling with excitement, was seated on a shady bench surrounded by a group of obviously admiring gallants, whilst Mme. d'Uverte, whom Marguerite had instructed to look after the Duc's betrothed, sat beside her, busily engaged in some embroidery.

"Gentlemen," said Marguerite, approaching the group, "you must go away. Or, rather, you can remain here and we will go away. For Mlle. Denise and I are taking a little walk and we wish to be alone."

Then, slipping her arm through Denise's, she led her away down a shady path to a little glade where Lent lilies shone in the grass and in the middle of which was a low stone seat.

"Now I have got you to myself at last," said Marguerite as they sat down. "Well, Denise—for I may call you that, may I not?—it is a pretty name and suits you so well—how do you like Tours? I do want you to be happy here," she added, a little anxiously, "and to enjoy yourself. Do you know that I feel just as if I had known you all my life? Almost as if you were my little sister. I have never had a sister," and the big blue eyes grew wistful, "but if I had I should have liked her to have been just like you. Shall we pretend that it is so, that we are sisters, dear?"

And Denise, flushing with pleasure at the subtle flattery, gave the hands which held hers a little squeeze.

"I should love to, if you will let me," she replied shyly.

Marguerite nodded with a soft laugh.

"And you will call me Marguerite and come to me with all your secrets, just as though I really were your sister? But no," she continued, checking herself suddenly, "you have Mlle. de Breux to confide in, you do not want me. Ah, Denise, how you must love your cousin. She is so beautiful, so charming, so kind. She looks like a queen."

And Denise, glad to find some one else who shared her admiration for Yoeland, smiled happily.

"I think she is the most wonderful girl in the whole world, I am so glad you like her, too—Marguerite."

"Like her!" cried Mme. de St. Caux. "Why, Denise, if I were a man, do you know what I would do? I would try and persuade Mlle. de Breux to marry me, though I fear that she would not consent. For I have a feeling that she does not like me, whilst I would give anything to have her friendship, and so I suppose that were I a man it would be just the same."

"But I am sure Yoeland does like you," cried Denise loyally, "she was saying last night that she thought you most beautiful."

Marguerite shook her head, smiling.

"Mlle. de Breux is too kind to say disagreeable things even of those she is not fond of. She may admire my face, but I do not think that she likes me, myself, at all, Denise. Heigho! 'Tis well I am not a man, for I fear that I should in that case die of a broken heart. Why, what can they all be thinking of, these gallants," she cried, "that they do not persuade her to love one of them, instead of wasting her affection in such a hopeless quarter. For

I fear that she will not be able to marry the man of her choice, from what M. de Vrieac said."

"But—but does Yoeland love somebody?" asked Denise in surprised tones. "I did not know."

Marguerite made a gesture of impatience.

"La!" she cried, "was ever such an imprudent tongue as mine. I shall never learn to keep other people's secrets, Denise. M. de Vrieac said particularly that I was not to mention it to any one. But as I have told you so much, you may as well know the rest now. Only you must promise to keep the secret better than I have done and never to betray your knowledge to Mlle. de Breux herself. And do not let M. de Vrieac know that I have told you, for he would, rightly, never trust me again. Will you promise that, little one?"

"Why, of course, most faithfully," replied Denise, whose eyes were round with curiosity.

"Then, listen," said Marguerite, drawing nearer. "You know, Denise, that M. de Vrieac and I are very old friends, so we can say many things to each other. Yesterday, as we rode I asked him plainly why he did not try to persuade Mlle. de Breux to marry him. For M. de Vrieac, I can see, admires her very much. And then I was sorry I had said that, for he looked so sad. 'Alas!' he cried, 'if I only could, but it would be useless. She loves another man, Marguerite, and though I would die to see her happy I fear that her feeling for him is hopeless.' Then he told me that he had discovered that your cousin loves a man she has only seen quite a few times. He is young and of good family, but poor, though that is not an unsurmountable obstacle to Mlle. de Breux who, when she marries, will, of course, have a large dowry. The tragedy is that this man, this blind fool, prefers another girl. But I have hopes that he may yet see reason and make her happy. For men are seldom constant to one love, and Mlle. de Breux would, in time, by her beauty and goodness, win any one's heart. How soon, though, depends on the man. M. de

Vrieac had not time to tell me what this one was like, but perhaps you know him, Denise? For he lives somewhere near Briege. His name is Philibert de Vois."

With a startled cry, white-faced and trembling, Denise sprang to her feet.

"Who?" she cried wildly.

"Philibert de V—— Why, little one, what is the matter?" Marguerite asked. Then horror slowly filled her eyes.

"Dear heart, what—what have I said? What have I done? Oh, Denise," she whispered, drawing the weeping girl into her arms, "not you, too? You do not love this M. de Vois?"

"All my life," sobbed Denise, her face buried against the other's shoulder. "And he loves me. It is I he prefers to Yoeland, I who am making her unhappy, though I never dreamed that she cared for him until now."

For a few moments there was silence, whilst Denise wept piteously, and Marguerite, softly stroking the bowed head, looked out across the glade with a smile of secret amusement.

Then altering her expression to one of compassionate concern she raised Denise's face between her hands, kissing the tear-stained cheeks.

"Hush, dearest, hush," she whispered, "do not cry any more. And, oh, Denise, to think that I, I who love you and Mlle. de Breux so much, should have hurt you like this. Can you ever forgive me, dear? But I did not know, denise, I did not guess. I gathered from what the Duc told me that your marriage was your father's arrangement, but I never thought that you loved some one else, that you did not care for your future husband."

"I hate him," said Denise simply, wiping her eyes. A sudden quiver of amusement moved Marguerite's lips, but was instantly suppressed.

"In that case, dear," she replied gravely, "you must not marry him. Oh, Denise, why will you? He has wealth and power, I know, but that does not give happiness. How can you choose wealth, when you might have love? M. de Vois may not be very rich, but if he were the poorest beggar it would not matter one jot, so long as you loved each other. You will never be happy with M. le Duc, in spite of all the splendors which will surround you, if you do not love him."

"Oh, I know, I know," cried Denise miserably. "But what can I do? It is my father's wish that I should marry the Duc and I must obey."

"Nonsense," Marguerite replied, with a toss of her head. "The Vicomte cannot realize your disinclination to do so or your love for M. de Vois, otherwise he would never press it, I know. No father would force his daughter into such a marriage, did he understand her heart. Why, 'tis like mating a dove with a wolf.

"Denise," she continued, taking the girl's hands and looking very searchingly into her face, "you must not marry the Duc, you must not. He is what I have just called him, a wolf. Savage, treacherous, cruel. Nay, a wolf is better, it can sometimes be tamed or cowed, but the Duc de Tours, never. His heart is black and fierce and full of hate; even when he seems conquered, in the end he always exacts a terrible revenge. Child, your life with him could be nothing but a living hell, though perhaps not a long one—for have you not heard? No, they must have hidden from you what all the rest of the world knows—that he poisoned his first wife after they had been married only three years, because one day he killed a favorite dog of hers, and she, driven desperate by his cruelty, railed at him."

With a deep shudder Marguerite paused for breath, and Denise, who had been listening with wide eyes of horror and surprise, drew a little nearer to her companion.

"But—but——" she faltered.

With a swift, impulsive movement Marguerite laid her hands across the girl's lips.

"I know what you would say," she cried. "How is it

that I, feeling so towards him, can be on such friendly terms with the Duc? Child, you understand nothing of the world. I hope you will never need to learn to smile and be gay when your heart is nearly breaking with anxiety for those you love; to shield them from harm by suffering the presence of one whom you loathe and dread. The Duc is very powerful and he is my husband's cousin. He is jealous of Ambroise—my husband—jealous of his strength, his good looks, his courage, his popularity. Oh, I think that to be a prince's favorite is a very hollow honor, it is also very unstable, yet my husband values M. d'Anjou's regard. The Duc has great influence at the Louvre, one word said by him against my husband would be sufficient to make Ambroise lose everything.

"So, when he started on this campaign, he begged me to win M. le Duc's liking, to give him no cause for offense. And because I would do anything for Ambroise, I promised gladly. I did not know then what a hard promise that would be to keep. Oh, how I hate Henri de Tours," she continued in a low voice, apparently forgetful of her listener. "How I loathe and fear him! I would rather feel the fangs of a snake on my hand than the touch of his lips! And yet I must not betray this. For the Duc never forgives those who show they dislike or scorn him, and, sooner or later, he repays them by ruin and misery."

She raised her eyes slowly, meeting Denise's troubled gaze and gave a violent start. For a second she remained motionless, her nostrils dilated, her mouth half-open as one who suddenly finds a bottomless chasm yawning before her feet. Then catching Denise's hands she clasped them feverishly, whilst she searched the girl's face with fear-haunted eyes.

"Denise!" she whispered, "Denise! Forget what I have just said! Ah, child, do you not see? Ambroise's future and my happiness are in the hollow of your hand. You have but to breathe one word of what I have just betrayed to the Duc, your betrothed, and my husband will be disgraced,

whilst I—perhaps M. le Duc will poison me as he did his
Duchesse," she ended with a high nervous laugh. The
next instant Denise had flung her arms round her.

"Oh, Marguerite," she cried reproachfully, "do you really
think that I would do such a thing? I would rather die."

"Would you, dear heart?" Marguerite replied, disengaging
herself gently from the girl's ardent embrace. "Can I trust
you, Denise? To keep my secret from every one, even
Mlle. de Breux? There, I know I can, little one. But
I have not your innocence of treachery, I have seen too
much of the world, and for a moment I was afraid. And
now, dear, how shall we let M. Philibert know that you have
decided to marry him? Though we will not break this fact
to the Duc for some time I think, till it is too late for him
to prevent the wedding. For you must not marry any one
but M. de Vois. And do not fret yourself as to how it
is to be done. Leave everything to me, I will manage it all,
and my wedding gift to you shall be—M. Philibert de Vois.
Oh, I am so glad to think that my little sister is going to be
happy and not married to that one-eyed wolf.

"And now, dear, I must go back to my guests. They
will be wondering if I leave them too long. Be just
your gay, sweet self, Denise, for remember that you are
surrounded by curious eyes and we must not let any one
guess what we have planned. Above all, do not, by any
change in your manner towards him, let the Duc suspect
anything. I think we will have to keep this a secret just
between you and me, Denise, for although of course she
wishes you to be happy it would be rather cruel to ask Mlle.
de Breux to assist us. And I am afraid that Mme. Charlotte
might, accidentally, disclose our plans to your cousin. The
fewer who know it the better a secret is kept. So we will
keep ours between you and me—and some one at Vois.
Now go, dear heart, and when you dream to-night of your
M. Philibert, remember that, very soon, you will see him
again, and after that you will never have to leave him any
more."

With a low, glad laugh Denise caught one of Marguerite's hands, kissing it lovingly.

"Oh, Marguerite!" she said, "it seems too good to be possibly true. You have been so sweet and kind to me. I do love you and I feel so—so happy."

Laughing softly, Marguerite held the girl in her arms, kissing the eager, pretty face.

"But it is going to be quite true, dearest. Only leave it to me. And now run away and find Mlle. de Breux, though remember, Denise, be very careful that you do not let her know we have discovered her secret. It might make her very unhappy, and she would not, perhaps, have wished you to know."

The smile was still in Marguerite's eyes as she watched Denise walk away up the glade, and ripened into a merry laugh as the slender figure disappeared beyond a clump of hazels. Then Marguerite yawned widely.

"La!" she murmured to herself, "my throat is as dry as one of the Abbé Bémile's sermons. I have talked myself quite hoarse, but I am certainly a most excellent actress. The girl believed every word, her eyes were as wide as the moon. That was an inspiration of mine to make Mlle. de Breux love her M. Philibert. I do not think there will be any more confidences between Denise and her cousin after that."

The last of the guests having gone and Mme. d'Uverte very wisely disappeared, Marguerite and the Duc strolled to a little summer-house covered with roses, where they would be absolutely undisturbed. Here Marguerite sank into a low-cushioned seat, heaving a deep sigh of content, whilst the Duc seated himself on the farther side of a little marble table, fixing his eyes expectantly upon his companion. For a second there was silence, then Marguerite, turning her head, met his gaze with laughter-filled eyes.

"Well, M. le Duc de Tours?" she said.

"Is it well, Mme. de St. Caux?" he replied, with a grave

smile. "Your fête was a vast success. I trust you were equally prosperous in your other undertaking this afternoon?"

"Yes, I think I was—beyond all expectations," she answered, with a little nod of her head as she helped herself to some sweetmeats on the table. "I should not be surprised if Mlle. Denise, now she has had leisure to think over something I told her this afternoon, almost hates her cousin by now."

The Duc leant forward with eager interest.

"And what did you tell her, Margot?"

"I told her," replied Marguerite, critically surveying a large bon-bon, "that Mlle. de Breux was secretly in love with M. Philibert de Vois and that I had had my information from no less a person than Rupert de Vrieac."

For a second the Duc looked at her, a smile spreading slowly over his face. Then he rose and, coming around the table, knelt at Marguerite's side, whilst he raised her hand reverently to his lips.

"Margot," he cried, "it was an inspiration. You are a genius."

"Just what I thought myself," she nodded. "And do you know, Henri, that I loathe and despise you, that I would sooner a snake bit my hand than that you should kiss it," she added gravely, though her eyes danced with mischievous amusement. "Listen, mon ami."

Then, very graphically, she told him of her talk with Denise, copying the girl's voice and expression and giving many details, whilst the Duc listened intently, shaken by silent mirth which broke into a grating chuckle when Marguerite related her condemnation of himself. When she had finished he kissed her hands again.

"Excellent! excellent!" he murmured, "why, Mme. Catherine, with all her practice, could not have done it better. Bravo, Margot! And that other little matter of Mlle. de Breux that I mentioned to you? Were you able to form any opinion on that point?"

Marguerite nodded eagerly.

"Yes. You were right, Henri, she does love Rupert de Vrieac. And this is how I know—because she hates me. Why should she do so? We have never met before and I have done my best to be charming to her. It is because she is jealous, because I was once the Huguenot's betrothed. She would not allow him here to-day. He was sent off to Briege, away from the possibility of seeing me, you observe."

"Sent to Briege!" said the Duc, with an evil smile. "Now why did she tell you a lie about that, Margot? A lie which is only a league from the truth and on the same road? And which, if my spies were not very sharp fellows, would have passed for the truth? I am afraid that Mlle. de Breux is suspicious, that her distrust is not as dead as I hoped. We must be very careful not to rouse it more, if I am to bring off my coup and you are to get your diamonds. Do you know where she really sent him? To Vois, with a letter for that puppy, de Vois? What she wrote to him I cannot say, but Philibert de Vois' reply, which de Vrieac brings back to-morrow, will tell us. It is always a good plan, when one is sure of a reply being returned, to let the outward dispatch through and capture the returning one, for in it you have the question as well as the answer. So de Vrieac got safely to Vois, but he will not find the way back so easy." And he gave a dry chuckle.

Marguerite's eyes grew alert at the sound of it, though her voice was carelessly quiet.

"Do you mean to have him killed then?" she asked.

The Duc held up his hands in simulated horror.

"Killed! De Vrieac killed! Why, Margot, you have let your wits go to sleep when you ask such a question. I would not kill him if his death gave me the crown of France. It is my constant care to preserve his life most carefully, in fact I have quite an army of men told off to guard it. What is the use of Yoeland de Breux loving him unless I can use his life as a condition to make her submit to my terms?

"Oh, no, he most certainly will not be killed—to-morrow. Only, as he rides back from Vois, he may fall amongst thieves, and of course they may take a fancy to his dispatches, as well as his money. No, ma mie, Rupert de Vrieac shall live until I will that he does otherwise, which is not yet. And now we must give Mlle. Denise a little time to think over your information. Indeed, there is nothing we can do until we get Philibert de Vois' letter to Mlle. de Breux."

CHAPTER XVIII

RUPERT DE VRIEAC, riding out of Tours by its northern gate, took the highway which, stretching like a broad gray ribbon across the country, would, had he followed it far enough, have led him ultimately to Paris, and turning his horse on to the grass along the road side, went forward at a long, swinging canter.

It was only eleven leagues to Vois, but it behooved him to push on quickly if he wished to reach his destination before dusk, after which it might be difficult to find his way along the woodland tracks. Besides, he had no need to spare his horse, as he intended to take a fresh one at Arc, a small town lying almost half way on his journey, picking up his own mount again when he returned the following day.

After careful consideration he had come to the conclusion that, were his suspicions correct, and some one in Tours did indeed wish to gain possession of his dispatches, it would be more probably on his return journey that he might expect trouble. But, experience having taught him the fallibility of human judgment, he rode forward with a wary eye open for possible ambuscades.

He reached Arc a little after noon, and having seen his horse comfortably stabled and chosen a remount from the half-dozen lean beasts offered by the landlord for his inspection, strolled into the inn and ordered himself a good meal. Then, having waited until the fierce midday heat had passed, he set out once more on his journey, the big raw-boned remount carrying him forward with a slow, tireless stride.

The sun had already set behind the wooded hills when Rupert at last reached his destination, and received a

Father Paul had fixed the rope of blankets to a beam.

delighted welcome from Philibert de Vois. Both his host
and Father Paul, for whom Philibert insisted on sending,
that he might also hear the news of Denise, had so many
questions to ask, and there seemed to be so much to discuss and relate that it was not until the dark, silent hour
before the dawn that the three men finally separated and
went to sleep.

In the morning Rupert rose for an early start. He had
grown uneasy and apprehensive with thoughts of what
might have happened at Tours during his absence, and felt
anxious for Yoeland de Breux's safety when he was not at
hand to guard her.

Just before setting out he followed Philibert into a little
room away from all prying eyes. There he again re-
newed his promise to protect Denise to the best of his
power, and there he also received Philibert's reply to Yoeland's letter, the contents of which he neither knew, nor
had Philibert offered to tell him. Taking the packet he
slipped it safely inside his doublet, smiling a little to
himself as he did so. For by its bulk and Philibert's very
certain slowness at writing, it was evident that the scribe
must have given the remaining hours of the night, after his
friends had left him, to its composition.

Nothing happened to delay him and he reached Arc
two hours before midday. Here, having had a meal and a
short rest, he took his own horse again and started forward, anxious to reach Tours as early as possible.

As he advanced he grew more alert, keeping his eyes
keenly on the watch, for it was at this stage that he guessed
an attempt might be made to stop him. He got within
three leagues of Tours, however, without seeing any hint
of danger. The road led up a long slope, at the top of which
a copse of larch and hazel grew on either side. It was a
good place for an ambuscade, and Rupert, who had been
saving his horse as much as possible for this effort, put it
full gallop at the hill, intending to pass through the danger
zone as quickly as possible.

He reached the first shade of the trees and spurred his horse on, glancing keenly from side to side for the glint of an arquebuse or any sign of an enemy. But he saw nothing, and reached the far end of the wood safely. Another three lengths would have brought him once more into the sunlight. Then a sharp whistle sounded somewhere in the branches above him, something fell over his head and, with a violent jerk on his throat, he was dragged backwards out of his saddle on to the road, as his horse, frightened and eased 'of his weight, dashed madly on.

For a few seconds he lay stunned and breathless whilst the thud of his horse's hoofs grew fainter in the distance. Then, opening his eyes slowly, he stared up at the half-dozen men gathered round him. Feigning more confusion than he really felt, he gazed from one to another of their unkempt, fierce-looking faces, but could not recollect having seen any of them before. They were just the. ordinary type of cut-throats who made traveling by even the most important roads unsafe in those times. Kneeling down, one of the fellows felt him over quickly.

"Only a little stunned," he said, slipping off the rope by which Rupert had been lassoed. "No bones broken. Holy Mother! but you made a good cast, Gaston. Here, lend a hand to truss him up before he gets his wits back, and then we'll see what he has in his pockets."

Turning Rupert over with more haste than ceremony, they bound his hands securely behind his back, and fastening his ankles together, drew them up to his wrists, so that he was powerless to move. Then they made a hasty search, transferring his money and small valuables, to their own pockets, grumbling the while at the smallness of their finds.

"Pardieu! He's a poor crow to pluck," said the man who had spoken before. "I thought from his feathers we should have found more. Better go through again to make sure we've passed nothing."

With large, blunt fingers he felt Rupert over carefully

and, just as he was about to give up the search, came upon
the thickness in his doublet which hid Philibert's letter.
A gleam of greed shone in the man's eyes.

"Ah! I thought so!" he cried with a satisfied chuckle.
"Our bird has a packet of notes hid within here. Give
me your dagger, one of you, and we will soon see what
they are worth."

Powerless to offer any resistance, Rupert could only lie,
cursing with impotent fury, as the man, ripping open his
doublet, slit up the lining and drew the packet out. A
murmur of disappointment came from him, however, when
he saw it was only a letter.

"Hum!" he muttered, turning it over in his hands,
"'To Mlle. Yoeland de Breux at Tours.' Never heard of
the lady, but you," he continued, looking down into Rupert's
furious eyes with an amused grin, "seem to attach value to
this letter, Monsieur. So I think I will take charge of it.
Perhaps when I have time to read the contents, I may
find it valuable also. Fare you well, my fine gentleman. I
am heartbroken to be obliged to leave you in what I fear
is rather an uncomfortable position, but no doubt, if you
wait long enough, some one will come and untie you. Hoist
him up, lads, somewhere into the shade."

Lifting him up by the knees and shoulders, two of the
men carried Rupert about fifty yards into the wood and
laid him, still bound but ungagged, to be rescued or not as
Fortune decreed.

His head aching violently from contact with the hard road,
tortured with cramp, and the hope of rescue very remote,
Rupert lay still, listening to the highwaymen's departure.
Then, the sound of their horses' hoof-beats having died
away, he turned his face into the soft moss on which he lay
and gave vent to a smothered shout of laughter.

About two hours later a miller, stopping to rest his team
on the hill, heard calls for help coming from a little distance
within the wood which skirted the road. Leaving his boy
to mind the horses, he went cautiously towards the sound

and soon found Rupert, enduring the agonies of cramp and almost giving up hope of rescue.

Very briefly, whilst the miller was freeing him, Rupert explained his misfortune and arranged to be conveyed to Tours on his rescuer's wagon. But when it came to walking, Rupert's limbs, numbed by the long strain in an unnatural position, refused to support him. So the miller, as a quicker solution than rubbing them back to life, hoisted Rupert across his burly shoulders like a sack of flour, carried him to the wagon and, depositing him on the top of the load, started the horses. So, with many jolts, they moved towards Tours.

As they neared the city gate, a party of troopers clattered out under the archway, breaking into a quick trot as they reached the high road. They had almost passed the wagon, when Rupert, sitting up suddenly, shouted to their leader to stop.

Blaise Blas, for it was he, did so all the more speedily since it was in quest of Rupert that the troop was setting out. Riding along beside the wagon as it creaked and bumped through the streets, he told Rupert that his horse had been found and brought into Tours by a traveler, and Blaise Blas, having seen it, had at once taken the news to the Duc, who had sent him off with a company of troopers to find its rider.

The wagon at last rumbled into the great square, and Rupert, very stiff and sore, climbed up the stairs to the little room where Yoeland was sitting alone. No news of his adventure had reached her, but she looked up with a quick sigh of relief as he entered.

"You are late, M. de Vrieac," she said, "I expected you two hours ago and had begun to fear something had happened."

"I was delayed, Mademoiselle," he replied gravely, "by a score of cut-throats who picked my pockets clean. But they took nothing of value," he added quickly seeing a sudden apprehension grow in her eyes. "I have brought M. de Vois' letter safely. Here it is."

And advancing, he gave her Philibert's packet.

A vivid flush swept over Yoeland's face as she took it; then, with a hasty word of thanks, she broke the seal and turned eagerly to read it by the light of the little window, whilst Rupert, a rather bitter smile on his lips, bowed gravely to her unmindful back and left the room.

Outside in the passage Blaise Blas was waiting, and taking him by the arm, Rupert led him upstairs to his own room. Then, the door shut and secure from observation, Rupert turned with questioning eyes.

"Well, Blaise?" he asked.

A slow grin spread itself over the soldier's face.

"I conveyed the news of your safety to M. le Duc and he seemed profoundly relieved, Monsieur. He bade me bring you the assurance that your assailants shall be found and punished, and also his felicitations on your escape. He will bring them to you personally later on. Was it as you suspected, Monsieur?"

"Yes. The fellows who stopped me were strangers, except their leader, and he wore a mask, but he had forgotten to remove one of his rings, and I have seen that ring every day since we came to Tours on the finger of one of the Duc's gentlemen. I know him. They took my money just as a blind, but it was a relief when they found the letter, I could tell, though they played their parts well enough. It never occurred to them that I could have another letter hidden in the sole of my boot. Dieu! What I would have given to see the Duc's face when he opened the packet they brought him. I hope he found it interesting."

Blaise smiled broadly.

"I fancy that had I brought Monseigneur the tidings of your death he would not have been broken-hearted, Monsieur."

Rupert shrugged his shoulders with a quick laugh.

"That is more than likely. Well, at any rate, we know now that the Duc is up to some devilment and is having a watch kept on us all. We must redouble our watch on him. We've fooled him this time, but we have also had to let him know that we are on the look-out, which is a pity. You have got those twenty extra men of ours ready at hand, Blaise?"

"Oh, yes, Monsieur. Three are in the Duc's hotel. Two are here, and the rest are scattered over the town. No one suspects they are from Vrieac, and I could call them all together within a few minutes."

"Good," Rupert replied. "We may want them, and your troopers also, to get us out of Tours at very short notice."

Yoeland found only a short letter for herself within Philibert de Vois' packet, but there was also a remarkably large one for Denise. So having carefully read and burnt her own, she took the other and went in search of her cousin.

Since Mme. de St. Caux's fête Yoeland had noticed a curious restraint in Denise's manner towards her, and had guessed instinctively who had been setting the girl against her. She was perfectly aware that in Marguerite de St. Caux she had a treacherous enemy who would not hesitate to decry her to every possible person, though she never dreamt by what a falsehood the poison had been sown in Denise's mind.

She found Denise in the central courtyard, watching the gold-fish in the fountain and trying to touch their elusive tails with a slim forefinger. Glancing round quickly to make sure that no one was watching, Yoeland went close to her cousin.

"Denise, dear," she said in a low voice, "here is a letter for you from M. de Vois. I should advise you, when you have read it, to destroy it carefully."

A quick flush swept over the younger girl's face.

"A letter from Philibert!" she cried sharply; "but how did it get here?"

"M. de Vrieac brought it in a packet for me," Yoeland replied and was startled by the jealous gleam which flashed in the blue eyes.

"For you?" Denise stammered angrily, moving a little nearer. "Why is Philibert writing to you, Yoeland? Did you send him a letter by M. de Vrieac? You told me M. de Vrieac was going to Briege."

And tossing back her hair she looked at her cousin with a white, passionate face. For a second Yoeland gazed at her in surprise.

"I do not understand what you are trying to imply or why you should be so angry, Denise," she said gravely. "I did not tell you that M. de Vrieac was going on to Vois because—because I thought it best that no one should know. You need not be angry about that, dear, and some day, quite soon, I think you will understand and be glad that I sent him."

And she turned away, a quick flush sweeping over her cheeks as she caught Denise's bitter little laugh.

Had Rupert had his wish and been present when the Duc received Philibert's stolen letter, he would most certainly have found the episode both amusing and satisfactory.

On the afternoon following her fête Marguerite de St. Caux was in her boudoir with the Duc when one of the latter's gentlemen arrived, asking for an immediate interview with his master.

"Show him in here," said the Duc curtly, adding, as the servant withdrew, "it is de Ganotte, whom I sent to relieve our dear M. de Vrieac of his dispatch, Margot. He must have got it safely, for he would not dare to show his face to me without it."

At that moment M. de Ganotte, whose appearance proclaimed that he had lost no time in returning with his booty, entered, and having bowed deeply to Marguerite, stood stiffly at attention.

"Well," the Duc asked sharply, "have you got it?"

"Yes, Monseigneur, here it is," de Ganotte replied, and,

advancing, he handed the Duc the packet of which Rupert had been robbed.

The Duc examined the inscription with a grunt of satisfaction.

"Good," he said. "And M. de Vrieac? You remembered my instructions not to harm him?"

"He is quite unhurt, Monseigneur. One of my men threw a noose and so got him unhorsed. We then easily found what he carried, although he made a fierce resistance. The packet was hidden in the lining of his doublet. Beyond a headache I do not think he will suffer any inconvenience from his fall."

"And he did not guess who, or what, you were?"

"No, Monseigneur. M. de Vrieac could have suspected nothing. He obviously considered us just common highway thieves. We left him tied up near the road and ungagged, so that he can call for help from the next passer-by. Shall I send and make sure that he is assisted, if he does not return by sundown, Monseigneur?"

"Yes," the Duc replied, "you had better do so. I wish him to come to no harm just now. You have done well, de Ganotte. You may go now. I will see you later."

Waiting until the door had closed and he was once more alone with Marguerite, the Duc quickly broke the seals of the packet. But a look of astonishment spread over his face as he opened out the sheets of paper within, and Marguerite, leaning over his shoulder, gave a little cry of surprise.

The pages were perfectly blank. For a second the Duc stared in perplexity. Then he shrugged his shoulders with a little laugh.

"Our dear M. de Vois is cautious! Will you tell some of your people to bring a light here, Marguerite? The fellow seems to have written in lemon-juice. We shall need heat to bring out the letters."

But although they warmed the sheets before a brazier, nothing appeared and gradually, as they unsuccessfully tried various methods for reproducing invisible writing, a fierce light of anger began to blaze in the Duc's eyes.

"Fooled!" he snapped. "They have fooled us, Margot. We may as well spare our trouble, there is nothing on the sheets. That fellow, de Vrieac, must have suspected something. I wonder if he had the other letter hidden on him somewhere, or if de Vois sent it by another messenger? Anyway, de Ganotte got the wrong one. I would to heaven I had stopped Mlle. de Breux's letter to Vois, unless that was a blank too. What can have made them suspicious? Or what can they suspect, for the matter of that? We shall have to go very warily, Margot, and I will have the watch on Mlle. de Breux and the Huguenot redoubled, and on Philibert de Vois too. They are up to something. We must find out what it is, but we shall have to work cautiously."

So when Yoeland rode out of Tours the following morning, Rupert, who escorted her, although he looked keenly at all whom they passed or overtook, found no reason to suspect that, the Duc having issued his orders, they were being both closely watched and followed.

Yoeland had not given Rupert any hint of their destination or her reason for choosing to ride abroad that morning, having merely expressed a wish for his company. Nor did she speak to him as, passing out of the Porte du Nord, they turned their horses along the road to Paris. Rupert, too proud to risk a possible rebuke, rode silent half a length behind her, and so they pushed forward at a sharp canter.

About half a league beyond the hill where Rupert had met with his adventure on the previous day, was a small tavern and, as they approached this, Rupert frowned with sudden surprise. Beneath a large chestnut tree which spread its branches before the inn, a big black horse was being led up and down by a stableman, and Rupert caught in his breath quickly as he recognized the animal as one belonging to Philibert de Vois.

Drawing up her horse before the inn, Yoeland turned

and addressed him for the first time since they had started.

"I am going in here, M. de Vrieac. I do not expect to be long. Please call some one to hold the horses and wait for me outside."

For a second Rupert thought of remonstrance and insisting on accompanying her into this strange place, but something in her face deterred him.

In silence he helped her to dismount and, still in silence, watched her follow the bustling landlady within. Then, having called a boy to hold the two horses he sat down moodily on a bench beside the door to await Mlle. de Breux's pleasure.

Meanwhile in the room above, Yoeland had met Philibert's greeting quietly. There was a determined look on her face as she watched him close the window, and then, having seated herself and appointed him a chair close by, she met his rather curious glance with steady, thoughtful eyes.

"I daresay you were surprised by my wish to meet you here, Monsieur," she began, her voice made a little brusque by embarrassment and anxiety. "Of course it is with regard to Denise that I desired to see you. M. de Vois, tell me truly, do you love her? Do you really wish to marry her? Because in that case I cannot understand why you do not do so."

"But, Mademoiselle, how could I?" cried Philibert, flinging out his hands with a protesting gesture, whilst a hot flush spread over his face. "The Vicomte would not consent to our marriage, and she is betrothed to the Duc. What would you expect me to do?"

Very thoughtfully Yoeland gazed down at her hand, turning a ring slowly round and round one of her fingers.

"I have heard of men who carried off their brides in spite of relentless fathers and a thousand obstacles, Monsieur."

"And I also would have done so, Mademoiselle," Philibert replied, shrugging his shoulders with a helpless gesture. "I have begged Denise to let me, but I cannot persuade her

to agree.   She is afraid of the Vicomte.   He has forced her
into this betrothal with the Duc and she will not go against
his wishes."

"And you let that deter you?   You took her refusal
as final?" Yoeland asked, looking up at him with a quiet
smile.   "Oh, M. de Vois, you do not understand women,
I can see!   If Denise would not come with you willingly
you should have carried her off just the same.   Afterwards
she would be only too glad that you had taken no notice of
her fears.   Now listen to me, Monsieur.   You love Denise
and Denise loves you.   On no account must she be allowed
to marry the Duc.   I was against that marriage before we
went to Tours, but now it seems to me a positive crime.
The Duc is not worthy to marry a witch, much less a sweet,
gentle girl like Denise.   What the Vicomte wishes or commands I do not care at all.   Neither need you.   I am determined that Denise shall not be sacrificed to his ambition
or stupidity.   She must marry you, for I am sure that you
will make the child happy.   She is just breaking her heart
now, and the sooner you take her the better.   So attend
to me very carefully, Monsieur, whilst I give you your
orders.

"You must ride back to Briege to-night and fetch Father
Paul.   You know the wood just beyond this inn?   On the
right there is a large white stone by the road, and from
there a bridle track leads down the wood to an old ruined
tower.   Very well.   You and Father Paul must be at
the tower an hour after noon to-morrow with good horses.
You must arrange also for changes of fast ones to be ready
at Arc and Luçon, so that you can get back to Vois as
quickly as possible.   I will make some excuse to take
Denise out riding to-morrow morning.   You must leave it
to me to decide whether I shall tell her the real object of our
expedition or not, as I think best.   Never fear, the result
will be the same.   She will be only too glad once she is safely
married to you.   All you have to do is to be at the tower
with horses and Father Paul an hour after noon to-morrow,

and Father Paul shall marry you and Denise there. I will
be one witness and M. de Vrieac will, I am sure, gladly
be the other. Then you can take Denise home. I am quite
prepared to break the news to the Duc, and the Vicomte
also, if necessary. After which I shall insist on Mme.
Charlotte returning with me to La Roche.

"Now I must go back to Tours. No, do not thank
me, Monsieur! You can do that—if you think of it then—
after you are safely married to Denise to-morrow. Remember the white stone on the right side of the road and
the change of horses at Arc and Luçon. I need hardly tell
you not to be late. You had better not appear now till I
have gone. Au revoir, Monsieur."

Outside Yoeland found Rupert waiting, a very gloomy
look upon his face. In silence he helped her to mount,
and in silence they turned their horses' heads towards
Tours. Absorbed in their thoughts, both rode forward unmindful of their surroundings. So that when half a league
from Tours, a horseman, going at a hard gallop, overtook
them, Rupert was too preoccupied to notice that he rode a
gray stallion, which, with Philibert's black and their own
two horses, had been waiting outside the inn under the
chestnut trees.

CHAPTER XIX

PHILIBERT DE VOIS was returning with all haste to fetch Father Paul and had almost reached Luçon, where he intended to give his tired horse an hour's rest, when he became aware of the sound of galloping hoofs behind, him. Absorbed in the prospect of his coming happiness, and grateful thoughts of Yoeland de Breux, it was some time before he paid any attention to them, or realized that above their clatter a voice was calling his name. At last it attracted his attention and, slipping out his sword, he pulled up, waiting for the oncoming horsemen to overtake him.

They were three in number. The first, a slight, boyish figure, mounted on a big roan horse and dressed in black doublet and hose over which was a long gray cloak, had been the one whose high, piping voice had called him. Behind followed two sturdy troopers. All three horses showed signs of having been ridden hard.

"Ciel! Monsieur," cried the rider of the roan, reining in beside Philibert. "I thought I should never make you hear. Your head was in the clouds, I fancy. But now I have stopped you, you are, I believe and most sincerely hope, M. de Vois?"

"I am, Monsieur, though you have the advantage of me there," Philibert replied, surveying the youth with suspicious eyes.

The other bowed courteously.

"We cannot talk, nor can I tell you my name here, M. de Vois," he said, glancing uneasily round. "Let us go on to Luçon, and in the inn there I can safely explain my errand to you. In the meantime I carry my recommendation—the name of the lady who sent me, Mlle. Yoeland de Breux."

199

So they rode forward the next half-mile in silence, a faint smile twisting the newcomer's face as he observed Philibert's motion for him and his troopers to go on first, and the certain and obvious mistrust with which their backs would be watched in the falling dusk.

On reaching Luçon, Philibert and the rider of the roan, having left their horses with the two troopers, went into a room at the inn where they could be alone and undisturbed. And here Philibert, turning to face his companion, started suddenly. Outside he had thought the other a youth, but now, in the brighter light of the candles he saw that it was a woman in man's clothes. She caught his look of surprise and, seating herself in a low chair, faced him with flushed cheeks.

"I thought it a safer way to travel after you, Monsieur," she explained, "and swifter. For there was need of haste. Draw your chair a little closer—there may be listening ears outside—and I will give you Mlle. de Breux's message. But firstly I must show my credentials. You will no doubt, Monsieur, recognize this ring as belonging to Mlle. de Breux? She said you would be sure to do so."

And Philibert, not liking to admit that he knew nothing of Mademoiselle's token, nodded gravely.

"Very good, Monsieur," continued his companion, slipping the ring back on to her finger with a curious little smile. "Then, secondly, I must present myself. My name is Marguerite de St. Caux. You may not have heard it before, as I have only known Mademoiselle since she came to Tours a few days ago. But one does not have to wait for months and years before learning to love her, and I hope, and think perhaps, that she likes and trusts me somewhat. For to-day she came to me in her need. Mademoiselle saw you lately, I think, M. de Vois, and made some arrangement? Very well. On her return to Tours, Mademoiselle discovered that all your plans had been overheard and had been reported to the Duc. Also, that to-morrow, should you go to the rendezvous, instead of Mlle. de Breux with Mlle.

Denise and M. de Vrieac, you would find awaiting you M.
le Duc de Tours and a score of his men-at-arms.   And you
do not need me to tell you, Monsieur, that you and your
companion would stand but little chance of escaping from
that meeting alive.   Mlle. de Breux had to warn you, but
whom could she send?   Her servants, M. de Vrieac, herself, were all no doubt being closely watched by the Duc's
orders.   Then she thought of me.   I am the Duc's cousin,
Monsieur, but that does not make him his friend, and Mlle.
de Breux knew that.   Also, at Tours I am a privileged person, no one dares to question my actions.   So I had no
trouble in coming after you, though I began to despair of
ever making you hear my calls and so stop and receive
Mlle. de Breux's message.

"At first Mademoiselle wished you to put off your marriage to Mlle. Denise, but then I pointed out to her that,
since this plot of yours had come to his ears, the Duc would,
in all probability, hasten on his own marriage to Mlle. Denise,
forcing her perhaps to wed him at a few hours' notice.
The best thing to be done was to prevent that by forestalling
him, and instead of delaying your marriage, to hurry it on.
So these are your orders from Mlle. de Breux.

"To-morrow morning the Duc goes hawking and Mlle.
de Breux, Mlle. Denise and I have accepted to join his
party.   But at the last moment I shall feign illness and Mlle.
Denise will insist on staying with me.   The Duc has no
idea that we have learned of his treachery.   He has arranged to return to Tours by noon and for a series of apparent accidents to prevent Mlle. de Breux and Mlle. Denise
from reaching the rendezvous with you until an hour or
more later.   Mlle. de Breux will go with this hawking party,
so the Duc will not guess that Mlle. Denise has any reason,
other than her anxiety for me, in staying behind.   Now
you, M. de Vois, must reach Tours, coming in at the Porte
du Nord, by ten o'clock.   Do not bring Father Paul, and
you need not, I think, even disguise yourself.   The Duc
will never dream of your daring to enter the city, and any

one who might recognize you will be away hawking. You must come to my house, which is on the south side of the great square. Take these papers, and if any one questions you pretend you bring them to me from Angers, they will give you a good excuse also for asking the way to my house. Arriving there, show this ring to my steward and he will bring you by a secret stairway to my apartments. Here you will find my own confessor waiting—and Mlle. Denise. And here you shall be married. In the courtyard a coach will be waiting, and afterwards you and Mme. de Vois shall drive away in it from Tours.

"As I have already told you, no one interferes with my actions. My outriders will go with you, you can sit well back in the coach and the guard at the gate will not dare to ask any questions. Once beyond the city my coachmen will take you quickly to Arc. Here you must arrange to have fast saddle-horses ready and on these you must ride to Vois as speedily as you can. You should have nearly reached there, or at any rate be well beyond his vengeance, by the time the Duc discovers what has happened.

"Now, do you quite understand what you have to do, M. de Vois? It is such a simple plan that I do not see how it can miscarry. So au revoir, until I have the pleasure of being a witness at your marriage to Mlle. Denise to-morrow, Monsieur."

And rising, she smilingly extended her hand to him.

Philibert, his heart overflowing with a great gratitude, dropped on one knee as he raised it to his lips.

"Ah, Madame, how can I thank you for all your kindness," he stammered, "you and Mlle. de Breux? Denise and I shall owe all our happiness to you, and I have no words to tell my gratitude."

With a queer little smile Marguerite de St. Caux laid her other hand lightly on his shoulder.

"Do not try and thank me, M. de Vois," she said. "I am only too glad to be of any service to Mlle. de Breux, or to do anything to defeat the Duc's plans. How I hate him!

If you knew how much, you would understand that I want
no thanks for helping you to save Mlle. Denise from him.
Now I must return. The gates of Tours will be open again
by the time I get there, though in any case I have a pass
which would satisfy the guard."

Philibert looked at her with grave anxiety.

"And what will happen to you and Mlle. de Breux after—
after we have left Tours to-morrow, Madame?" he asked.
"I cannot let you both run any risks, even to save Denise
from that snake. The Duc, cheated of one victim, is devil
enough to find substitutes."

But Marguerite turned to him with a quick laugh.

"You need have no fears for us, M. de Vois. The
Duc is, as you say, a devil who stops at little, but there
are some things which even he dare not do, amongst them
to harm Mlle. de Breux or myself. You may drive away
with your pretty bride feeling no qualms for us to-morrow."

They went down the stairs together, and Marguerite,
having swung herself lightly into the saddle without Philibert's proffered assistance, turned her horse's head towards
Tours and, followed by the two troopers, rode swiftly away
into the darkness.

It was still early morning when Marguerite, having
changed horses at Arc, rode into Tours. Going to her
rooms, she had a light meal, and having given orders for
her women to arouse her at eight o'clock, went to bed and
was soon in a deep, dreamless sleep.

Arising at eight she wrote a short note, and having
heavily sealed it gave instructions that it was to be taken
at once to M. de Vrieac. Then, her toilet having been
accomplished with great care, she went into her boudoir
to wait.

Very shortly Rupert was announced.

He entered the room, and having glanced round searchingly, bowed gravely, apparently unconscious of her extended hand.

A faint sparkle of anger gleamed for a second in Mar-

guerite's eyes; then, with rather a wistful smile, she sighed
and, seating herself on a low couch, gazed at him gravely.

"I am glad you have come, M. de Vrieac. I rather wondered if you would."

"I gathered from your note that it was advisable that
I should do so, Madame," Rupert replied, his eyes searching
her face questioningly. "Perhaps you will tell me why I
was favored with your command?"

Again Marguerite gave a little wistful sigh.

"Which you only obeyed because you thought that danger
threatened Mlle. de Breux and I could warn you of it?
Ah, Rupert! Once you would have come to my slightest
call just because *I* gave it. There! You must not look annoyed. I will not mention the past again, though I cannot help feeling sad that you have so changed. Yet, in a
way, you are right to be angry with me, for I changed first.
That is past, but I ask you to believe that I did love you,
Rupert, more than I have ever loved any other man, or ever
shall. I was not true to my love. But when a woman has
ever cared for a man like that, she can never lose interest in
him; there is always a corner left for him in her heart, drift
they ever so far apart. And it is because of that I have sent
for you now. Your face does not look as if you believe me,
but it is true nevertheless. I own that I treated you shamefully, but I was only a child, Rupert. I never knew the
whole shame of my act until too late. Cannot you forgive
me now, Rupert? Was it so great a wrong, Rupert? You
would never have been really happy with me. You would
have soon tired of my silly, vain childishness which once
attracted you. You should marry a clever, loyal woman,
for whom your love would never die away as it has for me,
a woman I mean like Mlle. de Breux."

Marguerite watched him with smiling eyes. Then, rising,
she crossed the room and laid her hand gently on his
shoulder.

"There, you see, Rupert, I have guessed your secret.
Oh, you need not think that so very wonderful! Any

woman could have done so the first time she saw you look
at Mademoiselle. And, Rupert, I am so glad, so very, very
glad. It seems to make my treatment of you not quite
so bad, for, had I never failed you, you would never have
allowed yourself to fall in love with Mademoiselle, perhaps? But I should still like to make what reparation I can,
and so I sent for you. Listen. You know that the Duc
is my friend. But you do *not* know what it costs me to
give him that position, how I hate and distrust him, how
revolting his presence is to me. Yet I must never show
this. Ambroise, my husband, is the Duc's first cousin.
Partly for his sake, I have hidden my real feelings for the
Duc, but lately, it has been principally for yours, Rupert
de Vrieac. Oh, you need not look so astonished or incredulous! In a few minutes you will understand.

"Did you know that the Duc hates Mlle. de Breux?
You cannot have known how much he does so or you
would never have allowed him to come near her. I guessed
this from the first and, so that I could learn if he ever meant
any active harm to you or her, I simulated hatred for her
also. I pretended—ah, Rupert, I could have laughed at my
guile sometimes did it not run so near tragedy—that I was
jealous because you had forgotten your love for me at
sight of her. As though I were the one to raise the cry
of 'Faithless!' But he believed me and would try to play
upon my jealous resentment by reporting attentions and
glances he had seen you give Mademoiselle, little guessing
how it pleased me to hear of them, how glad I was to
know that you had found some one really worthy of your
love. And then, last night, I was rewarded. The Duc told
me a plan he had formed against Mademoiselle, believing
that in me he had a willing accomplice. Yesterday you
rode out with Mlle. de Breux to an inn on the northern
road where M. Philibert de Vois was waiting, did you not?
Mademoiselle went in with him, whilst you remained outside. Do you know what Mademoiselle and M. de Vois
said to each other? Well, I can tell you, for the Duc's spies

overheard it all. Mademoiselle arranged that M. de Vois
should run away with Mlle. Denise. That he and a priest
should be waiting at an old ruined tower in a wood just
beyond the inn, and that Mlle. de Breux would bring Mlle.
Denise there at an hour after noon to-day. There the priest
would marry M. Philibert to Mlle. Denise and they would
then escape to Vois, Mlle. de Breux returning to Tours.

"Now do you know what would happen if those plans
were adhered to? Should Mlle. de Breux try to leave
Tours with Mlle. Denise, the Duc has arranged for a series
of accidents to delay them, but, should they not be deterred
by these, he is quite prepared to use force. And when
M. de Vois, with the priest, reached the rendezvous he would
find a score of the Duc's men-at-arms awaiting them. You
can guess as well as I what would be the end of that interview. Also that the Duc would not feel amiable either
towards Mlle. de Breux or his betrothed, and in such a mood
he is dangerous. I am trying now to make reparation,
Rupert, for the way I have disappointed and flouted you.
You must go to Mlle. de Breux and tell her immediately all
this. Let her send to M. de Vois and warn him to return
home and stay there, for a time at any rate. Then persuade
Mademoiselle to remain quietly at Tours with Mlle. Denise,
as though she neither contemplated any plans against the
Duc or guessed his movements. The Duc will leave Tours
with his company before Mlle. de Breux would have done so.
He will therefore guess nothing, and reaching the rendezvous,
will patiently await M. de Vois—who will not appear. So
Monseigneur will have to return baffled, and it will take him
some time to discover whether his spies have brought him
wrong information, or whether Mlle. de Breux purposely
let them overhear false plans, or whether, at the last moment, M. de Vois was warned.

"And in the meantime we can perhaps think out other
means of arranging Mlle. Denise's marriage, to M. de Vois.
Now go quickly, Rupert, and carry my warning to Mlle.
de Breux. But tell me first that you have forgiven the

wrong I did you and that I have done a little to atone?"

And then for the second time within twenty-four hours Marguerite, looking down at the bent head of a man who kissed her hands with gratitude, smiled to herself with scornful derision.

Leaving Marguerite's house, Rupert hurried in search of Yoeland. There was in his mind not the faintest doubt that Marguerite had been speaking truth, or the least suspicion that, instead of making reparation for her faithlessness, she was burning to punish him for allowing another woman's image to replace hers in his heart.

He found Yoeland alone in a little room overlooking the shady courtyard, and, with an eagerness which made his manner almost brusque, requested an interview. Then waiting neither to choose his words nor prepare her, he poured out Marguerite's story. So intent was he on telling it without loss of time that he failed to notice the expression which had gradually hardened his listener's face. Only when he had at last finished and paused, breathless, for her orders, did he observe it. And his heart leaped with a sudden fear. Very slowly Yoeland rose to her feet, watching him with eyes dark with passion and a great resentment. The jealousy which had swept over her when Anne claimed Rupert as her chosen companion was raging fiercely within her now. Rupert had seen Marguerite de St. Caux. By his voice, his words, he proclaimed his trust in her, his gratitude. He was obviously at that moment burning with admiration for her and expected her, Yoeland de Breux, to be so likewise. For a moment Yoeland stared at him, a dangerous little smile on her lips.

"So! Have you finished your story, M. de Vrieac?" she asked coldly. "Then perhaps you will tell me how you dared to discuss my plans with Mme. de St. Caux? When I took you with me yesterday, it was as an escort, not as a spy. What do you mean by coming to me with this tale of Madame and her efforts to assist Denise and protect me? I desire neither help nor friendship from such a woman as Mme. de St. Caux, and I do not wish to hold any intercourse with her in the future. Also, I do not remember having given you permission to call upon her this morning, M. de Vrieac? You will have the courtesy to mention the fact when you go out in future, and should you seek the society of Mme. de St. Caux, I forbid you to mention my name to her.

"As for this story of yours—and hers! Frankly, I do not believe it. And I am surprised that you should have been deceived by such obvious fabrications. Neither can I imagine what her real object can have been in inventing them. You do not seem to understand the insolence of what you have done; the presumption which you have shown in discussing my supposed plans and arranging for my future actions with Madame. I shall take no steps to verify her story. Both her actions and the Duc's are matters of complete indifference to me. And you, M. de Vrieac, will retire to your room immediately, if you please, and remain there until I send for you."

Completely surprised by the storm of her anger and utterly at a loss to account for it, Rupert made matters worse by a sudden tightening of his jaw.

"Pardon, Mademoiselle," he said quietly, "but I cannot do so now. There is danger threatened to you and Mlle. Denise, as well as M. de Vois. M. le Comte ordered me to guard you. Is it your wish that I shall ride and tell M. de Vois to avoid this rendezvous, or shall I send Carlote, and with some of our men-at-arms go myself to the meeting-place and wait for the Duc's company there? What are your orders, Mademoiselle?"

A very dangerous light burned in her eyes as she faced him.

"I have already given them, M. de Vrieac, and as I have told you, Mme. de St. Caux's intervention is not necessary for either my safety or M. de Vois' to-day. Perhaps it is not only the Duc who has had information by his spies."

Then, turning swiftly, she rang a small hand-bell.

"Send Carlote here and eight of the men-at-arms," she said to the woman who answered. "Now, M. de Vrieac, will you go to your room quietly or must the men drag you there? No! I want neither protests nor advice from you, only obedience. Carlote," she added, turning to the old trooper as he entered with his men, "I wish M. de Vrieac to go to his room. When he is within, you will lock the door and bring the key to me here."

So Rupert, seeing that her anger was something with which he could not cope and that there was nothing else to be done, turned with a shrug of his shoulders and left the room. A couple of moments later, Carlote, who had been in her father's service before she was born and took an almost parental interest in her doings, reëntered the room and, making no attempt to disguise the disapproval on his face, laid a key on the table beside her.

But Yoeland, although she was perfectly aware of his disapprobation and was already beginning to feel ashamed of her jealous outburst, took it up in silence, and Carlote, with a sorrowful shake of his head, went out, leaving her turning the key thoughtfully over in her hands.

CHAPTER XX

A S the door of Marguerite's boudoir closed behind Rupert, the thick curtain drawn across a small recess in one corner was pushed aside and the Duc stepped into the room. He met Marguerite's glance with a grimly amused smile and bending before her, raised her fingers to his lips.

"Ciel, Margot!" he cried, "you are altogether wonderful. But I would not be your enemy, ma mie. The poor young man! How basely you deceived him! And how the fool took it all for solid fact. Let us hope that he will be equally successful in convincing Mlle. de Breux of your truthfulness. And now, what next, Margot? For you are managing this play. I can only look on and admire profoundly the cleverest actress in all France."

With a soft, rippling laugh Marguerite swept him an elaborate curtsey.

"You flatter me, I fear, Monseigneur. You also forget that the victims of my guile were not very difficult to deceive. I was careful to mix some truth and a good deal of probability in my tales, and neither Rupert de Vrieac nor Philibert de Vois are amazingly clever, you will own. Had it been yourself, I fancy I should have had harder work to carry conviction of my sincerity. And now it is nearly ten o'clock. You must retire again to your recess and draw the curtain, whilst I clear the stage for the great marriage scene of M. Philibert de Vois. And when that is over, then my acting will be over also. The second part of the play is your affair. I shall only look on—to admire and be amused. So away with you, Henri. M. de Vois must not see even your shadow. You are supposed to be hawking, you know."

"And you to be upon a bed of sickness," laughed the Duc,

"I trust that your malady will soon cease, Margot. In the meantime where is your consoler and nurse, Mlle. Denise?"

"She is at present in my garden wild with jealousy and bitterness against Mlle. de Breux, for I told her that her cousin had been having secret meetings with Philibert de Vois. As soon as he comes I shall send for Denise and have them married. Then into the coach and out of Tours with them, to clear the stage for your play, Monseigneur. They will soon, no doubt, discover that there are many discrepancies in the stories I have told them both. But that will not matter then, and I do not suppose that they will greatly care."

"I am torn between my desire to kill this fool de Vois and my anxiety to enrage the Vicomte," said the Duc slowly, "but I think the latter is the stronger. Besides, I shall no doubt be able to do both. It will suit me just as well to kill de Vois some time hence, and it will be a strange thing if, sooner or later, I cannot get him into my power. So we will let this marriage go forward, and as soon as the fools are away from Tours, I will send a messenger to tell the Vicomte that de Vois has actually dared to carry off my betrothed from the heart of my own city, whilst Denise, ignoring her father's commands, has gone with him gladly. Dieu! how he will rave when he hears that all his grand dreams for making his daughter a Duchesse have crumbled to pieces. And he will never imagine that I have arranged it. All the world knows how anxious I was to marry his daughter; the whole town saw how, when we came from Briege, I made her ride in beside me that the people might acclaim my future wife. But some day I shall have a quiet talk with M. le Vicomte, and then I shall tell him the truth. Ah! I shall enjoy that interview, almost more than I shall presenting you with those diamonds to-night, Margot."

A swift avaricious gleam shone in Marguerite's eyes, but before she could speak a soft knock sounded on the panel hiding the secret stairway into her room. Silently the Duc fled to his recess, and Marguerite, having drawn the curtain across, cried, "Entrez !"

Softly the panel slid back and her old steward stepped into the room.

"M. de Vois is here, Madame," he announced, and standing aside, motioned to Philibert to come in; then, entering the stairway once more, he descended, closing the panel behind him.

With a swift glance round, Philibert crossed the room to Marguerite's side, bending to kiss her extended hands.

"You see, Madame, that I have come, but where—where is Denise, and—and—— ?"

Marguerite interrupted him with a soft laugh.

"You need feel no anxiety, Monsieur. Both Denise and the priest are close at hand. And all has happened as we hoped. The Duc is hawking, with Mlle. de Breux. He will not return until noon, by which time you and Denise will be safely away. I thought it best not to tell Denise that you were coming or what we proposed to do. She might have betrayed her happiness to some of the Duc's spies and made them suspicious. But now that you are safely here, M. de Vois, I see no reason for delay. So I will send for Denise—and Father Crezier."

A few minutes later, Denise, in answer to a message from Marguerite, came into the room. She paused with a startled cry as she caught sight of Philibert de Vois, and the next second was wrapped in his arms. Turning her head, she looked at Mme. de St. Caux with shining eyes.

"Oh, Marguerite, what a lovely surprise ! And you never whispered a word of it. But how has Philibert come? Is it safe for him to be here?"

And she glanced round apprehensively.

Crossing the room, Marguerite took the girl's face between her hands and kissed it softly.

"Yes, dear, you may rest at ease. Be very sure that I should not have allowed your M. Philibert to come had there been any danger. I have made certain that the Duc is safely away, and no one can interrupt us here. Now I will tell you why M. de Vois has come, little one. You know that the Duc is both cruel and cunning. He might—nay, he probably would—have tried to force you into a marriage with him either to-day or to-morrow, at a few hours' notice. There was only one way to prevent such a thing and that was for you to marry M. de Vois first. Therefore, I told M. de Vois to come here, and Father Crezier is waiting now to marry you to him, Denise. Then you shall both get into my coach, which is ready in the courtyard, and drive safely away to Vois, where you will live happily ever afterwards. Come, dear, the sooner this ceremony is over and you start from Tours the better, for you must be far away before the Duc learns what has happened. Stand here, Denise, and you beside her, Monsieur. Gilbert, my steward, and I will be your witnesses. Now, father," turning to the tall, thin-lipped priest who had silently entered the room, "we are ready. Have it as short as possible, for time presses."

So Philibert de Vois and Denise were made husband and wife, whilst Marguerite and the old steward stood by, and the Duc, peering through a slit in the curtain, watched the ceremony with a sour, derisive smile.

When the few words which had made them one were spoken, Philibert caught Denise to his heart.

"My little love. My wife," he whispered. "Thank God no one can take you from me now."

Then as the priest and Gilbert left the room, he turned and, one arm still around Denise, caught Marguerite's hand, raising it in a passion of gratitude to his lips.

"Ah, Madame, how can I ever thank you for all your kindness," he stammered.

And Marguerite, gently withdrawing her hand, gave a low laugh.

"By not attempting to do so, Monsieur. It is thanks enough for me to see your happiness. There, there, dearest," as Denise's arms clung round her neck and a soft cheek was pressed against her own, "you must hurry away now. There is really no time for delay. The coach is ready. Come."

"Oh, Marguerite, how sweet you have been to me. I never dreamt that I could be so happy. I am not going to try and thank you, for I never could. And must we really go now? Without saying good-by to Aunt Charlotte and—and Yoeland?"

"Yes, dear, I think you must," Marguerite replied gravely. "I will say good-by for you, and they will both understand and be glad, I know. I did not want Mlle. de Breux to be present now, for the reason you know, Denise, and I am afraid I never thought of Mme. Charlotte. Do not trouble yourself. I will explain all to them. You must both go now."

But Philibert hesitated for a moment.

"Mme. de St. Caux, are you quite sure that you run no risk from the Duc's vengeance for your goodness to us?" he asked seriously.

Marguerite nodded.

"I am quite sure," she answered, smiling quietly.

"And Mlle. de Breux? You will try and tell her a little of my gratitude for the happiness which I owe to her and you?"

Marguerite nodded her head again with the same quiet smile.

"Yes, Mlle. de Breux shall know everything very soon," she replied.

And then they went with her to the waiting coach.

When Marguerite returned from having started Philibert and Denise upon their journey, she found the Duc seated at a little table idly playing with some dice.

"Well?" he inquired, without looking up, as she entered the room.

"Have they gone?"

"Yes, they have gone," she replied, "they must be out

of Tours by this time. Do you know, Henri, I am glad
that you did not keep to your first plan of having M. de
Vois killed when he came here. They love each other
absurdly much, those two, and are so happy now. Their
devotion is, of course, extremely foolish, but I confess to
having found it also rather pathetic—and amusing."

The Duc glanced up at her curiously.

"You seem to have been quite moved by the touching
sight, Margot," he said. "It is perhaps a good thing that
you will not see those fools in a month's time, they will be
fighting like wild cats then."

Startled by her own momentary rush of feeling, Marguerite shrugged her shoulders.

"Oh, I dare say they have begun to quarrel already.
It is quite possible that, by the time they reach Arc, they
will no longer care for each other, and Denise may return
in my coach!"

"I sincerely trust that she will not," the Duc replied,
tossing out the dice across the table. "I have arranged
for another passenger to return in that, you know. Besides, I should wish that when the time comes for me to
pay my reckoning with Philibert de Vois, Denise should still
care for him. Why, I shall be robbed of half my revenge
if his death does not break her heart. And now, ma mie,
we have a little interval to ourselves before we can pass to
the second part of our play."

When Carlote had left Yoeland turning the key of Rupert de Vrieac's room absently in her hands, she stood for
a few moments thinking very deeply. Although in her burst
of jealous anger, she had professed not to believe his story,
yet in her heart she knew it was true. Her plans had undoubtedly come to the Duc's knowledge and she had, very
reluctantly, to admit that although Marguerite might have,
and no doubt had, deceived Rupert as to her motive for
betraying the Duc's counterplot, yet the solution for frustrat-
ing it which she had suggested was the only feasible one in

the short time left before Philibert would reach the rendez-vous. He must be stopped from going near the ruined tower, but how could she get a message to him?

She could, of course, send Carlote. He was faithful but rather slow-witted, and if he did not find Philibert at the inn, might arouse the suspicion of the Duc's spies, some of whom would surely be on the watch, and so make the position more desperate than it was already. There was also Rupert de Vrieac. He would accomplish the mission successfully, but a foolish pride deterred her from releasing him and owning that she believed Marguerite de St. Caux's warning. Pride and a growing shame at her treatment of him when his sole thought had so obviously been to serve her; in a man's blunt, unthinking way, he had touched a raw place in her heart, and she had lost control of her temper and common-sense—most unjustly, she now admitted to herself, since her great anxiety had been to hide her love for him and her jealousy of Mme. de St. Caux. Then why should she punish him for hurting a wound of which he did not know?

But although she admitted herself in the wrong, yet pride still kept her from confessing this to him: a certain self-distrust also making her afraid of betraying her heart's secret to the one man who she was determined should never know it. No, Rupert de Vrieac must stay where he was for a time, until she returned from seeing Philibert de Vois.

For she had decided to be her own messenger, fearing to trust such an errand to any other person. Sending for Carlote, she ordered him to get ready her palfrey and with Duras, the only remaining soldier of La Roche, to be her escort into the country.

Riding very slowly and making no effort to conceal her movements, Yoeland left Tours by its western gate and cantered quietly into the country beyond. But having reached the side of a low hill by which she was hidden from any watching eyes and made sure that she had not been followed from the city, she set her horse across country and, reaching the northern road about a league beyond Tours, turned in the direction of Paris; then, followed by Carlote and Duras, rode forward at a hard gallop.

On reaching the inn by the chestnut-trees, she was told that Philibert, with Father Paul, had been there, but that they had left shortly before her arrival, going in the direction of Arc. The landlord, who had been instructed by the Duc's spies what to say should any one come asking for M. de Vois, watched Yoeland with curious eyes as she rode away, then, looking down at the money she had left in his hand, laughed grimly.

"I am afraid you have some bad enemies, my lady," he murmured, "but it was no business of mine to tell you so." And shrugging his shoulders he went back into the inn.

Meanwhile Yoeland, riding towards the old ruined tower, smiled to herself at Philibert's impatience. He had gone to the rendezvous nearly three hours too soon, feeling no doubt that he could endure the torment of waiting for Denise better in the quiet of the woods than under the curious eyes of the inn people.

Poor Philibert de Vois! After all there was to be no marriage for him that day. How had the Duc learned of their plans, Yoeland wondered. His spies must have been at the inn and have somehow overheard her interview with Philibert. But why should the Duc have had her watched? Why should his spies have followed her? And who could they have been? The hostess had seemed such a jovial, homely woman; the host, a little wizened man with a dull, stupid expression, intent upon his work. Perhaps there had been servants or other guests whom she had not seen.

Involuntarily she looked behind. Spies might be following her now. But except for Carlote and Duras, not a soul was in sight, and with a little sigh of relief she quickened her horse's pace. If only she could meet this crisis

successfully and save Philibert from the Duc's plots!—
then, as soon as she returned to Tours she would release
Rupert de Vrieac and, frankly owning her contrition, beg
him to ride to La Roche and fetch the Comte.

They had reached the white bowlder by the roadside
marking the track down to the ruined tower, and Yoeland,
after glancing round to assure herself that no pursuers were
within sight, turned her horse under the cool shadow of the
trees, and followed by Carlote and Duras, cantered down
the grassy track. A few seconds later, reaching a small
clearing, she came within sight of the tower, and gave a
quick sigh of relief, for two horses were tied to the stump
of a tree, and within the deep shadow of the ruin their
riders, wrapped in heavy cloaks, were waiting.

Signing to Carlote and Duras to stop, Yoeland went
forward.

"M. de Vois!" she cried in a low, clear voice, pulling up
her horse.

The taller of the two figures came towards her. At the
same second she heard a fierce cry from Carlote, answered,
it seemed, by twenty others, as figures sprang out from
behind trees and thickets, and she found herself surrounded
by strange, fierce faces, whilst rough hands seized her
habit, dragging her from the saddle.

Turning her head, she saw Duras lying on the ground,
a dagger thrust between his shoulders, whilst Carlote, surrounded by his assailants and streaming with blood, was
still fighting gallantly. But even as she looked, a man behind
got in a savage blow on the back of his head and without a
cry Carlote crashed from his saddle, lying a still, limp heap
at his enemies' feet.

With a gasp of horror Yoeland looked desperately round.

"M. de Vois! Where is M. de Vois?" she cried.

The man whom she had mistaken for him, moved forward
to her side.

"M. de Vois is not here," he said, with an insolent smile,

and unfastening his cloak, suddenly flung its folds over Yoeland's head and shoulders, stifling her cries for help and
pinioning her arms securely to her sides.

"That was well done. Now into the coach with her," he
cried. And Yoeland felt herself half-dragged, half-carried,
apparently to the back of the tower.

Here she was lifted and placed on a cushioned seat;
some one, whose iron grip held the cloak still around her,
sat at her side; a door was banged, and the coach with
many bumps and creaks began to move forward.

The coach had lumbered away up the bridle track, and
gradually the peace of the woods, which had been so suddenly disturbed, settled down once more. A throstle in the
hazel bushes who had abruptly ceased his song to listen,
silent and frightened, to the sounds of conflict, burst forth
again into his clear, lilting melody. A squirrel peeped out
of his little house and withdrew his head quickly. Then,
after a pause, looked out once more. His quick eyes had
seen two strange, dark objects lying on the grass below,
which he knew had not been there before the loud, fierce
noises had sent him hurrying home. And the squirrel was
not going to run any risks by approaching those things until their harmlessness had been proved.

But a robin, whose instinct for danger was less keen,
because less needed, hopped down from a holly tree, his
curiosity aroused by the same sight. Perching on a branch
just above, he looked down with bright, alert eyes. "Peep!
peep!" he called cheerfully, but neither of the strange things
moved, lying silent with the dark stains on the grass beneath them and on their clothes and skins.

Two rabbits, hopping cautiously forward, joined the
robin in his survey, but none ventured very near, for both
birds and animals had caught the warm scent of blood
and were intently on the alert for danger. Then, in an
instant, the throstle's song was hushed, whilst, with a flash
of white, the rabbits vanished, the squirrel hurried to his

hole, and the robin fled, for one of the strange things had stirred. Just the slightest twitch of a hand, hardly a movement, but enough to scare the forest folk.

And then the robin, safe on a high branch of the tallest oak tree, cocked his head inquiringly on one side and watched Carlote slowly struggle back to consciousness.

At first he did no more than fling one arm out wildly, then gradually, with agonized effort, he raised himself on one elbow, gazing vacantly round. Sinking back on the grass once more with a gasping groan, he lay quiet for a long time, staring up at the trees above him. At last with many winces of pain he sat up, and in reviving consciousness examined his injuries, binding the worst up roughly.

Then, very slowly and painfully, he crawled over to Duras. But here was no chance of any revival. A deep knife thrust between the shoulders had put Duras beyond all further action.

For a moment Carlote stared down at the dead face, whilst softly but with bitter intent, he cursed their assailants. Then, lifting his head, he looked anxiously round. Beside him, deep in the grass, were two tracks—one coming, the other going—of a coach, that coach into which, whilst in a state nearly unconscious and mistaken in their haste for death by his assailants, he was dimly aware having seen men lift Mlle. de Breux. And they had driven her away in it, whilst he lay, a helpless log, unable to save her.

Well, he could move a little now at any rate, and it behooved him to see if he could not yet help his mistress.

So, very, very slowly, with many pauses and stifled groans, he began to drag himself up the bridle track towards the road.

CHAPTER XXI

BARELY twenty minutes after Yoeland had ridden out of Tours, Blaise Blas, having gained admittance to the house by an invented message from the Duc, knocked at Rupert's door.

"Monsieur! Monsieur de Vrieac!" he called almost imperatively, "it is I, Blaise Blas, and I must see you at once, if you please."

"Then you will have to open the door yourself, Blaise," Rupert's voice answered from within. "I am locked in. Can you see the key anywhere?"

"No, Monsieur, but if you will keep well back from the door I will burst it in," Blaise replied.

And picking up a heavy chair from the passage was soon as good as his word.

He stepped into the room, looking at Rupert with anxious, questioning eyes. But although he understood Blaise's curiosity and indignation at the affront put upon him, Rupert offered no explanation of his imprisonment.

"Well, Blaise," he asked, "what is it?"

Glancing hastily into the passage to make sure there were no listeners, Blaise came to his side.

"I thought perhaps you would wish to know, Monsieur, that Mlle. Denise left Tours by the Porte du Nord about half an hour ago with M. de Vois. One of my men was on duty at the gate and saw them."

"Mlle. Denise left Tours with M. de Vois!" Rupert cried incredulously.

"Yes, Monsieur, in a coach belonging to Mme. de St. Caux."

"But that is impossible, Blaise. I was with Mme. de

St. Caux not an hour ago, talking of M. de Vois. She would have told me if he were in Tours. Your man must have been mistaken."

Blaise shook his head.

"Your pardon, Monsieur, but I do not think so. Michel is no fool and knows M. de Vois perfectly well. The coach certainly belonged to Madame. The servants wore her liveries. It also started from her hotel, Monsieur."

"But—but—I do not understand what it means," cried Rupert, utterly at a loss. "I wonder if Mlle. de Breux knows? I must go and see her."

Blaise, however, stopped him with a respectful gesture.

"One of the servants told me as I came in, Monsieur, that Mademoiselle had gone riding about half an hour ago and had taken Carlote and Duras with her."

Rupert turned, looking at him with startled eyes.

"Where has she gone?" he cried sharply. "And why? Mon Dieu, Blaise, where *is* Mlle. de Breux!"

"I do not know, Monsieur," Blaise replied, surprised by the seriousness of Rupert's manner, "but I can soon learn which way she went from the guards at the gates. If you will wait here, Monsieur, I will find out and be back in a few minutes."

And not staying for permission he hurried off.

But to wait quietly was just what Rupert felt he could not do. So, having ordered his horse to be saddled ready, he went in search of Mme. Charlotte.

She could, however, tell him nothing concerning Yoeland's movements; and beyond the fact that she had gone riding, with Carlote and Duras for escort, the servants knew no more. But it was with a startled feeling of uneasiness that he learnt Denise had, a little before nine, gone with one of her women to Mme. de St. Caux's house and was, presumably, still there.

Just at that moment Blaise returned with the information that Mlle. de Breux had left Tours by the western gate, taking the road to Angers, but that she had turned off into the meadows behind the little hill just beyond the city and had disappeared from view.

For almost a moment after he heard Blaise Blas' report, Rupert stood perfectly still, staring at the ground wrapped in thought. When he looked up, Blaise was startled by the white intentness of his face.

"Pardieu, Blaise!" he cried in low, troubled tones. "Then Mademoiselle *did* believe Mme. de St. Caux's story, and she has, she must have, gone to warn M. de Vois. She took the western road to deceive anybody who was watching, she could easily go across country and strike the northern one. God alone knows what may have happened to her by now. Carlote and Duras are useless if she comes upon the Duc's men waiting for M. de Vois. We must follow her, Blaise, as fast as possible. Go and get as many of your men as are off duty. And send word to those other twenty to be ready for the slightest call. I will meet you and your men at the Porte du Nord in three minutes. Then we must ride after Mademoiselle. And pray God we shall not even then be too late."

He was just turning away, when a servant approached, bearing a letter.

"From Mme. de St. Caux, Monsieur, and I was to say it was very urgent."

Breaking the seals, Rupert read the brief contents quickly, a puzzled frown puckering his forehead.

"Come to me here at once. The Duc has changed his plans, and Mlle. de Breux is in grave danger. I have also important news to give you of Mlle. Denise. Come immediately.—MARGUERITE DE ST. C."

Folding up the letter, Rupert slipped it inside his doublet, and gave the servant a sign to withdraw.

"Blaise," he said gravely, "I must see Mme. de St. Caux. But do you take your men and go hard after Mademoiselle along the northern road. I will follow as soon as I can.

You may find her at the Inn of the Three Chestnuts, or if not there, at an old ruin amongst the woods on the right-hand side beyond the inn. I do not know the exact place, but I think there is a white stone marking the track down to it, about half a league further on the Arc side. When you have found Mademoiselle tell her your story about M. de Vois and Mlle. Denise (which from this letter of Madame's I gather is quite correct) and beg her to return to Tours to Mme. Charlotte. If she will not consent, you must still bring her back, Blaise, though you will, of course, only use compulsion as a very last resource. Go now and lose no time."

With a grave salute Blaise turned away.

"Yes, Monsieur," he said quietly, as though the orders he had just received were everyday affairs.

Then Rupert, telling a servant to wait with his horse outside Mme. de St. Caux's house, went to learn Marguerite's news.

Blaise Blas, having gathered a dozen of his men together, started off on his quest with all speed. About two leagues from the city he was surprised to see Mme. de St. Caux's coach, with six outriders, returning at a good pace. The blinds were drawn, so that he was unable to see if any one were within, and it did not seem his duty to stop and inquire. His master had given him no instructions concerning Mlle. Denise; it was therefore not his affair if she were inside or not. So letting the coach pass, he hurried on to the inn.

Here the fact that he was in the Duc's livery, and had very cunningly decided to give the weight of the Duc's name to his inquiries, made his task easy. The landlord, who knew considerably more than he appeared to do, answered his questions freely. The lady with her two servants had been there, but not finding the gentleman she sought, had ridden off to the woods on the right-hand side towards Arc. In which direction Blaise made all speed to follow her.

He soon reached the white bowlder, and having drawn his sword and warned his men to be ready for a sudden attack, rode cautiously down the bridle track.

He had not gone very far, however, when he saw a strange sight in front of him. Something, which at first he took for a log, was dragging itself forward, but as the riders drew nearer revealed itself to be a sorely-wounded man, who, raising his head, gave a feeble cry for help. The next second, slipping from his horse, Blaise ran forward and lifted him gently in his arms.

"Carlote! Carlote!" he cried. "What has happened? Where are Mademoiselle and Duras?"

But with closed eyes, Carlote laid his head feebly back against Blaise's shoulder and did not seem to have heard.

Holding him still in his arms, Blaise unfastened the collar of his tunic, and whilst one of the troopers attended to his wounds, carefully poured a little wine down the injured man's throat.

Revived, Carlote opened his eyes and looked round with a vague, puzzled glance. Very gently Blaise held the flask again to his lips.

"Drink some more," he urged, "and then tell us where are Mademoiselle and Duras."

A startled consciousness leaped into Carlote's eyes as he looked at the troopers and then up into Blaise's face.

"You have come too late," he muttered. "Duras is back there. Those devils killed him and they have taken Mademoiselle away in a coach, whilst I lay like a useless fool, unable to stir a hand for her," he added bitterly.

A deep flush of rage spread over Blaise's face.

"A coach!" he cried. "What coach?"

Carlote's forehead puckered in a desperate effort to collect his scattered senses.

"I think it must have been hidden on the far side of that tower," he gasped. "We never saw it when we rode up. And those devils were out on us like a flash. There were nearly a score of them. I think the postillions wore Mme.

de St. Caux's livery, but I could not swear it. I don't
know who the others were."

Then his eyes closed wearily and he sank back once
more into oblivion.

Blaise Blas laid him down very carefully, and rising to
his feet, cursed himself with dispassionate thoroughness.
It was plain now that, had he but known it, Mme. de St.
Caux's coach had had everything to do with his duty, that he
could not have done better than have stopped it. Whereas,
like a fool, he had let it pass on unmolested. The reason
for the drawn blinds was plain enough now, and who had
been concealed within.

Well, by singular good fortune and furious riding, he
might yet overtake it before Tours was reached. But
that would never be if he were hampered by a wounded
man. So, judging that Carlote could tell him nothing
further, Blaise left him in charge of two of his troopers,
telling them to make a litter and bring him into Tours
by easy stages. Then, ordering the rest to mount, he set
off in hot pursuit of Mme. de St. Caux's coach.

But, when at last, they reached the Porte du Nord, he
learnt from the guard that Mme. de St. Caux's coach had
entered more than a quarter of an hour previously.

Blaise had seen nothing of his master, and the only
thing to be done now seemed to seek him out and report the fruitless result of his quest and what had befallen
Mlle. de Breux.

But when Blaise reached the great square, the servant
who was still holding Rupert's horse and who was one
of those two men of Vrieac taking service in the Duc's
guest-house, stopped him with the surprising intelligence
that M. de Vrieac had not yet left Mme. de St. Caux's
house, adding that Madame's coach had just drawn into the
courtyard, the great gates being securely closed behind it.

It was midday, and the streets were deserted, the shutters of the houses being closed in the fierce heat.

Drawing into the deep shadow of a wall, Blaise and

his men held a brief council of war. It was plain that all was not well at the house of Mme. de St. Caux. For their master had certainly never meant to stay there so long. Besides, here was the coach into which Duras' murderers had hurried Mlle. de Breux driving into the courtyard, with Mademoiselle presumably still inside it. And M. de Vrieac's orders had been to bring Mlle. de Breux back to Mme. Charlotte. To do so it was their plain duty to get her away from Mme. de St. Caux's house.

But how to gain an entrance there? The great gates had been closed, and the men of Vrieac were not strong enough to storm them. No. If they were to enter it must be by craft. But how could they do so?

It was then that Pierre Gallon—Pierre Gallon, whose brother had been murdered by the Duc and whose own life had been saved by Yoeland de Breux's care and protection—found a way to pay his debt to both of them.

As Gallon, although he hobbled unsteadily and could do little, belonged to Mlle. de Breux's small, special retinue, and also because since he seemed to belong to her, Gallon included Rupert de Vrieac in the devotion which he extended to all things appertaining to Mademoiselle, Blaise Blas had eyed him with approval. Gallon's hatred for the Duc had been another link between them, leading Blaise at last to confide the secret of the men of Vrieac within the enemy's citadel. He, Carlote and Gallon, had often talked together, discussing plans for vengeance, and Gallon, having been some time in the Duc's service, was able to tell the others many secrets and important details.

It was Gallon who limped up to Blaise now, his face pale with excitement, and the tale he told was listened to in breathless silence.

For Gallon was to marry Angelique, one of Mme. de St. Caux's women, and had just learnt from her that not only were M. de Vrieac and Mlle. de Breux in her mistress' house, but that M. le Duc was there also, and, more ominous still, Angelo Lupi, that misnamed, evil-faced Spaniard who had entered the ducal service with a reputation of being one of the most skillful torturers in Spain. Moreover, all Madame's servants had been ordered to their quarters, and the door of the corridor leading to Madame's apartments was locked. There was something sinister and unusual being planned, and Angelique, who had obtained her information by adroit listening at key-holes and secretion behind curtains, was convinced that harm was intended to Mlle. de Breux, who, as the savior of Pierre Gallon, she adored. So she had sent Gallon forth to fetch help, and he, in a good moment, had found Blaise Blas holding his council of war.

They discussed plans in hoarse whispers for a few seconds. Then leaving the horses in charge of two troopers, Blaise Blas and the rest of his men followed Gallon's limping figure down a small, empty street. They met no one, and no one saw them enter a little gate in the high wall which surrounded Mme. de St. Caux's garden.

Meanwhile Rupert, having seen Blaise start on his quest, hurried across the square to Marguerite's house. Here he was instantly admitted by Gilbert, the old steward, who conducted him to a part of the house away from the great reception rooms. Leading him up a flight of stone stairs, Gilbert paused before a door at the top and knocked softly.

"Entrez!" cried a voice within, and opening the door, Gilbert stood aside to let Rupert pass.

His mind filled by anxiety for Yoeland, Rupert stepped absently over the threshold. The next second he received a strong push from behind, something caught his ankles and he fell forward heavily on his face, whilst from either side men sprang upon him, pinioning his arms firmly, binding his knees and forcing a gag into his mouth. Then lifting him, they placed him, helpless and flushed with rage, against the wall, and silently left the room.

Dazed by the sudden assault, Rupert blinked with vague eyes, then suddenly became aware that at the further side of the room, watching him with mirth-filled eyes, sat Marguerite de St. Caux and the Duc de Tours. A deeper red burned in Rupert's face and, as his blazing eyes met the Duc's the latter rose with a grave bow.

"Welcome! You are thrice welcome, M. de Vrieac. I hope you are quite comfortable? Those fellows have not pulled the thongs too tight or sent the gag too far down your throat? Very well then, Mme. de St. Caux and I wish to have a little talk with you. You fool!" he continued, all the suavity gone from his manner and a very cruel smile twisting his lips. "You meddling, insolent fool! And you came to the trap as easy as a fly!—To hear news of your dear lady of Breux, eh? Well, I have pleasure in telling you that I hope, I fondly believe, that she is at this moment on her way here, and when she comes I expect to spend a very amusing half-hour, with your assistance. Indeed, I fancy I can hear sounds of her arrival now. I must hurry out to greet her. You, M. Fool, will stay here with Mme. de St. Caux, who has, I believe, also a few words to say to you."

For a few seconds after he had left the room, Rupert and Marguerite gazed at each other in silence.

Then Marguerite rose, and coming very close, smiled down at him with mocking eyes.

"Yes, she is indeed coming," she said softly, "this haughty, beautiful Mademoiselle, whom you love very dearly do you not, M. Rupert de Vrieac?"

Then, as she looked into his grave, steady eyes, her own suddenly blazed with a furious anger. "And you thought I admired her and really wished your happiness with the proud hussy! You fool!" she whispered fiercely, "you fool indeed! I will show you that Marguerite de St. Caux is not so lightly to be forgotten and cast aside. By this, and this!"

And snatching up a little riding-switch she struck him passionately across the face. Then as Rupert, blinded and wincing with pain, leant his head back against the wall, Marguerite stood and surveyed him with cruel eyes.

CHAPTER XXII

IT seemed to Yoeland a very long time that the coach jolted and swung on its way. Once or twice, through the thick folds of the cloak, she fancied hearing a louder beat of hoofs, as though they were passing horsemen. But common-sense told her the uselessness of trying to attract help. The man at her side still held the cloak firmly round her and she could not tell how many more of her captors were also at hand. There was nothing she could do but sit still and wait—and think.

But though her brain was working desperately she could find no answer to the puzzle of her present position. Who her assailants were she could not guess, though she suspected that they must be the Duc's men. If that were so, had they been sent to the ruin to await Philibert de Vois and had perhaps, in the shadows of the wood, mistaken her company for his until too late to retreat and leave her unmolested? Or were they waiting there with a general order to carry off any one who came to that place within a given time? In any case her woman's heart felt gratitude that she had come herself instead of sending Rupert de Vrieac into the danger, for he might then have been lying still and cold like poor Carlote and Duras. And she shuddered, then smiled a little, as she thought of the key which was in her pocket. He, at any rate, was safe. Behind that locked door he could come to little harm. But how he must hate her! Never again could she scorn Marguerite de St. Caux for her treatment of him. Her own had been as bad, or worse. For she loved Rupert de Vrieac, whilst Marguerite had done what she did through lack of love.

And yet, although she had slighted and humiliated him,

he had never once shown the scorn and loathing he must feel for her. Self-controlled, unfailingly courteous, he had obeyed her slightest wish without a murmur, always clever, dependable, and how brave! She thought of him as he had been that night at Briege, when, desperately wounded, he held the stairway against the men of Tours, held it in her defense. And how had she repaid him? By cold disdain, because he dared to love another woman! He had certainly had little reason to love Yoeland de Breux. And so, jealous and unjust, she had heaped insults and humiliations upon him. She knew the pettiness of it all now. If she could only tell him, ask his forgiveness, bear something for him in reparation.

The jolting rumble of the coach seemed to be going on incessantly, but suddenly the pace slackened, and the coach appeared to pass over some wooden hollow structure.

Immediately after, the swaying and bumping increased and Yoeland's heart began to beat tumultuously for she knew that they had crossed a bridge and were rolling over the cobbled streets of a city. Then, quite abruptly, the coach stopped, she heard men's voices talking round her and suddenly felt herself lifted in a powerful pair of arms and carried up a long flight of steps. She made no attempt to struggle or free herself. If she were to go, and that was obviously unavoidable, pride made her wish to do so as dignifiedly as possible. Besides, it was useless to rebel, the arms which held her felt as though they had the strength of steel, although, being neither very small nor slender, it gave Yoeland a certain satisfaction to know that their owner could not find her a fairy weight. At the top of the stairs she was placed upon her feet and led down a seemingly unending corridor, then into a room and a deep, high-backed chair. Here the cloak was adroitly slipped off and she was able once more to see and breathe freely.

For a second she looked around her with dazed, puzzled eyes. The room in which she found herself was large and richly furnished, but entirely strange. Then as her eyes roved round, they fell upon the Duc de Tours, who, seated in a chair opposite, was quietly awaiting her discovery of him. As their eyes met he rose and swept her a stately bow.

"Welcome, Mademoiselle," he said quietly, "though I fear that you have had a somewhat—er—compulsory journey here. But I trust you will pardon that as a sign of our great desire to have your company?"

Yoeland looked at him with steady, alert eyes.

"Were those your men who brought me here?" she asked.

"They were, Mademoiselle."

"They have killed my two servants and treated me as though—as though I were a sack," she continued, a slight tremble of indignation in her voice. "I presume that they were carrying out your instructions, Monseigneur?"

"Yes, Mademoiselle, they were," he replied suavely. "At least, the instructions which I gave them if you chanced to come riding by the old tower this morning. I had made other arrangements should you send some one else, M. de Vrieac, for instance."

A quick little flush swept over her cheeks at his name. Thank God for that key in her pocket, and that he was safely away from harm! She spoke, however, in the same level tones.

"Indeed, Monseigneur, and why?"

The Duc smiled gravely.

"I have told you already, Mademoiselle. Because we were very anxious for your company here. And perhaps you will also permit me to ask you one question?" he continued, a little of the suavity dropping from his manner. "Why were you at the old tower this morning? Nay, I know the answer to that already. Why then did you meet Philibert de Vois yesterday and arrange with him to marry and take away Mlle. Denise, my betrothed?"

With a sudden quickening of her heart Yoeland realized that all pretense was at an end now, but she never flinched or altered her manner in the least as she faced him.

"Because I did not, do not, consider that you are capable of making Denise happy, Monseigneur, and I think M. de Vois is more suitable and worthy to be her husband."

The Duc shrugged his shoulders with a gesture of helplessness.

"Alas, Mademoiselle, I fear you have a very poor opinion of me, but I hope that you will believe me when I say that I too have thought the same. Therefore—and indeed, Mademoiselle, I trust that this may lead you to think a little more kindly of me in the future—I have ventured to forestall your plan and this morning, with the aid of that most accomplished lady, Mme. de St. Caux, I arranged for M. de Vois to come here and be married to Mlle. Denise. They left Tours in Madame's coach—the same, by the way, which brought you here, Mademoiselle—man and wife four hours ago and were driven to Arc. There they took horse to Vois, where they may, perhaps, live happily ever afterwards. I do not know. My part is done. I had them properly married."

A scornful little smile curled her lips as she looked at him.

"I do not believe you, Monseigneur," she said simply.

He threw out his hands in mock despair.

"Alas, Mademoiselle, I feared it would be so. And yet I am, for once, speaking honest facts. Mlle. Denise is at this moment indeed Mme. de Vois, riding home with her husband. I can call the priest who married them, the witnesses who were present, or send for the guard who saw them leave Tours. Will that convince you, Mademoiselle?" In spite of herself his manner carried conviction. Yet the thing seemed incredible, the very last action one would attribute to Henri de Tours.

"And why, supposing it took place, did you arrange this marriage, Monseigneur?"

He looked at her quizzically, a malicious gleam in his one eye.

"Shall we be inventive, Mademoiselle, and say that I

was touched by Denise's innocent beauty and breaking heart, so, rather than blight her life by linking it to my wicked and agéd one, I sacrificed myself and gave her to the young and handsome knight of unsullied record whom she loved? Or shall we speak the truth and say that as I no longer wanted her it suited me for another man to take her? I had really a number of reasons for my course of action, but you need only know three. The first I have just given you, Mademoiselle. Then secondly, I wished to annoy M. le Vicomte, and the news of his daughter's marriage to M. de Vois and consequent inability to become Mme. la Duchesse de Tours will, I fancy, do so very thoroughly. He is a proud, ambitious fool and hates de Vois. The third reason is that it will be necessary for me to have a good explanation to give the world for my conduct when, as I intend to do a few months hence, I get Philibert de Vois into my power and with Angelo Lupi's help, kill him— unpleasantly. We are becoming so particular in these days that one must have an excuse for killing a man in cold blood. But who could have a better than that he stole my betrothed from me? Why, St. Michael himself would not rest quiet under such an insult!

"No doubt the world, not knowing it was my pleasure to arrange the whole thing, will laugh when it hears how my betrothed was carried off by her lover from the very heart of my city of Tours. And because·I do not choose that it shall laugh, even mistakenly, at me, I have decided to show how little I care, by being married myself to another lady in a few minutes. It has been my intention to make her my wife for some time. Hence my willingness that Denise should become Mme. de Vois, since a man may not marry two women at once. You do not seem· at all surprised, Mademoiselle, or ask who ·my bride is to be?"

"No, Monseigneur, I feel no interest in your amours," she answered coldly.

A little flush of anger crept into his cheeks and his eye

flashed dangerously, though, when he spoke, his voice was very quiet.

"I am always loath to contradict a lady. But in this case you are mistaken. My 'amour,' as you are pleased to call it, holds great interest for you, since it is Mlle. Yoeland de Breux whom I intend to make my wife."

She lifted her head a little higher, watching him with grave eyes.

"I think you must be mad, Monseigneur," she said.

"Perhaps, Mademoiselle," he replied, with a careless shrug of his shoulders. "I know a man who believes that every one in the world is mad, except himself. Yet his friends are ready to swear that he is madder than anybody. We will let it pass at that. Though I must confess that your mode of receiving my—my declaration is unusual and rather disconcerting. I know of many a woman who, had I asked her to be my Duchesse, would have deemed me a man of good sense. But I ought to have expected that. For it was your difference from other women which first— charmed me, Mademoiselle. I should have put my—my wish another way. Let me do so now. Mlle. de Breux, I lay at your feet my name, my position, my wealth, begging that you will deign to accept them, together with my most unworthy self. Will you be my Duchesse, Mademoiselle? Will you marry me?" And coming forward, he knelt before her in an attitude of humble supplication. But with a quick movement Yoeland pushed back her chair, drawing her skirts away from his touch.

"I must decline, Monseigneur, since I would as soon marry Judas Iscariot," she cried. And for one brief instant they gazed at each other, the antagonism in both their souls laid bare. Then, with a shrug of his shoulders, the Duc rose from his knees and, flicking the dust from them, nodded his head gravely.

"Very good, Mademoiselle. I have tried to treat you courteously, but since it seems that you like plain speaking, I too will be honest and say that my request was a mere form. I was convinced that you would refuse. But I intend that you shall marry me, nevertheless. Your reference to the Iscariot, instead of angering me, as you no doubt intended that it should, fills me with satisfaction, since it implies that you will find marriage with me distasteful. And that brings me to my reason for making you my wife. You feel curious on that point? You must be, since such a project has, I feel certain, never occurred to you. And I flatter myself that it is quite a novel one. Mademoiselle, do you remember one day at Briege we went riding, you, Mme. Charlotte, Mlle. Denise and myself, and a child stoned Marcus? I meant to give the brat a lesson, but you prevented me—by a cut from your riding-switch. Again, the next day, when some one had removed the stepping-stones, I helped to carry you across a stream, and afterwards you mocked at my wet shoes? And do you remember that night when my rebel fellows went mad and tried to storm the stairway? You took no trouble to conceal your scorn of me because I did not dash out and do prodigies of valor beside de Vriac and the men of La Roche, thereby inflaming the attackers' fury and activity tenfold by the sight of me? And, once more, when I, in jest, proposed a plan to punish Pierre Gallon, you did not hesitate to tell me that I had a 'fiend's heart.' Indeed, you have never troubled to conceal your scorn and dislike of me. You have heaped a thousand other slights and insults upon me. And I am only a man, a madman if you will. I have, naturally, been angered and astonished by your treatment of me. No other woman have I ever met who would not, however much she loathed me, have concealed the fact to my face. But as I said just now, you are different from other women. You have courage and intelligence and opinions of your own—I have often wished that you would not display some of them quite so openly; I have been made bitterly angry and ashamed by your treatment of me—and also extremely curious—curious to know how strong your spirit is, how

much it would take to tame you. And for this reason I
wish to marry you. It will not be long before I find ways
to teach you that it is neither polite nor wise to show a man
how much you may scorn or hate him, especially when that
man is Henri de Tours. Now, Mademoiselle, I ask you
once more—will you marry me?"

"No, Monseigneur, I will not," she replied, looking at
him with steady eyes.

He shrugged his shoulders as though at the answer of
a petulant child.

"That is unfortunate, Mademoiselle, since it is my firm
intention that you shall do so. Therefore, if you will not
consent willingly, I shall be obliged to take steps by which
I may persuade you to—change your mind. I deeply
regret having to do so, but since your disinclination seems
to be strong, I cannot help myself."

Crossing the room, he rang a little bell. Instantly a tall,
swarthy man, Italian or Spanish by his looks, entered.

"Lupi," said the Duc quietly, "ask Mme. de St. Caux if
she will favor us with the pleasure of her company; also
Father Crezier. Then take your two men and bring M. de
Vrieac down here."

With a low bow the man left the room and the Duc
turned, to find that Yoeland had risen to her feet and
was staring at him with wide, apprehensive eyes. Cool
and fearless for herself, she had been overcome by sudden
panic at the sound of Rupert's name.

"M. de Vrieac, Monseigneur?" she questioned in a low,
strained voice.

"Yes, Mademoiselle. M. Rupert de Vrieac, your Huguenot—servant. We have him upstairs, and I bade Lupi
bring him down," he answered, watching her closely and
smiling with quiet satisfaction as he saw the fear in her
face.

"But how can you? How can he be here?" she cried.
"I had him locked into his room and here is the key. He
could not get out!"

"He has contrived to do so, however, Mademoiselle. Perhaps he had another key or climbed from the window. He is most certainly here. You will be able to see him for yourself in a few seconds."

Just then the door opened and Marguerite de St. Caux, followed by a tall, sallow-faced priest, entered the room. The two women gazed at each other without greeting, antagonism in their eyes. And so, for a few seconds, the four stood silent, waiting.

Then the door was opened again and two men, carrying the bound figure of Rupert de Vrieac between them, came in.

Crossing the room, they set him roughly in a large iron chair, as Lupi returned, bearing a brazier of burning charcoal and several iron instruments, which, although she had never seen them before, made Yoeland shudder convulsively, as their probable purport flashed across her mind.

Rupert was absolutely helpless, being securely bound and gagged, and the horrified look which leaped into his eyes when he caught sight of Yoeland was reflected in hers as she gazed at him.

Then Lupi, having closed and locked the door, the Duc turned to Yoeland with a deep bow.

"Now we are ready to begin. But first allow me to present some of the present company to you, Mademoiselle. Mme. de St. Caux and M. de Vrieac you already know, but this is Father Crezier, who married Denise to Philibert de Vois and is ready to do a similar office for you and me. And this is Angelo Lupi. You may not have heard of him before, but he has just returned from the Low Countries, where he had been serving the Spanish Army and. where he made quite a reputation for himself, with the aid of a brazier and a few instruments like those you see there, as a converter of heretics. Those two burly fellows are his assistants. Now, Mademoiselle, once more—will you marry me? I beg of you to think well before you answer."

"I have already told you, Monseigneur, that I will not

marry you under any circumstances," she replied quickly, hiding beneath a calm exterior the apprehensive doubts which filled her.

The Duc shrugged his shoulders carelessly.

"Very well, Mademoiselle, then we must see what we can do to persuade you to change your mind. Perhaps when M. de Vrieac has been in Lupi's hands for a few minutes you may think differently. You have á kind heart, I know, and it will not be pleasant for you to see him tortured—even though he is the—er—enemy of your house! Yet unless you agree to marry me now, that is what will happen. And 'Lupi has some very painful little tricks, I assure you. But the moment you consent to do as I ask and Father Crezier has married us, I give you my word of honor that M. de Vrieac shall be liberated and allowed to leave the city safe and unharmed. Now, Mademoiselle, what do you say?"

Now there was horror in Yoeland's eyes. "You are mad," she cried. "You dare not do this. You forget that I am not a common village wench, that I have powerful friends whom you can ill afford to raise against you. I warn you to be careful what you do, Monseigneur."

She looked very beautiful as she stood there, her eyes flashing with indignation. Henri de Tours glanced at her in admiration, then shook his head with a tolerant smile as though she were a petulant child.

"Pardon, Mademoiselle, but it is you who have a wrong estimate of my power. You forget that here in Tours I am as much king as Charles is in Paris. More so. For he cannot depend on the obedience of any, whilst my servants know better than to disobey my smallest order. As for your powerful friends, Mademoiselle——! The thought of their possible animosity does not cause me great alarm. I have said that I wish to marry you and I intend to do so. It is merely a question of how soon you will be sensible and yield to my—persuasions. But perhaps you do not believe that I will torture M. de Vrieac? Lupi!" he cried, turning

to the Spaniard, "give Monsieur a few turns of the cord,
to convince Mademoiselle that we are in earnest."

Yoeland caught her breath with a little gasp of dread as
Lupi, crossing to the helpless man, tied a thick piece of
silk round his temples, knotting it firmly at the back of
his head. Then, slipping a stick beneath it, he began to
twist the cord gradually tighter and tighter. She watched
in fascinated horror whilst the veins on Rupert's forehead
swelled and the cord, getting tighter still, bit into the skin.
Then, although he had closed his eyes and sat perfectly
still, a little pucker of pain began to gather on his forehead.
Marguerite de St. Caux, seeing it, slipped softly to the
Duc's side.

"Ungag the fool!" she whispered. "Do you not see
that one groan from him will move her quicker than anything else?"

And the Duc, with an approving nod, gave the order,
telling Lupi at the same time to remove the cord.

"Now, Mademoiselle!" he added sharply, all the suavity
gone from his manner, "which is it to be? Will you consent to marry me, or shall Lupi give M. de Vrieac something
a little more severe? That was a mere nothing."

"You coward!" she cried, trembling with anger and
horror, and would have risen, but one of Lupi's assistants
had, unnoticed, come behind her, and at a sign from the
Duc, slipped a rope over her shoulders. The next second
Yoeland found herself securely tied to her chair, her elbows
fastened helpless at her sides. With an evil little smile the
Duc turned to Lupi.

"What did you find brought those heretic converts of
yours quickest to their senses, Angelo? Try the receipt on
M. de Vrieac. Perhaps it will be equally effective in Mademoiselle's case."

And Lupi, a cruel light glittering in his eyes, gave a hoarse
chuckle.

"Why, Monseigneur, I think this little fellow, heated red
hot and popped into one of their eyes, was as good as any-

thing. There were not many who needed to have it in the other eye also," he replied, picking up a small skewer-like instrument, at the end of which was a little bulb with a sharp point.

"Very well, try that," said the Duc.

But as Lupi thrust the instrument into the brazier and his assistants, going behind Rupert's chair, caught his head, holding it back so that he could not move, Yoeland gave a little choking cry.

"Monseigneur! Monseigneur! You cannot be such a fiend. You cannot! You must not!"

There was a high note of fear in her voice, and the Duc, hearing it, laughed softly.

"Indeed, Mademoiselle, I think it will be the very thing to persuade you. A good idea of Lupi's. Therefore we——"

He paused, a little startled, for Rupert de Vrieac's voice interrupted him.

"Look away, ·Mademoiselle, and do not mind," he cried. "You shall not hear anything, I promise you. And on no account consent to marry that villain. You will save me nothing and condemn yourself to hell. For God's sake stay firm. They cannot keep you here forever, and your friends——"

Then his voice stopped suddenly, as Lupi forced the gag once more into his mouth.

Going to the brazier the Spaniard took out the little instrument, and having tested its heat on a piece of rag, returned to Rupert's side.

A deep silence fell over the room.

Rupert sat perfectly still, staring up at the ceiling with brave, steady eyes, whilst the Duc, his head thrust forward like a hungry bird of prey's, glanced from one to the other of his victims, playing absently with a tassel on his sword hilt.

Then Lupi, with an adroit movement of his finger and thumb, laid back one of Rupert's eyelids, and, the glowing instrument poised ready, bent over him.

At the same second a sharp cry rang through the room and Yoeland, making a helpless little gesture with her hands, looked up in the Duc's face, her own as pale as death.

"Stop him! Ah, stop him, Monseigneur!" she cried "I could not let any one endure that for me. Not that! Not that!"

Then as Lupi, at a sign from the Duc, laid aside his instrument with a regretful sigh, Yoeland continued more calmly:

"If I consent, you will let M. de Vrieac go safely from Tours, Monseigneur? You promise me that?"

"Yes, Mademoiselle," he replied, with a cruel smile. "The moment you are my wife he shall be set free and given a pass out of Tours. I swear that, on my honor."

"Then—then," Yoeland faltered, trying to check the tremble in her voice and keeping her face turned from the passionate protest which she knew was burning in Rupert de Vrieac's eyes, "then I will marry you, Monseigneur. But let it be now, at once, before I can change my mind," she added piteously.

"Pardon, Mademoiselle, but it need never be, unless you wish," said a deep, strange voice behind her.

And Blaise Blas, with his men-at-arms, stepped quietly out of the secret stairway into the room.

Yoeland, making a helpless gesture looked up into the Duke's face, her own pale as death.

CHAPTER XXIII

FOR a moment there was a tense pause. So engaged had all been on the conflict between the Duc and Mademoiselle that none had noticed the silent opening of the secret panel and the men of Vrieac's coming. Now, startled and surprised, all gazed at them in silence; only Rupert, behind his gag, muttered a deep "Thank God!" Then the Duc, his eyebrows drawn in an angry frown, came forward.

"What does this mean, Blas?" he asked sharply. "You had no orders to come. I did not send for you. Go back immediately with your men and do not dare to intrude thus again. You insolent dog, do you not hear my orders?" But Blaise made no motion to obey.

"Pardon, Monseigneur," he said coolly. "I do not take your orders any more. I am of Vrieac and obey Monsieur. I and my men did but take service with you to be near our master. Now, lads," he added, turning to the troopers and making a gesture towards Lupi and his assistants, "tie them up." Then drawing a knife he went over to Rupert, cutting his bonds and removing the gag, whilst a trooper untied the cord which held Yoeland to her chair.

The Duc stood looking on, helpless with surprise and rage, but Lupi was quicker witted. As his two burly assistants were struggling with Blaise's men, he ran to the door, and unlocked it quickly, with the intention of slipping out and raising an alarm. But on the threshold he fell back a pace, for outside three men of Vrieac with drawn swords were waiting. Seizing hold of him roughly, these entered the room and the door was locked once more.

So two minutes after Blaise Blas' coming Lupi and his assistants were lying bound and helpless, Rupert de Vrieac and Yoeland were free, and the Duc found himself standing, his hands securely pinioned behind his back, unarmed and conquered.

The priest, who had retired to the farther end of the room with Marguerite, had shown no signs of resistance, but to prevent any chance of his giving the alarm, they had bound and gagged him also. Then Rupert, who had been holding whispered converse with Blaise, came to Yoeland's side, looking at her with anxious eyes.

"You are not hurt at all, Mademoiselle?" he asked. "No? You are sure? Thank God for that! Then will you go with Blaise, Mademoiselle? I have given him orders and you can trust him implicitly. He will take you to a place of safety."

Now that danger to him was over, Yoeland had recovered her calm stateliness of manner, and fearful lest, in her terror, she should have betrayed her feelings towards him, she set her face with a cold indifference, although, as she noted the weals which Marguerite's whip and the cord had left on his face, her heart ached with love and compassion.

"And you, Monsieur?" she inquired.

Rupert gave an awkward little laugh.

"Oh, I shall stay here for a short time, Mademoiselle," he replied.

A swift flash of fear leaped into her eyes.

"No! No!" she cried sharply, laying a hand on his arm. "No, Monsieur, you must leave here now, or—or—I will not go. Why should you stay? It is madness. You must come away with Blaise and me."

He looked at her with a wistful smile, then, taking the hand which held his arm, raised it to his lips.

"I cannot, Mademoiselle," he said, with gentle firmness. "There is something which I must arrange with the Duc and which I cannot do till you are gone. But I will come, I will follow you very shortly. Blaise will take good care of you. With him and his men you will be perfectly safe.

So please go now, Mademoiselle. Every second you delay increases the danger."

She looked anxiously into his face.

"You will be quite sure to come?" she asked. "And quickly? You promise that?"

"Yes, Mademoiselle," he answered steadily, "I promise to come—as soon as possible."

For a second more she hesitated, searching his face with troubled eyes, then with a grave inclination of her head she turned towards the open panel where Blaise was waiting, and allowed him to lead her down the secret stairway.

Rupert stood perfectly still, watching her go with a strange, wistful little smile, but as the panel closed softly to behind her, he turned back into the room and the smile vanished from his face, leaving it very stern.

The rest of the men of Vrieac had already gone, but before doing so they had, at Rupert's order and much to her indignation, fastened Marguerite to her chair in the same position as that occupied by Yoeland a short time before. So Rupert was alone with his enemies.

Drawing his sword, he ran a finger thoughtfully along the blade, whilst he stood for a few seconds staring at the Duc's white, fearful face with grim enjoyment.

"Your feet are not bound," he said at last, "so come here." Then as the Duc advanced, Rupert caught him roughly by the shoulder.

"Now, Monseigneur," he said, "do you wonder why I did not order my men to slit your throat, as you deserve? Well, I will tell you. First, your death would not have been an edifying sight for Mademoiselle. And, second, I intend to kill you myself. Oh, no, do not shudder like that! I do not mean to stab you with your hands tied. You judge me by yourself when you think that. Besides, it would be too tame—and quick. No, I shall release your hands and give you your sword. Then we will fight and you can make a struggle for your life. But in the end I shall kill you. Be very sure of that. After what you have done to-day I would conquer you were you Bussy d'Amboise himself."

"In other words, you mean to murder me!" cried the Duc huskily, with a white-lipped smile.

Rupert shrugged his shoulders.

"If you like to put it so, Monseigneur, though I call it the justice of heaven on a villain. But no more words. Turn your back to me. Nay, man, you have less courage than a mouse! What do you fear now? I only wish to free your hands. There! Rub your wrists if they feel numb. Now go to that table and get your sword. But remember, if you attempt to give any alarm or attack me before I am ready, I will kill you like a rat."

Then Rupert glanced searchingly at the other occupants of the room. Lupi and his two assistants lay, securely bound and gagged, in one corner, the priest beside them. Marguerite, her hands tied before her, sat in a chair at the far end of the room. The door was locked. They were secure from interruption.

Turning to the Duc, Rupert ordered him sharply to clear a space in the center of the room, and knowing that failure to comply meant a thrust from Rupert's sword, Henri de Tours obeyed.

Now that death, from which only the greatest miracle could save him, was staring him in the face, the Duc showed a calmer bearing than Rupert had expected. The good blood which he inherited from a long line of warrior ancestors was asserting itself a little at the last. But as, the preparations over, Rupert allotted him his place and stood on guard, ready to begin the fight, the Duc made a last bid to bribe off death.

"Is there no price you would take in exchange for your—your revenge, M. de Vrieac?" he asked haltingly. "I have jewels upon me worth thousands of crowns. You could easily take them, bind me again, slip out by the secret stairway and be well away from Tours before the alarm was raised. In any case, I would pass my word not to have you followed."

But Rupert, looking at the white, drawn face opposite to him, laughed.

"I would not forego the pleasure of killing you for a sackful of jewels, Monseigneur," he replied pleasantly.

"But there is nothing certain in this world, and by chance I might kill or disarm you," the Duc persisted, more with the object of delaying the fight and so giving his servants longer chance to rescue him, than from any hope of being able to dissuade his enemy. "Your foot might slip, or your sword snap, or you might turn giddy. And even supposing you do kill me. What advantage will you reap? Revenge gives but a very transitory satisfaction. And, like Mlle. de Breux, I have powerful friends who will never rest until they have captured, and punished, my murderer; which they will do in a very unpleasant manner for him."

But Rupert's face set very sternly.

"You waste your breath, Monseigneur. Better keep it. You will want it sorely in a few moments. I am not so fond of my life that I should greatly care if you or your friends took it. But I am quite determined that there shall never again be any risk of your molesting Mlle. de Breux, and therefore I mean to kill you now even should the consequences to me be as pleasant as you suggest. So on guard, Monseigneur. Look to yourself and kill me if you can."

Then in silence, save for their breathing and the sharp clash of steel, the fight began. Now hope was gone from the Duc's heart and he fought desperately, knowing that the end for him was indeed death, that he had stayed it off so far only because it pleased his adversary to play with him. Dry-lipped, with wide, horror-filled eyes, he fought in a kind of wild desperation, and Rupert had several times to draw back quickly to prevent the Duc impaling himself on his sword.

Watching the drawn, livid face before him, Rupert laughed softly. This was revenge indeed! He felt that he was executing the justice of heaven very effectively and wished that Philibert de Vois might have been present. And Marguerite, watching them with fascinated eyes, was seized by a horrible dread. It was so evident that Rupert de Vrieac intended the Duc's death. And after that what would he do to her, the woman who had tricked and mocked him and who had betrayed him into his enemy's power? A violent shudder shook her and she looked round with desperate eyes. If only she could escape and summon help, could prevent Rupert killing the Duc. With his death all her golden dreams of wealth and power would crumble into nothing. She would even have to speedily leave Tours. For the Duc's brother, Louis de Lothes, who would succeed him, was a bitter enemy of her husband's and had openly proclaimed his opinion of herself in terms which had both enraged and frightened her. There would be neither jewels nor amusement to be had from Louis de Lothes.

Rupert was fighting with his back both to her and the secret stairway. If she could but unfasten the cords which held her and silently slip away down there, she could bring some of the Duc's men-at-arms back by the same way, and, with caution, they could surround and capture Rupert de Vrieac before he was even aware of their presence. Fiercely, silently, she began to work at the knots, careless that the cord cut her flesh, trying to loosen them with her teeth. The man who had tied them had not troubled to make the knots very firm, having a poor idea of woman's strength, and gradually, as she pulled at it, the rope binding her wrists seemed to grow slacker. Then suddenly her heart gave a leap of joy, for she realized that it was a running knot, that she had but to give a strong tug for it to loosen.

A moment later her hands were free and having untied the rope fastening her to the chair, she rose cautiously to her feet.

The cord which Lupi had twisted round Rupert's head had left it dazed and aching, dulling his perceptions, and engaged in watching the Duc's terror, with no thought of her escape, he was utterly unconscious of Marguerite's movements behind him.

Softly she crept forward towards the panel covering the secret stairs. But suddenly she paused, whilst a vivid gleam of excitement leapt into her eyes. Rupert, having lost his own, had not given the Duc back his poniard and it lay on the table by which she was standing. Very carefully she picked it up, glancing apprehensively at Rupert's unconscious back.

The blade was very bright and sharp. How easy to plunge it between a man's shoulders and so repay her debt of hate. Softly she stole forward. The Duc caught sight of her over Rupert's shoulder and, guessing her intention, was seized with panic lest Rupert should hear her. Making a desperate rally, he strove to hold all Rupert's attention.

Closer and closer Marguerite crept. But there was one man whom she had overlooked—if indeed she had ever known him—whom both Rupert and the Duc had ignored in their plans and whom even Blaise Blas had forgotten. As Marguerite moved slowly forward, the panel hiding the secret stairs slid back a fraction, and then more widely, as the white face of Pierre Gallon peered into the room. Having learnt from Blaise that the Duc was still in Mme. de St. Caux's boudoir Gallon had crept up the secret stairs, hoping to find him alone, and, with the long knife stuck in his belt, to avenge his brother's murder and the many wrongs he had himself suffered at the Duc's hands.

Marguerite was almost within reach of Rupert, and her arm was already raised to strike, when there came a sharp cry, the sound of running feet and Rupert heard a fierce scuffle going on behind him. A second later the Duc's guard was brushed aside, he gave a shrill, terrified scream, then his knees bent beneath him and he fell forward with Rupert's sword through his heart. Pierre Gallon, bursting out from the secret stairs, had caught Marguerite in his arms, but he was still weak, and, fighting like a wild cat, she eluded

his attempts to disarm her. As Rupert turned, she twisted
herself round in Gallon's arms, the dagger raised in her hand.
Then like a flash of light it fell, burying two inches of the
point in Gallon's throat. His hands relaxed their grip,
flinging Marguerite to the floor, and with a deep, choking
cry he fell back into Rupert's arms, the blood pouring from
his wound in a spurting, scarlet stream. Very gently Rupert
laid him down. There was nothing he could do. Already
death was glazing the poor fellow's eyes. Dimly he peered
round and Rupert, knowing his story, guessed his thought.

"The Duc is dead, Gallon," he said, speaking very distinctly. And a smile twisted the dying man's lips.

"It was well done, Monsieur," he gasped. "I wish I
had—— Madame there tried to stab you. I am glad I
stopped her. Mademoiselle would not have wished you
harmed and she—was very—good—to me."

Then his eyes closed and with a sigh Pierre Gallon was
dead.

For a second Rupert looked down at the still face, a
lump in his throat and great self-condemnation in his heart.
Gallon had saved his life and he had never even thanked
him. Ah, well! no doubt in the life he had gone to, that
brave deed would be put to Gallon's credit. And the living
still called for his thoughts. It was time to go if he wished
to escape from Tours before the Duc's death was discovered.
Rising quickly, he took up his sword and some rope which
lay on the floor and with a sternly set face approached
Marguerite. She had thrown herself into a chair, shuddering and sobbing, the front of her dress red with Gallon's
blood. As she heard Rupert coming towards her she
cowered back, a horrible fear in her eyes.

"No! No!" she cried hoarsely. "I did not mean to kill
you. I wanted to reach the Duc. Ah! I am glad you
have killed him and that you have escaped unhurt. I
never dreamt that he meant you harm or knew of your
coming when I sent for you. It was he who forced me to
plot against you and Mlle. de Breux, but I always meant

to save you in the end. I always think kindly of you, Rupert."

But there was contempt in Rupert's eyes as he answered her.

"Do you, indeed, Madame?" he asked sternly, pointing to the weals across his face and the bloodstains on her dress. "If those be tokens of your abiding love, then I could have wished that you had hated me. And I must trouble you to place your hands so, whilst I tie you to your chair, more securely than my fellows did. For I wish to leave Tours alive if possible, and your kind thoughts might lead you to set the Duc's men-at-arms on my heels as soon as I had gone from this room. I fancy there is small risk of that now, however. Those knots will take some slipping, and since your servants have had orders not to come till called you may look forward to several hours' quiet meditation. I do not think any of your companions will disturb you either. M. le Duc lies still enough. Oh, have no fear, I do not mean to kill you also. Traitress, apostate, murderess, you are still safe by reason of your sex; although in heaven, when you reach it, I fancy you will not find that saves you from justice, Madame."

Then turning, with a curt bow he entered the secret stairway, drawing the panel to behind him. And so Rupert de Vrieac passed forever out of Marguerite de St. Caux's life.

CHAPTER XXIV

FOLLOWING Blaise down the secret stairway, Yoeland passed with him unseen out of the house and into the great square. Here they found the rest of the troop already mounted and, having assisted Yoeland into her saddle and climbed nimbly into his own, Blaise gave the word to start.

Rupert de Vrieac had given Blaise orders where to take her, and since they were those of the man she loved Yoeland was quite content to follow them blindly. She was rather surprised, however, when they passed the Duc's guest-house—where Mme. Charlotte must be waiting and wondering what had happened to her and Denise—without stopping. Her surprise grew deeper as they turned down a street towards the southern gate of the city, beyond which was the Loire, and beyond the Loire strange country, roughly known as the Huguenots' Land.

"Where are we going, Blaise?" she asked.

And, with a deep light of pleasure in his eyes, "To Vrieac, Mademoiselle," he replied respectfully.

To Vrieac! To his own stronghold! She was being taken there, she, the girl who had mocked and insulted him, the hereditary enemy of his house, the sister of the man who had laid an intolerable, humiliating bondage upon him!

With a hot flush burning in her cheeks, and eyes gazing straight before her, she rode on. She knew now why Mme. Charlotte had been left behind in Tours. Rupert de Vrieac had the cards in his hands. Holding her a prisoner at Vrieac, it would be easy for him to arrange a compromise with the Comte, exchanging her liberty for his own. She knew his honor too well to think that he would break his oath to her brother, but it would not be difficult to force the Comte to accept any terms he might choose to dictate—to save his sister.

And then the red in her cheeks deepened. He had so much to resent, and revenge, not only, least of all, perhaps, from the Comte. It was she who had treated him most shamefully, who had urged her brother to surround him with annoying restrictions, who had tried to turn Anne against him, and had carried him off to Briege out of spiteful jealousy. And now she was being taken to Vrieac! Yet her eyes were very calm and thoughtful as she rode forward.

The dark had fallen some time. Overhead a small crescent moon and a few twinkling stars gave a faint, silver light. Before them through the gloom the road stretched dim and gray. No sound but the rhythmic beat of their horses' hoofs and the loud, mournful hooting of an owl as they passed his home in an old ivy tree, broke the silence.

On and on they went, and every stride of their horses was bringing them further into the Huguenots' Land and nearer to Vrieac.

At last, as they slackened their pace up a steep incline, Blaise Blas rode closer to Yoeland.

"Valens is just before us, down in the next hollow, Mademoiselle. It is only a little place, but there is a decent inn where you could rest. The road beyond goes through marshy woods which it would be better to pass in daylight. A couple of hours' rest would help our horses too, as we cannot get fresh ones at Valens. Would it be your pleasure to stop there then, Mademoiselle?"

She looked at him almost eagerly. Absorbed in her thoughts she had not been conscious of fatigue, but welcomed the suggestion of a halt very heartily, nevertheless.

"If it is safe to do so, I should be glad to stop there, Blaise," she replied.

And a very few moments later they rode down the cobbled streets of the little town.

Halting his company outside the inn, Blaise succeeded in arousing the landlord, and at last brought him, alarmed and disheveled, to the door. Matters were soon explained, and it was evident from the welcome accorded them that Blaise Blas was well known and liked at the inn.

Dismounting, Yoeland entered a little room bright with candles and a newly-lit fire. Here the bustling, kindly hostess set a hastily-prepared but excellent supper, whilst her husband attended to the wants of Blaise and his men downstairs.

But Yoeland ate very little. She felt neither hungry nor tired. At her orders the table had been placed near the window, and having drawn back the curtain, she opened the casement wide, leaning out—listening—into the night. But no sound, save the distant baying of a dog and the crowing of a couple of cocks, proclaiming the hour before the dawn, came through the darkness. With a little sigh she withdrew her head and went back to her supper.

Buoyed up with excitement and having an excellent constitution, the strenuous tangle of events through which she had passed in the last twenty-four hours had had no wearying effect upon her as yet. It had not been any desire for rest which had made her welcome Blaise Blas' suggestion of a halt. All through their ride to Valens her ears had been straining back to catch the sound of a galloping horse behind them, the sound of Rupert de Vrieac's coming. He had promised to follow quickly, he must be close, and so she had acquiesced in a two hours' stay at Valens to give him time to overtake them.

For several moments she sat by the window, listening intently for the sound which did not come. Then, rising with an anxious sigh, she summoned the hostess and, having given orders to be called in two hours' time, was shown to her room.

She did not, however, get into bed, but going to the window, leant out to try once more if she could catch the expected sound. Her brain was too excited and alert for sleep to be possible just then; and she stood for some time gazing up at the starlit sky, letting its peace and stillness flow over her soul.

Suddenly she turned, looking back into the room, listening intently, for she imagined she heard some one move outside her door. Picking up her riding-switch she crossed the room softly, and, slipping back the bolt, peered out into the dimly-lighted passage. Then with a little laugh she pulled the door wider. Blaise Blas, with sword ready, stood on guard outside, and her sudden appearance seemed to surprise him considerably.

He came to her with questioning eyes.

"Is something wrong, Mademoiselle? Shall I get you anything?" he asked.

But Yoeland answered his questions with another.

"Why are you out here, Blaise?"

"Oh, there is no danger at all, Mademoiselle," he replied quickly, evidently thinking that she was alarmed, "but it was M. de Vrieac's order that I should not leave you, and so I am here."

"But if there is no necessity, would it not be better for you to go and get some rest, Blaise?"

He shook his head. "No, Mademoiselle," he said with respectful firmness, "I am not tired; and, besides, those were Monsieur's orders."

So, seeing that she could not persuade him to leave his post, Yoeland wished him "Good-night" and returned to her room.

Here, having merely removed her boots and loosened the collar of her riding-habit, she blew out the candle and lay down on the bed, listening and thinking. One by one the events of the last three days arrayed themselves in her mind. First, her letter to Vois and the answer which Rupert de Vrieac had brought her. Then her interview with Philibert, her efforts to help Denise, and afterwards Rupert's warning from Marguerite de St. Caux, that false, treacherous warning which had made her so shamefully insult the man she loved, and had led them both into the trap prepared by their enemies. Then had come the Duc's attempt to force her to marry him by torturing Rupert, and the horror which grew in her eyes at the thought of that scene changed into a very soft and tender light as she remembered the courage and self-sacrifice with which Rupert had urged her to stand firm in her refusal and to pay no attention to the tortures inflicted upon him.

"Do you really think I would have let them do those terrible things to you," she whispered in the dim light, "even to save myself from the fires of hell?" Ah, what a God-sent relief the coming of Blaise Blas and his men had been, just in time! Then she had ridden out of Tours safe and free, whilst she knew very well that Rupert had stayed behind to punish the man who had tried to harm her. And now before her lay Vrieac and Vrieac's master.

For a moment her breath came quicker. "What Vrieac owes, Vrieac pays." That was the motto of his house. And what a debt of hatred, scorn and evil treatment he owed to her and her people! Yet she lay, wide-eyed, trembling but hoping for his coming, for the sound of a galloping horse bringing the man she loved to his revenge. Gradually, although she did not realize it, weariness crept upon her and so, still listening, she fell asleep.

It seemed to Yoeland that she had hardly closed her eyes before there came a loud knocking on her door and the hostess entered to announce that the two hours had passed.

Having washed, Yoeland smoothed her hair, put on her boots, and, taking up her hat, whip and gloves, went down to a breakfast of which she began to feel very much in need.

She saw nothing of Blaise Blas and his men, but heard the sound of their voices below and had already learnt from the hostess that M. de Vrieac, who seemed well known to her, had not been near the inn. After breakfast Blaise Blas appeared to recommend an immediate start, and at sight of him all the vague fears which had been gradually forming themselves in Yoeland's mind rose to her lips.

"Where is M. de Vrieac, Blaise?" she asked. "Why does he not come? He promised that he would follow us very quickly out of Tours. Can he have passed us while we have been here, do you think?"

"Oh, no, Mademoiselle," Blaise replied, shaking his head decidedly, "I thought of that. He has not gone through Valens to-night. The road to Vrieac leads straight past this inn. I should have heard his horse, I was listening for it."

"Then why has he not overtaken us? Perhaps he was not able to leave Tours, perhaps—ah, Blaise!—he has been caught there like a rat in a trap by the Duc's men?"

But again Blaise shook his head.

"I do not think there is any fear of that, Mademoiselle, unless something unexpected has happened. Monsieur would not take long to finish his little business with M. le Duc and then he would slip from the house, as we did, by the secret stairs. He would not likely be caught in Tours either, for there are still a score of our men there. Some of them were guarding the southern gate as we passed through. They were watching for Monsieur, and had horses ready for him and themselves, the rest were waiting in the square by Mme. de St. Caux's house. But I do not understand why Monsieur has not overtaken us. I made sure that he would. As soon as we get to Vrieac, if he does not come by then, I will take a couple of score of our men and go to meet him."

"But it may be too late then, Blaise," Yoeland cried apprehensively. "If M. de Vrieac is in danger he will want your help as soon as possible. Leave me one man to show the way to Vrieac, and go now, at once, back to Tours with your troopers and see what has delayed Monsieur."

But Blaise again shook his head.

"I cannot, Mademoiselle," he said with respectful firmness. "Monsieur's orders were that neither I nor any of the men were to leave you until you were safe at Vrieac. We must take you there first. It is only six leagues on from here and at Vrieac we can get fresh horses, so that we shall not really lose time. Besides it may not be necessary by then, Monsieur may overtake us at any moment."

But although Blaise's confidence had lessened her fears, they were not completely allayed, and she hurried the start and their pace to Vrieac, with the object of sending back help to Rupert as soon as possible. Blaise's refusal to leave her with only one soldier, and his watch outside her door, had taken another aspect in her mind. Rupert's instructions that she was never to be left out of reach of his soldiers had evidently been very definite.

"He thinks that I should slip away, or resist going to Vrieac," she thought with a tremulous, half-bitter laugh, "but he need not be afraid. What La Roche owes La Roche pays as well as Vrieac."

It was in the golden hazy light of noon that Yoeland and her escort, coming to the top of a steep slope, saw Vrieac lying before them on a high, wooded hill barely a league in front. At the foot of the hill, sparkling, gleaming in the sun, ran the Vienne, that beautiful, winding tributary of the Loire, flowing away to join the greater stream above Chinon.

As they rode down to the ford they could see the fields and vineyards which spread themselves before the steep, pine-topped sandstone cliffs. The village was gathered, as though for protection, at the foot of the red rocks, and high above it a great mass of stone curved outwards like a giant buttress, and on this the lords of Vrieac had built their home, part castle, part chateau, solitary, supreme, impregnable, with its wonderful view across fields and vineyards, river, woods and marshes, over the land which their valor, might and skill had won and held for them since the days of the first Louis.

They were expected, for Blaise had sent on a trooper whilst they rested at Valens, and Martin with Mamette, Rupert's old nurse, was waiting to receive Yoeland as she rode up the steep, narrow path to the castle.

As Yoeland looked into Mamette's shrewd gray eyes,

she smiled with a sudden, instinctive friendliness. Each of them, the toil-worn servant and the beautiful high-bred girl, loved Rupert de Vrieac, and so they met on common ground.

Too anxious to rest, Yoeland induced Mamette to show her the castle, listening with rapt interest as the old nurse told her stories of bygone Vrieacs, the beautiful women and gallant men whose spirits, Yoeland felt, must be watching with surprise this entrance of a de Breux of La Roche into their ancient stronghold. Were they very angry, she wondered, or would they understand that her presence was a consummation of all the revenge which, in their lifetime, they had desired against La Roche—understand and be glad?

There was a tremulous, wistful smile round her lips as she looked at the memorials they had left behind, at the calm, marble, carved faces in the little chapel and at the gleaming swords and weapons hanging in the great hall, some of whose edges must have been reddened with the blood of her own kin. Ah, they need not fear, those dead Vrieacs, that Rupert would forget the sword which lay between his house and hers. And she, with her own hands, by her own actions, had sharpened the blade. The feud held as strong as ever, an unsurmountable barrier between her and him. And now La Roche was to pay Vrieac's price.

So the two women spent the hours of waiting, while Mamette told little tales of Rupert's youth, and Yoeland with a fierce bitterness recalled her many acts of cruelty to the man she loved. And then, because the woman's part is very hard—to wait and hope for the man she loves, praying for his coming—they cried softly together in the foolish tender way of women, which nevertheless seems to give them comforting strength. And afterwards, drying their eyes, they went together to the top of the castle to look for news.

It had been past noon when Blaise Blas, with his freshly-mounted troopers, had started back to meet Rupert, but it was nearly sunset when the watchers at the castle saw his company returning. Even then they were too far off to distinguish the figure for which they hoped and waited, but it was evident by the increased numbers that Blaise had met the men of Vrieac returning from Tours.

Suddenly, as Yoeland and Mamette stood watching their slow approach, Yoeland clutched the older woman's arm.

"Mamette!" she whispered in a strained, dry voice. "Look! They have a litter with them. Some—some one must have been hurt!"

Love, however, had sharpened Mamette's eyes.

"Yes, Mademoiselle," she replied, "but it is not M. Rupert. See, he is on the gray horse there, riding by that lady."

And then both of them stared hard and suspiciously at the female figure at whose side Rupert was riding.

It was not until the company had reached the ford and were crossing the river, that with a sudden leap of her heart, Yoeland realized it was Mme. Charlotte, and that Jeanette and Marie, her women of La Roche, were there also.

She stood, silent and motionless, watching their approach. Why had he brought them to Vrieac? Why? Why?

When the company rode into the courtyard, she kept in the background, overcome by an unusual shyness. Only when Rupert, looking round eagerly, met her eyes, she went forward and flung her arms about Mme. Charlotte; then, still holding to her, passed him with a grave inclination of her head and went into the castle.

But very soon, having made Mme. Charlotte lie down to rest, Yoeland slipped out to the terrace which hung above the village and the river. She felt a restless, half-glad, half-miserable longing to see him, and so, leaning on the low terrace wall, she stood gazing down at the shadows in the water below.

And in a moment it came, the step for which she waited, on the flags behind her. Yet she did not move, and Rupert, thinking she had not heard him, stood irresolute, undecided how to make his presence known without startling her.

Then, slowly, she turned and faced him with grave, questioning eyes.

For a second they gazed at each other, whilst a wave of despair swept over Rupert's heart. He had dared to hope, a light he had caught on her face when he rode into the castle yard and their eyes met, had made him think that perhaps—— Ah, well, that had been foolish presumption. He fell on one knee before her, as, taking her hand, he raised it to his lips.

"Welcome to Vrieac, Mademoiselle," he said, "though I should have bidden you that sooner, should I not?"

Withdrawing her hand, she turned back towards the river.

"Why did you not come before, Monsieur?" she asked in low tones. "I—we began to feel alarmed, to fear that something—had happened to you."

He watched her with puzzled eyes.

"That was not necessary, Mademoiselle. We left Tours very shortly after you, but had to travel slowly on account of Carlote."

The set look in her face broke as she turned to him eagerly.

"Carlote!"

"Yes, Mademoiselle, Carlote. The Duc's men killed Duras, but Blaise found Carlote alive when he went to look for you at the ruin, and took him back to Tours. And of course I brought him with us when I fetched Mme. Charlotte and your women. But his litter made our pace necessarily slow."

She stood looking away over the river into the gathering dusk.

"And the Duc?" she asked slowly.

Rupert's face set with sudden sternness.

"The Duc is dead, Mademoiselle," he replied gravely.

She turned suddenly, looking at him with steady eyes.

"And—and Mme. de——" she began, then paused, ar-·
rested by something in his face, and changed her intention
quickly. "And Mme. de Vois?" she asked.

He laughed, shrugging his shoulders.

"—is indeed Mme. de Vois. How, or why, Philibert
was allowed to come to Tours and marry Mlle. Denise I
do not know. It seems incredible, yet it is perfectly true.
Also that they are now safely at Vois. I imagine that the
Duc must have had some scheme of vengeance to play on
them afterwards. Well, he cannot carry it out now."

They stood silent for a few moments, whilst the grave
look in Yoeland's eyes deepened. Then she turned to
Rupert with quiet dignity.

"M. de Vrieac," she said in a low voice which she vainly
tried to keep steady, "I—you were right yesterday when
you warned me of the Duc, that he had learnt of my plans
for M. de Vois and Denise. I knew at the time that you
were right, but I—I——" She paused for a moment, it
was not an easy explanation to make, then continued bravely,
"I was angry and I treated you——"

He had been listening in silent surprise. Now, with a
deprecating gesture, he interposed.

"Mademoiselle, if Blaise had not come when he did, you
would have married the Duc just to save me a little pain,"
he said quietly moving a step nearer to her. "I do not know
why, or for what, you are apologizing to me. There has
never been any need, you have never done anything for
which I should have to excuse you. You are over-tired
after these last few days. It is I who must beg your forgiveness for my presumptuous interference, my idiotic self-
satisfaction, which brought me headlong into the Duc's trap,
and but for which you need never have seen Lupi and his
—arrangements. I behaved like a fool, Mademoiselle. I
nearly got the punishment of one. I ask your pardon."

"Oh, Monsieur," she cried, pressing her fingers over her
eyes with a sudden shudder as she recalled those loathsome
preparations of torture, "it was horrible!"

"Do not think of it any more, Mademoiselle," he said gently. "Think of something else more pleasant—of Mlle. Anne and how glad she will be to have you back again at La Roche. I am sorry," he continued, "that I could not have sent you straight there from Tours. But the gates were shut and my men were only on guard at the southern one, so we had to go by that, we could not have got out through the others. I thought too, that if—if what had just happened were discovered before we got well away, the Duc's people would be less likely to follow if we went south. However, we can start for La Roche early to-morrow morning. We shall, of course, have to make a long detour and cross the Loire lower down to avoid the Duc's country, and Carlote's litter will make our pace slow. But we ought to reach La Roche in four, or five days, at the latest."

Yoeland had taken her hands from her face and stood listening in wondering surprise.

"Start for La Roche to-morrow!" she murmured. "We— I thought——"

Her voice sank into silence as, leaning forward, Rupert gazed at her keenly, reading in her eyes something of what her thoughts had been. For a few seconds there was a tense pause. Then he turned, looking up at a coat-of-arms roughly carved on the castle wall.

"Do you see the words beneath that, Mademoiselle?" he asked quietly, pointing to it. " 'What Vrieac owes, Vrieac pays.' It is the motto of my house. You forget, I think, that my oath binds me to La Roche for four years more."

A primeval instinct, a sudden longing to break the cold restraint of his manner, to force some feeling from the man she loved, stirred within her, coupled with a desire to hurt, to punish him for the inadequacy, the injustice of his judgment. It was true that she had thought he would not return to La Roche, but there were other things which she had expected also.

"No, Monsieur, I have not forgotten," she replied coldly,

"but you, I think, have overlooked the fact that, although it is not on the device of our house, yet we of La Roche pay our debts also."

Something in her voice, some meaning in her words which he could not, dared not understand, made him miserably angry.

"Yes, Mademoiselle," he answered, looking straight into her eyes. "No one should know that better than I."

And then, as a burning flush leaped into her cheeks, he turned, ashamed and wretched, leaning silent over the wall.

And so they stood, each gazing out into the gathering dusk, whilst there was a long pause. Rupert, his hands fiercely clutching the rough stone barrier, his face unnaturally stern and cold, was fighting with an almost overmastering desire. If only he could turn, and catching her in his arms, kiss her hair and eyes and lips, whilst he poured out the love and worship and passion which was consuming him. And she, standing motionless like a saint's image, clasped her hands in an agony of longing. If only he would kiss her, take her in his arms and letting her tell all her love and remorse, lean her head for a moment against his breast in absolute surrender. What did the feud between their houses matter, or his love for Marguerite de St. Caux? Nothing, if only he would kiss her once.

And so they stood, each unconsciously wishing the other's desire, until, when the man's endurance had almost snapped, Yoeland broke the silence.

"It is getting cold and as we start early to-morrow I think I will retire. Good-night, Monsieur."

He kissed her extended hand in silence, not trusting himself to speak; and then, like a white moth through the dusk, she was gone.

He stood for a long time staring out into the darkness, but at last rousing himself, entered the castle, and went up to the little room where he knew Mamette would be waiting for him.

Entering, he caught her up in his strong arms, hugging her as he had done when he was a boy.

"Of course you are not at all glad to see me again, Mamette?" he asked gravely, though a smile was twitching his lips, as he set her down.

And Mamette, smoothing out her crumpled apron, looked up at him with adoring eyes.

"Ah, little master, you know that I am not," she answered laughing, as she gave him the pet name of his childhood. "But must you go—go back there to-morrow, back to La Roche for four years?" she added, the smile dying from her eyes.

He nodded his head with grave decision.

"Yes, Mamette, I must. My oath to the Comte still holds."

Yet although he could not own it to Yoeland, and would not to Mamette, or hardly to himself, it was not all for the honor of Vrieac that he went back to La Roche, nor would it be to the same intolerable bondage. For she would be there. However much he must conceal his feelings, hide and suppress his longing, yet she would be there. For four years he could see her, hear her voice every day. No doubt they would go by all too quickly, those years whose passage he had once dreaded as interminable. But, if the substance were beyond his reach, let him at least creep into the shadow of happiness whilst he could.

And then once again he recalled Yoeland's words, "We of La Roche pay our debts also." What had they meant? Something beyond the construction he had given them, something which had made her eye suddenly soft and large and her lips curve into an almost friendly smile. But what did the real meaning matter since it could never be the only one which he desired.

With a sigh he sat down on the ground at Mamette's side, and as he had done when a boy, tired or in trouble, leaned his head against her knees. And Mamette's wrinkled hand stole down, clasping his comfortingly, just as it had always done in those far-away days.

Looking up into her face he laughed softly.

"Tell me a story, Mamette," he said.

For a moment she hesitated, gazing down at the dark head resting against her with very tender eyes, and then, as though to the little boy of long ago, she began softly:

"Once upon a time there were two gentlemen of France who both loved the same beautiful lady, and one of these gentlemen she loved and one she hated, yet her father forced her to be betrothed to the one she did not love. But the night before she was to be married her real lover came, and, carrying her off, married her himself, and so they lived happily ever afterwards. But from this a bitter feud arose between the two gentlemen's families and went on and on for many years. And then once again there were two gentlemen, one of each family, and they hated each other very much indeed. But one of them had a sister. She was very good and beautiful, and having met and learned how brave and fine a gentleman he was, she grew to love the one who was her brother's enemy. And as he loved her, they were married and lived happily ever afterwards. And so at last the feud between the two houses was ended."

As Mamette finished Rupert looked up at her with a bitter little laugh.

"That is a very nice story, Mamette," he said gravely, "but it is not like real life. Listen, and I will tell you what would have happened if those people had been real men and women," and kneeling before her, he took her hands, looking seriously into her eyes.

"Once upon a time there were, as you say, two men who loved the same woman. One she married—and one she did not. And from this a feud grew between her husband's family and his rival's, which lasted for a long time. Indeed, everything happened just as it did in your story, until we come to the time when there were again two men who hated each other very much indeed. And one of these men had a sister, who, as you say, was good and beautiful—and more. Well, her brother one day brought home the man he hated as a prisoner to his castle. But from there real life would differ from your story, Mamette. For how can a flower love the blight which kills it or a woman give her heart to a man whose fathers for generations have fought with and slain her own? It was a heritage of hers to hate and scorn her brother's prisoner, and she did so. And yet, because he could not help himself, he worshiped the ground she stood upon. But he knew his love could never be satisfied, that it was hopeless, because between them lay the curse of the dead and the hate of the living, because he was a prisoner, a servant, in the house of his foes.

"And in course of time she, I suppose, would marry some great and splendid gentleman. And he, her brother's enemy, would go back to his castle, and there live perhaps to be a very old man. But because he loved his beautiful lady too well to marry any one else, when he died there would be no one to carry on his name, and, since it takes two to quarrel, the feud between the houses would have, of course, to die out.

"That is what would happen to your story in real life, Mamette. And now, good-night. I must go and see Martin. To-morrow we must start as soon after sunrise as possible. There, there, do not cry. Why, I shall be back again in four years' time to plague you, and then we shall be happy, just as we were before I went to Paris."

And kissing her wrinkled old cheeks softly, he went quickly from the room, not trusting himself to think of the real desolation that the return to Vrieac would be when it came.

CHAPTER XXV

FIVE mornings later, Rupert, with Yoeland and Mme. Charlotte, riding out of the beech-woods, saw the castle of La Roche two miles away across the valley. Grim and impregnable, it frowned down over the fields and village at the river which lay dimpling in the sunlight below it, just as it had done ten months before when Rupert saw it first. Yet how absolutely different from what they had been then were the thoughts in his mind, as pulling up his horse, he sat for a moment gazing at it! It seemed no longer a prison, somber and forbidding, but the castle which held Love and all that made life to him worth having. A light almost of affection shone in his eyes as he looked at its gray walls.

Then turning, he beckoned to Blaise Blas who was in charge of the forty troopers that accompanied them. Traveling from Vrieac by roundabout and little-frequented ways, they had met with no attempts to molest or stop them, the strength of their escort inducing a disinclination to interfere with them. But now that they had safely reached the Comte's land and La Roche stood before them, there was no necessity for the troopers to come further. So having hired a couple of peasants to carry Carlote's litter, Rupert gave Blaise the order to return to Vrieac, and with Yoeland, Mme. Charlotte and the two serving-women, rode on towards the castle.

In the days since they had left Vrieac, Yoeland had hardly exchanged a dozen words with Rupert. Riding in front with Blaise Blas he had seemed to shun her, and although his solicitude for her and Mme. Charlotte's comfort had been untiring, yet there was a constraint in his man-

ner towards herself which Yoeland was quick to feel.   But
as, Blaise and the troopers left behind, they rode up the steep
ascent to the castle she received a sudden surprise.   Turning to watch a hawk her eyes rested on Rupert's face as he
rode behind her.   She had expected to see dejection, gloom,
almost despair written there, but, although his expression
was unusually grave, there was a light like that of joy burning in his eyes as they met hers for the fraction of a moment.
And yet he was returning to wear the shackles of servitude
in the house of his enemy for four long years!

Her face was almost as grave as his, although a new-
found hope had set her heart beating quickly, as they
clattered into the castle yard.   Here welcome warm and
eager was waiting, in the midst of which Rupert, standing
alone grave and thoughtful, felt a hand grip his shoulder
and, turning, found the Comte looking at him with a grim
smile.

"Welcome back to La Roche, my dear de Vrieac.   This
is an almost unexpected pleasure, for I own that I felt
grave doubts as to whether we should ever see you again;
whether, once away, you would return.   You are, of course,
delighted to be with us once more?"   And Rupert, looking coldly into his enemy's face with no sign of having
caught the insult in the other's words, bowed.

"Of course, Monsieur," he answered quietly.

A mocking light shone for a second in the Comte's
eyes, then he shrugged his shoulders.

"I will speak to you presently," he said, turning away.
It was not, however, until nearly two hours later that Rupert, in answer to a summons, went to the Comte's room
in the west tower.   Entering, he laid the sword which the
Comte had given him at the start for Briege on the table
before his enemy and stood silently waiting.   The Comte
fingered the hilt for a few seconds without speaking, then
looked up quickly.

"I owe you an apology, de Vrieac.   What I said to
you in the courtyard just now was not true.   I knew

that your honor would hold. Had I not done so I should never have allowed you to leave La Roche. I was simply trying to make you angry. I am sorry. Mademoiselle has just been telling me what happened since you went to Briege and Tours," he continued, not giving Rupert an opportunity to speak. "It seems that I owe you thanks also, that but for your courage and resource and the help of your men my sister might have found herself in very serious difficulties. You have guarded her well and as a sign of my gratitude I hope you will keep this sword— and return to Vrieac. No, wait one moment!" Holding up an imperious hand as Rupert was about to speak. "Let me make the position quite clear. I am not proposing that we should end the feud which exists between our two houses, nor do I ask for your friendship. I simply wish to absolve you from the oath which binds you to my service for four years more. I will be frank, and own that my plan of revenge has been disappointing. I have not derived the satisfaction from it that I expected. I think that you and I could carry on our quarrel better if you were free. The state of France and difference in our religions will provide plenty of scope for encounters between us, no doubt. Therefore to-morrow I shall supply you with an escort and you can go back to Vrieac, or wherever you wish, a free man."

A look of consternation had been gradually spreading over Rupert's face and now, as the Comte paused, he shook his head. Return to Vrieac, leave La Roche, when by staying he could for four years be near her, could hear her voice and see her face every day! His lost liberty and the Comte's mastership, nothing, could count against that.

"Thank you, Monsieur, but I would rather not. I— I—there are reasons, which I cannot explain, which you would not understand, which make me wish to remain at La Roche."

"Make you—what?" exclaimed the Comte, staring at him incredulously. Then suddenly he shrugged his shoulders. "Ah, I see! It is your confounded pride, de Vrieac. You will not take your liberty as a gift from my hands. Why, man, it is only justice. Cannot you understand? Your freedom in exchange for Anne's life, which you have twice saved, and for all that you and your people have done for Mademoiselle while she has been away. You have earned it, heaven knows! Take it and go with an easy mind. I am only yielding you your right."

But Rupert still shook his head.

"That is not my reason, Monsieur. I cannot explain, but—oh, I beg you to let me remain."

The astonishment in the Comte's face deepened, then with a short laugh, he shrugged his shoulders once more in complete mystification.

"It seems strange. However, you know your own affairs best. But human plans are very uncertain, so, should you ever change your mind—to-day, next week, next year—remember that my proposal holds good for as long as you are here. You have only to mention the fact and that escort will be at your disposal. Now tell me how you killed Henri de Tours."

Relieved that the Comte had not pressed his point, Rupert did so with relish, only omitting all mention of Marguerite de St. Caux, whilst the Comte listened intently, nodding his head in silent approbation.

"Good!" he said, when Rupert had finished. "That is another devil in hell. You made a clean piece of work there, de Vrieac. And I do not think you have much to fear from his brother, de Lothes, who succeeds him. Of course if you fell into his hands he would, for the sake of appearances, have to kill you. But keep out of his way and he will not trouble you. The two brothers fought like tigers and de Lothes, who was none too rich before, must think of you now as his best friend. I should like to hear about that fight on the stairs at Briege, when the Duc's men attacked you all. I have had Mademoiselle's account. Give me yours."

Very bluntly, making little of his own part in it, Rupert described the affair, whilst the Comte smiled quietly to himself. His sister's version had been so much more elaborate and to the glory of Rupert de Vrieac.

It was nearly an hour before the Comte had finished his questions, and having impressed on Rupert that his offer of an escort to freedom stood open indefinitely, dismissed him.

Leaving the tower, Rupert made his way to the door of Anne's room. He had not seen the child since his return, for her sister had been with her, but now he hoped to have her to himself. Knocking softly, he entered the room and had almost reached the bed before he realized that Yoeland still knelt beside it.

Stopping abruptly, with a murmured apology, he would have withdrawn, but Anne's voice, clamorously imperative, called upon him to stay, whilst from her eyes shone a rapturous welcome. Returning obediently, Rupert knelt down by the bed as Anne flung her arms round his neck in an embrace which almost choked him.

"Oh, I am so, so glad you have come back, M. Rupert," she cried, nestling against his shoulder. "Yoeland says you have had lovely adventures and that you took care of her beautifully. You got safely through all the witches and dragons. And I know two stories in the chronicle quite by heart. Where is my token?"

With a quick catch of his breath Rupert gently unclasped her arms and stood up.

"Alas, Mlle. Anne, I—I have lost it," he stammered. "It was hidden in my doublet and one day—it was gone."

"Gone!" Anne cried, a pucker gathering round her lips. "But knights never lost their ladies' tokens, they guarded them with their lives and always——"

Very softly Yoeland's hand clasped the child's.

"Hush, darling, for one moment," she whispered, then looked up at Rupert with dark, troubled eyes. "Was Anne's token a curl of hair—that you lost after you had been wounded on the stairs at Briege, Monsieur?" she asked.

"Yes, Mademoiselle, I never found it after—after Jeanette mended my doublet."

Very slowly Yoeland stood up, facing him across the bed with grave eyes.

"No, Monsieur, you could not possibly do so, for—I burnt it."

"You burnt it, Mademoiselle?"

"Yes, I thought—I thought it was Mme. de St. Caux's."

"But it wasn't," Anne interposed shrilly. "I had to give M. Rupert some hair, the knights' ladies always did, and he would not let me cut my own. So I took a curl off the doll Charles brought me from Paris."

But the two looking at each other across the bed were not listening. Very quietly Yoeland faced Rupert—waiting. In her eyes was pride and shame and something else—something whose sound had been in her voice that last evening at Vrieac, stirring him almost to madness, something which made him now catch his breath with a sharp cry as he made an almost unconscious movement towards her. He forgot that he was a prisoner, a Huguenot, the enemy of her house, everything—except that he loved her.

And then through the shadow in her eyes a smile broke. And as he caught its sparkle, the mask of indifference fell across his face and he drew back sharply. But he knew that in that instant he had laid his soul bare before her, that his secret had been written plain for all to read —and she had smiled, smiled in the knowledge of victory, that she had forced her enemy to love her.

Ah, what a truly magnificent revenge was this for her, and no doubt, one which she would not fail to use for his hurt. Fool that he was, for he had, by his own act, put the weapon to wound him into her hands. This would make La Roche intolerable, he could not endure the four years near her now, with this knowledge of his secret between them. If only he could get away and never see that smile of scornful amusement in her eyes again. And then he remembered the Comte's offer.

Abruptly, without a word, he unclasped Anne's protesting hands and, bowing gravely to Yoeland, left the room.

But once outside the door his calmness of manner deserted him, and with frantic haste he hurried to the Comte's room. Bursting in unceremoniously, he paused for a moment to recover his breath, whilst the Comte surveyed him with surprised eyes.

"What is the matter? You seem excited, de Vrieac. Is the castle on fire?"

"No, Monsieur, but I have changed my mind and have come to——"

"Oh, I understand," the Comte interposed, glancing at him keenly. "You want the escort? Very well. It shall be ready in an hour. I dare say you can fill up that time saying good-by to Mme. Charlotte and Anne and—and—Carlote. And see here, de Vrieac, take this sword. I am sorry that I broke your own that night in Paris, but this has served you well already, and you will find opportunities to test it again soon, no doubt. Very likely you will try and run it into me one day. There, there, man," as Rupert, touched by the Comte's manner, stammered out his thanks. "We shall be liking each other and forgetting all about our feud soon, if we are not very careful!"

And taking Rupert by the shoulder with a quiet laugh, he pushed him out of the room.

An hour later Rupert stood on the steps of the terrace, with a gloom on his face utterly preposterous under the circumstances. Overhead a lark sang joyously of freedom; in the courtyard the men who were to escort him back to Vrieac were busily making ready to start. He, a prisoner so long, was about to return home to his own land, and yet he stood looking utterly miserable.

He had said good-by to Mme. Charlotte, who, smiling very kindly, had given him her blessing. Carlote, that hardened old soldier, slowly recovering from his encounter with the Duc's men, had wrung his proffered hand in silence and then turned quickly away, to hide the tears in his eyes. Anne had made no secret of her grief at all, and raised indignant protest at his going. Indeed it was only when he had taken a solemn oath that she and Mme. Charlotte should, the Comte willing, come to Vrieac the next summer and that he would most surely send her back by the escort a certain brown spaniel to be all her own, that Rupert could induce the child to release his hands and let him go. And as he remembered her face, tear-stained and wistful, a lump rose in his throat, whilst desolation surged over his heart.

It was like going from his own home, this leaving, so utterly different from the glad release he had pictured it when first he came to La Roche. Even the serving-maids and men-at-arms seemed sorry, for, unconsciously, Rupert had made them all fond of him.

Five minutes had passed since Yoeland sent him a message, asking him to go to her in the old garden before he left La Roche, and still he had not obeyed. For an instant the craven idea of riding away without seeing her came to him. Then, squaring his shoulders, he walked quickly down the path leading to the little wicket in the high yew hedge.

With his hand on the latch he paused, looking into the garden beyond. At the far end of the lawn, her dark hair shining against the gray of the old stone seat, Yoeland sat, working a piece of embroidery, whilst before her on the grass sloping down to the fountain, strutted Charlemagne the peacock, in all the pride of his splendor.

For a moment Rupert stood absorbed, gazing with wistful eyes, impressing every detail upon his memory, storing the picture of her for the lonely years to come. Here he had seen her first, distant and beautiful, here again he saw her, more beautiful and infinitely further away from him, for the last time.

Did she remember that first meeting, too, he wondered.

Was that why she wished to see him in the garden again? She had been coldly, insultingly contemptuous then; what would be her attitude now?

He swung open the gate and walked quickly across the lawn towards her. Then paused suddenly, for on the grass at his feet lay a knot of ribbon, cherry-red, such as Yoeland was even then wearing on the whiteness of her dress. She was bending over her work, Charlemagne had turned his back, there was no eye to see him.

Stooping quickly, Rupert picked it up and pressing it for a second to his lips, slipped it inside his doublet, then went forward to the old seat. Although she must have heard the click of the gate, Yoeland made no sign. Not until his shadow fell across her work did she look up.

"Ah, Monsieur!" she said, putting her embroidery carefully aside and intimating by a gesture that he might be seated, though, bowing his acknowledgment, he chose to remain standing before her. "Ah, Monsieur, are you starting now? How glad you must be! Does it not seem almost too good to be true, that you are going back to Vrieac? What a day it will be for Martin and Mamette when they have you again! Dear old Mamette," and her face softened, as she took up a little packet beside her, handing it to Rupert. "Will you give that to her from me? I feel I should like to send her a little token of how much I love her sweetness. You do well to be fond of her, Monsieur, for she adores you. Have you said good-by to Anne? The poor child! She will feel desolate without you. Indeed, we shall all miss you," she added, looking up at him with a grave smile.

And Rupert, too miserable to speak, bowed coldly. He had expected sneers, perhaps insults, and had steeled himself to meet them. This courteous, almost friendly manner, the regret in her voice, was something utterly unlooked for and which tried his self-control dangerously.

For a moment there was silence, silence which threatened to become interminable, whilst he stood before her, fearing she would hear the beating of his heart.

Then throwing back his head in the way she knew so well, and looking at her with steady, indifferent eyes, he begged permission to take his leave.

It was such a different parting from what in moments of hope he had dared to dream of, or in his humiliation had dreaded. His going left her utterly indifferent. He had been a fool to fancy that her terror for him at Mme. de St. Caux's or the light which he had surprised in her eyes when he came safely to Vrieac, were prompted by more than the anxiety which her kind heart would feel for anything in danger. And as for his secret which she had learnt in Anne's room, that was evidently to be ignored, she was treating his presumption with silent contempt. Well, he would match her manner with his if he could, and he would be indifferent too, though the sooner this miserable scene were over the better, lest, losing all self-control, he should catch her in his arms and tell her how he loved her.

"Adieu, Mademoiselle," he said, bowing gravely.

And in a voice as cold and steady as his, she answered, "Adieu, Monsieur."

Then, as he raised her fingers to his lips, he heard her catch her breath, and glanced up quickly, hoping against hope. But she was only looking with grave concern at her sleeve as it fell back, loose and untied, from her wrist.

"I have lost my ribbon," she explained seriously, meeting his eyes. "'Tis very strange. I could have wagered that it held my sleeve a moment ago. It must be somewhere near and I must find it, for my dress will be spoilt without it. Have the goodness to see if it is near the gate, M. de Vrieac."

And Rupert, the ribbon lying against his heart, turned dutifully to do so. He knew that he ought to return it to her, and once, his back to her, drew it out for that purpose, but at the thought of those lonely future years without her, slipped it back again, and returning to Yoeland, reported that it was nowhere to be seen.

She seemed much concerned at her loss, but Rupert could not bring himself to give up the only token he had of her.

"I wish that I could find it," she said, "though it is very selfish of me to keep you looking for a lost ribbon, when you must be so anxious to start. Adieu, M. de Vrieac."

It was obvious that he should make some gallant speech, protesting that there was never any haste to leave the presence of Mlle. de Breux, but he could not trust his voice to keep steady. For a second he raised her fingers, lying cool and soft in his, to his lips, then releasing them, bowed low, and without a word turned away, whilst Yoeland, standing very still, watched him in silence.

But he had not gone a dozen paces when he faced round quickly, having caught a slight sound behind him. Yoeland still stood, tall and straight, by the old seat, her hands clasped loosely before her, her head thrown proudly back, but in her eyes the tears had gathered, and her lips were quivering piteously.

Neither spoke. Only Rupert, catching his breath sharply, held out his arms, and with a sob of relief, Yoeland came to him.

"Dieu!" murmured Rupert a few moments later, as they sat on the old stone seat, her head against his shoulder, his arms round her. "And I was just going to leave you without ever guessing! Sweetheart, how can you love so great a fool?"

But Yoeland laughed and drew closer to him, seemingly well content.

"Do you think I should have let you really go, because you thought I did not care?" she asked. "And fancy not guessing! M. de Vrieac, you are too humble-minded. 'Tis the fault of most men that they cannot believe that there is one woman in the whole world who does not, or would not, adore them. But I prefer you so," she added with mock gravity. Then, her face hidden against his shoulder, "Mamette guessed," she whispered, "and—and I think she was glad."

Although this did not surprise Rupert, yet he was several minutes explaining to Yoeland why not only Mamette, but all Vrieac would be glad, whilst she listened with a smile of great content.

"But what will M. le Comte say?" Rupert asked, struck by a sudden thought.

Yoeland, lifting a charming, blushing face, laughed softly.

"He knows already. I told him that—that I loved you."

"Heart's desire! And what did he say?"

"He said you were a gallant gentleman, worthy of a better fate, and that you were greatly to be pitied."

Then they both laughed in the happy, spontaneous way of lovers and children.

"When will you marry me?" he asked.

"When you wish," she replied.

So they settled that it should be some time very soon. Presently he took out the cherry ribbon and laid it in her hands.

"I had it all the time," he said, kissing a curl which had strayed against his lips.

Yoeland laughed softly.

"I know. I put it there for M. de Vrieac to find. I—I wanted to see what he would do with it."

And in the light of this explanation Rupert sat very still, understanding several things which had greatly puzzled him.

"Little witch," he murmured fondly, putting his finger under her chin and gently tilting back her head, so that he could see her eyes. "Why did you take me to Briege? Why did you burn Anne's ribbon? Why were you so unkind to me?"

Then bending his head he kissed her gently, for in her eyes he read the answer to all.

"When did you love me first?" he whispered.

Yoeland shook her head gayly.

"I shall not tell you, for you should have known long, long ago. I do not know myself," she added, growing suddenly serious. "I think it was the night when Anne was so ill and you carried her—do you remember?—but I would not own it even to myself, for I thought she loved you more than me and that you still loved Mme. de St. Caux and it made me jealous and cruel. Ah, forgive me, Rupert. And you—when did you——?"

"The first time I ever saw you, here in this garden, I thought you the most beautiful lady I had ever seen, and it was then, I think, though you were so wonderful, so—so cold, so far above the reach of a poor prisoner, but I too tried to bar Love out, and would not acknowledge that it was so even to myself till long, long after, and then——! Ah, Yoeland!" he cried, slipping off the seat and kneeling beside her, whilst he withdrew his arms from around her, "I am the most unworthy man that ever lived. What have I done that you can possibly love me? It cannot be true. This is an enchanted garden and that shameless villain, Charlemagne, over there is the ogre who has bewitched you. Listen, I am only a plain Huguenot, not very rich, not famous, not worthy to kiss your hand. And yet I dare to love you. Yoeland, Yoeland, how is it possible that you can care to marry such a worthless fellow as I?"

Then Mlle. de Breux, a very tender light in her eyes, bent towards him and laid her hands upon his shoulders.

"Even if you were such a worthless person, or worse, I should still want to marry you, because—because——" and her smiling lips were very close to his, "because I love you—Rupert."

The Comte de La Roche, having heralded his approach with considerable noise, found them still in the garden half an hour later. He came across the grass and, standing before them, looked sternly from his sister's happy, blushing face to her hand which was still held by those of Rupert de Vrieac, and then into his enemy's eyes.

"I have, Monsieur," he said, "given orders for the men to unsaddle. You have been so long saying 'Good-by' to—to every one that it is now too late to start for Vrieac to-day. Your journey must be postponed."

Without releasing her hand, Rupert took a step in front of Yoeland and faced her brother boldly.

"M. le Comte," he began steadily, "we—Mlle. de Breux and I—have—have——" and there he stopped, for it was so obvious what arrangement they had made.

An amused smile broke over the Comte's face.

"I think I understand," he said, "although your explanation does not go very far, de Vrieac."

Then crossing to his sister he kissed her gently, and with an arm still round her, held out his hand to Rupert.

"I am very glad," he said. "I would not trust her to the keeping of every man, de Vrieac. Therefore, although neither of you care one sou if I give it or not, you have my consent. I wish you both much joy."

So, out of the ashes of vengeance, Love arose glorious and triumphant, and the feud which had begun with the marriage of Raoul de Vrieac to Yvonne de Marbleu was ended by that of Yoeland de Breux with Rupert de Vrieac. For, as the Comte said, how could he and Rupert fight? Whatever the result, the victor would undoubtedly fall under Mme. de Vrieac's displeasure, which was a condition not to be risked by any man.

THE END

www.ingramcontent.com/pod-product-compliance
Lightning Source LLC
Chambersburg PA
CBHW030939260626
47169CB00002B/537